After graduating in Spanish and French, Chris Lloyd lived in Catalonia for over twenty years, first in Girona and then in Barcelona, where he taught English and worked in educational publishing and as a travel writer. More recently, he worked as a Catalan and Spanish translator. He has also lived in Grenoble – researching the French Resistance movement – as well as in the Basque Country and Madrid.

Banquet of Beggars is his third novel set in Paris, featuring Detective Eddie Giral. The first, *The Unwanted Dead*, won the Historical Writers' Association Gold Crown Award for best historical novel of the year, and was shortlisted for the Crime Writers' Association Historical Dagger Award.

BANQUET OF BEGGARS

Chris Lloyd

ORION

First published in Great Britain in 2024 by Orion Fiction,
an imprint of The Orion Publishing Group Ltd.,
Carmelite House, 50 Victoria Embankment
London EC4Y 0DZ

An Hachette UK Company

3 5 7 9 10 8 6 4 2

A CIP catalogue record for this book
is available from the British Library.

ISBN (Hardback) 978 1 4091 9035 6
ISBN (Trade Paperback) 978 1 4091 9036 3
ISBN (eBook) 978 1 4091 9038 7

Typeset by Deltatype Ltd, Birkenhead, Merseyside

Printed in Great Britain by Clays Ltd, Elcograf S.p.A.

www.orionbooks.co.uk

For Helen and Malcolm

Entrée

I

Three hours in and I was ready to kiss the cellar wall.

With my fingertips I traced the cold bricks for the dozenth time. Water from a leak somewhere had run down them and along the gridlines of mortar and had frozen there, its texture uneven but smooth, a patina of ice over the coarse grain of the sand and lime. I touched it a moment longer than I should have. What lingering warmth I had in my hands melted the ice. I felt the water between my fingertips and almost weakened.

I had nothing to drink. Forget the whisky I could no longer get; right now water would have been a gift from the Teutonic gods. My mouth was so parched I was tempted to lick the wall for its moisture. But I held back. The grit embedded in the ice would have had me choking and gasping for proper water the moment I tried. There was a lesson to be learned there, but I couldn't be bothered to go looking for it.

There is one thing I will say. The one good thing about being thirsty is that it takes your mind off the sheer, numbing, incessant cold. The gnawing ache that worms its way through to the bones and freezes the mind.

A shiver ran the length of my body. All I'd been given was a single grey blanket that was as thin as a Nazi promise and a palliasse sparsely filled with ancient straw. I had my coat, but no scarf and no gloves, so I'd wrapped the blanket round my legs and pulled the old overcoat tightly around my upper body, trying to tuck my ears and nose down into the collar. My bed of hay and sackcloth at least shielded me from the cold of the stone floor. I tried to ignore the scratching noises that came from inside it. The water on my fingers was beginning to freeze again. I wiped them dry on my coat and shrank them up into the sleeves. I lay back, resigned, and tried to let my senses do the work for me.

As I calmed again, my nose began to bristle. A scent of mushrooms withering in the dank earth stung my eyes. I blinked twice and the tears froze in their ducts. Sighing, I accidentally filled my nostrils and was surprised to find myself savouring the aroma. In the cold and dark, it wasn't a sense of decay, but a memory of forgotten meals. I could almost hear the butter sizzling in the pan as, in my mind, I fried a reducing heap of freshly picked ceps. The sort I remembered from my childhood in the Pyrenees. My older brother, Charles, and I would go out to pick them, my mother would clean them and my father would cook them. I'd cooked them in Paris since. They were good, but they never had that sweetness that distance and longing gave them. I imagined now that I could taste the butter, rolling its gentle sheen around my tongue before biting into the tender flesh. It was a sad lifetime ago. My mouth began to water – finally – but then the hunger in my belly came knocking.

Smell and taste. I'd chosen the wrong senses.

In vain, I opened my eyes and stared at what lay above me.

Outside, it had been just a day or two short of a full moon. The last one before Christmas. A bomber's moon, some called it. A night when whatever air force might be lurking overhead could see what they were looking for, even in cloud. A night when the city was vulnerable.

Not that I could see any of it. I was in complete darkness.

I shivered at the thought. That brought other memories.

Instinctively I looked around me, despite the pitch black of my world. There were no windows to let in any light or to give me a glimpse of the night outside. No bars made this prison. My ears strained to hear if there were any planes circling. During the day, we heard little but the incessant drone of Luftwaffe aircraft patrolling the sky. So much so, we'd ceased to notice them. But at night, the friend became the enemy and the enemy the friend. We wanted the RAF to bomb the hell out of the Germans. Just not in Paris. Not when we were around.

'Quiet tonight,' a voice nearby said.

I nearly jumped. I'd almost forgotten where I was.

'Like last month,' a second voice replied.

Elderly voices. Women. Talking in hushed tones across the blackness. Somewhere to my right.

'Shh,' a man's voice admonished them.

A fourth voice joined in. Another man, behind my head. Close. 'Not like last time, mind. In November. The sirens.'

'The Boches,' one of the women agreed. 'Playing a prank on us. Sounding the sirens when there wasn't any air raid.'

'I heard it was so they could get all of us underground so they could see what Paris felt like with just the Germans in it,' the man behind my head replied.

'They wanted to search our homes,' the second woman piped up.

The other man shushed them again. I just sighed. Nothing like the Occupation to get the imagination going. It's not just truth that's the first victim of war. It's thought as well.

I sighed again and buried my face further into my coat. The low voices and occasional shushing were surprisingly sedative, and I felt myself drift off.

In one way they were right. There had been no sirens. It wasn't an air raid. Or even a German prank like so many believed. That wasn't the reason why we were all in this cellar.

5

2

I heard movement around me before the sound of the warped old door scratching sharply on the cellar floor, setting my teeth on edge. The first noise had ended my hunger-induced dream of butter melting in a giant pan. The second had made me start, suddenly fully awake.

A serpent of light from a faint bulb outside on the steep staircase slithered into the room. Enough to make out shapes in movement. Not enough to distinguish individuals. I looked for last night's conversationalists, but had no idea who they were. There were too many of us in the cellar, almost all now rushing to get up and make for the door. A sense of urgency filled the dank gloom, overcoming the stiffness brought on by the cold. Untouched by the same spirit, I lifted myself slowly from the palliasse, surprised to find myself resenting being torn away from its relative warmth and comfort. Figures funnelled past me to the door, most of them silent, some of them grumbling, one or two emitting eager sounds.

Then I remembered why I was there, and began to find the same urgency as my unknown companions.

An impatient queue had formed at the door, the stairs up to the ground floor narrow and sharp. I held onto the wall on either side as I climbed. I wanted the person in front of me to hurry up, not for the same reason as everyone else, I imagined, but because I needed to be out of the cold, damp ground. I tilted my head down so I couldn't see the walls or sloping ceiling, just the scuffed shoes of the elderly lady ahead patiently edging up the dark flight.

The concierge was waiting at the top when I got there. She was checking everyone, no doubt making sure no one had sneaked their way in somehow in the previous night's curfew. Wearing the same thick brown housecoat she'd been wearing the evening before, she sniffed at me as I went past. Her coarse grey hair was tied in a plait and wrapped around her head like a Cossack hat. Underneath it, her eyes were colder than her cellar and more avaricious than Adolf eyeing up another country to invade. I tried to think what I could arrest her for, but nothing came to me.

'Very comfortable,' I told her. 'Can't think why I haven't stayed here before.'

She sniffed again. I wished I could get that much scorn into my mucous movements. 'No one forced you to come.'

'That's arguable,' I told her, choosing not to.

She ignored me as I passed her and turned her open contempt to the man behind me. Just as she'd done with everyone else who'd spent the night in the cellar, she'd taken my franc for the heady pleasure of a night on a palliasse in the pitch black and was keen to get rid of us all now. Until the next time.

If the cellar had been cold, the outside world was polar. In the early-morning gloom, I shivered and tightened my coat around me. With the weight I was losing thanks to rationing, it was well on its way to becoming double-breasted. If they cut the meat allowance any further, I might even become fashionable.

A queue had formed by the corner of the street, just a few metres to my left. Before I had a chance to move, an old dear with whiskers and halitosis jostled past me out of the building and joined the end. I hurried to get in line behind her but was beaten to it by a man twice my age and half my height. I had to make do with third in my private race. Hunger took us all differently, I supposed.

'Thieving bastards,' the man muttered to no one in particular.

I recognised his voice. He was the one shushing the others in the night. A young woman two places in front of him turned and agreed. Another woman who'd come to stand behind me joined in.

'A franc,' she grumbled. 'For a louse-ridden sack in a wet cellar.'

I kept quiet but had to agree.

'I heard there's a concierge over on Rue de Prague who's charging two francs,' the man replied.

We all tutted at that.

'And all for butter,' the woman behind me said.

'From Brittany,' the old man piped up. He said it with the glee of anticipation, a non-sequitur in misted breath.

Slowly we shuffled forward. There was some commotion ahead, at the front of the queue. Snapping out of my thoughts, I leaned out to take a look, but saw nothing behind the line of some twenty souls ahead of me waiting their turn.

'I haven't had any butter since the summer.' The elderly woman spoke, in a hushed tone, for the first time.

'None of us has,' I couldn't help replying.

But I'd thought about it. Almost endlessly. And even more so since the rumours of a local grocer getting a consignment of it today had started to do the rounds. So here we all were. On a miserable December morning in the first winter of the German occupation of Paris, queueing in the cold for something we'd all once taken for granted. Butter. That's all. We'd each paid our franc to spend a night in a cellar of the building next to the grocer's so we'd be first in the queue. This is what we'd become under Nazi rule.

The commotion up ahead had turned into a ruckus. People squabbling over a pat of fat. Risking my place, I left the queue to see what was going on. Outside the door to the small shop, a crowd was gathering around a man in a brown cotton coat. I didn't recognise him, but I knew he had to be the owner. He was holding his hands up, placating the people slowly thronging towards him. His look was an odd mix of scared and uncaring.

'I know as much as you do,' he was telling two women who were pressing on him the most.

'All night we queued,' one of them told him.

He shrugged. 'That's not my problem.'

I thought for a moment that one of the women was going to take a swing at him, so I stepped in.

'What's going on?' I asked him.

He eyed me up and down, evidently thinking better of coming back at me with a smart retort. There's nothing like a night in a cold cellar to sharpen a mean gaze. Or it might have been because I was a good head and shoulders taller than him.

'There's no butter,' he said after a moment's hesitation.

A murmur of discord ran its way along the queue to the stragglers at the back. The crowd began to bunch up as the ones at the rear came forward to see for themselves.

'What do you mean, no butter?'

The grocer shrugged again. Under his work coat I could see a thick roll-neck sweater and trousers that didn't dance on thinning hips like everyone else's did. An unshaven neck emerged from the coat and held up a head that was just that bit too big and a face that was just that bit too small, like a child had drawn a tiny face on an overblown balloon.

'It hasn't arrived. I was promised it would be here.'

'When will it be arriving?'

'I don't know.'

'Where's it coming from? And don't say Brittany.'

He looked uncomfortable. 'I can't tell you that.'

'It's black market, I take it?'

He pulled himself up to his full height and gave me a scornful look. He was evidently more afraid of whoever he bought the butter from than he was of me.

'You really don't want to know.'

I pulled out my police ID and showed it to him. 'Yes, I really do want to know. I'm a cop.'

He looked at my ID incuriously and shrugged again. One more shrug and I'd let the woman at the front of the queue slug him.

'So arrest me. You're not supposed to be buying from me anyway. You're not registered with me.'

He had a point. 'Who were you supposed to be getting it from?'

'Black market. That's all I know.'

'You must know who you're buying it from.'

'I don't. I just spoke to some guy who said he knew where to get some. He wouldn't tell me who he got it from and I didn't ask. I'm telling you, they're not people you want to know.'

I turned away in frustration. 'I paid some money-grabbing concierge a franc so I could get this butter.'

'That's my wife you're talking about.'

'Why doesn't that surprise me?'

'What are you going to do about it?' the woman in the queue asked me. 'You're a cop. Make him pay us back.'

The grocer snorted. 'Yeah, sure, pay back what you didn't pay me because you wanted to buy something on the black market.'

'I could arrest you for selling on the black market,' I told him.

He looked around in an exaggerated gesture. 'You see any black-market goods here? You've got nothing on me.'

I had to hide my frustration. 'I will,' I promised him.

'You can't threaten me.' Again the snort.

I smiled brightly at him and addressed the crowd. 'No butter,' I told them, pointing to the grocer. 'There never was. Here's your man. The concierge you all paid a franc to is his wife.'

He blanched. 'You can't do that.'

The disappointed butter buyers turned their angry gaze on him as I started to walk away.

'I just did.'

3

I walked back past the angry failed shoppers, now more of a scrum than a queue, and pulled my coat tighter around my body. Hunger made you cold, I was learning.

For one idle moment I wondered if my snipe at the hapless trader had been right. That it had all been a ploy with his wife to con us all out of a franc for butter that was never going to materialise. I decided not. That wasn't the sort of ruse you could pull more than once. In fairness, he was probably telling the truth and had been conned himself by whatever black marketeer he was dealing with. I turned, with half a mind to go back and demand one more time who his supplier was, but he'd retreated into his shop and pulled the shutters down. The butterless mob milled around outside, unsure what to do, blocking any way in or out.

Instead, I carried on along the street. I was on the Right Bank, not my part of town. As a cop, I knew pretty much all of Paris, mostly the bits you didn't want to know, but this was one neighbourhood I'd never had much call to visit, despite being just over the river from my own home in the Fifth.

It was early. Too early to go to Thirty-Six, the police headquarters on Quai des Orfèvres, and my icy office on the third floor. The commissioner was threatening to assign me some run-of-the-mill burglary case, so I was in no hurry. After buying butter, I'd planned on going home to drop off my treasured purchase and grab a shower before heading back out to work. With a shiver, I recalled the sound of what I'd imagined to be insects crawling inside the palliasse of straw I'd slept in last night and decided I would go home to wash after all. My shirt collar felt like it was moving independently of my neck, and something I didn't want to know was dancing a tango on my scalp. I shivered again, and not just with the cold.

But first I needed coffee. I had none at home. None that you could call coffee anyway. Looking around, I could see no cafés open, and I didn't know the surrounding streets well enough to know where to find one.

I was heading along the narrow road towards the hospital that gave the quarter its name. Quinze-Vingts. Supposedly named after the number of beds in the eye hospital, founded in 1260 by old Louis the Prudent to house three hundred poor, blind Parisians. As a schoolkid in Perpignan, I'd always been taught that good King Louis had been the one to pull France out of the Middle Ages, so it's a pity Paris chose to remember him and his hospital with the archaic vigesimal counting system of the time. *Quinze-vingts*. Fifteen-twenties. Three hundred. And they insisted it was us lot from down south who were behind the times.

My mind was wandering with the cold, I realised. I yawned deeply and pulled myself together. Beyond the hospital was Place de la Bastille. I knew places there I could get a hot drink, maybe even some bread and a thin sliver of ham if my luck was in.

As I quickened my pace and gathered my thoughts, my annoyance returned. Not with the grocer. He'd just been trying to feed a need and got stung in the process. Butter was the new cocaine. As were a lot of things we'd once dismissed as everyday essentials. My anger was at the black marketeer who'd cheated us all out of our fix of fat. We could have done with it. I pulled my coat even tighter around me and hunched my head down into the collar, like some old guy shuffling home after a game of cards and too many wines.

Two things hit me as I walked towards my fate with coffee. The first was the faint smell of glue. It was sweet and somehow comforting in the cold air. Almost warming. I slowed as I came to the tiny enclosed entrance to Passage du Chantier. Its dingy depths had been home for centuries to cabinet-makers, and there was always the soft aroma of wood glue and tanned leather to entice you in. It was deserted now, but later it would be bustling. In warmer weather, old men would cheekily sit for a rest on the armchairs displayed outside the various makers' workshops and chew the fat, commenting on the people passing by, using the alleyway as a shortcut. I stopped and inhaled deeply, my eyes shut.

The second thing to hit me was a fist.

4

The back of my head stung from where I'd been thumped.

Two other hands shoved me from behind into the narrow alley. One of them slapped me on the head again for good measure. The other tried to turn me around to the right.

'Give us your butter,' a voice snarled at me.

Since I didn't have any to give, I twisted around to the left instead and lashed out with a roundhouse punch. The oath it caused told me it had connected. That and the sudden sharp pain in my right hand.

I turned and looked at my assailants and paused in surprise for a moment. I knew them both. Brothers. As a cop, I'd come across them over the years more often than their own mother had. This wasn't their part of town either. Jacquot, the younger of the two, was lying on the ground, blood streaming from his mouth.

'Bastard,' he cursed again, and scrambled to his feet.

His older brother, Firmin, who I'd always seen as the brains of the two, although that was relative, had to try and step over Jacquot to get to me, so it was a moment before he looked up and saw me.

'Fuck, Eddie, it's you.'

He stopped in his tracks, straddling his brother, who almost toppled them both over when he tried to get up. They sorted themselves out and stood side by side in front of me. In the shadow of the passage, I couldn't see their expressions clearly, but I could sense their shame. I'd arrested them so many times when they were younger that I was the nearest they had to someone who cared. In the gloom, I could see the years hadn't been kind to either of them.

'What the fuck are you playing at?' I asked them.

'Sorry, Eddie,' Firmin replied. 'We didn't know it was you.'

'What with the coat and everything,' Jacquot added, his voice muffled. He cupped his hand under his chin to catch the blood pouring from his mouth. The last time I'd seen him, he'd been a snot-nosed kid. He'd grown up into a snot-nosed adult.

I pointed to the wound. 'Sorry about that, Jacquot, but what the fuck do you think you're doing hitting me?'

'It was your butter we were after,' Firmin explained, like that would make it all right. In the gloom, I could see his teeth, grey and chaotic, like tank traps in a swamp.

'It was nothing personal,' Jacquot agreed. Gingerly he waggled one of the few ceramics left in the front of his mouth and winced. 'You still pack a punch, Eddie.'

'You should know better than to try and steal butter off a starving cop. What made you think I had any?'

My eyes had grown used to the dim light filtering through into the passage and I saw the look the brothers exchanged with each other.

'Nothing,' Jacquot said.

'Everyone knew,' Firmin contradicted his brother.

'Everyone knew I had butter?'

I waited for a reply. I'd learned years ago that if you waited long enough with the brothers grim, they'd almost always give something away without meaning to.

'Not you, Eddie,' Firmin said after a moment's thought. 'Everyone knew there was a load of dodgy butter going on sale today.'

'So you thought you'd steal mine?'

'Not just yours,' Jacquot spoke up. The blood had stopped gushing now, and he was cleaning his mouth on his coat sleeve. Firmin turned to shut him up.

'We knew people would be buying black market butter,' Firmin clarified, 'so we thought we'd have some of it.'

'By nicking it from people who can barely afford it and who'd queued all night in the cold to buy it? Nice.'

'Got to live.' For the first time, I recognised the old truculence in Firmin's voice. I was tempted to slap it out of him like we used to in the good old days.

'How many people have you taken butter from?'

'None, Eddie, I swear. Our hearts weren't in it. What with the Germans being here and all.' That was Firmin. He even tried crossing the spot where he thought his own heart would be.

I withered him with a look. 'Cut the crap. It's because no one had any.'

'Yeah, we noticed,' Jacquot muttered. His voice was bitter. Firmin hit him across the head and told him to shut up.

'Try not to talk, Jacquot,' I told him. 'You're giving the game away. No one had any because there was never any butter in the first place.'

'That's what you know,' Jacquot crowed. 'We saw it. Not so smart now, are you?'

I turned to look at Firmin. 'You see how easy it is? Where did you see it? Not the grocer's, I take it, so whoever was selling it to him.'

Firmin gave the slightest of tics. I could see the nervousness in his eyes. 'Don't know what you mean, Eddie.'

'And you're scared of whoever it is, so that means you won't want to tell me who it is or what's going on.'

'Fucking right we won't,' Jacquot swore.

'So I reckon we'll have to do it the hard way.'

I saw the brothers tense, ready for fight or flight. I reached out and slapped Firmin gently on the cheek.

'Don't worry, boys. I'm not going to hurt you.' I glanced around us at the passage. 'Bit of a way from home, aren't you? You're still around the Porte de Vincennes, I take it? South of Cours de Vincennes. Unless you've come up in the world. So my money's on you having seen this butter somewhere around there, wouldn't you say?'

I kept up eye contact with Firmin all the time. The flicker his eyes gave at each of my comments told me I was right. That was always how I'd caught him out in his younger days. Some crims never learn, not at this end of the food chain.

'Please don't ask, Eddie,' he begged me.

'I'm not asking, I'm just passing the time of day. You see, I reckon if you'd seen the butter, it had to be at wherever it's being kept. And that's where you got the bright idea. You know, the one about stealing butter from some black marketeer who scares the shit out of you.'

To my left, Jacquot snorted, but it was the half-hearted derision of someone slowly being caught out.

'On the back foot, Jacquot?' I asked him, my eyes still on Firmin. 'So how come you were in the black marketeer's place in the first place. Buying?'

'We don't buy butter,' Jacquot said.

'So you work for him.'

Firmin's eyes danced a waltz and I knew I was right.

'We're not saying a word,' he told me.

'No, but it seems to be working.' We stared at each other for a moment. I shook my head. 'Tch, stealing from your employer, boys, that's not a good thing. Bit too close to home.'

We waited in mutual stand-off for a few moments. My mind ran through my options.

'So what are we going to do? You see, the problem here is that

I've run out of clever ways of tricking you into telling me what I want to know, and I'm a bit tired and not a little grumpy at not getting the butter I'd been so looking forward to.' I shrugged expansively. 'So I guess we're just going to have to go old-school on this.'

Still looking Firmin in the eyes, my face centimetres from his, I whipped my left fist out and caught Jacquot squarely in the mouth again. The loose tooth finally gave up the fight. So did Jacquot. He staggered back, holding his jaw and screaming.

'You next, Firmin. What do you say?'

I backed him against the wall of the narrow alleyway. He looked sideways at his brother then back at me. Jacquot was still on his feet, moaning now in pain and spitting more blood onto the ground.

'Impasse Vassou,' Firmin whispered. He gave me a street number. 'Please don't ask me for a name.'

'No good. You know I need a name. Is it Julen le Basque?'

I studied his face. Julen le Basque had been the *grand fromage* in Porte de Vincennes in my day as a young cop and had kept half the criminal youth in terrified thrall. Firmin just looked surprised.

'Julen lost it years ago. Doesn't know his own name these days.'

'Who then?'

'It's no one you know, Eddie, I swear.'

'Someone new?'

He nodded his head vigorously. 'Ever since the Boches came.'

'So give me a name.'

A movement to my right, at the entrance to the small passage, distracted me. I half turned to see an elderly man shuffling past. He glanced at us as he passed but slowly went on his way.

I felt Firmin shove me. I stumbled on a cobblestone and lost my footing, falling backwards onto the opposite wall. The two brothers took their chance. Firmin grabbed Jacquot by the coat and dragged him away, before they both broke into a shambling run along the passage towards Rue du Faubourg Saint-Antoine, at its northern end.

I regained my balance and watched them go. I was far too old to bother giving chase.

'Catch you later,' I told their now-distant backs.

5

I decided to forgo my shower. Paris would just have to endure its suffering a little longer.

Instead I followed in Firmin and Jacquot's footsteps along Passage du Chantier. It was still too early for the local cabinet-makers to wheel their wares out onto the cobbled lane, so I was spared from weaving my way past comfy armchairs and sweet-lacquered cupboards, and old men in trousers to their armpits staring resentfully at anyone too young to remember the Franco-Prussian War.

The wider Rue du Faubourg Saint-Antoine at the top end was noticeably colder when I emerged. The passage, narrow in parts and completely covered in others, filtered out not just the sunlight in summer but the cold in winter. I felt a moment's reluctance to leave it. Luckily, the entrance to the Metro was a bare ten paces away, and I sank into its warmth.

This time in the morning, the carriages were mercifully empty. Just a few workers, lucky enough to have a job still, on an early shift. No German soldiers in sight either, which cheered me almost as much as the graffito on a tunnel wall when I changed line: *Watch out, it's the Greeks!* That brought a smile to me and a man walking alongside me, although we looked away in distrust rather than be caught enjoying Mussolini's misfortune. Greece had recently pummelled the Italians and most people in Paris had celebrated in silence.

Impasse Vassou was the crock of gold at the end of a journey that took you down a dingy flight of steps and along the wintry canyon of Rue de la Voûte into the sepulchral dead end of an alley lined with tattered and fading buildings. Only without the gold.

I found the building I wanted. All the way on the Metro, I'd had to ask myself if my eagerness to track down the black marketeer was because I knew Firmin and Jacquot knew more than they were letting on, or because I was simply curious to find out who the new kid in town was. Either that or because I really wanted some butter.

Still undecided, I pushed open the door. It led into a dank hallway that smelled of damp and decay. My eyes adjusted to the light. There were no doors off the hall, just a flight of stairs leading up into the darkness. Feeling either side of the entrance door, I found a switch and turned it on. A weak light came on in the hallway, but the stairs were still shrouded in black. Old Julen le Basque had lived in relative squalor considering the clout he'd wielded back in the day, but this place gave poverty a bad name.

In the jaundiced light cast by the ancient bulb, I saw the plaster, blackened and brittle, peeling off the walls. The wooden stairs were scored and gouged, their centres worn down to a smooth and sulking bottom lip. Functional at best, the balustrade was rusted and missing some of its spindles. The front door swung closed behind me. The smell of neglect filled my nostrils. I rubbed my fingers. They felt sticky from the caked-on grime of the light switch.

I paused, wondering again why I was here. For one brief moment I considered giving up and going home for a shower.

You can solve the mystery of the butter another day, I told myself. I knew I didn't mean it. Firmin and Jacquot had seen to that, with their comment about the black marketeer being someone I wouldn't know. The Occupation had brought with it a new generation of chancers. Small-timers out to earn an easy sou, coexisting with the bigger gangs so long as they didn't pose a threat. Just one more of the benefits life under the Nazis had given us. I was determined to find out who it was. And what the deal with the missing butter was.

Hearing no noises in the building, I climbed the stairs. The first-floor landing was in darkness, and I felt along the wall for the light switch. I flicked it, but nothing happened. I tried a few more times in that way that you do but got the same result you always get. A semi-landing I'd passed halfway up the stairs where they did a U-turn meant little light from the ground floor penetrated this far. There was no skylight in the ceiling two floors above to shed any light either.

I edged away from the stairs. I sensed the shape of a door set into the far wall in the middle of the landing. Feeling my way with my hands and feet, I went further into the blackness. My foot crunched on something and I jerked back in reflex. Treading forward again, I got the same crunch. It sounded like glass. As I felt the door frame with my fingertips, the sound underfoot became a symphony of tiny crackling.

I had no gun on me. I wasn't yet on duty, and our masters in their nice new uniforms were touchy about our being armed, even though we were cops and supposed to be helping them keep the peace, whatever that meant these days, so I'd left mine at home last night just in case. Normally I didn't care, but I figured that being caught carrying a pistol while buying dodgy butter might just tip the balance and make the Germans decide to take my gun off me. I pushed against the door and wished I'd carried on not caring.

It opened. Just a crack, but it opened.

My fingers felt the handle and found a neat hole underneath in the middle of the lock. That puzzled me.

Pushing the door open further, I was surprised at how heavy it was. I peered into the room beyond. It was still in darkness, but I could make out cheap blackout curtains covering the windows. They let in a rectangle of light around the edges, which was enough for me to discern the layout of the room.

Listening for any sound, I reached for the light switch inside the door. This one worked, and cast a sullen light on a prairie of scuffed floorboards and row upon row of shelves rising from floor to ceiling. Every single one was empty.

I remembered my earlier thoughts about the new kids in town coexisting with the original gangs who'd taken it upon themselves to supply the city with black-market goods.

'Coexisting,' I said in a low voice. 'So how long's that going to last?'

I pushed the door to behind me and went into the room, initially treading carefully but soon giving up as the ancient boards moaned and complained with every step. Running my finger along a shelf, I found no dust on it. They'd been recently cleared of whatever it was they'd been storing.

Two doors led off at the far end of the room, one to the right, the other to the left. I went right first, and found two much smaller rooms. The first revealed the same panorama of bare shelves, but the second was what evidently passed for an office. There was a small desk, a telephone, a mismatched chair and a battered old filing cabinet.

'I'll come back to you in a minute,' I told it.

Retracing my steps, I tried the door on the left and lost myself in a maze of rooms, each one the same as the others – floor-to-ceiling empty shelves.

Except for one.

I stopped and stared at it.

'Now I wasn't expecting that,' I said.

Plat Principal

6

It was a guinea pig.

Standing on its hind legs on a shelf, looking at me, its nose twitching, its black eyes sizing me up. I stared back at it. One of us had to say something.

'What the hell are you doing here?'

It ignored me.

A movement on the floor caught my eye. It was another one, brown and black and matted with dust, tentatively crawling out from under a shelf. A third one peered around the edge of a door into another room. I heard scratching beyond the threshold. Mystified, I followed the third guinea pig next door and found at least a dozen more, shuffling in the dirt around the shelves. Had Dante written about rodents, this would have been the first circle of hell.

Only I wasn't looking at them.

I was looking at the man lying scrunched in a zinc bathtub in the middle of the floor among the shelves, the captain of a small ship steaming through a cavian sea. His knees were bent almost up to his chest so he could fit in the small tub. It looked unnatural and uncomfortable, although I didn't think that mattered to him.

In his mouth was a huge pat of butter, solid in the cold. His eyes bulged, his complexion red and scored with broken veins under the skin. I stared at him for a few moments. He seemed to be looking back at me, but there was no sight in those eyes. I wasn't going to need Bouchard, the pathologist, to tell me he'd choked to death.

I checked the rest of the room, avoiding crushing its furry denizens, and returned to the office. Picking up the phone, I called Thirty-Six to tell them what I'd found. They put me through to Commissioner Dax, so I described the scene to him and asked for some more bodies to help with this one.

'Gang killing?' he asked. The guinea pigs hadn't impressed him.

'Looks like it.'

'Great. How come you found it?'

'Let Bouchard know too.'

I hung up and took another tour of the rooms. The floor throughout was covered in dust, scuffed and churned by what must have been dozens of feet. Whoever had killed the man had done a good job on his stock. The place had been gutted. All I found were some empty sacks in one room and a couple of small wooden crates, both cleaned out of olive oil, according to the labels. I felt a sudden pang of hunger. I still hadn't had any breakfast.

To quell my need for food, I decided to take a look at the door and the hole through the lock. By opening the blackout curtains and turning the electric light off, I allowed the winter sun in. Even if its glow was weak, at least it was a hue that didn't give me a headache. Going to the door, I examined the neat little hole. It was completely smooth. I'd never seen anything like it before. I was surprised to find a second hole, higher up, through another lock.

Staring at the two holes, I had the fanciful idea that whoever had got in had done so by drilling through the locks. I pictured a brace and bit and dismissed the idea. It would have taken an age to do that to just one of the locks, let alone both, not to mention the muscle power in cranking the handle with enough force to drill a hole through something so dense. That would have needed the whole of the night and a team of people taking turns. It would have been easier to batter the door down. At least that was what I thought until I took a closer look at the door. It was the one part of the entire building that was new. That and the two locks. All three pieces were heavy-duty, their sole purpose to keep undesirables out.

'Well, that went well,' I muttered.

Peering out onto the landing, I saw that what I'd trodden on was indeed broken glass. Tiny pieces of it, crushed almost to a powder. Looking up, I saw that the bulb had been removed from its fitting. That was why the light switch hadn't worked. I spied the metal screw base squashed on the floor amid the debris.

Looking back into the room, I saw that here and there among the dust were tiny motes that glinted in the light from the windows. At first I thought it was the glass from the bulb, but then realised it was metal. Minute filings scattered in the dirt, dissipated by countless footprints.

I started to give some credence to the idea of a team of people using a brace and bit to drill through the locks. If the treasure on the inside was rich enough, I could imagine a rival black marketeer deciding it was worth the effort. They were probably struggling to find enough goods to trade in as the rest of us were to feed and clothe ourselves. It would take some brute force, though.

Next I checked the office, but the filing cabinet didn't offer any clues. An empty bottle of brandy and two glasses in the top drawer, some ancient papers that revealed nothing in the middle, and a dead spider shrivelled up in the corner of the bottom one. The desk drawer just held some more pieces of paper that shed no light and some old pens and drawing pins. This wasn't a business that generated much paperwork. Under one blank piece of paper I found a superannuated packet of condoms.

Learning nothing more, I went back to take a closer look at the dead man in his bath. His skin was as greasy as his walls, his hair as dusty as his floors. He'd evidently adopted a hairstyle that had been big twenty-five years ago and gone with it. What was left of his crinkled locks was slicked across a balding dome with pomade. Flecks of dandruff powdered his collar. He'd also had a hygiene problem in life. Little wonder the condoms were unused.

Crouching to reach inside his jacket pocket, I found his wallet. It was empty of money but contained his ID papers. Joseph Cartier. Firmin had been right. It wasn't a name I knew.

The door downstairs banged open and I heard a voice call up.

'Eddie?'

'First floor,' I shouted down.

Leaving his wallet and ID on the floor, shooing away a curious guinea pig, I looked inside the bathtub. I couldn't help letting out a gasp when, underneath the man's knees, I saw a pat of butter, similar in size to the one in his mouth.

The downstairs door banged open again and other voices drifted up the stairwell.

I looked back at the butter. It was lying in what I took to be guinea pig shit, but the top was clean.

Footsteps sounded on the steps from the half-landing.

I ran to retrieve one of the small pieces of sackcloth from the floor and hurried back to the bath. I nearly stumbled to avoid stepping on my inquisitive friend.

More footsteps echoed on the stairs.

Crouching down, I had to reach underneath the man's legs to get to the butter. It slipped out of my hand. Despite the cold, it was starting to soften. I reached again, my shoulder edging the man's legs out of my way.

'After you, Doctor Bouchard,' a voice came from outside the front door.

I grabbed the pat – it had to be half a kilo – and quickly wrapped the sackcloth around it, fumbling in my haste. I stuffed the packet into the side pocket of my jacket, underneath my coat, and wiped my hands on the seat of my trousers.

'What you got there, Eddie?'

I looked up to see Bouchard rounding the doorway and coming to a stop in front of the bathtub. He stared at me hard through his semi-lunettes and ran a tired hand through his greying hair above his deep forehead.

'What do you mean?'

He nodded at the man at his toilet. 'Who's our friend?'

7

'What were you doing there, Eddie?'

I stood warming my hands by the stove in the detectives' room at Thirty-Six. The temperature had plummeted to colder than a police commissioner's humour and the outside world had taken on a stark blue-white sheen like its own mood was about to break.

Police Commissioner Dax stood beside me, rubbing his own hands to get some warmth. I hoped it would do some good for his humour. His gaunt face was made all the more angular in its reflection in the curved stovepipe, his glasses exaggerated and predatory like an owl's eyes. He was a thick paunch on a thin frame after years of cassoulet, wine and anxiety.

We were the only two at the heat oasis. The other cops had shied away first at my presence, then at his.

'How did you know this Cartier had been murdered?' Dax insisted.

I stared at the flames licking the blackened top of the stove before answering.

'I didn't. I had a tip-off about a black marketeer operating out of Impasse Vassou in the Twelfth, so I thought I'd better take a look.'

'And found him dead?'

'And all his stock gone.'

I suddenly remembered that in my eagerness to get warm, I'd forgotten to stow my new-found butter in my desk drawer. I shifted my body to ensure the pocket with it in was away from the fire.

'Who gave you the tip-off?'

'Couple of brothers I used to nick most weeks back in the day. Firmin and Jacquot Bouvier. Their part of town.'

'So why'd they give you the nod about this guy? Rivals?'

'Not these two. They couldn't run a bath, let alone a business.'

'Could they have done it?'

'And then told me where to find him? Unlikely.'

Sifting the truth from my own explanation – and the fact that I'd thumped the information out of Firmin and Jacquot rather than it being a tip-off – I wondered briefly if the brothers could have been responsible for Cartier's death. I still thought it unlikely. They were as petty as they came, but they weren't killers. Not when I knew them, anyway. Also, why would they be attempting to steal butter from shoppers if they'd already killed Cartier and emptied his warehouse? Only I couldn't mention that to Dax.

I sensed him shrug next to me. His physical expressions were always in exaggerated contrast to his verbal reticence.

'Things have changed,' he said, unwittingly expressing the same doubt I'd just posed to myself. 'Now the Germans are here. No one's acting the way you'd expect.'

A copy of *Au Pilori* lay on a desk beyond the stove. A far-right and anti-Semitic weekly newspaper since 1938, now the Nazis were in town it had grown in strength and regularly featured articles by Louis-Ferdinand Céline, who'd been far-right and anti-Semitic for even longer. I nodded at it.

'Not every leopard has changed its spots,' I commented.

Dax grunted. 'Heard the news? Marshal Pétain has sacked Laval. He's put him under house arrest.'

I gave a low whistle. Laval was the Vichy government's prime minister and foreign minister. The only thing growing apace with his clout with the Nazis was the hatred for him felt by the rest of us. Even Dax was slowly losing his love for Pétain and his acolytes, although he'd never admit it.

'So the crooks are falling out with each other,' I said. I looked around to make sure no one was listening before carrying on. 'Any other news?'

Dax knew what I meant. 'Jacques Bonsergent?' The Germans were about to execute a French civilian for the first time in Paris. It wasn't yet common knowledge. He shook his head. 'Nothing.'

The impotence we both felt sliced through the warmth from the stove like an ice-cold dagger.

Dax grunted again. 'It's snowing in Vichy,' he commented, changing the subject.

'Good. At least they've got it worse than us.'

I picked up the copy of *Au Pilori* and shoved it in the stove. The flames flared orange and yellow as they engulfed the rag, and I warmed my hands with renewed vigour.

'Best use for it,' Dax said quietly. His re-education was almost complete.

'I still don't think Firmin and Jacquot are likely suspects.' I took up the reins again. 'Doctor Bouchard says the victim took quite a beating before the butter was shoved into his mouth. Those two would crack your skull for twenty centimes, but I can't see them handing out a sustained battering like that. And the thing with the butter's just not their style.'

'Not even for a black marketeer? They're not anyone's friend these days. Can't say I blame whoever killed him.'

I turned to face him and quickly turned back, remembering the butter in my pocket. 'You don't mean that?'

He sighed heavily. 'No. Just suffering like everyone else. I can't drum up much sympathy for this Cartier.'

'So what do you want me to do about it?'

'You mean you'll pay any attention to what I say?' He let out a small laugh. He had a point. 'Find out what's going on. I don't care what happens to scum like Cartier, and I'm frankly not too bothered with who did it, but I am concerned about what might come next. Is Julen le Basque still around?'

'Past his prime, I hear. He had a son, though. I'll see what he's up to, if he could be behind it.'

'All right, but I don't want any shooting matches because of it and I don't want any reprisals or gang wars. Keep a lid on things, Eddie.'

I nodded. In the past, I would have argued. Justice was justice, regardless of the victim, but needs must when Adolf shits on your doorstep. The last thing we wanted was the Germans breathing down our necks with black marketeers at each other's throats. Especially when the Occupiers were the biggest racketeers of them all.

We carried on warming our hands and I told Dax about the holes through the two locks in the warehouse door. 'That was obviously how they got in.'

'How in God's name did they do that? Hammer and chisel?'

'Too clean. And it would make too much noise. Brace and bit, I was wondering. Drill through the lock. It would take one hell of a time, though.'

He shook his head. 'You'd need an industrial drill to do something like that. But they're huge, much too big and heavy to carry around. I don't see it.'

'Maybe not.'

Dax cleared his throat. I waited. 'We've got someone new starting in the department on Monday. A woman.'

'A cop?'

'You know that's not possible, Eddie. You can't have women

cops. A secretary. Office help now we've got all the extra paper-work to keep on top of because of the Boches.'

I watched the flames briefly flare at a particularly stubborn piece of newsprint. There'd been women working as secretaries and typists in the Paris police for the last ten years or there-abouts, but Dax had always been reluctant to take one on when offered. Like him, the powers-that-be still wouldn't countenance a woman as a beat cop or a detective. I watched two of the old-timers, echoes of a bygone age, shamble past us to stare out of the window, and I couldn't help wondering if it wasn't such a bad idea after all.

'We need the help,' I agreed.

'You all right with it?'

'Completely.'

'I'm glad to hear that. She'll be sharing your office.'

I was silent for a moment. Dax had played me. I'd had a room to myself ever since the Germans had arrived in town, and I'd got used to not having to put up with anyone's foibles. Of my two former cellmates, one had fled the city before it fell to the Germans and had simply never returned, the other had taken it as his chance to retire. Good job. If he hadn't jumped, I'd have pushed the useless bastard. I considered the loss of that privacy.

'Fine,' I told Dax. 'Just make sure you keep Boniface out of her hair. And mine.'

We both laughed at that one. Boniface was another detec-tive who'd fled the city along with thousands of other people, but in his case, he'd returned. There were days I reckoned his prime motivation in coming back had been to irritate me. And to seduce any woman who hadn't yet succumbed to his heavily rationed charms.

Dax looked thoughtful for a moment. 'One other thing. There's been a series of burglaries that's been running our detec-tives ragged. We've been chasing our own tail for over a month trying to catch some burglar who's been robbing apartments in the Sixteenth and the investigation's getting nowhere. It needs a new pair of eyes to take it over.'

I hid a sigh. 'What's this got to do with me?'

'Nothing. You've got this murder now. So I'm thinking I might assign the burglaries to Boniface instead.'

I couldn't help breaking into a smile. 'I'm thinking that's the best idea I've heard since the Germans got here.'

'You would.' Dax sniffed. 'But don't hold your breath. He's still working under you until a decision is taken.'

'Take it soon.' Oddly, even as I was saying it, and relishing the thought of not having to put up with Boniface's prattle and preening, I felt a reluctance to lose him. He was a pain in the arse, but he was a pain in the arse who was also a good detective.

I left Dax warming his own arse by the stove to take myself off to my flat for a wash. I also needed to get my butter away from the heat. He had one last parting shot.

'Oh, and Eddie, make sure you behave yourself tonight.'

Neither of us laughed at that one.

The first thing I did at home was inspect my cache of fat. Some of the fibres from the sack had stuck to it, so I picked them off. The underside, the bit that had been face-down in the bathtub under Cartier's knees, was polka-dotted with guinea pig droppings, so I took a knife out of my kitchen drawer and scraped the thinnest of layers off before putting the butter away in a bowl in a cupboard. It would have been pointless using the cold box outside the kitchen window, as it would freeze in this weather. The temperature was steadily falling as the morning wore on.

I washed and put on an extra vest and long johns. I was still feeling the effects of my night in the cellar, and my flat was nowhere near as warm as the stove in Thirty-Six had been. The fireplace in my small living room grinned back at me like a blackened and toothless mouth. I was glad I had a murder to investigate. It got me out of the cold.

The relief didn't even last the time it took me to get out of my building. My downstairs neighbour was just returning home from his own queue. He had a couple of leeks firmly embedded under his left arm as he unlocked his front door with the right. I couldn't help staring at them. Leeks weren't rationed, but they were almost impossible to come by. I hadn't seen one in months. They'd go lovely with butter.

'Morning, Inspector Giral,' he greeted me through his clipped moustache and thin lips.

Our relationship had been permanently at the formal, awkward stage for over ten years. I hid a groan. He was one of a new breed spawned by the Occupation. He believed nothing of what he read in the newspapers, which was a healthy trait, and everything he heard in a queue for food, which was not.

'Morning, Monsieur Henri. Won't stop.'

'You'll have heard the news. The British are bombing the castles in the Loire Valley.'

'Is that so?'

'And they've landed at all the major ports. Not that we'll be any better off here.'

'You don't say.'

He gave me a knowing look and disappeared into his apartment.

'Except you do say,' I added to myself as I descended the stairs. 'Ad fucking nauseam.'

8

'I'm looking for your boys.'

'Scrounging little shits.'

'Nothing like a mother's love.'

'You should've locked them up and hurled the key into the Seine when you had the chance, Eddie Giral. Save a poor mother's woes.'

The source of such maternal pride was Georgette Bouvier. The scrounging little shits were her sons, Firmin and Jacquot, so her logic was essentially faultless, if harsh.

I'd come to the brothers' part of Paris, a crummy apartment block near the Gare de Charonne goods station. Even past its nineteenth-century prime, the station and the railway it served still managed to blacken the quarter's streets and dead ends with soot. Through the grimy window of their mother's flat, I saw the railway lines of the Petite Ceinture stretch north and south. The circular railway had been built the best part of a hundred years ago to supply the city's defensive ring with troops and arms. Now wouldn't that have been a good idea? Giving off an air of decline, it was just used for goods now, as passenger trains had stopped using it in the mid-thirties.

'Save a poor mother's woes?' I nearly choked. 'You taught the thieving little bastards everything they know.'

'Not everything. They always get caught. I never did.' She

said it with a fond melancholy, like they'd only just failed to get into the Sorbonne. 'Useless pricks. Swapped at birth, must have been.'

'Both of them?'

'I reckon so. Although the younger one's not as hopeless as the older one.'

'Only a mother would know that.' Or even see it. Her words surprised me. I wondered if she knew which son was which, but gave up on that line of thought. 'So what is it they've got themselves into now?'

She shrugged and tapped the ash off her cigarette. 'Who knows. You know what they're like. Nicking fifty sous here and losing a franc there. As bad as their father, wherever he is.'

We both knew he lived three streets away, happily married to a hairdresser, and was now a successful – and straight – businessman. I thought of the two sons. If ever a gene had skipped a generation, they were it.

'What sort of thing?'

'Bad crowd. Taking advantage of people's misery.'

'Black market?'

She shrugged a second time. 'This and that. I don't ask. They'll fuck it up like they always do.'

'Do you know Joseph Cartier?'

'I know of him. Slimy little runt.'

'He's dead. Murdered.'

'I know. Good riddance.'

'Do your boys work for him?'

'How would I know? All three are as bastardingly useless as each other, so they might. The way flies find shit. But you'd have to ask them that.'

'So where can I find them?'

She stubbed the cigarette out straight onto a kitchen table already pockmarked with burns and craters. 'You think I'd tell you that? What sort of a mother do you think I am?' She stood up and pointed to the door. 'Now piss off.'

Leaving mother of the year to her little corner of paradise, I tried a few of the cafés around her block, but no one would tell me where the brothers were. In all honesty, I hadn't expected much joy there. Instead, I headed south, towards the Cours de Vincennes, the wide road that acted as the border between the Charonne and Bel Air quarters, and the streets around Impasse Vassou. I figured I might find out more in the neighbourhood of the warehouse where Joseph Cartier had stored his black-market goods than in the brothers' neck of the woods.

My walk was through a part of the city I'd never loved. I had a choice between taking the Boulevard de Davout, part of the Boulevard des Maréchaux, the old military route encircling the city, each section named after a First Empire marshal, which I'd always found grey and soulless; or the Rue des Pyrénées, which I couldn't face. It was the opposite end of a long road, I know, but Rue des Pyrénées was where I'd first lived in Paris long ago with my wife and son. It was a time in my life when I'd followed a path that had almost killed me. And when I'd hurt the two people I shouldn't have.

And the rest, I reminded myself.

I took a third option and cut through the soot-filled railway tracks and the narrow streets that criss-crossed between the two bigger roads. Eventually I reached the Cours de Vincennes, next to a school, where I was stopped in my tracks by the sight of a pair of German army lorries parking outside. A couple of dozen soldiers climbed down from the two trucks and slowly entered the building, chatting like kids on a school outing. Puzzled, I waited a few minutes to see what was going on, but no one emerged.

Unable to move on without knowing what was happening, I went into the main entrance and found an office. A woman with white-grey hair and warm eyes sat behind a desk, filling in forms. I showed her my ID. She told me her name was Isabelle Collet. A low hum of children's voices permeated the building.

'Is there a problem?' she said.

'That's what I came to ask you. I saw German soldiers and wondered if there was anything wrong.'

She gave a laugh, as bitter as it was short. 'Only that in their wisdom, the Germans have decided to billet their soldiers in the school.'

'And they haven't relocated the children? That's what they've done with other schools.'

'No. And this is a girls' school. It's absurd.'

It was my turn for the mirthless laugh. 'How do they think that's going to work?'

'We do what we can. Fortunately, the soldiers are in a separate wing, so it could be worse.' She looked at the form she was completing and scratched her head. 'But it's still one of the stupidest things I've seen in twenty-five years of dealing with the Ministry of Education.'

With nothing I could do, I left her to her headaches and crossed the road to enter the *impasses* of Bel Air. The first place I tried was a bicycle repair shop on Rue de la Voûte, a stone's throw from the entrance to the dead-end lane where I'd found the black marketeer.

'Don't know what everyone's complaining about,' the owner, a wiry man aged anything between forty and seventy, said. All I'd done was ask how business was. He was busy doing something greasy with a chain and an upturned bike. 'I've never had it so good. Everyone's buying or repairing bikes now the Germans are here. No fuel, so no cars on the road. Never had so much work. Lovely.'

'Well, as long as you're all right.'

'Never better.' Sarcasm is lost on some people.

I showed him my ID and nodded in the direction of Impasse Vassou. 'What do you know about Joseph Cartier, the man who was killed?'

The smile faded, like the tan on his paper-thin cheeks. 'Nothing.'

'Nothing?'

'Well, I mean, everyone's talking about it. The murder, that is. Or whatever happened. But I didn't know him.'

'You never bought goods from him?'

'Didn't even know he was there.'

'So if I were to check what's in your kitchen, it would all be above board? Nothing bought on the black market?'

He paused before replying. 'Well, no. I mean, I buy on the black market. Everyone does. But not from him. Not that I know of, anyway.'

'Who from, then?'

'I don't know. Just in cafés, like.'

I stared at him, his expression increasingly more uncomfortable. 'Sure you don't want to tell me any more?'

He shrugged and said nothing.

I tried a couple more places on Rue de la Voûte and knocked on a few doors in the Impasse Canart, which gave off the road opposite the alley where Cartier had operated, but the response was similar. Few would admit to knowing there was a black marketeer in their neighbourhood, let alone to buying from him.

I had more success the further away I moved from the crossroads. Two men – one middle-aged, one younger – were loading tools into a van parked outside an electrician's. I showed my ID to the older of the two. He called the other one over.

'Yves Ferran,' the first one said. 'This is my son, Pierre.'

'And you work here?'

'I own the business. My son's working for me.'

I asked them the same questions about Cartier that I'd been

asking everyone else. 'It looks like no one had ever heard of him.'

Yves snorted. 'Of course they had. We all knew Cartier.'

'You won't find anyone around here who didn't buy from him at some time,' Pierre added. 'You had no choice.'

'Did he have any enemies?'

'He was a parasite,' Yves told me. 'A profiteer. No one liked him, that comes with the territory. But enemies? Not that I know of.'

'He was a bastard,' his son agreed. 'But a necessary one.'

Yves pointed at the buildings around him. 'We didn't like having to buy from him, but we're screwed now he's gone. The whole neighbourhood. Who knows how we're going to manage for food now.'

'Until the next one takes over,' Pierre said. 'And wait and see what they're like.'

'True enough. At least Cartier was an evil we knew.'

'Have you seen anyone trying to take over his business?' I asked them.

They looked at each other and shook their heads. 'Not that we know.'

I described Firmin and Jacquot and asked if they'd seen them around.

'Couple of guys, mid-thirties, here a few times,' Pierre told me. 'Could be them. I assumed they were buying.'

They finished loading their van and Yves walked to the driver's door. Looking at his father's retreating back, Pierre turned to me and put his hand on my forearm. He went to open his mouth.

'Come on, son,' Yves called to him impatiently. 'Work to do.'

Pierre let go of my arm and joined his father in the cab. I watched them go. 'Now what did you want?' I wondered aloud.

Next door to their business was a café. I hadn't seen it when their vehicle had been in the way. My need for coffee was suddenly greater than any urge to find who had killed a black marketeer. I'd get back to him.

The guy behind the counter was my age, a veteran of the last war like me. You can tell by the look. And because of the photos on the wall of a younger version of him in uniform in a trench. An old German officer's Luger lay on a low shelf behind the bar. I had one at home just like it.

'Nivelle,' he explained.

'I was already in a German prison by then,' I replied. 'Verdun.'

'Bad luck.'

'I survived.'

He grinned. A big, broad crease that carved deep lines about his eyes and mouth and gleamed like his coffee machine. 'Something to be said for that.' He reached across the counter and shook my hand. 'Ulysse Lavigne.'

'Eddie Giral. Now about that coffee ...'

'*Café national*, I'm afraid.'

I waited until he'd served my drink. *Café national* was the name the government had given to the excuse for coffee served up because of rationing and shortages. Another fake patriotic virtue to attempt to distract us from how bad things really were. It was one part coffee, two parts roasted barley and acorns, three parts vile. I took a sip and tried to hide a grimace.

'No offence taken,' Ulysse said. 'It tastes worse than anything we ever had in the trenches.' He reached under the counter and pulled out a bottle of brandy. Hidden from view, he poured a small measure into a glass and gave it to me. 'Just don't let the cops know.'

'I am a cop.'

'I know.' Again the grin. 'It's all people have been talking about all day. That and Cartier getting a taste of his own butter.'

I took the smallest sip of the brandy and felt it tingle on my tongue and in my mouth before reluctantly swallowing it. The burn in my throat was two parts pain and pleasure in a balance that *café national* would never achieve.

'Any thoughts on Cartier?' I asked Ulysse.

He flicked his tea towel over the counter. 'I saw death in the last war. I lost friends. I don't wish ill on anyone, no matter what they've done.'

'Very noble.'

'But I'm sure as hell glad someone did for that evil little shit.'

9

The Hotel Lutetia at this time of year always put me in mind of a Christmas tree. The undulating balconies swathed in light both inside and out were reminiscent of ribbons strung from branch to branch. The top-floor windows with their arches were the pine cones. The gentle and welcoming lights on the ground floor were like the red apples of temptation. As a child, I'd always been told that the tradition of the Christmas tree as we now know it dates to refugees from Alsace bringing the practice with them to Paris. This was during the Franco-Prussian War. Another time our neighbours across the way decided they liked us so much they wanted to own us.

Only this was the second Christmas of the war and the first under Nazi occupation. So there were no lights, no music, no joy. The building was in darkness. The once-bustling crossroads where it sat was still as a stagnant pond, all life choked out of it by the weeds that had invaded it. And from where I was standing, the red apples of temptation were few and far between.

The Hotel Lutetia was the chosen home of the Abwehr, German military intelligence. Every time I went in, I wondered if or how I'd come out. Tonight was no different, although perhaps irrationally so.

I'd been invited. Not invited as in the 'we want to question you until you fall into our trap' way that I'd got used to with the

47

Abwehr, but invited as in 'find your least scruffy suit and come along for a perfectly jolly evening together'. I'd have been hard pushed to say which of the two was the less welcome. Especially at the end of a very long day trying to find anyone who cared about a black marketeer being force-fed butter in his own ransacked warehouse. I recalled Dax's exhortation to behave myself. I still wasn't laughing.

'Édouard, so glad you could make it.'

Crisp and imposing in his best uniform, Major Hochstetter was waiting for me in the bar near the foyer. He beckoned me over and ordered me a whisky. The sort that was illegal for the rest of us, ever since our marvellous Vichy government had banned the sale of alcoholic drinks over sixteen per cent proof in the summer. We couldn't even drink away our sorrows efficiently.

I sat down and paused before sipping it. We all have our moral hills to climb, but whisky is whisky in anyone's Occupation, and this was good stuff. Only the best for our Major Hochstetter.

'I wouldn't have missed it for the world,' I told him. I meant the whisky.

'I know.'

He said it in that way he had of a wolf sharpening its fangs as an aperitif to the main course of jugular. Providing the wolf had studied at the Maurice Chevalier school of charm. Hardly the model Aryan of Adolf's wet dreams, Hochstetter was nonetheless striking, with dark hair, chiselled cheekbones and deep brown eyes as cold as a shark's. And an urbane sophistication that simply accentuated an undercurrent of menace.

I surreptitiously scanned the room to make sure no one I knew was lurking amid the potted plants and field-grey uniforms.

'You're safe here,' he told me, reading my thoughts.

'That would be a first.'

He had the grace to laugh. 'Most droll. If you don't mind,

we'll wait a moment longer before leaving. We have a companion for the evening's entertainment.'

'I'm intrigued.'

'That's because you're a policeman. You trust nothing and no one, so you use the word "intrigued" to justify that.'

The only answer I had was to nod sagely and drink some more of my whisky. Someone had got out of the Lutetia's crisp white sheets on the wrong side that morning. Hochstetter was something high-up and shadowy in the Abwehr, which I now knew, thanks to his insistence, was the intelligence service of the German army, not of the Nazi Party structure. That honour went to the Sicherheitsdienst, or SD, with its sibling organisation of the Gestapo. The SD and the Gestapo didn't always get on nicely, but they both hated the Abwehr, which hated them back. Hochstetter was always at great pains to point all of this out to me. I still don't understand how we lost. Actually, I do.

I was sitting in the bar of the Hotel Lutetia because the day after the Germans had marched into Paris, Hochstetter had been assigned to act as a liaison between the Occupiers and the French police. More specifically, the criminal police, the bit that had me in it, so I was the lucky winner of my very own watchdog in a grey uniform. I'd quickly learned to be guarded with what I said to him.

'Why the foul mood, Major?' I asked him. 'Adolf not happy with the way things are going?' I didn't say I always applied that learning.

'You would do well to temper your witticisms this evening, Édouard.' He took a long drag of his cigarette. Tobacco and Hochstetter were never far apart. 'I apologise. I am somewhat tense about tonight's command performance.'

'Why're you going? More importantly, why am I?'

He chose not to answer my question. Instead he asked one of his own. 'What investigations do I need to know about?'

One thing I really had learned was that it was pointless trying to keep everything from him. The secret was to feed him slightly more of anything that he'd be likely to know to appease him and pass all his tests, while keeping as much of the really important stuff to myself as I dared. I told him about the black marketeer being found murdered. He wanted to know more.

'In the Twelfth Arrondissement. The Bel Air quarter.' I answered his next question and tried to change tack. 'How has your day been? Have you all finished what you came to do?'

'Do you think a rival criminal was the perpetrator?'

'Probably.'

'Was he part of a larger organisation?'

'You seem very interested, Major.'

'It is my business to be interested. You know that.'

'So why have I been invited to this thing tonight?'

He lit another cigarette and adroitly flicked the dead match into an ashtray.

'The same reason I have. To get to know one's enemy.'

Momentarily surprised by his comment, I was only partially aware of a figure who came and stood by a third armchair set at our low table. I glanced across and saw a grey uniform. In the moment before he sat down with a cool grace, I saw that it was a tall, slender man. I turned to look at Hochstetter to check his reaction. His head cocked to one side, he had a smile on his face. Genuine, not the mocking half-smirk I'd grown used to.

The newcomer sank into the chair and took his hat off, throwing it onto the table in front of him. It landed with its peak obliquely facing me, and I hid a low gasp. A death's head leered at me from above two lengths of braid, set slightly apart in a rictus grin over the brim.

'This is your policeman, I take it,' he said to Hochstetter in German.

I looked at him more closely. I now saw that the field-grey

uniform I'd assumed a moment ago was Wehrmacht was giving me a message I'd missed. On the man's right collar as I faced him were three diamonds and two sets of tramlines, symbols that meant nothing to me. On the left was a symbol that did – SS. The letters were like two lightning bolts that left me stunned.

'You may speak German to Inspector Giral,' Hochstetter told him. 'He picked up enough to get by during his time as a prisoner in the last war.'

The man looked at me and nodded a greeting.

'Édouard,' Hochstetter addressed me, 'allow me to introduce Martin. He is visiting Paris and will be accompanying us this evening.'

I was still transfixed by the skull on the cap badge. 'You know each other?'

'Indeed we do. Martin is my brother.'

IO

I was surrounded by stained glass and nymphs. Mirrors and statues. Belle-époque curlicues and mauvais-époque waiters.

And field-grey uniforms.

I was one of only four not in uniform. Eight were in varying shades of Wehrmacht field grey, and one, Hochstetter's brother, was in the spectral grey of the SS. There were thirteen of us in all, seated around a table in Maxim's piled high with glasses and plates and military formations of polished steel cutlery waiting to see action.

'So whose Last Supper is it?' Hochstetter had whispered to me when we'd arrived at Paris's poshest restaurant.

'Very cheery,' I'd replied.

He had recognised one of the others in the group and gone over to sit next to him, greeting him warmly. The man looked of a similar age to Hochstetter, too young for the last war and not old enough to challenge the present one. He had the same greyish-green uniform as the others, but I noticed the bits of adornment on it were different. I was adrift in a sea of epaulettes and stripes.

Seated to my left was one of the other mufti diners, a tall, cadaverous man with a receding hairline and hangdog expression. Surprised to hear me speak in German – faltering as it was – he introduced himself as Dietrich Falke and gave me a card with an address on Avenue Foch on it.

'A businessman,' he added cryptically.

'What sort of business?'

'Oh, I trade. You know the sort of thing.'

'Yes, I certainly do. I met one of your fellow traders this morning.'

'German?'

'French. But he had a good line in butter.'

His interest gone, he grunted and turned away.

To my right was a face I recognised. High cheekbones and thoughtful blue eyes under a mop of blond hair that was slightly at odds with the Wehrmacht uniform below.

'Eddie,' he greeted me in German. 'Peter. We met at a jazz club in Montparnasse a month or so ago.' He grimaced. 'And at the opera.'

'I remember. A fellow jazz-lover.'

He smiled, seemingly touched that I'd remembered. The opera had been one of those nights when Hochstetter had tried to educate me in German culture and forced me to watch an entire warble-fest. I'd met Peter there, an officer in the Wehrmacht and equally reluctant to be present. I'd sensed at the time that he was also rather reluctant to be taking part in Adolf's operatic fantasy in general.

'Maybe we could cut loose and no one would notice,' he suggested as the others around the table began to look at their menus.

I felt the same appalling sorrow I'd felt the last two times I'd met him that we'd been forced to come together because his country had invaded mine. Our similarities far outweighed any differences we might have had.

'How come we've all been invited?' I asked him.

'Who knows. Our host is very much a law unto himself, I've heard.'

Our host chose that moment to speak. 'Put your menus away,

gentlemen. I have chosen for us all. Only the best for my guests.'

He issued an order in fluent French, and a stream of waiters emerged from the shadows with trays piled high with dishes. Steam and desire rose in tendrils from the fine china.

I took a sneaky look at the host. He was third in the quartet of those of us not in uniform. Instead, he was in a shiny suit that probably cost more than I'd ever spent on clothes in a lifetime of looking crumpled. He had dark hair slicked to one side, an elongated oval face and eyes that were set too far apart. There were few of the blond gods that Hitler seemed to insist on seated at the table.

He was Otto Abetz, the new German ambassador to Paris. A little over twelve hours ago, I'd awoken in a cellar to queue for some non-existent black-market butter, and now I was sitting in probably the most expensive restaurant in the city surrounded by food and champagne and people who would without a moment's thought scrape a week's ration of butter onto a family's ration of bread.

I looked at my fellow diners. Each one was in muffled conversation with their neighbours. The food on the table meant nothing to them. A rarefied fantasy for an entire street of Parisians was simply the side dish of just another meal they saw as their birthright as the master race. My stomach growled quietly, giving away both a hunger and an anger I felt rising in my core. Another sensation arose in me. Panic. Panic at the thought of temptation.

I had to look away from them, my gaze inevitably going to the food on the table, the object of their indifference. There were garnishes that would have made anyone outside the room weep with envy, the meat and fish they were there to adorn too elusive a memory for most Parisians to recall.

I looked at the men around the table once more.

I had no idea why I was here.

I only had marginally more of an idea who or what Abetz was. He was a Nazi, that was no surprise – Hitler's envoy to France was never going to be anything but a dyed-in-the-wool believer, even though he'd only joined the Party late in the day – but I also knew he was married to a Frenchwoman and thought of himself as an ardent Francophile and lover of Franco-German rapprochement. That was probably why he'd been chucked out of France for political meddling just before the war broke out. Which is how come I'd got to hear of him, as we'd been instructed at Thirty-Six at the time to investigate some of his activities, although I'd never actually met him. And now here he was back with us. Only this time I didn't think we were going to be booting him out again any day soon.

I studied him for as long as I dared before turning to look at the man seated on his right, the final civilian in our unlikely tetra. He was unknown to me, but I knew from the shape of his mouth as he spoke that he was French. That surprised me. From the deep confabulation he was holding with Abetz, they obviously knew each other well. A snippet of their conversation drifted over the table to me. It was indeed in French, but I couldn't make out the words. The man raised his head and looked towards me.

Peter patted my arm and passed me a bowl of prawns. I simply stared at them. Someone else placed a platter of salmon in front of me. I looked at the food and wrestled with my conscience. And with my self-control. Most Parisians were going without; many would have sold their souls or anything else they had for just one of the dishes on the table. There were those who would have killed for a taste of what was in front of me. And it was being handed to me. By our Occupiers, invaders, Nazis.

Placing some of each on my plate, I passed the dishes on but left my knife and fork untouched either side of the ornate porcelain. I don't know if it was my excess of hunger or my conscience, but my hands simply wouldn't go to the cutlery. The food was too fine. My head fluttered as hungrily as my stomach as I watched the others feast. It was grotesque, a ravenous mutilation of mouths and teeth and saliva that would have made Rabelais eat his tongue.

For some reason, I had a sudden image of the whisky I'd had at the Lutetia with Hochstetter and his brother. It was another luxury – or staple – denied to the French, yet I'd happily drunk it. It was a question of degree, perhaps. I looked again at the food on my plate, the aroma rising off the prawns and salmon and filling my nostrils.

'Have you recently been posted to Paris, Hauptsturmführer?' I heard one of the younger Wehrmacht officers ask Hochstetter's brother from across the table, a welcome distraction from the self-loathing of my temptation. There was a palpable under-current of distrust among some of the army men at the sight of the SS uniform, and Abetz had seemed oddly displeased with Hochstetter at bringing his brother along.

'I am simply visiting,' Martin replied. 'Just here for a Christmas break to see my brother.'

He nodded at Hochstetter, and I saw a couple of cogs fall into place around the table at the young Hochstetter's reason for being there.

'From Berlin?' a second officer asked him, a bouncy-looking type with rosy cheeks and fine hair like a baby's.

Martin finished shelling a prawn and chewing it before replying. The table was silent as he did so, which seemed to please him. Taking his time to wipe his hands on his serviette, he shook his head.

'I came via a brief stay in Berlin, but I've been serving the Führer in Poland. I return there after my visit to Paris.'

I glanced at Hochstetter to gauge his reaction. I'd learned in the staff car that had brought us from the Lutetia to Maxim's that his brother was some seven years younger than him and a hauptsturmführer, which appeared to be lower down the pecking order than a major, although you wouldn't think it to listen to Mini-Hochstetter. When he'd got onto boasting about his service in Poland, an uneasy Hochstetter had silenced him before glancing at me. We both pretended otherwise, but we both knew the stories that had come out of Poland about the way the SS had acted there.

'So how are you enjoying *die Stadt ohne Blick*, Martin?' the first officer, a lugubrious counterpoint to his cheery fellow interrogator, asked.

Martin looked confused, so a third officer explained. 'The city that refuses to look at you. The Parisians. They try to pretend we're not here, so they completely ignore us in the street.'

'Do you find it as disconcerting as we do?' the first one asked, his voice as grey as his manner.

Martin paused in his disembowelment of a second prawn and looked at each of his questioners in turn. The scorn was apparent in his eyes long before it reached his mouth.

'You call yourselves Germans? You find the French ignoring you disconcerting? Does it hurt your poor little feelings?' He snorted and chewed on his prawn. 'I've come from Poland. No one ignores us there. Not the Poles, not the Jews. We know what to do with them.'

'That's enough, Martin,' Hochstetter told him quietly.

His brother laughed, fine specks of prawn spitting from his mouth. 'You are soft. All of you. Look at you, all this food, all this luxury. It is lucky for Germany that we have the SS to do your dirty work for you while you skulk about in Paris with your fine restaurants and whores. You grow as fat and as effeminate as the filthy French scum you mix with.'

He was brought to a halt by a loud bang on the table. Everyone turned to see Otto Abetz, his face red with anger, as he slammed a plate down a second time, shattering it and sending shards scattering over the food in front of him. The metamorphosis from charming diplomat to enraged beast was as rapid as it was shocking. Staring at a defiant Martin, he calmed equally quickly, although his voice was filled with subdued ire as he spoke.

'You are a guest in this country, Hauptsturmführer, you would do well to remember that.' Martin was about to reply, but Abetz cut him short. 'Need I remind you of my position? Not only in Paris, but in the Party?'

The two men stared at each other for a moment before Martin finally nodded a grudging acknowledgement and ostentatiously deliberated over a slice of smoked salmon.

Four waiters hurriedly removed the food that had pieces of china in it – the dishes they took away would have fed a family for a week – and quickly replaced them with fresh plates of salmon and lobster, turkey and veal. I watched transfixed as a large pat of butter quickly melted over a bowl of boiled potatoes. Oddly, they seemed to me to be the greatest luxury. Like leeks, potatoes weren't rationed, but I hadn't tasted any in a while. I caught myself on the verge of laughing, a tense, nervous reaction. I was surrounded by dishes that would have been sumptuous even before the Occupation, and it was the potatoes that I coveted.

And it was the potatoes that finished me. Mechanically, remotely, I took some from the bowl and put them on my plate. Ignoring the salmon and prawns, I picked up my knife and fork and cut into a potato, taking in its scent before placing it in my mouth. I could have wept at the tenderness of the flesh, the oiliness of the butter, and I took another piece. I figured it would be no insult to my countrymen to eat foods they could still get, albeit with difficulty. So I ate the rest of the potatoes on my plate.

And then I ate a prawn. And I took a large draught of the

champagne that had been poured into my glass and I accepted some more from the waiter at my shoulder. And I took some salmon. And some lamb when it was offered to me.

And I ate the first piece of veal I'd tasted in over a year, and I chewed as Abetz spoke, his voice a silken dagger.

'My dear Hauptsturmführer,' he addressed Martin Hochstetter again, 'do not for one minute think that I am criticising your passion for the Führer and the Fatherland. That could not be further from the truth. I have nothing but admiration for the work you in the SS are doing. At home, in Poland, in Czechoslovakia, indeed in all our conquered lands. But France is now part of the Reich. And as such, it merits our respect. A valuable addition to the thousand-year Reich, in fact. One with a cultural legacy even greater than ours that has made an immeasurable contribution to mankind. A society that enriches us all with its art and literature, its thinkers and philosophers.'

'For all the good it's done them,' another officer chimed in, his first contribution to the evening. 'Doktor Goebbels is right. Our goals should be to crush this so-called French cultural supremacy. Let others know their place.'

I ate my food and held my tongue. Instead, I examined the new speaker, a myopic scholarly type with round glasses and hair parted sharply in the centre, and mused on how unfortunately easy it was to lead people to believe anything and do anything you wanted them to by belittling or destroying the achievements of others. I noticed the younger Hochstetter nod in agreement with him.

Abetz smirked indulgently. The officer had more than his fair share of pips and braid on his uniform, but I imagined Hitler's ambassador to Paris was above having to worry about such hierarchical niceties.

'*Au contraire*, Herr oberstleutnant,' he replied. 'Our goal is to win the French over. If we are to continue to be victorious on all fronts, we must subdue our conquests and make them safe to allow good patriots like all of you seated around this table to make further gains for the Fatherland elsewhere. Your way and Herr Doktor Goebbels' way would simply incite resistance and unrest. No, we must seek collaboration by seduction to win the French over to our way of thinking. That is the way to weaken and divide France and bend its people to our will.'

Next to me, Falke broke into a smile for the first time, like a skull jangling. It was every bit as unnerving as the badge on Martin Hochstetter's cap.

'I must say, I'm very happy with the way we're seducing the French,' he commented. 'I can barely keep count of the Reichsmarks I'm raking in.'

'Just so long as you're happy,' I told him, emboldened by the succulence of potatoes.

Hochstetter glared at me.

'Oh, I am,' Falke replied.

Abetz looked triumphant and gestured to my neighbour. 'You see? Our friend here is the perfect example of just how much we can do for the Fatherland by working with the French. For my part, I am immensely pleased to have been able to replace Jean Paulhan as editor of *La Nouvelle Revue Française* with Pierre Drieu La Rochelle, a man who is more in tune with the sort of Franco-German collaboration I seek. And the values of the Party. The first issue under his tenure has just this month been published.'

'And have you read it?' I asked, this time emboldened by champagne.

Abetz appeared to notice me for the first time. 'I beg your pardon?'

'This month's *Nouvelle Revue Française*. Have you actually read it? The only thing of value in it is the ink it's printed with.'

Ink was another commodity in short supply, so it had seemed a pity to waste so much of it.

My comment was met with a stunned silence, which was worth it alone. I saw the look Hochstetter gave me. It was colder than the champagne bucket sweating into the tablecloth.

'Ah, the policeman,' Abetz said with a smirk. 'My journal not to your literary or intellectual taste, is it?'

'I was sorry to see Paulhan go. He was a good editor.'

'And you would know that, would you? You are evidently an unusually cultured policeman.'

That earned him some sycophantic sniggers from various points around the table.

'No, I'm only a cop. I just like the bit where Paulhan spoke of Rhetoricians, those who have confidence in the ability of language to express what it is they have to say, and Terrorists, the ones for whom language is an obstacle to expression. It just strikes me we have an awful lot of Terrorists in town right now.'

There's a silence that tells you when you've gone too far.

'Terrorists?' the myopic oberstleutnant muttered, a menace in his voice that was at odds with his appearance. If not his uniform.

I saw them look at each other, a cauldron of annoyance at this interloper in my own land beginning to come to the boil. I'd provided them with a diversion from their discomfiture at Martin Hochstetter's scorn. An epicentre from which their anger could quiver and rumble.

One of them half rose from his seat. 'I will deal with this man,' he told Abetz.

Instinctively I held firmly onto my knife and put the fork down. I stared him in the eyes as he continued to stand up. It suddenly occurred to me that I was at a table with at least nine men – ten if you counted the mysterious Frenchman – who had the power of life or death over me. At a darker time in my life,

I'd had a ritual with a Luger and a dud bullet that I used to hold to my head. This felt awfully similar, only the bullet wasn't a dud.

We were all surprised by a noise. Laughter. Gentle at first, but rising in crescendo. As one, the men at the table turned to look in astonishment at the ambassador. He was laughing to the point of tears running down his thin cheeks. He waved at the officer to sit down and dried his eyes, looking directly at me.

'I like you, policeman. Touché.'

My grip on the knife relaxed as cautiously as the tempers around the table. Next to me, Peter let out a little laugh and clapped his hands gently. The tension eased like a slowly deflating balloon.

Hochstetter rose from his chair and beckoned me. 'Édouard, a word. Would you come with me a moment?'

I took my glass of champagne with me just in case.

II

I washed my hands and looked at Hochstetter's reflection next to me in the mirror. He wasn't happy. Although I will say, the gentlemen's toilets in Maxim's are spotless enough to eat off. I dried my hands on a small towel thicker than my mattress at home and drank some more of my champagne, any pangs of conscience cowering in the corner of my dissipating hunger.

'I didn't know you had a brother,' I told him in a last-ditch attempt to head him off.

'I have warned you, Édouard. This is not the place for your supposed humour.'

I was surprised to find his voice calmer than I'd expected. He stepped back from the washbasin and lit up a cigarette, flicking the dead match into a bin and inhaling deeply. I looked away. I'd been unable to contemplate the idea of smoking since experiencing gas attacks in the last war. Perhaps it wasn't entirely logical, but it was good enough a reason for me.

'I brought you here to assist me,' Hochstetter continued. There was a hint of resignation in his voice. 'You might be surprised to hear, but I value your judgement. You have the instinct of a survivor and, when it suits you, the guile of a feral cat. Despite your evident faults, your experience among the dregs of this city means that you are able to read people and situations. I need you to observe and to listen. What I don't need is your puerile insistence on provoking a reaction.'

I was surprised. Not entirely flattered. But surprised.

'Assist you in what?'

'You asked me why you were invited. And you were quite right to do so. I have asked the same question about myself. Why has Otto Abetz invited me, an officer in the Abwehr, and a number of other senior Heer and Kriegsmarine officers to one of his infamous soirées? Although I will state that it is not as luxurious as I'd been led to believe by all the stories.'

Heer, I remembered. The German army. Even though we all called the army the Wehrmacht, including the German army themselves, really they were the Heer. The term Wehrmacht embraced the army, navy and air force. I know all this because Hochstetter had impatiently told me every time the mood had taken him. He only used the term when it suited him.

And the Kriegsmarine was the German navy. That would explain the different bits of fruit salad on Hochstetter's friend's uniform.

'Maxim's not good enough for you, Major?'

'I will ignore that. I will simply observe that this evening's event is out of the ordinary for Abetz, in so many ways. I know it's in Maxim's, but it is still a more muted affair than his normal celebrations.'

I pictured the table we'd temporarily left and recalled the queue for butter that morning, and I tried to imagine how this could in any way be construed as muted. 'You mentioned something about knowing your enemy. What did you mean?'

He gestured at the door leading back into the restaurant. 'This whole meal. Otto Abetz is no friend of the Wehrmacht, and much less of the Abwehr. He is a Party man through and through. He has the ear of the Führer and is Foreign Minister von Ribbentrop's man in Paris. Hitler has already removed all responsibility for political matters relating to the press and the arts in Paris from the Wehrmacht and given it to Abetz.'

'So he's to blame.'

'Please curb your attempts at humour, Édouard. His dinner guests are normally the great and the good of the Party structure and the pro-German French elite, not a random assortment of army, navy and military intelligence officers. Paris is still currently under the control of the military authorities. My instinct tells me that one of our ambassador's avowed goals is to further undermine Wehrmacht influence here so that his friends in the Party and the SS can take over.'

'Who's the other Frenchman, next to Abetz?'

'I have no idea.' He waved his hand dismissively.

'So why do you think you're here tonight?'

He looked at me frankly. 'No, Édouard, you tell *me* why you think I'm here tonight.'

I stared back at him for a moment and visualised the diners around the table. They were like the pieces in a child's jigsaw. 'Know your enemy. He wants to know who he can count on and who he should see as his enemy.'

'Precisely.'

'He's arranged this whole thing so he can see which Wehrmacht officers are more pro-Nazi. Which ones he can put in his pocket. And which ones he should keep a close eye on.'

'I'm Abwehr,' Hochstetter said. 'The head of army intelligence, Admiral Canaris, will not allow senior officers to be Party members. I think we both know where that places me with Ambassador Abetz.'

'Collaboration by seduction. He hopes to see if you're amenable to being won over.'

'Quite possibly. As with everything, Édouard, there are varying shades of commitment, and Abetz knows that. You can win even the most reluctant of people over to your side through the right combination of persuasive measures.'

'I'll bear that in mind.'

That earned one of Hochstetter's smiles. Not the warm beam at the sight of his brother, but not the wolfish glow of the predator either. I recalled Abetz's displeasure at the sight of Martin in his SS uniform.

'That's why he wasn't too pleased to see you turn up with your brother,' I said. 'Although in the end it's worked in his favour. Martin's views, if I can call them that, have been the right provocation for Abetz to gauge the response.'

'The response being?'

'It's the ones who don't speak who are the ones you have to watch. The Goebbels-fan oberstleutnant is an obvious contender for seduction, but there were two more who said nothing but who nodded along to what your brother was saying. Abetz would have singled them out. One to your left and the other between the oberstleutnant and Abetz.'

He smiled for a third time that evening. 'This is why I asked you to come along. You pick up on these things.'

'I'm surprised our Otto agreed to let you bring me.'

'A tame senior French detective? I imagine you're yet one more of his possible targets for seduction.'

'That's going well, then. So you brought me along to observe?'

'And to shake things up a little, I must admit. Which you have done admirably. Up to a point. But please do not go beyond that point.'

'I think young Martin has taken on that challenge. I really didn't know you had a brother. And one who's so different from you.'

'There is no way you would know. And I could say likewise. I have no idea if *you* have a brother.'

I drained my glass of champagne and avoided my reflection in the mirror. 'I don't. I did. He was older than me and also very different. But he died in the last war.'

'I am sorry to hear that.'

*

'We should maintain a bank of hostages,' the oberstleutnant was saying when Hochstetter and I returned to the table. 'Detain groups of civilians at random who would then be made available for public retribution in any further cases of violence against our troops.'

I knew what they were talking about. I also knew it had just got that bit harder for me not to go beyond Hochstetter's point.

'I fully agree.' One of the two silent supporters I'd pointed out to Hochstetter finally joined the conversation. 'This Saint-Jean or whatever his name is should be an example. We should be going further.'

'His name is Bonsergent,' I told him. 'Jacques Bonsergent. If you're going to execute a man for jostling a German soldier, the least you can do is get his name right.'

The man turned on me. He had a bright red complexion and a uniform one size too small for him. 'I really don't think we need the opinions of the losing side.'

'All opinions are valid here,' Abetz interrupted him. He really was hedging his bonhomie bets to see who was on his side. He turned to me. 'It was more than jostling, surely.'

'It wasn't even that. A group of friends on a night out got into an argument with some drunk German soldiers a few days after the Armistice Day demonstration. Someone raised a fist to a feldwebel. That was it. It was the most trivial of incidents. And it wasn't even Bonsergent, according to witnesses.'

'So why would we be executing this Bonsergent if he were innocent?'

'Because you've chosen to make an example of him precisely on account of the riots. And because he refused to name the other people with him. This is not the seduction you talk about.'

Hochstetter caught my eye. He raised one hand very slightly to indicate that I should pull back.

'I think that listening to our French guest, we can all agree with the need for hostages,' the oberstleutnant commented, looking at me with disdain.

'General von Streccius was right.' One of the younger officers took up the baton.

'General von Streccius?' I whispered to Peter. Partly to calm myself.

'Chief of the Military Administration,' he explained in a low voice. 'Before von Stülpnagel took over from him in October. Be careful.'

'Hostages cannot simply be random,' the young officer carried on. 'They should be carefully selected to have an especially close solidarity with the criminals. Communist hostages to receive retribution for Communist outrages. A working-class individual attacks one of our soldiers, we execute ten working-class individuals that we have previously detained as an example.'

'Quite right,' an older officer agreed. 'This would at least be in keeping with your desire to collaborate with the French, Otto. Why alienate all of French society? Simply focus on the ones who cause us headaches. I am sure the rest of the population would welcome this.'

I glanced at Hochstetter and held my tongue. It was extraordinary how the most repugnant of attitudes could be expressed with such a sheen of rationality.

'Nonsense,' Martin said forcefully. 'You are too soft. The French are a conquered nation. You need to behave as their conquerors. In Poland, we shot forty or fifty *Untermenschen* for the death of just one German. It is the only thing they understand.'

'Reprisals are the only way.' The oberstleutnant nodded. 'There have been far too many attacks on our men for us to allow the situation to go any further.'

'Agreed,' the one in the tight uniform said. 'The culprits

responsible for the murder of the NCO last June near the Porte
d'Orléans have never been brought to justice.'

'Or the ones who planted the bomb that killed the soldiers in
Sarcelles. The first victims of the cowardly Parisians.'

I glanced at Hochstetter and decided to ignore him, the bass
notes of anger rising in my voice. 'The first victim, as always, is
the truth. Your NCO was not murdered. He was knocked over
by a train because he was drunk and on his way back to barracks
from a brothel. And the soldiers in Sarcelles were killed when
they ran into a pile of German landmines stacked by the side
of the road. An accident with no French people involved. Your
own investigations proved this.'

'My dear Otto,' the oberstleutnant said, 'do we really have to
put up with this insolence?'

I rounded on him. 'You already have French hostages, more
than you will ever need. Random or otherwise. Only you call
them prisoners of war. Nearly two million of them. Half a
million of those are from Paris. And you haven't released them.'

'Precisely. They are prisoners of war.'

'There is an armistice in place. They are being held as hostages.'

'No, they are being held as prisoners of war,' Abetz interrupted, 'which is what they are. There might be an armistice, but
there is no peace treaty. Until there is, they will continue to be
regarded as prisoners of war and they will continue to be held
in Germany.'

'And this is your idea of seduction?'

We stared hard at each other, but were stopped from talking
further by a commotion at Hochstetter's side of the table. A
candle had toppled over and ignited a pool of brandy on the
tablecloth. The officers hurriedly got out of their chairs and stood
back from the flames which were gathering pace on the linen.
A waiter came over with an ice bucket and threw it over the

small fire. A second waiter appeared and beat out the remaining flames with a serviette.

Hochstetter looked at the others and then at me before speaking.

'Well, that was close.'

12

'I don't think I went beyond a point in particular,' I told Hochstetter in the staff car that drove us back across the river away from Maxim's.

'Only because I set fire to some brandy.'

Hochstetter's brother had decided not to come with us back to the Lutetia.

'It is my first time in Paris,' he'd told his older brother when he'd offered him a lift. 'I wish to go out. I cannot leave without sampling the delights for which it is famous.'

'You'll find most of those have gone,' I'd told him, which had earned a stern look.

I was glad now that he wasn't in the car. As we crossed the Seine, the Assemblée Nationale building loomed up ahead of us. Adorning its façade was a huge white banner, ghostly in the fake twilight cast by the almost full moon. Picked out on it in black letters was the message *DEUTSCHLAND SIEGT AN ALLEN FRONTEN* – Germany is victorious on all fronts – put there to let us know how well it was all going. I doubted I could have put up with young Martin's crowing at it without doing a spot of jostling of my own.

'For once it is your anger you need to curb, Édouard, not your supposed humour.'

I looked again at the banner and turned away to stare out of the side window at the low carved stone walls on the Pont de la Concorde. Through the spindles, I caught glimpses of the river glistening black and silver in the moonlight.

'How come you don't get angry?' I asked him. 'With Abetz playing you all like that?'

'Oh, I do get angry. Don't make the mistake of thinking I don't. I merely bide my time with it.'

He dropped me off outside the Lutetia without offering to get his driver to take me back to my flat. It didn't surprise me. I'd served my purpose for the evening. I checked my watch. Since November, the Germans had pushed the curfew back to midnight and the Metro would still be running.

I walked to the nearest station. The city was surprisingly busy for a Saturday under German occupation and with a bright moon in the sky to tempt the RAF. It was nothing in comparison with the time before the Germans had come, but the numbers of Parisians willing to chance their luck with the bombers and able to push thoughts of foreign soldiers on the streets out of their heads never failed to astonish me. I thought of my argument with the Wehrmacht officers and realised we all sought our outlets where we could.

My anger hadn't dissipated by the time I was underground. It was simply simmering as I sat down in a carriage filled with German soldiers and young Parisians carefully trying to avoid eye contact with them. Since the demonstrations by schoolkids and students on Armistice Day, over a month ago now, and the energetic response of the Germans – and some of the French cops – the atmosphere had become that bit tenser.

As the clacking of the rails and the spectral image of myself blurring in and out of focus in the grime-blackened window tried to lull me to calm, I spotted something. Tucked into the metal surround of the wooden bench next to my shoulder was a piece of paper. I glanced around to check no soldiers were looking my way – that was another thing we'd quickly learned – and pulled it out. It was a single-page leaflet, black ink on coarse white paper, with just one message crudely printed on it. Making sure once again that I wasn't being observed, I scanned what it said.

I'd seen it before, in the early days of the Occupation, as part of a much longer pamphlet, and the BBC had broadcast parts of it in October. Then it had been called *Conseils à l'occupé* – tips for the occupied – and I remember it containing over thirty pieces of advice on passive resistance. Things like not giving a truthful answer to a German, pretending not to understand them and keeping contact with them to a minimum. Its writer needn't have worried, I thought, we'd all done that naturally. Unless, of course, we'd all seen the pamphlet when it had first come out and followed its manifesto. Its final paragraph had been to call on people to copy it and spread the word.

I read the simple message again. Oddly, it reminded me of Hochstetter's words in the staff car, about merely biding his time with his anger. My simmering temper reduced instantly to a slow stew.

The single line on the piece of paper told us to save up our anger. Not to use it until we needed it.

I folded the leaflet carefully and put it back for the next person.

13

I was eager to get home. I wanted to sit in my ice-cold living room and read Jean Paulhan's *The Flowers of Tarbes, or Terror in Literature*, to relive the Rhetoricians and the Terrorists and to allow my gently bubbling anger to find a place in which to be contained.

But first I had to get past Monsieur Henri outside his apartment door.

'You know who's living at the Hotel Majestic now, don't you?' he demanded of me.

'No, but I'm sure you'll tell me.'

'Only Adolf Hitler. That's who. Their bloody Führer. Got tired of Berlin and come to live here.'

'I really thought you'd be in bed by this time.'

He sniffed at me. 'Bed. I thought you were home too. Sounds like someone moving about up there.'

I couldn't help glancing up at the ceiling. I heard nothing. By the time my gaze came back down, my neighbour had already gone inside and closed the door behind him.

I climbed the stairs slowly, listening out for any noises. I didn't have my gun on me. It was safe in the bedside drawer in my bedroom. Hochstetter had banned me from bringing it along to the evening's jollity. That had probably been a wise decision.

Pushing the door open as silently as possible, I found the lights on and the sound of singing coming from the living room. A gentle lullaby sung in a soft, harmonious voice. Entranced, I paused to listen for a brief moment and clicked the door shut behind me. The singing stopped.

'In the living room,' a voice called.

Wrapped up in a blanket on the more comfortable of my two faded armchairs, Dominique looked up at me when I walked in. She smiled. Thoughts of Jean Paulhan and his essay were gone in a moment.

'You were singing,' I said.

'No, it was the radio.'

I let it ride. 'What are you doing here?'

'Aren't you happy to see me?'

'Of course I am. I just thought we said I'd come to your flat tomorrow. I wasn't sure what time I'd finish this evening.'

'How was it?'

What? Dinner with a dozen German officers and the Nazi ambassador to Paris? It was a riot.

Except I couldn't say that. I hadn't told her where I was going. I knew she wouldn't be happy with the thought of me hobnobbing with the Occupiers.

'It was all right,' I said instead. 'Trying to track down someone who murdered a black marketeer.'

'Ugh, I hate those people. Parasites.'

'Worse than their murderer?'

'As bad as each other.'

I always marvelled how some people had very clear ideas on what was right and wrong. Where the line was drawn. I suppose my time in the last war and as a cop had put paid to any certainties I might once have had.

'What are you doing here?' I asked her again.

'I didn't want to be on my own at home.'

'So you came and sat here on your own.'

'Yes, and it's freezing in here.'

Despite her words, she shed the blanket and stood up, coming to me for a hug and a kiss. It was a long kiss. We were still at that stage and I wasn't complaining.

'I've got some butter,' I told her. 'I queued for it.'

She laughed with delight, a joyous peal that worked almost as well as an anonymous leaflet in cooling my temper, although infinitely better in warming my spirits.

'And I've got something for you. For us. Wait here.' She went into the kitchen and returned a moment later with two small round objects, one in each hand. She opened up her palms to show me. 'I found these in my local greengrocer's.'

'Apples,' I said.

'I can't remember the last time I ate an apple. We can eat them now.'

I stared at them. I was full. After the mountain of food and sea of champagne on offer at Maxim's, the thought of any more food made me bilious. I looked up and saw her face beaming with happiness.

'Lovely,' I said.

'Come on.'

She gave me the larger of the two apples and sat down in my armchair. I sat in the chair next to her and tried to swap my fruit for hers.

'You have the larger one. You found them.'

'Nonsense, Eddie.'

She took a hefty bite and began to savour it, chewing slowly. I looked at mine and took a deep breath. I had no appetite, but I could see no choice. Part of me said I had to save it, let her eat it tomorrow. Another part of me knew that that would upset her. She was too excited at the notion of sharing them. I had to eat it now. I took a small bite and chewed, forcing it down.

'Aren't they wonderful?' she asked.

'Wonderful.'

Dominique pulled her blanket around herself again, but I was too hot. The surfeit of food – a feeling I'd never thought I'd experience again – was bringing me out in a sweat.

'Aren't you cold, Eddie? I'm freezing.'

'I'm fine. This is relatively warm after being out all evening.' I struggled through another mouthful of apple.

'I've been thinking about it. While I've been sitting here waiting for you. I couldn't find any coal in your flat and I realised you didn't have any.'

'I've used up my ration. Fifty kilos a month doesn't go far. Not in this weather.'

'Me too. I'm nearly out of coal as well. We should combine our two rations.'

'How would that work?'

'We live in one of our flats instead of spending time in each other's. That way we only have to heat one place and we can pool our coal rations.'

'Live together?' I put my half-eaten apple down on the occasional table and looked at her.

'Only while this cold lasts.'

'How's that going to work? It's hard enough keeping this a secret as it is.'

'I've thought about it,' she said, taking the last bite out of her apple and savouring it for a moment. 'We'd have to live in my flat. Another Frenchman entering my building isn't going to attract any attention. But a Senegalese woman coming and going in your block, people will notice that. Especially with you being a cop.'

I gazed at her for a long minute. Her words made so much sense, but the Nazis and their racial laws meant it was a risk, even though it was a risk we were already taking just by being together. Vichy hadn't explicitly pronounced on the matter – although the removal from office in September of Henry Lémery, a minister from Martinique, as Vichy's Colonial Secretary, had given enough of a clue – but we both knew Pétain's government would go along with whatever the Occupiers wanted.

Looking away, my eye alighted by chance on the Paulhan book. I suddenly had an urge to read it, to hide. Dominique was the love I'd never had when I was younger. I'd first met her in 1925, when we'd both been married to other people. I'd been moonlighting on the door of a jazz club in Montmartre. Dominique had been one of the resident singers. Nothing had happened at the time, despite what we'd both obviously felt. It wasn't until just a few months ago, shortly after the Germans had taken over Paris, that she'd come back into my life.

Unwillingly, my gaze shifted automatically to a photo at the far end of the bookshelf surrounding the empty fireplace. It was of my son, Jean-Luc, taken three months earlier. I'd walked out on him and his mother at the same time I'd met Dominique, although not because of her. He was six when I did it. I hadn't seen him again until he'd come to me for help when France had fallen to the Germans and he was a soldier on the run. I'd helped him escape Paris. The last I'd heard of him was over a month ago. He'd still been stuck in France trying to get over the Pyrenees to join the Free French in London.

All I had of Jean-Luc was a single baby shoe in a box I kept firmly shut. Besides that, I had nothing but two photographs of him up to the age of five, then none until the picture on the mantelpiece, taken secretly by someone who had wished him – and me – harm. I had no letters or notes from him. For someone who loved books, it was odd that I had no idea what his writing looked like.

But at least I had my son. Dominique's son, Fabrice, a year

older than Jean-Luc, had gone missing in battle. That was why she'd come back into my life, when she'd asked for my help in finding him. From what I'd learned, he was almost certainly dead.

'What are you thinking, Eddie?'

'I think we should do it.'

'I was afraid you'd say no.'

I could sense the relief in her voice. I picked up her finished apple from the table and took it out into the darkened kitchen. Standing at the sink to try and fathom what I felt, I heard the same lullaby from before, sung in a low voice. Dominique told me she no longer had the heart to sing, but I would occasionally catch these moments. Moving to the door between the kitchen and the living room, I stood in the shadow and listened. Her song had a melancholy quality to it that shook me to the core.

She stopped before I went back into the room.

'Come and sit down, Eddie. You haven't finished your apple.'

14

I had another date with Hochstetter the following night. And with history, if the Occupier were to be believed. Not that anyone cared.

But before that, I had my own little date with prehistory.

The city's criminals are an unadventurous bunch. They always stick to their preferred routines and places to unwind. And the two I was tracking were less than intrepid even by those heady standards. I wasn't even sure the place I was looking for still existed. A generation would have come and gone since I'd last frequented its marble halls, but I figured that if it had shut up shop, I'd just follow my nose to find what I wanted.

It was still there. On Rue d'Avron, north of Cours de Vincennes. And it hadn't changed. Les Quatre Chats was one of those odd places that did not appear as it was. It had large windows giving onto a busy working street, the glass adorned with elaborately painted signs advertising the joys in the interior, and tables and chairs in serried rows like any other respectable bistro. Just another café in a bustle of everyday life outside it. An unsuspecting stranger to the Bel Air quarter would quite easily have strayed in looking for an anis or a wine before realising their mistake. The first clue would have been the framed boxing photos around the walls. That was always a bad sign in some parts of town. And then the owner, Claude, a former featherweight champion who was as wired as he was wiry, his temper sharper than his surprisingly unbroken nose. And finally, the clientele. They seemed to scurry about the tables like rats in a respectable sewer, swapping furtive glances and murky packages.

But not the bar. The bar was reserved for drinking and eyeing each other up. Whether it was for a fight or a fuck was often moot. Sometimes it was both. The first thing I noticed was that the brass bar running the length of the counter was still there. Back in the day, some of the tougher villains would strap themselves to it with their belts so they could drink themselves unconscious without falling over. As I said, Les Quatre Chats was nothing like as salubrious as it liked to make out.

Pouring wine into two adjacent glasses, Claude stared at me for a few moments, trying to place me. It had been a long time, but he got there in the end, slopping the wine over his steadying hand in surprise. I saw his hand shake slightly; the years of getting hit in the head had caught up with him.

'Evening, Claude,' I told him. 'The usual.'

'I have no idea what that is.'

He had a point. I looked along the counter. Vichy's ban on strong liquor and the fact that wine was one of the few pleasures not yet rationed meant that that was what everyone was drinking. There was a faint smell of acorns from the few brave enough to try a *café national*.

'Wine,' I told him. 'Red.'

'Long time no see, Police Inspector Giral,' he replied, his voice appreciably louder on the last three words. He reached for a glass without taking his eyes off me.

'Subtle. Well done.'

I turned my back on him to face the room. Suddenly no one was reaching into coat pockets for packages, or, indeed, talking. Four men at the door hurried out, only half as unobtrusively as they imagined, their glasses of wine unfinished. A young tough who'd forgotten to button a collar onto his shirt like every other young tough in the city started giving me the mean-eye. An old-timer next to him, a safe-cracker I'd nicked a dozen times in the past, put his hand on his sleeve to warn him off.

'Very wise,' I mouthed to the older one. I'd had a reputation in my younger years that sometimes actually stood me in good stead even now.

Looking around, I found the two I was looking for. Bless their hearts, they were sitting at the far end of the café and hadn't noticed my arrival. I turned back to the counter and looked at my half-filled glass.

'And the rest,' I told Claude. 'I'm off to chat with a couple of friends and it could be thirsty work.'

He reluctantly topped it up and I wandered off to where the brothers were sitting. Firmin saw me first, when I was almost upon them, and made to stand up. I put my hand firmly on his shoulder and pushed him back into his chair.

'Stay with me, boys, I get lonely.'

There was a third man with them. Not someone I knew. He had a rough face that looked like it had tried and failed to appear urbane, with a thin moustache modelled on Fernand Gravey under a nose as broken as Jean Gabin's. His black hair was slicked back with a hair oil so pungent it would have stung a bee.

They had a bottle of wine on the table and two glasses, along with some cured ham they were eating from a cloth bag that they were hiding from Claude's view. Even without that little detail, it could only have been dodgy. The other man took a piece of ham and stood up.

'Something I said?' I asked him.

He ignored me and spoke to the brothers. 'I'll see you later.'

Without a glance in my direction, he left and headed for the door. Two other men, a snake-hipped charmer with hard

82

eyes and a thickset type with a nose so crooked it looked like a dirt track snaking down a hillside, peeled off from the bar and followed him out. Before they did, the first one looked across to me and asked Claude something.

'We don't know anything,' Jacquot said, interrupting my observation. The gap in his mouth from the tooth I'd knocked out was keeping the other dark spaces in there company.

'I could have told you that.'

I sat down in the chair their companion had vacated and put a slice of the ham in my mouth.

'Who's your friend?'

'He just came to talk to us,' Firmin told me.

'We don't know him,' Jacquot added.

I looked from one to the other and took another piece of ham. They were lying.

'Good stuff. Your new friend give it to you?'

'No, Eddie.'

'From Cartier then, your old boss?'

Their glance to each other told me that was a yes.

'We stole it from him,' Firmin admitted.

I took a third slice and ate it. They didn't object. 'Was that when you cleared out the rest of his stuff? You know, when you force-fed him butter like a goose until the old guy choked?'

Firmin looked shocked. 'That wasn't us, Eddie.'

'We found him like that,' Jacquot added. 'After we tried stealing your butter.'

'You found him? And so you decided to help yourself to his goods?'

'No,' Firmin said. 'It was all gone when we got there. The place was empty.'

I poured myself a bit more wine from their bottle and nodded at the ham. 'So what's all this then? And where did you get the money from for a bottle of wine?'

The brothers looked at each other again and shrugged. Neither of them knowing what to say, neither wanting to take the lead.

I shrugged along with them. 'Of course, if you want to be guillotined for Cartier's murder, that's all the same to me. No need to say a word.'

'We stole the ham before,' Jacquot said after a pause. 'We sometimes took stuff. He never noticed. It was just him there and he had more than he could manage.'

'And the money?'

'We found it.'

'Try again.'

'Really, Eddie. When we found him dead. There was all this money in his safe.'

'So whoever killed him and took his stock decided not to take his money?'

'They couldn't have seen it. We knew where it was. It was underneath the floorboards next to the filing cabinet. We knew he kept the key in his desk, so we looked and found some money.'

'There wasn't much,' Jacquot added.

I studied each of them in turn. They were no angels, but they weren't killers. Or at least they hadn't been when I knew them.

'Julen le Basque had a son. Seen him lately?'

They both looked surprised. 'Not for years. Doesn't live here any more.'

I took that in. 'So what was it you did for Cartier?'

Firmin shrugged that bit too nonchalantly. 'We helped out. Earned a bit of money.'

'And the thing with the butter?'

'Nothing, Eddie, honest. We just knew there was a load of butter that Cartier had sold to the grocer, so we thought we'd take it. Sell it on.'

'Great idea,' I told them. 'Only it wasn't yours.'

Firmin looked aggrieved. 'Why wasn't it ours?'

'I love you, boys, almost like you were my own delinquent sons, but proud as I am, even I know you couldn't work out your own names without a year's learning at the Sorbonne. Who told you to do it? Someone trying to take over Cartier's business?'

'No one,' Firmin argued. 'I told you, it was so we could sell it again.'

I stared hard at him for a moment. He was nervous, but I reckoned that was my doing. It wasn't because he seemed afraid of anything. Or anyone. There was something about this I couldn't get a handle on.

'Again? You said so you could sell it again?'

'I meant sell it on.'

'So who got you to do it? Your friend who just left?'

The brothers shrugged and avoided making eye contact with each other.

'We really don't know,' Firmin insisted. 'It might not have been someone out for his business. Maybe someone just got mad at not getting the butter and they killed him.'

'If you're working for someone and they killed Cartier, you need to tell me. I can help you.'

'We don't know anything, Eddie.'

I looked from one to the other. 'Because it's either that or the blade.'

While my words hung in the air, I felt rather than heard the room fall into silence. It was punctuated by a harsh knocking sound on the wooden floor. I turned to see what was going on.

A wizened old guy with even fewer teeth than Jacquot and hair that clung to his thin skull like cobwebs to a rotting apple walked across the room. People grinned as he made his way. Every step he took clacked on the floor like a tap dancer who'd given up. I recognised him as Jules le Requin – the Shark – a hard-nosed fence back in the day who used to specialise in gold jewellery and dirty postcards. He gave a little flourish every now and then, which set the whole bar off laughing.

'Get a load of Bojangles,' one wag called. He was a bruiser in a grey cloth cap with a dog-end surgically attached to his bottom lip that sprayed burning ash as he spoke.

'I like the armistice shoes,' another one shouted.

Mercifully, Jules le Requin found a chair and the tuneless tap stopped.

I looked at the old-timer and his shoes. In the armistice talks in June, the Germans had made the French government agree to send all the country's shoe leather to supply the German army. That meant we had none for us, so just a few days ago the Vichy government had passed a law banning the sale of leather-soled shoes, which meant that cobblers were forced to sell shoes with wooden soles. They were immediately called armistice shoes.

'You'll never get me in a pair of those,' the first wag took up the joke again.

'No, you won't be able to sneak up on people.'

The rest of the café burst out laughing, but the bruiser took offence, reaching for a bottle. Claude put paid to any nonsense with a firm hand on the man's arm, and he put it down, pretending to see the joke.

'Well, that's enough entertainment for one night,' I told the brothers, and got up. 'One last question. What's with the guinea pigs and the zinc bath?'

'What guinea pigs?' Jacquot asked in reply.

'We saw the bath,' Firmin added. 'Never saw any guinea pigs.'

'So why would there be guinea pigs and a bath there?' I insisted.

Jacquot shrugged. 'Maybe he liked guinea pigs.'

I took a couple more pieces of ham and left them. Outside, I scanned the dark night. The man with the broken nose was on the opposite corner, evidently unable to hide even in a blackout.

I crossed the road to him. He stared impassively at me as I spoke.

'So why would you be waiting for me all this time?' When he didn't reply, I pointed to one of the few cars in the street. 'That's my car over there and I'm heading back to the police station if you want to come with me.' It wasn't and I wasn't. I snapped both hands out and grabbed hold of his collar. 'Tell your boss that. What was his name again?'

Behind me, tyres screeched, and I half turned to see a Renault Novaquatre drive up. I felt myself pushed back as the heavy shoved me away and got into the car. I watched it roar off.

'Now that's not going to arouse any suspicions,' I told its retreating echo.

15

'I hate this bloody snow,' Penaud, the uniformed cop standing next to me, complained in a low voice.

'Call this snow?' I whispered back. 'I'm from the Pyrenees. Coco Chanel could go sunbathing in this.'

He grunted and pulled his collar up around his ears.

I squinted up into the night sky. The weather had turned by the time I'd left Les Quatre Chats, and a sharp sleet was falling, flecked with snow, that got into your eyes and stung your cheeks. Some flakes had settled on the ground and on the roofs. I stamped my feet against the cold. Penaud and I had both exaggerated in our own way.

It was an hour past curfew, and all sensible Parisians were in their beds. The dumb ones like us were standing in a powdered courtyard surrounded by a ragtag bunch of French officials and a couple of hundred Republican Guards, all waiting for a box of ashes.

'With all these Guards, we could fight back,' the cop told me.

'Good luck with that.'

We'd been there over an hour already, outside Les Invalides. The Guards were each holding a flaming torch, which spat and fizzed angrily in the steady fall of sleet. I looked around me. The flickering red shadows they cast on the church wall seemed infernal, grotesques and monsters approaching and retreating.

Some of the usual suspects were in attendance. Oddly, the most expected ones weren't.

One who was there, among a small coterie of officials, was the Frenchman I'd seen the previous night at Ambassador Abetz's pleasant *soirée à treize*. I pointed him out to Penaud.

'Do you know who that is?'

He squinted through the night and shook his head. 'No one I know.'

Besides the mystery man and the regulation generals and admirals, I spotted Marcel Déat, a right-wing journalist who had taken over a left-wing pacifist newspaper, *L'Oeuvre*, and turned it into a rabid mouthpiece for toadying up to the Nazis. As the son of booksellers, I was unhappy to see a few writers waiting in the courtyard, including Abel Bonnard, a member of the Parti Populaire Français, which was as savagely Fascist and anti-Semitic as its masters in Berlin. There were even a couple of aristocrats I thought we'd got rid of a century and a half earlier, and Sacha Guitry, an actor and director who'd roll up to the opening of an envelope. A bomber's moon shone down on them all through the sleet.

'Where's the bloody RAF when you need it?'

The absences were Marshal Pétain, the head of the Vichy government, and Pierre Laval, the prime minister he'd just placed under house arrest.

'Have you heard?' Penaud said. 'Pétain was on the radio earlier. He said that Laval is no longer a part of his government, or his successor. He's put Flandin in his place.'

'For Christ's sake, he's even more pro-German.'

'I don't care. Just so long as that amoral, deceitful dog's arse Laval is gone.'

A messenger turned up and said something to the men in redundant braid and medals. Admiral Darlan and General Laure approached the open gates just as a small stream of German staff cars pulled up on the other side. The two Ottos – Abetz and von Stülpnagel – got out and took up their places in the front row.

Behind them, a gun carriage slowly appeared out of the swirling gloom. Bugles sounded in the night, a tearing tone that stung through the cold. It was a funeral cortège.

'Ashes,' Penaud whispered. 'Waste of bloody time.'

'As if anyone cared,' I agreed with him.

I felt a presence next to me and turned to find Hochstetter standing there.

'A fine gesture from the Führer, Édouard, don't you agree?' he asked.

'If you say so.'

Penaud mumbled something and moved away.

'L'Aiglon's ashes are finally home with his father's,' Hochstetter continued. 'A kind gesture by the German people to the French. Surely that is some cause for celebration.'

We both fell silent as some twenty German soldiers lifted a heavy bronze casket off the caisson and carried it to the entrance to the church, where they set it down on a podium. They saluted and vanished into the darkness.

L'Aiglon was Napoleon II, Bonaparte's son. His ashes had been kept in Vienna, but Hitler had ordered them to be placed in Les Invalides on the night of the fourteenth to fifteenth of December, a hundred years to the day after his old dad's ashes had been interred there. A gesture, we were told. We had a few of our own.

I nodded to the odd assembly of dignitaries.

'Our Otto doesn't look too happy.'

Abetz's face glowed redder than the spectral light. If young Napoleon hadn't already been ashes, the ambassador's look would have fried him in an instant.

'Marshal Pétain was supposed to be here. Indeed, Herr

Doktor Abetz was counting on it. And Prime Minister Laval. Our ambassador is a great supporter of his.'

Hochstetter turned to face me after speaking, as if daring me to respond. I could have said that Abetz liking Laval was all anyone needed to know about our prime minister. I decided it was best kept to myself.

Abetz chose that moment to give a speech to mark the occasion. I switched off, but caught his words in praise of Laval: 'It is he who created the atmosphere of collaboration and who is, for us, its sole guarantor.'

'He's not wrong there,' I told Hochstetter.

He merely held a finger up to me to be silent and moved closer to hear the words being spoken. Behind me, I heard voices speaking German. I half turned to see two of the officers who had been at Abetz's soirée the previous night.

'I see Hochstetter's brought his policeman boyfriend along,' one of them said.

The other one sniggered. They were like two privileged school-boys with guns and a conquered country to play with. 'Well, he is divorced. You know what they say.'

They both laughed at that, but hushed when Hochstetter returned to stand near me. For my part, I'd learned that he was divorced. Another piece in the jigsaw I was trying to fit together.

We waited through a few more bland words and then, after the speeches had been made, a dozen or more Republican Guards slowly marched forward. Picking up the casket, they carried it in through the gates between two rows of Guards bearing torches and into the chapel. Drums played in slow time with their march as the procession disappeared from view.

People stood around, unsure what to do. Some began to drift away into the night like the sleet.

'So,' Hochstetter said, turning to face me. 'You have the ashes.'

I shivered in the cold.

'We'd sooner have coal.'

16

Monday morning and I was in a room full of men who'd never seen a woman before.

'This is Mademoiselle Sarah Chevalier,' Dax announced to the assembled detectives, who stared at the young woman next to the commissioner. 'She will be providing secretarial assistance to the department.'

I stood in the doorway to my office and looked out across the smoke-filled detectives' room. One or two younger cops surreptitiously brushed their hair with their hands. The older ones eyed her with a spectrum of emotions from hopeless lust through disdain to indifference. One or two at least looked welcoming for the right reasons. One small mercy was that Boniface was absent. He'd no doubt make his grand entrance later.

A slight figure with neat brown hair that looked like it would go its own way at the drop of a hat and blue eyes that took in the room at a glance, the woman looked tiny next to Dax. Young and wary, she studied each of the cops in turn as the commissioner spoke.

'Welcome to the lions' den,' I said under my breath.

'She will be sharing an office with Inspector Giral,' Dax concluded.

Some of the detectives made jokey comments about lucky me, but then turned to stare at their feet when they caught my look back at them. Dax signalled to Sarah that she should take up her new home now and left her to go back into his own office. Without taking her eyes off me, she crossed the floor. I thought at first it was to lay down a challenge, but then realised it was to avoid the stares of the men she passed on the way. I stood back and let her in.

'Which is my desk?' she asked.

I pointed to my own paper-strewn table. 'Any one but that one.'

She nodded and looked at the other two available, finally deciding on the one with its back to the window. She took off her coat and hung it on the hook by the door before sitting down.

'What do you want me to do? Commissioner Dax said I should get to know the procedures first. And the department.'

I was glad Dax had thought of that. I pointed to the filing cabinet.

'Everything you need's in there. Who's who in the team and who's working on what.'

'What are you working on, Inspector Giral?'

I cast a hand over the files on my desk. 'A black marketeer. In Bel Air. Murdered.'

'By another black marketeer?'

I looked across at her. 'You'd think so.'

'Even if it isn't, it won't be long before a rival does move in.'

When I didn't reply, she nodded and got up to start looking through the files in the cabinet. I caught myself watching her and looked away. I was having to get used to giving up the private domain I'd enjoyed for the last six months or so. Another safe haven gone. My humour was darker than the sky louring behind her desk.

I'd left Dominique's flat in Montmartre much earlier than I would have had to leave my own place in the Fifth, which was just over the river from Thirty-Six. When they'd arrived last June, the Germans had made us put our clocks forward an hour to Berlin time, and it made the winter mornings seem unnaturally dark. It was the first Monday I'd had to make the journey and I'd allowed myself longer so I could take a round-about route from the Right Bank that would take me across to the Left Bank before turning up at work on Île da la Cité. That way, it would look to anyone watching as though I'd come from my own apartment in my own part of town.

The snow from Saturday night had melted to slush and all but gone, but it was still bitterly cold and I wasn't in a morning sunrise sort of a mood after facing the Metro. I could walk from my place, so sharing the start of my day underground with half the city wasn't my idea of heaven.

I'd never loved the Metro ever since moving to Paris to become a cop after the end of the last war, but I'd never disliked it as much as I had this morning. I'd recently read a report that said that ten times more people were using it now than before the Occupation. From three hundred thousand in June to three million in December. It was about the one thing I'd read lately that I did believe.

The reason was because there wasn't enough fuel to run as many buses as before. And the Germans had requisitioned most private cars, so even if we could find petrol, most of us no longer had a car to put it in. I still had mine, a concession from Hochstetter, but I used it very rarely now as I never knew when I'd be able to refill it. Among the very few others to be allowed to keep their cars were doctors and surgeons, which was either a good thing or a disturbing thing depending on your way of looking at it.

I also didn't want to keep my car in Montmartre. I'd had to hide my relationship with Dominique ever since we'd got to-gether, but living in her flat had brought all the subterfuge – and anger at the need for the subterfuge – to the fore, and my car being seen where it shouldn't be felt like a risk too far, so I'd left it parked by my own home.

After an hour or so trying to piece together what information we had about Joseph Cartier, I heard Sarah ask a question. 'Who else is working on the black marketeer investigation?'

I nodded to the cabinet. 'It's all there, in the files.'

'They're on your desk, Inspector Giral.'

I looked at the papers sprawled in front of me and let out a sigh. 'Detective Boniface. You'll meet him soon enough.' I checked my watch. 'We're expecting the photographs of the crime scene. Would you find out what's happening with them? And when you get them, catalogue them.'

She paused for the briefest of moments before nodding and turning her attention to the folders on her desk. I got up to go to Dax's office.

'Joseph Cartier,' I told the commissioner, closing his door behind me. 'The black marketeer.'

I brought him up to date with the investigation so far, not that there was much to tell.

'Any thoughts?' he wanted to know.

'It's either a killing by a disgruntled customer or it's another gang looking to take over his patch. I'm looking at the Bouvier brothers, who used to work for him. They don't know much, but I might get something out of them about any rivals he might have had. Besides that, there's a shopkeeper I want to have a word with. See what he knows. He owns a grocer's and was let down by Cartier, so he might fit in with the angry punter avenue.'

'My money's on the latter,' Dax said. 'The rival gang.'

'Mine too, to be honest.'

'Was there anything else?'

I told him about the ceremony on Saturday to return Napoleon II's ashes, but he wasn't overburdened with interest about it until I told him that neither Pétain nor Laval was there.

'Neither of them?' he said. 'I haven't read a thing about that.'

'Looks like there's been a complete news blackout. Not even *L'Oeuvre* has mentioned it, and Déat has done nothing but criticise Vichy every chance he gets.'

'It's a way of getting at Pétain. He doesn't dare go for the marshal, so he attacks Vichy instead.'

'The papers haven't even said anything about Laval being arrested.'

'Word is,' Dax said, his voice low, 'that Pétain reckoned Laval wasn't doing enough to get concessions from the Boches to make collaboration look beneficial to France, so that's why he had him put under house arrest. That's why all the Laval toadies are having a roundabout go at Pétain.'

Dax was one of the few I bothered arguing with about Vichy these days, but I could see he was still clinging to his love of the marshal.

Walking back to my office, where Sarah was just coming out, I heard a snigger to my right. I turned to see three cops seated at a table looking at her and then back to each other. They hadn't noticed me.

'Looking for a chair, darling?' Lafitte, a middle-aged bruiser from Belleville, called over to her. 'I've got something here you can sit on.'

His two friends laughed. I stopped in front of him, in his eyeline but far away enough for the room to hear. He looked at me, his expression challenging.

'Stand up,' I told him.

'It's just a joke, Giral. She doesn't mind.'

'Stand up and get your coat.'

'What do you mean?'

'You're married, aren't you? So stand up and put your coat on. You're going home to fetch your wife.'

He finally stood up, but only to face me. 'You leave my wife out of this.'

I took one step nearer, but made sure my words were heard around the room. Out of the corner of my eye I saw Dax open his office door.

'Fetch your wife and bring her here. And then you're going to stand where you are now and say exactly the same thing to her that you just said to Mademoiselle Chevalier. And your friends sitting there are going to laugh at it.'

'You're fucking insane, Giral.'

'Are you going to do it?'

'Of course I'm not.'

I took his coat from the rack and threw it at him. 'Then get out of my sight.'

He made an attempt at bravado, but no one in the room would meet his eye. Staring me out, he put on his coat and left the room. I stood where I was long enough for the others to look up at me to see what was going on.

'Anyone else got anything to say?' Not one of them spoke. Dax retreated back inside and closed his door. 'No? Good. Get back to work.'

17

A respectable-looking middle-aged couple were leaving the Metro station as I was entering. For some reason, they caught my eye, so I saw what happened. I spied them glancing quickly at each other and timing it so they let the door swing into the face of a German soldier behind them. To all intents and purposes it looked unintentional. The soldier, a shiny young gefreiter every inch the innocent abroad, rubbed his nose and cheek while the couple walked on, their heads down.

I watched them go and shook my head slightly. Save up your anger, I thought.

I was saving up mine. My anger with Lafitte. My anger with the city being under occupation. And my anger at having to take the bastard bloody Metro again so soon.

I didn't want to take my car and use up my petrol, but as I was going alone to Quinze-Vingts, which wasn't far from Thirty-Six, and I wasn't planning on arresting anyone, I couldn't justify taking out a pool car. Even the cops were having to use our petrol ration sparingly, and I couldn't be bothered to put in a request for a car and argue the toss with Dax.

The grocer was even more rattled than I was, and that was before I'd walked into his shop. He didn't recognise me at first, until I showed him my police ID. I was surprised again by the overly small features on his round face. The shop was empty of customers, the morning queuers gone by this time. Most of the goods too by the look of his shelves.

'You were here on Friday,' he recalled. 'Did you get the bastard who cheated me?' He was rattled but truculent.

'You mean the black marketeer you tried to buy illegal butter from? That bastard?'

He had the grace to look sheepish. 'Well, did you?'

'What do you know about him?'

'Just a black marketeer. And a con artist.'

'Where did you buy his butter? From his warehouse?'

He looked surprised at that and glanced nervously at the front door. 'I don't know where his warehouse is. He came here and offered me the butter.'

'But you went to see him when he failed to turn up with it?'

'How could I? I don't know where he is. But I tell you, when I do see him, he's in big trouble.'

His threat somehow didn't seem to go with the underlying anxiety I could sense.

'Big trouble? What would you do if you saw him?'

'I don't know, but he wouldn't be happy, I can tell you that, my friend.'

As he spoke, I studied him to try and sense what he knew.

'You do know he's dead?'

He looked shocked. 'Dead? How?'

'Murdered.'

Again he glanced at the front door. He was hiding something, but I didn't for one minute think it was Cartier's murder. It wasn't me he was afraid of.

'What do you know about his murder?'

He shook his head vigorously. 'Nothing until you just told me. This is the first I've heard of it. I'd never done business with the guy before. But he offered me this butter and it seemed a good price, so I thought I'd give it a try.'

'You hadn't heard about him from other shop-owners?'

He laughed for the first time, a bitter sound. 'That's not how things work these days.'

'You mean anyone could walk through your door?'

He couldn't help looking at the front door a third time.

'Expecting someone?' I asked him.

He shook his head again, slowly this time. I figured whoever had been coming through the door had already done it and gone.

'Anyone else been offering you butter?' I carried on. 'Or anything else for that matter?'

He recovered a little and some of his earlier defiance came out. 'There's always someone offering something these days. You tried buying black-market butter from me. You know the score. It's the only way to get hold of anything.'

Despite myself, I had to agree with him. 'If anyone does, you call me. At Quai des Orfèvres.'

He laughed. We both knew that was never going to happen, but I had to go through the motions.

I left and stopped a moment in the doorway on my way out. There was a faint smell lingering in the cold air. One that I knew but couldn't place.

I turned to see him staring at me before he turned away to restock an empty shelf. The truculence was well and truly back in place, but in the brief moment our eyes met, I saw a fleeting glimpse of the anxiety I'd picked up on earlier.

18

Another Metro, another moment of irritation, another moment of storing up anger.

'What is your name?'

Eschewing the first-class carriages that were free of charge to them, two German officers had taken up residence in the cars set aside for the rest of us. What was even more annoying was that they were sitting in seats reserved for the elderly or for pregnant women. Both leaning forward, they were staring intently at an attractive young Frenchwoman opposite them.

'What is your name?' the first officer repeated.

In reply, she reached into her bag and pulled out her papers. Without a word, she held them up for the officers to see. Her interrogator turned to his friend and said something in German that I didn't catch. He turned back, the smile slowly disappearing from a face that was used to getting its own way.

'I am not interested in your papers. I would like your name.'

His friend joined in, leaning so far forward he was almost on top of the woman. He had a slight sneer and an overbite that reminded me of one of the grotesques on Notre-Dame. 'We merely wish to engage in conversation with you, mademoiselle. Perhaps invite you for a drink with us.'

'You hold your ground, girl,' an elderly lady two seats away said.

'This does not concern you, old woman,' the first German snarled at her.

I took a deep breath and wrestled with what to do. As a cop, I had no say over what German officers said and did. If I spoke out, I had no idea what their reaction would be. Would they make an example of me? Insist the young woman go with them to prove a point?

'Your name?' the German repeated.

As I debated, we stopped at a station and an old guy got on, shuffling his way with the help of a walking stick. Putting her papers away, the young woman stood up and gestured to her seat.

'Sit here,' she told him.

She went and stood near the door while the old man struggled to lower himself onto the wooden seat. Looking straight into the German officers' eyes, he hawked violently and coughed up into his handkerchief, displaying all its glory for the officers to see.

'I've got my papers if you want to look at them,' he told them.

At the end of the journey from the grocer's shop in Quinze-Vingts to the Bel Air district, it felt a strange relief to get out of the grinding heat of the Metro and into the biting cold of Cours de Vincennes. From one extreme to the other – hell really had frozen over.

The two officers had got off at the next stop while the young Frenchwoman had stayed on the train. The occupants of the carriage had waited until the Germans had gone from sight and let out a low cheer. The young woman curtseyed to gentle clapping. I neither cheered nor applauded but stared at the seats vacated by the two men, telling myself I was storing up my anger.

Once above ground, the first place I wanted to see was Cartier's old warehouse on Impasse Vassou. The lock hadn't been repaired and the door swung open when I pushed it. I edged forward carefully, but there was no sign of life. Or any sign that anyone had been here since Cartier had eaten his last butter. Not surprising, as there was nothing in here to steal any more.

The guinea pigs had gone too. Rounded up by half a dozen uniformed cops who'd sworn and sweated while catching them after Bouchard's initial examination of Cartier's body in the zinc bath.

I found the piece of floor by the filing cabinet that Firmin and Jacquot had mentioned. It was well hidden, so no surprise we hadn't come across it in the police investigation. That and because we were a bit distracted by a dead black marketeer with a face full of butter. I found a paper knife in a desk drawer and levered out a section of two parallel floorboards. From the marks on the paper knife, that had obviously been its sole purpose. The panel came away stiffly. You'd never have seen it by chance unless you knew what you were looking for. I thought of the Bouvier brothers.

'So far, so good, boys.' My voice echoed amid the empty shelves.

A safe was ensconced underneath, its door facing upwards. It hadn't been fully closed, and the key was sticking out of the lock. Pulling up the heavy piece of metal by the handle, I opened the strongbox and tried to peer inside, but it was too dark to see anything. Gingerly I put my hand in and felt around. Nothing but the bare steel walls of the safe. I closed the door again and replaced the floorboards.

'So it looks like you were telling the truth,' I said to the absent Firmin and Jacquot.

Dusting myself down, I took another look around the dingy room, but found nothing else that we'd missed the first time. I had to agree with Sarah. It wouldn't be long before another black-market leech moved in to suck everyone dry, but if one already had, they certainly hadn't taken over Cartier's old place.

It was too late for queues outside shops, but I tried all the same.

'Nothing,' the woman in the bakery near the dead-end alley told me. 'And I'd give them short shrift if they did.'

She stared at me defiantly through thick glasses that made her squint and wrinkle her nose, baring her teeth at the same time, as she tried to focus on my face.

'Do you know if any other shops on the street have been approached by someone trying to sell them anything?'

'No one.'

'We don't need the likes of Cartier round here,' a customer chimed in. 'Weaselly little bastard.' She was tiny and wizened and my money would have gone on her over ten rounds with anyone at Les Quatre Chats. She and a less wrinkled version of her had been chatting to the owner when I'd walked in.

'We look after ourselves in this neighbourhood,' the second woman agreed. I was in no doubt they did. She was the first customer thirty years earlier.

In need of a friendly face, I dropped in at Ulysse's café. The father and son electricians were seated at the bar when I went in. Seeing them drink coffee together, I had a momentary pang that I'd never done that with my son. I had no idea if I ever would.

'How's the investigation going?' Ulysse asked me.

'It's going.'

He grinned and served me my *café national*. From under the counter he pulled out the same bottle of brandy and poured me a large tot.

'Don't tell the cops,' he repeated from last time, his grin even broader.

'I'll drink to that,' Yves said, holding out his own glass for a top-up.

'Found who did for Cartier yet?' Pierre asked me. His gaze lingered on my face. I remembered him being on the point of saying something to me on Friday.

'Oddly enough, we haven't,' I told him.

'Bet you won't find many people wanting to help out.'

'True enough,' Ulysse added. 'No one's mourning that piece of shit.'

All three of them raised their brandy glasses. 'To Cartier. May he rot in hell.'

Ulysse was called away by another customer and I was left alone with the father and son.

'Did you have much in the way of dealings with Cartier?' I asked them.

It was Yves, the father, who answered. 'Just what we said. We bought food from him. We all did. He was a conniving bastard who robbed us blind, but we needed him.'

'What are people doing now for food?'

He simply shrugged and mimed tightening his belt.

'So how's business for you?' I asked.

'For me, all right. People still need electricians. No one's doing new stuff at the moment, but everyone needs repairs. It keeps me going. We had to give up our flat in Ménilmontant and live above the shop, but we're getting by.'

Ménilmontant. My old part of Paris when I was still with my wife and son. Another pang, another memory.

'I thought you worked together.'

'We do now.'

'I work for Citroën,' Pierre explained, 'but the Boches put us on a twenty-four-hour week and I can't earn enough money that way, so I help my dad out.'

'Not that I can afford to pay him much. But he's one of the lucky ones. Over half a million unemployed in Paris. At least between us we can get by. Do you know what he had to do before my work picked up and I could help him out? Sold his ration tickets so he could pay his rent. Sold them to poor little rich people who obviously can't go hungry just so he could make it to the end of the month. It's a self-fulfilling evil. Salaries are only just over half what they were before this capitalist war, so people like my son are forced to sell their tickets and end up having to buy everything on the black market, which means they're paying even more into a corrupt system. And then his landlord turfed him out when he couldn't make the rent, so now he's living with me again. Does that seem right to you?'

'You sound like you're ripe for joining this de Gaulle,' I told him. He didn't, but I like to provoke. It's sometimes the only way to get answers.

Sure enough, he snorted derisively. 'That bastard. If he wants to fight, tell him to come here and do it instead of sitting on his arse in London.'

'Ask him,' Pierre suddenly said to him, nudging his elbow, but his father ignored him.

'We're Communist and proud,' Yves carried on. 'The whole family. This is a capitalist's war, not a working man's war.'

'You should probably be careful who you say that to,' I warned him. 'Plenty of Communists are coming out of hiding and getting themselves arrested.'

'You think I don't know that? The only disgrace bigger than the Nazi–Soviet pact is the French police arresting us when we assume that because of the pact it's safe for us to stand up and be counted as good Communists. French police like you.'

'Somehow I don't think it's police like Eddie here,' Ulysse said. I hadn't noticed him come back to our end of the bar.

'Ask me what?' I said to Pierre, turning my full attention on him.

'Waste of time,' Yves told his son.

'It's my sister,' Pierre said. 'The Boches have arrested her.'

'What for?'

'Protesting,' Yves butted in. 'Against the Boches and for French working people. Like you should be doing.'

'And what are *you* doing?' I snapped at him. 'Apart from sitting here drinking coffee and illegal capitalist brandy and moaning? What have you done today to make the Germans leave? Or to improve the lot of the working people?'

He made to answer, but his son interrupted him. 'She took part in the Armistice Day protests. She was at the Place de l'Étoile when the Boches went in with the bayonets.'

Yves grunted. 'Bayonets. It's not the person at either end that's the problem. It's the bastard who placed it between them.'

Ulysse served him another brandy to shut him up.

'Where is she now?' I asked.

'We don't know. But as far as we do know, the Germans have got her, not the French police. We've asked the police to do something, but they say they have no jurisdiction over the Boches.'

'That's true, we don't.'

'Told you so, boy,' Yves said to his son. 'Waste of time.'

'It's been over a month,' Pierre insisted. 'All her friends have been released. She's the only one still being held.'

'Have they said why?'

'Nothing.'

I exhaled slowly, imagining her alone in a German prison. I felt powerless. 'If it's the Germans who arrested her, there isn't an awful lot we can do.'

'There's got to be something.'

'I don't see how. I'm sorry.'

Pierre's expression was one of quiet disgust that was more powerful than his father's angry rant.

'Her name's Marie. She's eighteen years old.'

19

On the Cours de Vincennes, the queues had started up again for the food shops. Smaller this time, more cowed. They were made up entirely of Jewish people. The Nazis had ruled that Jews could only shop between four o'clock and five o'clock in the afternoon, when what little food had been there in the morning had all gone. I walked past to an unbearable silence.

It was something else I could do nothing about.

I saw the entrance to the Metro and stopped in despair. I wished I'd held out for a pool car, or even sacrificed some of my own hard-saved petrol, rather than enter the beast's maw for the fourth time that day.

Something caught my eye. Another new feature of the city since the Germans had come to play. Parked by the side of the avenue was a sort of sedan chair rigged up to the back of a tandem. Two guys stood around smoking cigarettes and waiting. With the lack of fuel and so few buses and taxis on the road, the bicycle had become king. By extension, a few enterprising individuals had taken to providing a taxi service using these contraptions under the name of *vélo-taxi*. They weren't the most comfortable, or the quickest, but they did, which was as good as you could hope for these days.

'How much to Quai des Orfèvres?' I asked them.

One of the two took his cigarette out to speak and cupped

it in his hand. His fingers were stained the same yellow as the neckerchief he wore with a serge jacket and workmen's trousers. Only this guy wasn't another laid-off worker or taxi driver looking to get by. His constant eye movements and darting glances up and down the road told me that if he hadn't already been a customer of ours, he would be one day.

'How much do you want to pay?' he asked.

I groaned. Another of the joys of Occupation was the return of barter and haggling. A piece of meat for a watch repair, ten francs instead of two, a lump of coal for a blow job in a doorway.

'Ten francs,' I told him.

'Thirty.'

I was tired, so I climbed into the chair at the rear and showed them my police ID.

'Tell you what. Five francs and I won't arrest you for pissing me off.'

'I'm not Mademoiselle Chevalier, Inspector Giral. I'm married.'

I looked up from the mass of papers on my desk to see Sarah taking a break from typing, her face a mask.

'I'm sorry, Sarah. Commissioner Dax called you mademoiselle, so I assumed you were unmarried.'

'He was incorrect.'

'So how come you're able to work here?' a voice from the doorway asked.

I looked back to see Boniface filling the frame. He had a way of standing arms akimbo and pelvis forward when women were around as if to invite compliments on his genitals. His jet-black hair was greased either side of a severe parting with the adornment of a film-star quiff over his right ear that I always wished would unravel in a high wind. I glanced at Sarah. Her face was entirely impassive, which I hoped was a good sign.

'Sarah, this is Detective Boniface,' I told her. 'Avoid him.'

'The Vichy government has said that married women can't work in the state sector if their husbands are employed,' Boniface insisted.

'If their husbands are employed,' Sarah replied. 'Mine isn't.'

'What does he do then if he doesn't work?'

'Have you really not got any work of your own to do, Boniface?' I asked him.

'Don't worry about me, Eddie. Plenty of it coming my way.'

'Well, here's some more. I want you to look at the records we have for Firmin and Jacquot Bouvier. They're as petty as they come, but I'd like to know about their known associates. Files with mugshots, everything.'

'Leave it with me.'

'That's what I'm doing.'

He winked at Sarah, one of his most frequent and least endearing traits, and she pointedly returned her attention to the document she was typing. Next to her on the desk was a pile of photographs. I assumed they were the crime-scene pictures that I'd asked her to categorise.

'Off you go,' I reminded Boniface. 'And I want you here early tomorrow morning. You're coming with me to Charonne and Bel Air to look for signs of a new black marketeer moving into Cartier's old turf.'

'Will do, Eddie,' he said, and turned to go with one last, longing look at Sarah. He knew better than to wink in my direction.

'I notice everyone calls you Eddie, not Inspector Giral,' Sarah said. Her tone was neutral.

'You might as well call me Eddie too, if we're going to work together.'

She didn't reply.

The city outside my office had long turned black, the windows misted and cold, when Boniface reappeared at the end of the day. He'd taken the time to smarten his appearance and was entering the room like he was his own favourite film star, his coat slung over one shoulder.

'That's me for the day,' he announced. 'Anyone coming for a drink?' He asked the question in general but was looking at Sarah as he said it.

'No thanks,' she said without glancing up.

He shrugged and came further over the threshold to put his coat on. As the heavy woollen fabric settled around his shoulders, a waft of air sent a strong aroma my way. One that I recognised. I'd smelled it in the grocer's earlier that day, but there was somewhere else too that I should remember.

He finished smoothing his coat down and ran a hand through his hair, fluffing the side quiff in passing. He'd evidently layered a new coating of oil before coming in and had to wipe his hand on a linen handkerchief he took out of his trouser pocket. It left a trail of grease on the bleached white fabric. I stared at him.

'Your hair oil, Boniface. Is it a common brand?'

He gestured to himself. 'Nothing I wear is common, Eddie.'

'All right, but is it a brand you can get anywhere?'

'It's pretty exclusive. All the way from Argentina. As I said, only the best for me.'

I got up and sniffed at his hair.

'What the hell?' he said, backing away from me.

He looked at me in shock as I stared at the oil separating each strand of his dark locks. The man with Firmin and Jacquot, I remembered. The one sitting at their table in Les Quatre Chats, who took a piece of ham and said he'd see them later. Who had been accompanied by two heavies he'd obviously told to keep an eye on me. The hair oil that would have floored a skunk. And I'd smelled it again in the shop today, when the grocer had been visibly rattled before I'd got there. I tried to recall the face of the man I'd seen with the brothers. He wasn't someone I knew, but he had distinctive features, so I was certain I'd recognise him again.

'Where do you buy it?'

'I get it at Galeries Lafayette.'

'Is there anywhere in Charonne that would have it?'

He looked offended. 'Gomina Argentine? Hardly?'

I sat down behind my desk. It was to get away from the heady aroma more than anything. I carried on staring at his head. 'Good. Once you've taken a look at the Bouviers' known associates, check with me.' I explained about the man with the brothers in Les Quatre Chats. 'He's about your height, broken nose, thin moustache, snappily dressed, dark wavy hair. And lashings of hair oil. Looks a bit like Pépé le Moko trying to look chipper.'

'Ah, Gabin was great in that film, wasn't he?' Boniface nodded nostalgically, then immediately snapped out of it. 'And when we get a mugshot that matches, I'll check with the places that sell this brand to see if any of them recognise him.'

Casting one final look at Sarah, he left. I watched him go. Not for the first time, I had to admit that he was a good cop. There were times I wished I could like him more. Times I almost did.

'I categorised the crime-scene photographs, Inspector Giral,' Sarah told me. She was pulling the cover over the typewriter on her desk.

'Eddie,' I said absently, my mind still on Boniface and the man with the Bouvier brothers.

'Have you thought of talking to women, Inspector Giral?

I turned to face her. 'I beg your pardon?'

'You and Detective Boniface. When you go to Charonne and Bel Air tomorrow, you could try talking to the women in the queues outside shops. Women are the ones the government are reluctant to allow to work, so women are the ones who end up queuing for food. They're the ones who are going to be approached by anyone trying to get in on it, and the ones who know all the local gossip.'

I looked at her but said nothing. She finished packing up and putting her coat on. I spotted the piles of papers next to the typewriter and was shocked at the amount of them.

'Have they kept you typing all day?'

She glanced at the piles and shrugged. 'It's what I was hired to do.'

Scanning her desk one last time, she put her gloves on and stopped in front of mine.

'About earlier, Inspector Giral. The comments. I can stand up for myself. I don't need you to do it for me.'

'I've no doubt you can. But so can I, and they were annoying me.'

20

For those who aren't in the know, Luigi's in Montparnasse is a dump.

For those who are in the know, Luigi's in Montparnasse is still a dump, but it's a dump where criminal information goes to be sold. And I was buying. It was my piece of heaven between finishing work and going to Montmartre and Dominique.

'No trouble, Eddie, please,' Luigi, the owner, told me. 'Not tonight.'

His face had fallen visibly when he'd opened the heavy blackout drapes and the glass door to reveal me standing in the gloomy alleyway outside. With his broken nose and bushy moustache, his face really didn't need to fall any further.

'Why? What's special about tonight?'

'Nothing.'

'Let me in, Luigi, it's freezing out here.'

With as much ill grace as he dared, he pulled the drape aside and stepped back to let me in. Luigi wasn't his real name, but he was Italian and that seemed to be good enough for his clientele, which wasn't renowned for its discernment.

A wooden bar counter topped with zinc ran the length of the far wall and Luigi scurried behind it to safety. Opposite was a serried rank of low alcoves separated by wooden panels and glass panes, their denizens shadowy in the dingy light. A layer of smoke lay across the ceiling like a low storm cloud. At the far end, a piano stood idle, Luigi's one attempt at culture to curry favour with the Occupiers having failed dismally. It now served as a bar against which half a dozen prostitutes leaned in bored anticipation. They brightened at the waft of a newcomer, but then saw it was me and looked as tired as the walls again. In the space in between, a few wooden tables had unsavoury occupiers of their own – thieves and burglars, drug dealers and pimps. Half a dozen local gang members moved like sharks through the bar, each one wearing a white shirt and thin black tie, with a cloth cap angled over one eye.

The place had been an instant and surprising hit with the ruling German classes immediately after they'd entered the city, eager to sample a taste of Parisian lowlife, but their patronage had soon moved on. Now, the only Germans in the place were runty gefreiters and oafish feldwebels – privates and sergeants – doing deals with all the bright lights illuminating the Montparnasse night.

No informants in sight, though. Standing as far as possible from any flapping ears, I turned to Luigi behind his bar.

'Go and get Pepe for me and I won't arrest you.'

'What are you going to arrest me for?'

'I'll think of something. Go and get him.'

I suddenly realised that Pepe was skulking at the far end of the bar, on the business side of it. Gone was his usual white shirt and pencil-thin black tie. In their place was a thick roll-neck sweater that was much too big for him, over baggy black trousers. He'd also lost the gang cap he always wore, set jauntily at an angle over his right eye, itself every bit a uniform as Hochstetter's field grey. His bald head shone under the fluorescent lights beneath the shelves containing the bottles Luigi dared leave on display. I knew that tucked under the counter were the cupboards with the kind of drink I wanted. He was trying to avoid being seen, so I called him over. He took longer to reach me than butter from Brittany.

'I'm working here now, Eddie,' he told me. He might have lost the gang livery, but he still had the same weaselly whine. 'Earning an honest living.'

I glanced from him to Luigi. 'Whisky.'

Luigi looked apologetic, the way a praying mantis looks pious. 'Can't, Eddie. It's illegal. You should know that, what with you being a police officer.'

'Whisky. From the cupboard on the left, because that's the stuff you don't water down.'

To give him his due, he didn't attempt to pursue it any further and poured me a healthy slug. It made all the right noises as it went into the glass. I took a small sip and turned my attention back to Pepe, staring at him until he felt he had to fill the silence.

'I've gone straight, Eddie. Honest. Luigi's given me a job. I'm working.'

'Information. Now.'

He did the same act that Luigi had just failed with. 'I can't, Eddie. I told you, I've gone straight. I don't move with those crowds now, so I haven't got any information for you.'

I nodded and beckoned him over. Reluctantly he shifted his weight and shuffled over to where I was standing. He stood as far back from the bar as the shelves behind him would allow.

'Closer.'

He moved forward very slowly, and I reached out for his collar, catching it before he could back away again. I tugged the coarse wool down to reveal an old-fashioned wing-collar shirt and narrow strip of black tie underneath.

'So what's this, Pepe? Working undercover?' I pulled on the tie and tightened it, drawing him towards me. His eyes were centimetres from mine, his face turning red. I nodded to the remaining part of his gang uniform lying on the shelf to his left.

'A tip. If you're going to go undercover, don't forget to hide your cap.'

'I don't have any information, Eddie,' he said, his eyes bulging.

I released him and let him flop back. 'I'll be the judge of that. And if it's any good, I might even give you some money this time.'

As he caught his breath, I spoke in a low voice, describing the man I'd seen with the Bouvier brothers in Charonne and asking him if he recognised him.

'I don't know Charonne so well, Eddie.'

'Yes you do, Pepe. You know every part of the east side of the city, Left and Right Bank. That's why I love you so much. Who is he?'

He thought for a moment and finally shook his head. 'I really don't know. It's not someone I've come across. What do you want him for?'

'I want to put him on my Christmas present list. He possibly works with the Bouvier brothers, ring any bells?'

He snorted, his criminal pride affronted. 'What are you wasting my time for with those two? If he's anything to do with them, it's not surprising I don't know him.'

'How about a couple of other guys? A pretty boy with eyes like a snake. And a big type. Nose that makes Luigi's look as straight as a parson. Know them?' They were the two companions who'd been told to follow me outside Les Quatre Chats.

He shook his head. 'What's this about? If you tell me, I can maybe be more helpful.'

'Nice try, Pepe. Forget it. You know what I need you to know, and at the moment, that seems to be fuck-all. One last chance for the money. Julen le Basque. His son, Aitor. What's he been up to lately?'

'This a history lesson, Eddie?' He laughed.

'Don't try humour, Pepe, you're risible enough as it is.'

For some reason, that seemed to please him. 'Aitor le Crochu? He's out of the game. He lives in Montmartre now. Run out by some other gang after Julen le Basque started peeing himself in public.'

'Run out of Porte de Vincennes? So he might be ready for a comeback in his old stamping ground now things have changed. Where can I find him?'

'Pilou's place.' For once, Pepe suddenly looked genuinely thoughtful. He leaned in towards me to make sure no one could hear. 'There is one thing, Eddie. Henri Lafont.'

That surprised me. 'What about him?'

'I don't know.'

I moved back and slapped him across the head. 'You do know how being an informant works, Pepe? You tell me things you do know, not things you don't. We'd be here all night if that were the case.'

He seemed hurt, his eyes plaintive. 'No, I mean it, Eddie.' He stared out into the murk of the bar and then back at me. 'It's like he's vanished off the face of the earth.'

21

'Where did you get all this butter, Eddie?'

Dominique was holding what was left of the half-kilo block I'd taken from Cartier's warehouse. I'd brought it over to her flat rather than let it go to waste at home.

'Grocer in Quinze-Vingts. I stopped the bad guys from extorting money from him and he gave me that to say thank you.'

'Why don't I believe you?'

'Because you are all too aware of my roguish charm.'

That explanation seemed to work as well as it ever would. You should always keep a lie as near to the truth as possible. Even if someone thinks they know you well enough not to believe you, there'll always be a shadow of doubt somewhere in their mind.

'We don't need all this,' she said.

'What do you mean, we don't need it? It'll last.'

'It'll go off.'

She put it down on the table in the living room. The fire was burning low in the grate, but it was still quite warm.

'It will if you leave it there.'

'You decide, Eddie.'

She went into the kitchen and came out with a stew made of swede and onions. We ate it with my bread ration and a small glass of red wine each.

'This is good,' I told her.

Despite the lack of ingredients, she'd managed to make the meal tasty. Swede was another of the foods not rationed, and it was everywhere. Before the war, we'd only ever fed it to cattle to fatten them up; now we were vainly feeding it to ourselves and doing everything we could to try and find some flavour in it.

I asked Dominique about her day and what she'd done.

'This and that,' was all she said.

There was a sadness in her voice. She couldn't get work as a singer any more, and the government had gone full-on in its desire to see women in the home rather than in jobs, so it was putting increasingly tougher obstacles in their way when it came to getting work. The problem was our friends in Vichy weren't exactly hurling cartloads of cash at the women in this situation as a way of helping them get by. I knew that although Dominique got some money in social assistance, she was largely forced to live on what she'd saved over the years. I could sense some days grew longer than others.

I didn't press, so she asked me about my day. I told her about my concern that a new black marketeer would soon take over in Bel Air and Charonne, and about the Ferran family of electricians and Marie being held by the German authorities.

'What are you going to do about it?' Dominique asked me. 'This Marie? You say she's only eighteen.'

'There's not a lot I can do. If the Germans have got her, she's out of our control.'

'What about this major you know? Hochstetter? Can't he help?'

'I'm going to ask him, but you never know with Hochstetter. He'll only do something if it suits him or if he can get something out of me in return.'

The record that was playing on the gramophone came to an end and began to click insistently. There was a silence between us as she got up to put the needle back in its cradle. It was Marie

Ferran she was talking about, but I sensed it was her son she was thinking of.

'Then you've got to do it, Eddie.'

With her back to me, she found another record and put it on. I was having to become accustomed to music being played constantly. In my own flat, I lived in silence among my books. I'd always loved the jazz she listened to, but so much of it had gone out of my life at the same time that she had – and for the same reasons – and I was no longer used to it.

'You understand me, Eddie? You've got to do whatever it takes.'

'I usually do,' I said quietly.

She sat down and we carried on with our meal.

'What are you going to do about the butter?' she asked.

I was hoping she'd forgotten. I knew too well where it was going.

'Do you want to give half to your neighbours?' I asked. 'The Goldsteins?'

I knew that like all the Jewish people in Paris, her elderly neighbours struggled to find enough food to feed themselves and that Dominique often helped them out.

'Oh Eddie, you can't just do something good to assuage your guilt at doing something bad. It's not a case of putting something wrong right. It's a case of not doing something wrong in the first place.'

'That's not the way things are now, Dominique. There's a new reality.'

'Only if you allow it to become that.'

'So what do you want me to do about the butter? Give it to the Goldsteins or not?'

'Give it to them. But I'll take it. They feel safe with me.'

She sliced the butter in half and put one of the pieces on a small plate, which she took with her across the landing. When she was out, the record came to an end and I replaced the needle but didn't put another disc on. I welcomed the moment's silence and longed for a book. Dominique didn't understand my need to read to cope with what was happening to us. The lack of other thoughts to read made my own come rushing in a jumble into my head. As always, I wanted to disagree with her, but deep down there was the nagging doubt that she was simply voicing my own worries.

I relished the silence. In the quietest moments, I had to admit to feeling a greater sense of calm when I was in Dominique's flat, but not always when she was in the room with me. Here, there were none of the memories of years of loneliness and self-loathing, and a far too fleeting rediscovery of Jean-Luc in the summer, to pull me down into unforgiven depths.

She came back after ten minutes or so and chose a new record to play. It wasn't a tune I knew. It was called 'That's What Love Did To Me', and I recognised the clarinet style of Sidney Bechet straight away, which I loved, although I didn't know the voice of the woman singing. It wasn't really my type of song.

Dominique stood in front of me and held her hand out to me. She began to sway in time to the music.

'Why don't you sing?' I asked her.

'You know I don't sing these days, Eddie. Get up.'

I shook my head. 'You know I don't dance.'

She pulled me up and led me away from the living room.

'Who said anything about dancing?'

22

I was on my way out of my office with Boniface the next morning as another cop was on his way in. He was carrying a pile of loose papers, which he dumped on Sarah's desk.

'For five o'clock,' he told her, and walked out.

Sarah looked dispassionately at the new pile, alongside a couple of equally untidy stacks, and started to take the cover off the typewriter.

'Get your coat,' I told her. 'You're coming with us.'

She shook her head. 'I've got too much work.'

'It's squared with Commissioner Dax, it'll be fine.'

Boniface looked as mystified as Sarah did. She followed us out of the office and down the stairs. As there were three of us, I could justify using a police car – and police fuel.

'Where are we going?' she asked as I told Boniface to drive out of the yard and head east. 'I refuse to get into trouble with Commissioner Dax.'

'Stop worrying. Where are we going? Well, I'm going to Charonne, Boniface here is going to Bel Air, and you're going to both.'

'What's going on?'

I turned in my seat to face her in the back of the car. 'You mentioned listening to the women in the queues outside shops to find out what people are talking about. Boniface and I can't do that. Everyone knows us there as cops. But they don't know you.'

'Christ's sake, Eddie,' Boniface said, his eyes on the road.

I saw Sarah nodding, taking in what I'd said. 'They'd also be more likely to open up to another woman.' I could see the idea appealed to her more than a morning spent typing up Lafitte's rantings.

'That's settled then.' I turned to face front.

'And Dax has agreed to that?' Boniface asked in a low voice.

'Probably.'

I told him to park up just off Cours de Vincennes, by the girls' school where the Germans were billeted, and we all arranged to meet back there in three hours. I figured that leaving the car near where occupying soldiers were quartered would make it less likely that one of the local villains would try to steal it. Oddly, it was a sentiment partly shared by Isabelle Collet, the school administrator I'd spoken to the other day.

As I walked past the school, a large group of girls were clustered by the doorway, crying. Isabelle was standing on the steps, and I went up to her.

'Problem with the neighbours?' I nodded at the annexe where the Germans had been stationed.

'Inspector Giral,' she said, recognising me from before. 'Not in the way you think.' I could see her eyes were red from crying too.

'Do they cause you any headaches?'

She shook her head. 'Their senior officer came to see me and gave me his word that his men have strict orders not to approach or accost our pupils. He said any soldier disobeying that rule would be severely punished.'

'Are you never tempted to make an accusation? Have them billeted elsewhere?'

'There are some boats that aren't worth rocking.' She looked at me. 'Oddly, their presence affords us some protection. We see little of the interference other schools get. In that way, at least, it serves us.'

'So what's going on?'

As I asked, a middle-aged man came out and walked down the small flight of steps. Looking like he was close to tears himself, he nodded to all the girls. Isabelle Collet gave his hand a squeeze and watched him hurry away from the school building. I stood by as she rounded up the girls and ushered them back in through the door.

'That was Monsieur Stein,' she told me. 'One of our teachers. He taught philosophy. Today is his last day with us, after over thirty years.'

'Jewish?'

'Jewish. He is no longer permitted to teach here.'

We both turned to watch the small figure dwindle in the distance. The Nazis had decreed that all Jews working in the state sector had to resign by the end of December. Monsieur Stein – and the children he taught and the people he worked with – was one of very many in the city to be affected by the new law.

'Where is this going to end?' Isabelle asked, disappearing into the school.

By the time I got to Les Quatre Chats, I'd made my mind up. From the shops I'd gone into and the conversations I'd heard, I knew there was a new kid on the block, a new black marketeer supplying the local people. The first thing I noticed as I walked through the café door wasn't the angry glances from some of the hardened patrons, or the two men who immediately hurried out of the front door once I'd reached the counter, or even the scowl Claude was serving up for me with relish.

It was the smell. I'd clocked it the moment I pushed the

door open. A waft of warm air engulfed me after the cold of the street outside, and it carried with it the aroma of coffee. Not *café national*, not acorns and chicory, but coffee.

'Coffee. A large one,' I told Claude when he came and stood in front of me. 'And make sure it's the good stuff. I will know.'

I watched him make it, just to be sure it was the only liquid he put in the cup. He was torn between making me wait and serving me quickly so I'd leave sooner. It meant I got better service than I would have got in most other places. He put the coffee down in front of me, and I stared at it for a few moments, taking in the bittersweet scent and watching the tendrils of steam rise slowly from the cup. I took a sip and forgave Claude for pretty much all the ills befalling the city right then.

'Where'd you get this?' I asked him.

'Been hoarding it. Saving it for a rainy day.'

I looked pointedly at the street outside. 'One, it's not raining. Two, you're lying. Where did you get the coffee?'

'A merchant. He just happened to come across some.'

'And the merchant's name?'

'I forget.'

'Not one you've known long then?'

I tried to catch a flicker in his eyes to see if they gave him away, but he was so punch-drunk after a largely unsuccessful career in the ring that not even Adolf Hitler walking in with a dozen dancing girls would have got a response.

'Not to worry,' I carried on. I looked up at the photos on the wall to see if the man with the hair oil I'd seen with Firmin and Jacquot featured in any of them. He didn't. 'Miss the boxing, do you? I remember seeing you back in the day pummelling that Basque, what was his name?'

'Iturria.' Claude turned and took down a photo of two men in shorts hitting each other. He looked at it fondly before showing it to me. 'That's us, in 1922. I beat him in three. Nice guy.'

'There was another boxer. More recent. Broken nose and thin moustache. Not sure if he was Basque, though. Might not have been. Know the one I mean?'

'Casal? I fought him the year after Iturria.'

'No, this one was after your time. Younger. I'm sure I saw him in here the other day.'

Claude took one last look at the photo and gave a big sigh. He hung it back on the wall and turned back to me. 'I may have taken one hit too many in the past, Eddie, but I still know when someone's bullshitting me.'

I gave up on the sucker punch and went straight for the jab. 'Man here on Saturday night with the Bouvier brothers. Hair slicked back. He left when I arrived. Who is he?'

'Doesn't ring any bells.'

I finished every last sip of the coffee and left to try chez Bouvier, but no one was home. I banged on the door for a good ten minutes, then waited in silence for another five, but no heads peeped out of the door to see if the coast was clear. Not even the Bouviers were that good at hiding. I knocked again for good measure.

'They're out,' a neighbour shouted at me from across the landing.

'Thanks for that.'

Boniface and Sarah were waiting in the car when I got back. I climbed in and blew on my hands to warm them, but the air inside was only slightly less polar than outside. Some of the girls were coming out of the school, a lot of them still red-eyed. I explained about Monsieur Stein.

'Happening to a friend of mine,' Sarah told me. 'He's with the local *mairie*, but he's got to give up his job this Friday.'

'A couple of cops at Thirty-Six, too,' Boniface agreed. 'It's a steady drip-drip.'

We gazed out of the car, trying to get warm and avoid thinking too much of the slow erosion of life in the city.

'Well, it's pretty clear-cut as far as I can see,' I said, half turned in my seat so I could see them both. 'We've got someone new selling black-market goods. Best quality too, if the coffee in Les Quatre Chats is anything to go by.'

Boniface looked surprised. 'Seriously? I haven't seen a sign of that in Bel Air. Nothing in the shops, same old queues, no one talking about anything new.'

I studied him, taken aback. Boniface was all manner of annoying, but he would have picked up on anything different. Sarah spoke before I could reply.

'You're both right. There's definitely something happening. I stood in four queues in Charonne. The very first queue I stood in, I heard a woman say she'd only come out for one or two things now she could get the essentials elsewhere. And it was the same all over. One woman said she'd been able to buy some soap, another one had got cheese. No one was very happy, though. They were all saying everything was more expensive.'

'That figures,' I said. 'New marketeer moving in and putting the prices up now people realise how much they want their goods.'

Boniface was shaking his head. 'I saw none of this in Bel Air.'

'It was a different feel,' Sarah agreed. 'I heard some talk of black-market buying in one queue, but nothing like in Charonne.'

I signalled to Boniface that he should start the drive back to Thirty-Six. 'The question is why. Why in Charonne and not in Bel Air? Cartier controlled both districts.'

'A new player setting up there in a small way?' Boniface suggested. 'Going to expand into Bel Air once they've got the Charonne market cornered?'

'Could be. I just hope it's not going to be two rival gangs setting up so close to each other. Did you get any names, Sarah?'

'Nothing. People were talking, but they were cagey with it. No one opened up to me, as they don't know me, so I just stood and eavesdropped. I asked in one place where I could get stuff, but it just made them all suspicious, so I left.'

'More than we would have got,' I told her.

Boniface nodded his agreement. 'Any idea who it might be in Charonne?'

He stopped to let a German truck pass. Two bored gefreiters stared out of the rear and we let it move on rather than be stuck behind their sharp, unsmiling faces for the next kilometre or so.

'There's someone I'm interested in. He's one of the associates of the brothers I asked you to look into. I don't know who he is or what his name is, but he could fit the bill. But I don't know why he'd only be operating in Charonne.'

'Starting small?'

'I don't know so much. He didn't look the sort to go small. There's another face, Aitor le Crochu. His father was the leading light in Porte de Vincennes back in the day. I want to know what the son's up to.'

Another troop lorry hove into view, so Boniface let that pass too. The Germans seemed to spend their days driving themselves around the city.

'Would he be up to killing Cartier to take over his business?' Boniface asked.

'I have no idea. Years ago, maybe, but he was run out of town and I don't know what he'd be capable of nowadays.'

'These days anyone's capable of anything,' Sarah commented. Her words hung in the cold air.

Dax was waiting for me when we got back to Thirty-Six. He called me into his office. I'd dragged my heels through the detectives' room, not because I was worried about whatever it was the commissioner had to say, but because it was the only place with a heater. The temperature dropped noticeably when I closed the door behind me. I wished I'd kept my coat on.

'What is it?' I asked him when I'd sat down.

'It's Sarah.'

'What about her?'

'Nothing about her. It's about you.'

'Me?'

'You, Eddie. She's here to help out with secretarial duties, typing, taking notes, keeping the stove going. I don't want you using her as a cop.'

'She was listening, taking notes. That's secretarial work.'

'You took her with you on an investigation. That's police work. It's not what she's for. I don't want it happening again. I won't tell you a second time.'

I got up to go. 'Is that it?'

He motioned me to sit back down again. 'No. You've been summoned by the judge. You're to see him in the Palais de Justice. Now.'

'Judge Clément? He's never summoned me in his life. What does he want?'

'One way to find out.'

23

Judge Clément's name had been taken down from the dark wooden door into his chambers. There was a thin oblong of lighter grain where the old plate had been removed. As I stood outside the room, a man in work blues was preparing to affix a shiny new one. I leaned my head to read the name and he held it for me to see more clearly.

'Judge Rambert,' he whispered, nodding his head at the door. 'Good luck.'

I knocked and went in. Instinctively, I knew exactly who I was going to find on the other side. Looking out of the window in the far corner of the chambers was the Frenchman I'd seen at Ambassador Abetz's dinner on Friday evening, and then again at the return of Napoleon II's ashes on Saturday. His room was hotter than the stove in the detectives' room back at Thirty-Six. The coal shortage evidently hadn't reached this far.

Without a word, or indeed even looking at me, he pointed at the chair in front of his desk. I remained standing.

'Where's Judge Clément?' I asked him.

He finally dragged himself away from the view outside and sat at his desk. It looked far bigger than the one I remembered in Clément's day, like a small mountain plateau guarded by a vulture in a black gown. I sat down in front of him.

'He's retired.'

'I didn't know he was retiring.'

'Neither did he.'

His face broke into a smile. It wasn't the kindest I'd ever seen. Every part of his being was angular and rapacious, a creature of beak and talons that would rip and tear at the slightest weakness.

'You wanted to see me,' I reminded him.

'We haven't been formally introduced, Inspector Giral. We were both at Ambassador Abetz's fine dinner last week, but the opportunity for you to introduce yourself to me didn't arise. As you now see, I have replaced Judge Clément.'

'Is there a reason for that?'

He smiled again, the raptor unfurling. 'It was felt that Judge Clément was very much the old order.'

'And that's a bad thing?'

Rambert studied me. 'The Bouvier brothers. That's your investigation, is it not? I want them arrested.'

'They need to be questioned,' I agreed, surprised at the abrupt switch in conversation, 'but I don't think we're near the point of being able to arrest them.'

'You don't understand, Inspector Giral. I want the Bouvier brothers arrested and charged with the murder of Joseph Cartier.'

'We don't have the evidence to charge them. I also don't think they're responsible. They're thieves and chancers, they're not killers.'

Rambert picked up a paper knife from his desk and played with it. 'I'm afraid that's not your choice to make, Inspector. I am the judge, I am instructing this case, and I want these two men arrested for the murder of Joseph Cartier.'

I was struggling to keep my annoyance in check. Everything he was saying was right – under French law, as judge he was in charge of instructing my investigation – but over the years I'd come to an understanding with Judge Clément. He'd realised I knew what I was doing, so he left me and Dax to run investigations as we saw fit. More so after the Germans had entered the city and justice, such as it was, had drained into the sewers. The idea of that changing was troubling enough, but changing to accommodate this new judge was beyond disturbing.

'Then the case will fail,' I told him. 'There isn't sufficient evidence to arrest them, let alone convict them of murder.'

'That's where we would disagree. I have issued you with your order to arrest the Bouvier brothers. I expect it to be carried out. You may leave now.'

'It's a mistake.'

He looked sharply at me, any false smile gone.

'The mistake is yours, Inspector Giral.'

24

I had a visitor waiting for me in the entrance to Thirty-Six when I got back from seeing Judge Rambert. My mood hadn't lifted during the short walk back from the Palais de Justice.

A young man in a heavy coat and scarf stood up and walked over when I entered the building. It took me a moment to recognise him while he unwrapped the layers of warm clothing. My anger had to abate quickly.

'Inspector Giral,' he said. It was Pierre Ferran, the son who now worked for his father's electrician business in Bel Air.

'What can I do for you, Pierre?'

I led him over to a bench away from the handful of other people waiting in the entrance and we sat down.

'It's Marie.' Nervously he fiddled with the ends of the scarf hanging down to his lap. 'We've had news of where she is.'

'Where is she?'

'Cherche-Midi.'

I couldn't help letting out a deep sigh. Cherche-Midi prison had always had a tough reputation. Not far from Hochstetter's Abwehr headquarters, on Boulevard Raspail, it had been a French military prison up to two days before the Germans had entered the city, but we'd emptied it in time and sent all our prisoners to a camp in the Dordogne. The problem was that after they'd got here, the Germans had steadily repopulated it with prisoners of their own, mainly anyone proving to be too vociferously opposed to their presence in the city. When it had been a military prison, it had been harsh even by those standards, with inmates kept in solitary confinement and forbidden to speak to each other. By all accounts, it hadn't improved any under its new landlords.

'Have you been able to see her?'

He shook his head. 'The Gestapo are holding her.'

I left Pierre Ferran with a promise to do what I could and climbed the stairs to the third floor. Secretly I held out little hope that I'd be able to do anything. The Gestapo tended not to pay too much attention to my finer needs.

The detectives' room was raucous, the noise of cops going off shift and chewing the fat after a long day. Not even the stove to warm my hands could tempt me. I saw that Dax's door was closed, but his light was on. That was another reason to hurry into my own office, to avoid him.

Sarah had left work by this time. On her desk, I saw that the pile of papers waiting for her to type up had grown. On my own desk, Boniface had left a folder with my name on it.

'And what's your name, sweetie?'

The disembodied voice made me jump. I turned to see Boniface at the third desk in the room. He was on the phone. I calmed down quickly to my usual feeling of unhurried annoyance when he was around. He put the phone down.

'Finding out who stocks the hair oil,' he explained to me.

'Can't you do it in the other room?'

He gestured to the door. We both heard the loud chatter.

'All right. But don't get used to being in here.'

I sat down and picked up the folder he'd left on my desk, tuning out his prattle from across the room. He was alternating between making phone calls and giving me a running commentary on each one. I knew he'd happily talk away while I ignored him. That was one good thing with Boniface – you never had to make any polite noises. Not that I ever would.

He'd left a note inside the folder on top of a series of files with photographs. As always, I had to be impressed at how thorough he was. When the Germans had been about to enter Paris, we'd sent all our police files floating down the Seine on a barge to keep them out of their clutches, and we'd never really got any order back into them since. He'd done a good job gathering all this information. I glanced across the room at him. He was evidently talking to a young woman on the phone, judging by the tone and words he was using. He ran his fingers through his hair as he spoke. If only people were as un-irritating as I wanted them to be.

I turned back to the folder. Going through the mugshots and rap sheets on the known associates of Firmin and Jacquot Bouvier, I was struck by just how many minor thugs the brothers had got to know over the years. All of them local to Charonne.

And they say it's travel that broadens the mind, I told myself.

Something Boniface said finally got through to me.

'That's me done for the day,' he said, putting his coat on and peering out into the murky darkness beyond the window. He stood in front of my desk, an oddly sheepish look on his face. 'The hair oil, Eddie. Gomina Argentine. It's in a lot more stores than I thought it would be. Even with a mugshot, I don't think it's a line worth pursuing.'

'Not as exclusive as you reckoned.'

He sniffed and turned away, unable to avoid glancing at Sarah's empty chair, no doubt glad she wasn't there to see his lapse from grace. For a moment after he'd gone, I missed his noise. It was like when the steady crump of distant shelling in the trenches suddenly stopped and the silence became too loud. I shook my head and concentrated on the papers on my desk.

The December gloom outside filled every corner of the room, lit only by the lamp on my desk. I couldn't help feeling a sense of dismay at the life that had been dished up to the brothers. When I'd known them, they hadn't been malicious, they'd just never had the chances. I wondered how different things might have been had they left with their father instead of staying with their mother. While Gérard Bouvier might have been no Jean Valjean, at least he'd got out of crime. Georgette, on the other hand, had most definitely stayed cast in the Madame Thénardier mould.

I put the last file down in the pile on the left and sat back in my chair. The photograph I'd been looking for wasn't there. I considered trawling through them one more time in case I'd missed something – no moustache, the nose not yet broken, a different haircut – but I knew it would be pointless. The man I'd seen with the brothers in Les Quatre Chats and whose pungent hair oil I'd smelled in the grocer's was simply not among the photographs in the folder Boniface had put together. Boniface was right – trying to find him through the shops would be a hiding to nothing.

'So who are you?' I asked out loud.

I thought of the Metro to Dominique's flat in Montmartre and looked glumly at the dark sky out of the window. There were questions to which I wanted answers.

Was the man I was looking for a new kid in town, here to take over Cartier's old business? And if he was, who was he? Where was he from? And why only in Charonne? More importantly, did he kill Cartier?

That was the problem. I had no idea how he operated, or if he was capable of force-feeding Cartier his own butter. As I'd told Judge Rambert, I didn't see the brothers being responsible for it, but this new sharp-dressed thug? I knew nothing about him.

The other question was whether he was part of someone

else's set-up. Had Aitor le Crochu felt a stirring in his loins and decided to ride forth and win back the ancestral sewer lost by his father? And if so, was it with or without the mystery man's help?

The other thought that came to mind was Pepe's surprising comment about Henri Lafont. I would have been very happy not to see his involvement in any of this. As Henri Chamberlin, he'd been as petty a crook as they came, but somehow the Germans coming to town had significantly improved his fortunes. He'd changed his name and got himself mixed up with the Abwehr, along with a motley gang of career criminals, which won him a potentially catastrophic level of immunity. The Abwehr, but not Hochstetter, I had to remind myself. The major appeared to be opposed to working with gangsters, which was all well and good of him. The one consolation was that Lafont was probably out of the league of a small black-market operation in Charonne, wherever he was. As far as I was concerned, he was one criminal who could stay missing.

I picked up the folder again and threw it back on my desk in frustration.

I knew that if I was to ensure Judge Rambert didn't pin the murder on the brothers, as he seemed intent on doing, I had to find out who the mystery man with them was. Oddly, thinking of the judge, another figure sprang to mind. Falke, the German trader I'd met at the dinner with Otto Abetz. Another chancer come to Paris to make a killing.

I got up and decided it was time to face the Metro. But first I had to face another form of blackout, and then satisfy my curiosity with one person I did know.

25

'I usually go to Le Rex, down on Boulevard Poissonière, but of course we can't now.'

Dominique clung to my arm in excitement and held on tightly for a moment before remembering and suddenly tugging her arm out of mine. It felt the greatest loss. We didn't dare hold hands, kiss or touch in public because of the rules set down by the unwelcome guests. Or our uncertainty about how those rules could be interpreted. Better safe than sorry was fast becoming our new answer to everything as we tried to go about being a warm couple in a city gone cold.

It was for the same reason that we couldn't go to Le Rex, Dominique's favourite cinema. It had been turned into a *Soldatenkino*, requisitioned by the Occupier and reserved exclusively for German soldiers. And just in case you were in any doubt, they'd put up a massive unsightly painted *Deutsches Soldatenkino* sign, managing to turn the beautiful Art Deco façade into a thing of ugliness.

'I heard French people can go if they've got a pass,' Dominique said, reading my thoughts. 'No thank you. I'll wait until they've gone. Then I'll go back there.'

I smiled to myself. To Dominique, they were always 'they', never Germans, or Nazis, or Boches. They. It helped her de-humanise the invader. My smile faded immediately. The thought that Adolf's minions and believers could make someone as compassionate as Dominique seek to dehumanise another person was profoundly saddening. It reminded me oddly of the last war. One of the ways many soldiers used to survive the trenches and be able to shoot and bayonet the enemy was to blot out their ability to see the men on the other side of the mud as humans. As Yves Ferran had said, it's not the person at either end of the bayonet that's the problem. It's the bastard who placed it between them.

We had to venture farther from Montmartre into the city centre to find a cinema. I hadn't been to see a film since before the Occupation began, but Dominique wanted to go.

'It takes me away from all this,' she'd explained.

We went into the cinema separately. It was strange. As friends, I probably wouldn't have had any problem going in together, but the moment we'd become lovers, the fear of authority and its power over us became infinitely more acute. We were both, no doubt, much more cautious than we would have been under other circumstances. It was the fear of loss.

Once inside, we found each other and sat together. The cinema was full. The movies were flourishing this winter, not because they were making great films, but because it was one of the best ways to get warm when you couldn't heat your home every day. Two hours of someone else's coal ration while being warmed, informed and entertained suddenly became a sweet temptation.

Before we could get to the entertainment part, though, we had to endure the informing bit. There was never a word so cruelly misused. Photo reels of Adolf visiting German soldiers somewhere we cared nothing about, images of Pétain walking, looking severe and then walking some more, and the believable news that the RAF no longer had any planes. As the newsreel came on, Dominique squeezed my hand in the dark and leaned in to whisper to me, her voice gleeful.

'Wait and see what happens now.'

The moment Hitler hit the screen, almost everyone in the cinema began to cough long and loud. Any narration was drowned out. Next to me, Dominique joined in and motioned me to do the same. Looking around, I thought why not and coughed along with the best of them. An usherette hurried down the aisle, shushing everyone and shining her torch on the audience. The coughing fell silent.

But then Pétain came on and the noise started up again. This time it was sneezing, like a cinema full of flu patients on a day out. Dominique began to sneeze too, trying to suppress her laughter. I joined in with her, the tears running down our faces. It was a release we rarely experienced under a grey Occupation.

As the sneezing increased in intensity for the stories of the Luftwaffe's gains and the RAF's losses, the lights suddenly went on. The noise abated only slightly. A man walked onto the stage, his brown suit looking as tired and harassed as he did. He waved his hands up and down, asking for silence, and tried to speak. In our seats, Dominique and I found ourselves glancing around to see if anyone was looking at us.

'Please.' The man on stage finally got a word in. 'Please, I am the manager. I beg you not to make a noise during the newsreel. The German authorities have threatened to close down my cinema and arrest me if I can't control the audience. They mean it. They are shutting cinemas for a week at a time. This is my livelihood. I don't want to be arrested.'

The noise died down quickly after his words, with just a few sporadic sounds here and there. One man coughed and apologised, swearing it was genuine.

'If the noise doesn't stop,' the manager continued, 'I'll have to leave the lights on for the rest of the performance. Thank you.'

He walked off to a more subdued audience and the film started up again. Mercifully, the newsreel was ending and the main feature was about to start. It was a film that Dominique had chosen. After ten minutes, I realised that the last thing it would do was take her away from all this, as she'd wanted. It was about a group of workers building and repairing barges while living in barracks, an air of claustrophobia and distrust permeating every scene. I sighed as silently as I could. The title – *Campement 13* – should have been warning enough.

Unable to get into the film or warm to any of the characters, my mind started to wander. I thought of Judge Rambert and his order for the Bouvier brothers to be arrested for Cartier's murder. Not for the first time, I felt sorry for Firmin and Jacquot, at the hand that life had dealt them. I couldn't help feeling that they were being set up. They were easy prey for the mystery men and the Lafonts of this world. Suppressing a wry laugh, it occurred to me that the jackals needn't have bothered. Judge Rambert was more than happy to do their job for them and convict the brothers without the niceties of evidence, guilt or even a fair trial.

In the dark, Dominique suddenly squeezed my hand and I nearly jumped. I looked at her to see her smile glowing from the light on the screen.

'Are you enjoying it?' she mouthed at me.

I nodded my head and smiled back. We all had things to hide.

26

After the film, we re-emerged from the Metro in Montmartre and entered its streets, the tension we'd felt in the city centre and then underground gently diminishing amid the narrow lanes and winding hills. This was Dominique's part of town and I was already beginning to feel a sense of ease in parts of it. I'd spent just a few days living here, but I'd been visiting her for a couple of months before that, and we'd grown to learn the areas where we were less likely to see German soldiers sightseeing. Areas where we felt calmer being in each other's company.

'I'll take you home,' I told her. 'There's somewhere I need to go.'

'Where?'

I mentioned a bar and she turned to face me. 'Oh no you don't, Eddie Giral. If you're going for a drink, I'm coming with you.'

'It's work. Police work.'

We carried on walking. Dominique felt bold enough to take my arm and not let go. 'I'm still coming with you.'

We came out by the Moulin de la Galette and stopped in our tracks, instantly moving apart. Outside the old cabaret, two German trucks had pulled up and soldiers were jumping down from the tailgate.

'A raid?' Dominique asked.

We looked more closely. All young, they were in party mood, their hair neatly combed, their uniforms pressed. Their laughter rumbled across the cobbles and shattered the wintry night sky like thunder on a summer's day.

'You could call it that.'

We let them make their raucous way inside, young men as conquerors in a foreign land eager to taste the forbidden delights of Paris. In the meantime, Dominique and I skulked past, putting a couple of streets between us and them.

'Do you think they're going there to see the settings of Renoir's paintings?' I asked.

Dominique shook her head. 'Van Gogh. Got to be.'

We joked, but the sight of the soldiers had broken the moment and we walked the rest of the way in silence. Luckily, the bar we were looking for was very unlikely to be on the junior Wehrmacht holiday trail. Outside a dingy entrance, we stopped and looked at the walls shedding slivers of stone and the door dripping strips of varnish.

'You really know how to show a girl good time,' Dominique told me.

'I warned you it was work.'

Just once, I thought, I'd like to go somewhere nice, where criminals weren't bartering their souls for a slice of each other and some young thug wasn't out to make a name for himself by trying to batter a cop half the city remembered as a bastard. Then I reminded myself that I'd just been to Maxim's with Nazis and occupying soldiers and decided there was nowhere nice these days.

Montmartre might have been on every tourist's map and beloved of artists, bohemians and Dominique, but it was also home to one of the seediest dives this side of Gestapo headquarters, filled with a wildlife that was almost as blindly savage.

Secretly I loved it. It meant I didn't have to behave.

Our shoes stuck to the wine-soaked floor as we descended the narrow steps and crossed the smoke-filled bar. This place was so far down the circles of hell that I didn't even get dark looks from its denizens; they were too submerged in their own misdeeds that they assumed everyone was down there with them, including a cop.

'Eddie, good to see you after all this time,' the owner told me. I think he actually meant it. 'And Dominique.'

He beamed a genuine smile and bent down to kiss her hand. A legend in his own back street, he was Pilou. It was said he'd sold the family farm in the Ardèche in the 1920s because he couldn't be arsed to till the land and had spent every last sou he earned from it on this place. Some people just aren't cut out for business. Good-looking in a disturbing distortion of a matinée idol sort of a way, he had a pronounced widow's peak and large incisors that made him look like he was Bela Lugosi wishing he was Charles Boyer.

'What can I get you, Eddie?' he gushed a little more. 'And Dominique. You must sing for us. Please say you will.'

'You do know this bar isn't on the Champs-Élysées, don't you?'

He punched me playfully on the arm, the more than light tap a sign of the strength hidden in him. 'You are a tease.'

'Aren't I just? We'll have two whiskies, and yes, I know you haven't got any because it's illegal and you'd never break the law, but we'll still have them.'

'Your very best, please, Pilou,' Dominique added. In just five words, she'd wooed him even more than he already was.

He led us to a table sandwiched between a pair of pimps and an ageing aristocrat who'd lost all his money in the Stavisky scandal in the 1930s and now painted nudes for a meagre living because it was what he'd always wanted to do.

'Here on business, Eddie?' Pilou asked when he brought our drinks.

'I've seen what I came here for, thanks.'

He looked around in puzzlement but had no idea what I meant. Dominique stared at me, her expression equally quizzical, but I didn't enlighten her. Instead, I waited for Pilou to leave and clinked her glass with mine, taking a cautious sip of the whisky. I hadn't been here since Vichy had banned liquid joy in the summer and I wasn't sure what to expect of Pilou's contraband liquor.

'Don't worry, Eddie, it's good,' Dominique said, reading my mind.

It was. After so many years as a cop in Paris, it still amazed me how there were always people walking among us who could break the law in so many enterprising ways and get hold of something like whisky when everything else was in horribly short supply. I clinked glasses again and put mine down after taking a second, longer draught.

'Back in a moment,' I told Dominique, getting up.

'Where are you going, Eddie?'

'I told you. Work.'

Leaning heavily against the far end of the bar, vainly trying to convince a prostitute to treat him on tick, Aitor le Crochu was exactly the charm-school dropout I'd come looking for. The years since I'd seen him last hadn't been kind. His lank hair was slicked back in a grease more of his own making than the refinements of Argentinian oil, and while most of us were wearing clothes that were too big and threadbare for us, Aitor's were just a few more hellish circles of ill-fitting unkempt.

As I approached him from behind, I heard him threaten to hit the woman when she wouldn't succumb to his wiles. His words were slurred on Pilou's least salubrious red wine, the cheapest he stocked. I reached out to grab his upraised arm, but she was quicker and punched him full in the face twice before picking up her bag and walking away. Aitor was even more surprised than

I was. She would have given Claude from Les Quatre Chats a run for his money at his peak.

'That's got to hurt,' I told Aitor.

He was sagging heavily against the wall and turned at my voice. His face dropped when he recognised me. Blood was running in a steady stream from his nose, but he was so out of it, he was doing nothing to staunch the flow.

'Fuck off, Giral.'

'Not nice, Aitor, when I've only got your well-being at heart.'

I prodded his nose and he closed his eyes briefly with the pain. Opening them, he looked at me with even more loathing. A waster by anyone's standards, Aitor le Crochu had always ridden on his father's coat tails back in the day when senior had still had the wit to wear them, and he'd used his old man as a shield for his bullying. It was little surprise that the empire had folded when junior had taken over the family flick-knife. I just hadn't expected to see him fall this low.

'Things don't seem to be going too well, Aitor. Why's that?'

'Why do you want to know?'

'Goodness of my heart. Still longing for the days of Porte de Vincennes? Or are you happily reliving them?'

That was a question that had already been answered. I could see immediately that poor old Aitor was to organised crime what Boniface was to humility. He sneered at me, which was no mean feat. His nickname of le Crochu was down to his hook nose, which always made him look like a vulture having a bad day. He laughed. It wasn't the most musical of sounds, especially bubbling through the blood in his nose and mouth.

'I'm doing all right.' He belched loudly, his breath fetid, and looked longingly at another prostitute.

'Well, that's good to hear.'

'What is it you want?'

'Social call. Just wondering if business was booming or not.'

'Think I'd tell you, *poulet?*'

I flicked his nose one last time and turned to leave him. He yelped in pain.

'You already have.'

I wiped my hands and made my way back to Dominique. As I steamed a course through bleary-eyed representatives of each of old man Alighieri's circles of hell, it was evident that Aitor was less likely to be behind any black-market takeover in Charonne than my neighbour Monsieur Henri was. If he was, he was hiding it, and no one could hide it that well. The Aitor of old would have been shelling out francs for every prostitute in sight if he'd had even the slightest whiff of ill-gained cash. Which was both good and bad. It meant I could rule him out of the running, but it also meant I was no nearer to finding who killed Cartier or getting the Bouvier brothers off the hook. I quickened my pace through the crowd. I had an illicit whisky waiting for me.

Back at the table, Pilou was cajoling Dominique.

'You must sing,' he was telling her. 'Everyone is asking you to.'

'I can't.'

I could see she was tempted, starved as she was of the chance since the Nazis had hit the jazz clubs while telling everyone else not to, but there was a determination in her refusal that surprised me.

A chorus ran through the bar, spreading to one end then the other. 'Sing, sing.'

She smiled but wouldn't budge. I saw her exchange a look with someone, an old guy I recognised from my days on the door of the jazz club. I couldn't quite fathom what the look meant, but he stood up and went to the piano in the farthest, darkest corner of the room. She smiled at him as if to say thank you. He nodded and flexed his fingers over the keyboard, finally knocking out the opening bars of a tune far more melodiously than the place would warrant, like an angel's harp in hell.

The room fell silent. Some still thought Dominique might sing, but I knew she wouldn't. From the corner, when it became apparent that she wasn't going to, a voice started up the song. Good, but not Dominique. A second joined in, then a third and more, until the crowd forgot their disappointment.

More voices entered the fray, until almost everyone in the room was singing, not always tunefully, but always whole-heartedly. Thug and pimp, hooker and mugger, thrill-seeker and bag-snatcher, all fell under the spell of the haunting lines of 'Un Jeune Homme Chantait'. All around me, grown lowlifes went teary-eyed as they sang, their voices thunderous in the low-ceilinged cavern.

I watched Dominique out of the corner of my eye and saw no reaction to the singing. Like me, she listened to the patrons of one of the sorriest dens in Montmartre come together in their own anthem, but showed no response. Her silence filled me with a sadness deeper than anything Dante could ever dream of.

Looking away, I thought of all the time gone – all the time going – and I thought of Dominique, and I felt as deep a passion as I had since losing myself in the last war.

But I missed my home and my books.

27

I had two favours I needed to ask of Hochstetter. At best, he'd grant me one of them. I had to decide which one I wanted more.

He would also only be likely to grant me the one he thought I needed less. If I asked for first one, then a second, he'd assume the second was the more important to me as I was placing less emphasis on it. But then he'd know I'd know that and would swap the order accordingly. In the end, neither of us knew what to do.

Which just goes to show. If life under Occupation was stressful, living with Hochstetter made it more so.

I also had to get past a brand-new Rottweiler behind what was once the reception desk at the Lutetia, who insisted on inspecting my ID and calling up to Hochstetter's office.

'Can I go up now?' I asked the hauptmann behind his very own Siegfried Line. If you can imagine petty bureaucracy in a tight collar and a severe haircut, this was your man.

'When I receive Major Hochstetter's permission, Inspector Giral,' he told me.

I stared at him to put him off his work as we waited for the phone to ring. It finally did, and he waited a full minute after putting it down before telling me I could go on up.

'You're most kind,' I told him.

The naval officer who'd been at the meal with Ambassador

Abetz was in Hochstetter's office. He looked up when I walked in and gave me a cheery greeting.

'Inspector Giral, a fine morning. Good to see you working so closely with Major Hochstetter.'

'Isn't it just?'

'He will be along in a moment. Some business to attend to.'

I went and stood by the window to look out at the junction below. The lack of traffic in the city took me by surprise every time, and the view from above simply accentuated how few vehicles and how many bicycles and pedestrians there were. It was one of the dozens of small moments I experienced in a day that felt immeasurably sad, our home altered beyond our will.

'Do you have a meeting with Major Hochstetter?' I asked him.

'No, simply a social call. We know each other from Hamburg.'

'Hamburg?'

'That is where we are both from. We went to different high schools, but our families knew each other socially when we were growing up.'

'I see.' One more snippet of information for the mental Hochstetter file. 'And you've both been posted here?'

'Indeed. Albeit in different branches of the forces. Major Hochstetter eschewed his maritime upbringing for the army, and military intelligence.'

'Maritime upbringing?'

'Hamburg.' He stood up. 'But where are my manners? We weren't formally introduced on Friday. I am Korvettenkapitän Johannes Thier. But please call me Johannes.'

'Korvettenkapitän?'

'The equivalent of a major in the army. Our rivalry is so keen that we occupy the same rank.'

Hochstetter chose that moment to enter.

'At the same age, Johannes,' he added. 'Édouard, to what do I owe this pleasure?'

'Well, this is all very jolly, isn't it?'

Hochstetter sat down behind his desk and I took the upright chair in front of him. Thier was behind me, on one of the sofas, under an unfortunate reproduction of *The Raft of the Medusa* – also known as *Shipwreck Scene* – by Géricault. I turned to see him return to the magazine he'd been reading, a fortnightly affair to show German soldiers their way about the city. Besides pointing them in the direction of the tourist sights, it included all the shops, restaurants and attractions most Parisians could no longer afford.

'Going somewhere nice?' I asked him. I couldn't help myself.

Not waiting for an answer, I turned back to see Hochstetter give me an amused look.

'As I said, Édouard, to what do I owe this pleasure?'

Which was my cue to decide which favour to go for first. I glanced sideways at Thier.

'Would you prefer me to leave?' he asked.

'It is perfectly all right, Édouard,' Hochstetter said. 'You may speak freely in front of Korvettenkapitän Thier. We have been friends since our youth.'

'So I gather,' I said to give me the time to gather my thoughts and make my choice. 'Marie Ferran.'

'Should I know her?'

'She was one of the students arrested last month during the Armistice Day commemorations.'

'Or riots, as we might call them.'

I let that one slide. 'She is still being held at Cherche-Midi without charge or trial.'

Hochstetter couldn't help glancing out of the window in the direction of the prison. 'By the German authorities, I presume?'

'The Gestapo.'

He gave a slight shake of his head. 'You know I have no authority over the Gestapo, Édouard, or indeed any great deal of influence.'

'But you have some. More than I would.'

'And what precisely is it you want me to do with this supposed influence?'

'Have her released. She's a student. She's only eighteen years old.'

'She rioted, she was arrested.'

'She marked a commemoration. Your soldiers and our police turned it into a riot. There is no argument whatsoever for her to continue to be detained. Others who were arrested have been ordered to report to a police station every day. I don't see why the same treatment shouldn't be handed out to her.'

Hochstetter lit a cigarette and dropped the spent match into a full ashtray on his desk. 'I believe students from outside Paris were sent home.'

'That's precisely what happened. They were sent home. As I say, there's no reason for the Gestapo to keep her. She's not a threat.'

He took a long draw on his cigarette, the flakes of tobacco crackling red. 'I'm afraid that that is never an argument that appears to hold much water with our friends on Rue des Saussaies. Please don't tax me any further on this. I see no purpose in my antagonising the Gestapo over such a matter. It would do little to serve me.'

I left it there. Another thing I'd learned with Hochstetter was that I sometimes asked for something, he'd dismiss it, and then he'd come back to it later and offer it in exchange for something he needed in return.

I heard Thier behind me put down his magazine. 'Are we finished?'

Hochstetter looked frankly at me. 'I presume there is another matter?'

'Your role in assisting me with my investigations, Major. It's invaluable.' That won me a wry smirk. 'I'm seeking the leader of a criminal gang and supposed you might clarify a few things for me. There is a new black-market operation in the Twelfth Arrondissement, as I mentioned to you the other day. It might possibly be run by someone new to Paris. I wondered if your intelligence had thrown up any new criminal activity.'

The sarcastic smile hadn't dropped from his face one iota. 'Surely this is your area of expertise, Édouard. For you to know and inform me, not vice versa.'

'I felt you should be aware, that's all. So that we can assist each other in upholding law and order.'

'Most laudable, although I rather get the impression that this is merely another of your wearisome obsessions.'

I looked frankly at him. 'Is the Abwehr aware of any new criminal gangs in the city? Someone like Henri Lafont, perhaps?'

The sucking of breath might have been a long draw on his cigarette, but I prefer to think of it as an expression of shock, or irritation. I like to subject Hochstetter to both emotions. He stubbed his cigarette out forcefully. 'I simply would not know.'

'Criminal gangs?' Thier asked from behind me.

'Édouard is convinced that the Abwehr is in some way working with the city's gangsters,' Hochstetter explained. 'Common criminals. And now it appears that yet another French criminal is operating on our behalf. None of it is true, unfortunately, but his tiresome obstinacy will not allow him to accept that as a fact.'

'I really wasn't implying that,' I told him. 'I'm simply asking you if you'd learned of any unusual arrivals in the city.'

'Is this Otto the inspector is referring to?' Thier asked.

Stunned into silence, I turned back to Hochstetter and caught a glance from him to his friend, indicating that he shouldn't say any more.

'Otto?' I repeated.

'I have no idea who your new favourite criminal is involved with or who this Otto is,' Hochstetter told me. 'And I'm sure Korvettenkapitän Thier does not either.'

I looked from one to the other. 'Not any more he doesn't.'

'If that is all, Édouard.' Hochstetter pressed a button on the intercom on his desk and asked someone to come in. The door opened and the young officer who lived behind a desk in the antechamber entered. 'Leutnant Braun, please would you escort Inspector Giral from the building. His business here is concluded.'

I drove away from the Lutetia neither angry nor dispirited.

That was the way it was with Hochstetter. You cast your bread upon the waters. Sometimes it came back with interest, sometimes it fed the ducks, most times it sank to the bottom, a congealed mess.

Driving past an entrance to the Metro, I was glad I'd weakened and taken a pool car, even though it was only me using it. I figured that seeing Hochstetter meant I was on Occupier business, so use of the car was justified. And my next visit was to do the judge's work. More or less. So that was reason enough too. Besides, I'd had more than enough of being underground to last a lifetime.

Georgette Bouvier was in when I went calling. Shrugging when she saw me, she let me in and led the way to the same lunar table in the kitchen. A pot was on the stove, the smell of coffee emanating from it real. She turned it off but didn't offer me one or pour a cup for herself before sitting down.

'Smells good,' I said. 'Going up in the world?'

'What do you want, Eddie?'

'It's your sons I've come to see.'

'They're somewhere. Up to no good, and being no good at it.' She lit her first cigarette of the visit. She had a voice like barbed wire trapped in a mangle, hardened by forty Gauloises a day. She caught me eyeing it with distaste and bristled. 'Gauloises. The cigarette of our brave soldiers. Doing my patriotic duty as a Frenchwoman.'

'We all do our bit. Seriously, Georgette, I need to catch up with Firmin and Jacquot. It's important you tell me where they are.'

'What have they done now?'

'Nothing, I hope. It's just that there's a new judge in town, and he wants them arrested.'

'For this Cartier thing? The black market?'

'For his murder.'

She snorted and took a deep drag, all but finishing the Gauloise in one go. 'Oh, come on, that's not them. They're thieving little bastards, but they're no killers.'

'I agree with you, but the judge thinks differently. He's new and wants to set an example.'

'And my two boys are the example?'

I nodded. 'I need to talk to them, Georgette. They have to tell me their side of the story. That way, I've got a chance of protecting them from the judge. If they won't cooperate with me, there's nothing I can do.'

She lit a second cigarette from the dog-end of the first. 'I really don't know where they are, Eddie. I'll tell you when I see them.'

I got up to leave. 'Call me. Tell me where I can meet them. Don't let them come to Thirty-Six. I'm counting on you.'

She followed me to the door and leaned heavily against the frame while I stood on the landing.

'You know my boys, Eddie. They wouldn't swat a fly.'
'I know they wouldn't.'
She backed away to close the door.
'They'd be too fucking stupid to hit it.'

28

'Work for you,' a man's voice said.

I looked up. Sarah had stopped typing and was warming her hands inside the sleeves of her cardigan. The price I paid for privacy was no stove in my office, just the afterglow of the one in the detectives' room, so on overcast days at this time of the year, the room got cold.

'I need it by five today.'

Lafitte had walked into the room without knocking, his arms laden with loose bits of paper. He dumped the lot on Sarah's desk. Some of it overflowed and fell to the floor, but he didn't bend down to pick it up. He gave me the briefest of nods and made to leave.

'Detective Lafitte,' I called to him. 'Come back in here.'

He returned as slowly as he dared and stood in front of my desk. His one contribution to the conversation was a questioning nod of his head.

'You don't tell Madame Chevalier what time you want the papers typed. She tells you what time you can have them. And then you come and collect them when she says. Is that clear?'

He looked from me to Sarah. 'When then?'

'Five o'clock,' she told him. He looked back at me in triumph until she spoke again. 'Tomorrow.'

'Got that?' I asked him. 'And don't forget to pick the papers up off the floor before you go.'

Sarah and I watched in silence as he gathered up the overflow of documents and placed them in exaggerated tidiness on her desk. He turned and left without looking at either of us, his walk a self-conscious swagger.

'You like making friends, don't you, Inspector Giral?' Sarah said to me once he'd gone. There was a coldness to her voice.

'Eddie,' I reminded her.

'Commissioner Dax reprimanded me. For assisting you yesterday. He said that if I did it again, he'd dock me a morning's pay.'

'I'll have a word with him.'

'You said that last time.'

She picked up a document and began to type. At no point had she looked at me when we'd been talking. Without a word, I got up and went to Dax's office. I had to speak to him about other things anyway.

'I don't think you should have reprimanded Sarah,' I told him. 'It was my decision to use her, but it was necessary. We got much more than Boniface and I could have on our own.'

He waved at me to sit down. 'I reprimanded her, Eddie, because it's pointless having a go at you. You never listen. I don't want you using Mademoiselle Chevalier for police work, and the only way to stop you is to punish her.'

'That's hardly fair on her.'

'Get used to it. Do it again and she will be the one to be sanctioned. Now, get out or tell me something I want to hear.'

I told him instead about the new judge and his order to arrest the Bouvier brothers. His reaction was the same as mine.

'There isn't sufficient evidence to arrest them.'

'I don't think his plans for their future end there,' I told him. 'I get the feeling he's pretty clear they're his first and last suspects.'

Dax shook his head. 'God preserve us from crusading judges.'

'Especially when they're crusading on the wrong side. Do you know anything about him? Why he's been sent in to replace Judge Clément? And where he's been sent from?'

'I don't know, Eddie, but I'll make it my job to know.' He looked at a pile of files on his desk and sighed deeply. 'The burglaries. We're getting nowhere. And I don't want this new judge telling us to arrest the nearest scapegoat.'

'What's going on?'

He scratched his head. 'It's a whole string of them. All in the Sixteenth Arrondissement in flats left empty by families who fled the city before the Germans came and haven't come back, mainly Jewish owners. When they left, they only took what they could, so there's still plenty of rich pickings. None of them have been requisitioned by the German army, so the burglars know where to target. And we often don't hear about them for some time, as unless the neighbours notice something, there's no one to report them.'

'Good plan.' I had to be impressed. 'Are you still thinking of giving the investigation to Boniface?' I realised with a shock that I wasn't too happy at the thought of losing him.

'Probably. Any news on Cartier's murder? Real news, I mean, not the judge's.'

'Some leads. There's evidently a new black marketeer operating in Charonne, but oddly nothing in Bel Air.'

'Show me.'

He came with me to my office, where I went through the files and photos we had. I called Boniface in to add his thoughts, but I made sure not to ask Sarah what she'd learned the previous morning.

A uniformed cop knocked on the door and entered carrying a wooden box. A scratching noise was coming from inside it.

'The guinea pigs,' he said nervously. 'From the warehouse. What are we going to do with them?'

He pulled a piece of sacking off the top and I looked in.

About a dozen of the creatures were dozing or moving slowly around the bottom of the small crate. I had no idea what I was expected to do, and Dax and Boniface were silent for once. After a moment, Sarah spoke up.

'Give them to me. I know what to do with them.' She cleared a space on her desk and the young cop put the box down and scurried away.

'What is it with the guinea pigs?' Dax asked.

'We don't know.'

Out of the corner of my eye, I saw Sarah look expectant and then, in silence, roll her eyes and turn back to her typewriter.

'Meet me at this address in an hour, Inspector Giral. And bring them with you.'

I looked up to see Sarah standing in front of my desk. She'd covered the typewriter for the night and was wrapped up in her coat and scarf. She placed a folded piece of paper in front of me, along with the box containing the guinea pigs. Without waiting for an answer, she turned and left.

Checking the address she'd written down, I caught the Metro to Montmartre. The box and all its scratchings sat quietly on my lap all the way. Some old guy was about to ask me something, but I withered him with a glance and he kept his question to himself. A younger man looked away when I gave him a challenging glare. Luckily, the address was at the bottom of the hill, well away from Dominique's flat. I walked through narrow streets past German soldiers looking for the female companionship their officers had prohibited them from having. It was a strangely muted feel.

Finding the building, I stood outside for a few moments, glancing up and down the street. I had no idea why Sarah wanted me to meet her there. I checked my gun in my shoulder holster and went in, climbing a steep, dark staircase to the third floor. With one last look for anything untoward, I knocked.

The door opened a fraction and Sarah peered out. Seeing me, she opened the door fully and beckoned me in. She didn't smile or say a word.

'Is this your home?' I asked her.

She shook her head and led the way into a small living room. A wood-burning stove occupied the centre of the room and gave off a little heat. It was welcome after the cold of the streets, but I didn't stop to warm my hands. They were both still full with the box of guinea pigs.

A woman of about Sarah's age was sitting on a faded sofa. She looked up. I could see the nervousness in her eyes.

'It's all right,' Sarah told her. 'You won't get into any trouble.' She turned to me. 'Do I have your word on that at least?'

I nodded, not knowing what I was agreeing to.

'You stay there,' she told the woman. 'I'll show Inspector Giral. We'll be quiet.'

Mystified, I followed her into a tiny bedroom that led off from the living room. A baby was asleep in a cot. On the floor on the far side of the room from the cot was a zinc bath. I stopped in surprise. I heard scratching from inside it. Sarah motioned me forward.

I took two tentative steps towards the bath and peered in. It was filled with guinea pigs. I looked at Sarah in surprise, and she gestured me to empty the box into the bath before following her out of the room. Back in the living room, the other woman had gone. I heard her moving about in the kitchen.

'What's all this about?' I asked.

'The guinea pigs. In Cartier's warehouse. People breed them. They keep them in zinc baths. Like my friend.'

'Why?'

'Why do you think, Inspector Giral? They breed them and

sell the meat. On the black market. Which is why I made you promise my friend wouldn't get into any trouble.'

I looked back to the bedroom. 'So Cartier was breeding guinea pigs? With all the goods he must have had on the shelves?'

'That's the thing. I don't think he would have been doing that. This is a poor person's black market. Cartier wouldn't have needed to sell guinea pig meat.'

'How do you know about this?'

'Because I have to and you don't. Rationing isn't the same for you as it is for me.' She nodded at the kitchen door. 'Or for her.'

29

'Of course I've eaten guinea pig. You probably have too.'

I put down my fork with the piece of meat on it. I had no idea what the meat was. I nodded at it. 'Is this ...?'

Dominique laughed. 'No, Eddie, it's beef.'

I picked it up again and sniffed it. 'Black market?'

'From my butcher. He had a small delivery and I got up early to be in the queue in time.'

'Have you heard of a lot of people eating guinea pig? I knew there were some who were breeding rabbits on their balconies in the autumn, but I hadn't heard of anyone selling guinea pig.'

'Not a lot of people, but enough.' She tidied the plates away. 'And it's only going to get worse.'

'How do you know where to find it?'

'Because we talk to each other. When we're queuing. You're too busy fighting this war or catching criminals to hear.'

'I hear things.' I was about to tell her I'd learned of the butter and had spent all night in a cellar to queue for it, but I remembered the lie I'd told her about how I'd come by it, so I kept quiet.

'How did you hear about this?' she asked.

'Sarah. She's come to work at Thirty-Six as a secretary. She took me to a woman who breeds them.'

Dominique looked at me sharply. 'You're not going to arrest her, are you? For selling on the black market?'

'Of course I'm not.'

I waited until she sat down again. I'd managed to buy a bottle of wine from a grocer's on the walk home from the woman's flat further down the hill in Montmartre. I'd waited until Sarah had disappeared from sight by the Metro and taken a roundabout route to Dominique's. I dreaded to think of wine being rationed. I poured us both a little more.

'Steady,' she said. 'It's got to last.'

'Is rationing different for you?' I asked her after a while.

She looked at me, a smile playing about her lips. For the first time, I noticed the lines either side of her mouth where her face had got thinner.

'This whole Occupation thing is different for me.'

I recalled the young woman and the two German officers on the Metro a couple of days earlier. 'What about the Germans?'

'Them? They ignore me.'

'That's good, isn't it?'

'Is it, Eddie? Why do you think they ignore me?'

'I really don't know.'

'Because I'm dirty. I'm subhuman. They're not allowed to consort with me, so they leave me alone. Except for the ones who spit on the ground when I walk past. It's your nice French-women who get the attention.'

'And isn't that good?'

'Do I really need to tell you if that's good or bad?'

She drank her wine.

'You need to open your eyes a bit more, Eddie.'

30

Pierre Ferran was waiting for me in the entrance to Thirty-Six the next morning.

'I'm going to be here every day until you get the Germans to release Marie,' he told me.

I had no answer I could give him.

Upstairs, Boniface was infesting the office I shared with Sarah. He was talking and she was learning to drop the pretence of listening.

'So if your husband doesn't work,' he was asking her as I hung my coat on the hook, 'what is it he does do?'

'Haven't you got any work of your own to do, Boniface?' I asked him.

'You need a husband to look after you,' he insisted.

In reply, she looked at him with an expression that would have turned a gorgon to stone before shattering it in the icy cold. Boniface didn't notice. He was about to open his mouth again when I interrupted him. I was in no mood to reason.

'Door's over there, Boniface.'

He left and I sat down.

'You don't always have to be so blunt with him,' Sarah told me.

'I do. It does me good.'

She shrugged and carried on typing.

I left the glacial wastes of my office and went to see Dax in his. First I stopped off to warm my hands at the stove in the detectives' room, hoping the memory of warmth would linger. I had a lot of questions to ask him, and I knew I might be gone from the heater for some time.

Dax had a question of his own. I'd barely sat down. 'What's happening with this black-market investigation?'

'I've got a couple of avenues I'm exploring. There's a man I'm trying to find, not someone I know, who's of interest, who I saw talking to the Bouvier brothers.'

'Anything else?'

'I was talking to Hochstetter. A German naval officer who's a friend of his mentioned an Otto in relation to my question about criminal gangs. I don't know what it was about, but Hochstetter shut him up before he could say anything more.'

'Do you know who Otto is?'

'Unfortunately, I might. The German ambassador to Paris is Otto Abetz. He's a card-carrying Nazi. If it's him they're working with, that's a whole new level of pain.'

'Have you just come in here to cheer me up?' He reached for his secret stash of whisky – a gift from Hochstetter that had noticeably not come my way – and poured us both a glass. I'd had worse breakfasts lately. 'The German ambassador. And I've got you and Boniface digging around in it all.'

'Thanks for the vote of confidence.'

'Don't get me wrong, Eddie. You're both very good cops. It's just that neither of you is the most diplomatic.' He looked wryly at me over the top of his glass.

'One thing that *will* cheer you up. The quality of the goods we were finding in Charonne was very high. Real coffee, for one thing, not this *national* muck. I think that means there has to be a German connection. I don't see how French black marketeers would be able to get their hands on such good stuff.'

'I thought you said it was going to cheer me up.' We stared at each other in silence for a few moments. 'Judge Rambert. I was talking to someone who works with the police prefect's department. No one in Paris knows him. He's come from Lyon, which is strange, seeing as that's in the Unoccupied Zone. The word is he's pro-Nazi, has been for years. They say he even visited Berlin a few times before the war broke out.'

'So how come he's taken over from Judge Clément?'

'I was told he was a Vichy appointment.'

'Great. And he must have German backing at least – if not Otto Abetz's – to be allowed into Paris, and to be invited to Abetz's soirées.'

I left Dax to yet another exhortation to tread carefully. I returned to my room to news from Sarah that was about to make that harder.

'You've had a phone call, Inspector Giral.'

'Eddie.'

'The Bouvier brothers have been arrested. They're in custody.'

31

'I'm afraid our German allies did your job for you, Inspector Giral.'

The judge was in his chambers, drinking coffee in an armchair by the window. It was real coffee; the aroma had almost reduced me to tears when I'd walked in. He offered me neither a seat nor a cup. I studied him. He was thin and wiry, but he didn't give off the dull glow of hunger the rest of us did. He was another one for whom the Occupation was different again.

'What happened?'

'It appears your Bouvier brothers are as stupid as their reputation suggests. A German patrol caught them out after curfew. Drunk. They were taken to the nearest police station, where one of the French officers recognised them.'

'Where are they now?'

'In Fresnes. Awaiting trial, which I intend to be imminent.'

'That will be a first.'

'Indeed it will, Inspector Giral. And that is exactly what I seek in my mission.'

'What have they been charged with?'

'They have been charged as I ordered you to charge them. With the murder of Joseph Cartier.'

'Despite a lack of evidence. Or even anything resembling due diligence.'

Judge Rambert turned to face me sharply, the first time he'd bothered to acknowledge my presence in the room. 'Your attitude precedes you, Inspector Giral, but I can tell you that it won't wash with me. I expect you to do your duty as a French police officer.'

'So do I, Judge Rambert. Only there are already enough people trying to prevent me from doing that.'

He turned back to his view through the window. 'I will, of course, be advocating the death penalty for these two men. I wish it wrapped up quickly. We must show our German allies that we will not tolerate crimes by French civilians.'

'This is not how we do things, Judge.'

'This is how we do things now. This is a new opportunity for France. A chance to sweep away the old.'

'You mean things like justice and law?'

'Wasters and hopeless people. The ones who offer nothing and take everything.'

'I've got a few names for you.'

He turned to me a second time. 'Don't make an enemy of me. And I will tolerate no backlash from their execution.'

'Execution? They haven't been tried yet and you're talking of their execution?'

'Do not interrupt, Inspector Giral. As I say, there will be no unrest resulting from their execution. Reprisals may be taken. Against a similar class of the people undertaking these actions.'

'And who are you expecting to carry out these reprisals? Our police?'

'If called on to do so, yes. If not, our allies are more than sufficiently capable of carrying them out.'

I fought down an urge to slap the coffee cup from his hand. 'Finally, something we agree on.'

'It matters nothing whether we agree. One other thing. It has come to my attention that you've been employing civilians to do police work. That will stop.'

It certainly stopped me. My immediate thought was how come he knew of my getting Sarah to help with talking to people in Charonne and Bel Air. I showed him nothing of my doubts.

'When can I question the Bouvier brothers?'

A raptor's smile crossed his face. 'Whenever you wish. But you'd better make it soon. Before the guillotine claims them. In fact, I would suggest you go now.'

32

'The Eighth? What were you doing in the Eighth?'

Jacquot was slumped at the table in the interrogation room. He and Firmin were being kept separate. I'd wanted to talk to Firmin first, as I thought he'd make more sense. I looked at Jacquot trying to work out my question and I realised I was right. He was still drunk from the night before.

'Drinking,' he said, giggling. 'We went to the Eighth for a drink.'

'That's the other side of the city, pretty much. Why there? And why let yourself get caught drinking after curfew?'

'It was fun. They have different bars there.' He belched. The fumes would have kept my car going for the next year.

'So what happened?'

'The Germans came along. Arrested us. We were only drinking.'

'And then what?'

'They took us to the police station. In the Eighth. And they let us go in the morning.'

'They didn't let you go, Jacquot. That's why you're here. The Germans handed you over to the police, who arrested you for Cartier's murder.'

'Cartier. What a bastard he was. Glad someone did for him.'

'They're saying it was you. They want to execute you for it.'

He shook his head. 'It's all right. We didn't do it. They can't execute us.'

I sighed and looked into his bloodshot eyes. 'You need to help me help you, Jacquot. Who was the man I saw you with in Les Quatre Chats?'

'Strange accent. Funny name. He offered us a job, I think.'

'Doing what?

'Heavy lifting.' He smirked.

'By heavy lifting, I take it you mean enforcement?'

He flexed his puny arms. 'Me and Firmin. Tough guys.'

I tried one last question, knowing it was a fool's errand. 'Does the name Otto mean anything to you?'

He brightened up. 'Is that who he is?'

'No,' Firmin said. 'We were caught near home. We'd gone out for a drink and lost track of the time, that's all. They'll let us go when we've sobered up.'

He was slightly less drunk than his brother, but sat hunched up on the chair. In the end, I was glad to get to speak to him second, as he was clearing up some of the more unlikely things Jacquot had said. I thought they wouldn't have been as far from home as the Eighth.

'They're not going to let you go, Firmin. They've charged you with Cartier's murder. The judge wants to make an example of you.'

'We didn't do it. We've never killed anyone, you know that, Eddie.'

'Yes, I do, but I need your help to convince the judge.'

I could see him trying to pull his thoughts together, but he was all over the place after a night on the tiles.

'Who was the man I saw you with in Les Quatre Chats?' I asked him.

'He was Breton. One of those names from up there. Morvan,

that was it. He said we could do some work for him, earn some money.'

'Did he say who it was for? Does the name Otto mean anything to you?'

'A Boche? He never said anything about working for the Boches.'

'But did he mention this Otto?'

'No.'

I gripped the edge of the table to keep calm. 'Is there nothing you can say so I can help you?'

'I told you. We've done nothing wrong.'

'Like Cartier, you mean? The butter didn't melt in his mouth either.' I couldn't help my frustration coming out.

It took him a moment to catch it, but he laughed out loud when he did, a nervous braying sound. 'Butter. That's good, that is, Eddie.' He seemed to sober up for a brief moment. 'That was Cartier.'

'What was?'

'The butter.'

'What do you mean?'

'It was him who made us steal the butter. From the people who'd bought it.'

'He made you steal his own goods?'

Firmin nodded. 'He paid us to steal back as much as we could so he could sell it again.'

I sat back in my chair, dumbfounded. 'And no one would know it was him. Crafty old bastard.'

'It was a good plan. He sold some stuff three times. No one ever suspected him of doing it.'

I sighed and looked into his eyes.

'Until someone killed him.'

33

After the drive back from Fresnes, I left the car at Thirty-Six and called it a day. Without thinking, I crossed the river on foot to the Fifth, my side of the Seine. Really, I should be heading for the Metro and Montmartre, but I carried on walking. The sights and smells of my part of the city were comforting, the grey buildings my grey buildings. On impulse, and for no reason that I could think of, I went into the grocer's allotted to me by the local *mairie* since rationing had come in and used a ration ticket to buy a tin of meat. I had no idea what it contained.

Dragging my heels through the familiar streets, I fetched up outside the Palais du Luxembourg. The finery of the Italian-influenced Louis Treize palace was stunted by huge swastikas hanging limply like shrouds in the frozen air from the ornate balconies. Red and black sentry boxes were positioned either side of the entrance, their residents frozen and bored, their breath misting in clouds in front of their cold faces.

A staff car was parked outside, its engine running. Two officers emerged from the building and busied themselves marshalling four Frenchmen acting as porters. I watched as they ferried dozens of boxes and bags bearing the labels of the most select shops in Paris to the car and a second one that had pulled up behind. The two officers, senior ones by the look of all the buttons and bows on their sleeves and collars, laughed amicably with each other as they waited for their lackeys to finish. When they were done, one of the officers took a few notes out of his wallet and paid them off. The Germans then took their leave of a couple of other officers on the palace steps and were driven off in the first car, the second one following them. Their erstwhile servants passed near where I was standing and I called them over.

'What was that about?'

The oldest of the quartet spat on the floor and cursed the Germans. 'Going home on leave for Christmas. Taking presents they can't get there and we can't get here. Filthy Boches.'

They walked on, dividing the notes between them.

I looked bleakly at the tin of meat I was clutching in my right hand.

'I do hope you're not guinea pig.'

I stopped off at a café for a cup of coffee before taking the Metro to Montmartre. No real coffee here. We really could do with a better class of black marketeer on the Left Bank. I held my nose against the aroma of chicory and acorns and sipped the drink to get warm. It was the only purpose it had.

A radio was playing in the café. Dance music. At least it wasn't the latest political lies, but I still had to fight down an urge to ask the owner to turn it off. I wanted silence. I wanted my books. Most of all, I wanted an evening without the gramophone playing.

For the first time, I felt an odd dilemma facing me. I could catch the Metro to Montmartre and Dominique, like I was supposed to, and an evening of music filling the quiet. Or I could go home to my cold flat and to books and silence and the time to think.

Paying for my coffee, I made my choice, but I had one last hurdle. Monsieur Henri was on the stairs. I never knew what it was he seemed to find to do there.

'The Germans have invaded England,' he told me. 'But not to worry, the Americans have entered the war and should be here soon.'

'I've even missed you,' I told him.

I'd visited my flat over the last week to fetch clothes and make sure the pipes hadn't frozen, but it still felt as cold and bitter as the winters I'd spent in the trenches. Fetching a blanket from my bed and my copy of Paulhan's *The Flowers of Tarbes, or Terror in Literature* from the shelves beside the fire, I sat in my armchair. The one that knew me, the one that had moulded to my shape over fifteen years. It was the first time I'd sat in it since Dominique had started spending her evenings with me and before my week-long-and-counting sojourn in Montmartre. The chair had become my Alsace, annexed by a visiting force, no longer mine, and I hadn't realised how much I wanted it back. It embraced me like an old lover.

In the silence of my room and the comfort of my sparse furniture, I forgot the tin of meat I'd bought. The phone in the small hallway caught my eye. I'd been avoiding looking at it. Dominique didn't have one in her flat, so I had no way of telling her I wouldn't be in Montmartre tonight. That was a guilt and a consequence I'd face in the morning.

Instead, folding myself in the protection of my old blanket, I took one last look at the cobwebs and fading chill of the room and opened the pages of my book.

34

The following morning, I found Lafitte braying louder than a donkey on heat. He and a couple of other cops were crowded around a newspaper in the detectives' room like a trio of school-boys with a stash of smutty pictures.

'Don't go anywhere near, Eddie,' another cop, Barthe, told me. 'You really don't want to see it.'

I watched him shuffle back to his desk and then turned my attention to the prial of cards. Barthe's words had had the opposite effect. I really wanted to see what it was that was exciting Lafitte so much. I approached and he looked up at me, a sly grin on his face.

'Listen to this one,' he told his friends before reading aloud from the newspaper. '"Use them to make leather goods. I can see myself in shoes made from the skin of a Lévy."'

'Let me see that,' I told him, holding my hand out.

'Here you are Inspector Giral,' he said. 'You'll enjoy reading this.'

He handed the paper over. My heart sank when I saw it was *Au Pilori*. It was running a competition offering three pairs of silk stockings to the reader coming up with the best proposal for what to do with the Jews. Another of the ideas sent in was to burn them all in a crematorium, from babies to the elderly. My stomach turned when I saw the words. I crushed the paper in my hands and fed it to the flames in the heater.

'No,' I told him, 'but I can see you do. Get out of my sight, I don't want to see you.'

He bowed low and made a show of leaving.

'Anyone else want to go?' I asked the room, especially the other two who had been clustered around the rag.

Dax came in as I was turning away from them and asked what was going on. For the first time, I understood Barthe's reaction.

'You really don't want to know,' I told him.

'You and Boniface, in my room, now.'

I gathered the garrulous one and we followed the commissioner into his office and closed the door behind us. Dax kept his coat on to maintain some of its warmth and looked at us both in turn.

'I'm giving the burglaries investigation to Boniface. It's going nowhere, so I think we need some new eyes on it. Eddie, that means he won't be helping you with the Cartier case.'

I glanced at Boniface. The excitement on his face shone out.

'I want Boniface to remain with me,' I told Dax. They both looked shocked.

'This is my chance to lead an investigation,' Boniface said. 'You can't deny me that.'

'No can do, Eddie,' Dax agreed. 'The burglaries need a boost. I'm putting Boniface in charge. No arguments.'

I protested once more, but to no avail. Boniface being taken off my investigation should have warmed me like a bucket of black-market coal, but it didn't. He annoyed the hell out of me, but he was a good cop. I'd miss his insight and doggedness. Especially now that I needed a result if I was to save Firmin and Jacquot from the blade.

Dax looked at us both. 'Off you go then. Boniface, I've given you your orders already.'

Boniface left, but I lingered a moment. Dax looked at me quizzically as I closed the door. I began by bringing him up to date with my meeting with Judge Rambert and his eagerness to see the Bouvier brothers executed for Cartier's murder.

'Without bothering too much about things like trials or proof,' I added.

Dax rubbed his eyes. 'So it begins. Do what you can, Eddie. We can't open the door to this sort of thing.'

I agreed with him and paused before carrying on. 'I wanted to ask something else. Did you tell anyone about Sarah? About her taking part in the Cartier investigation?'

'About you going behind my back and using her to eavesdrop in queues, you mean? No, I didn't. Why?'

I explained how Judge Rambert had known about me using Sarah on an investigation.

Dax wasn't concerned. 'You know this place – and the Palais de Justice and every other police department in Paris, for that matter – has more leaks than our navy. I'm not surprised he heard about it.'

'What do you know about Sarah? Her background?'

He looked surprised. 'Very little. She was foisted on me by someone in the prefect's office, their bright idea to use women in the police. Why? Are you not happy with her?'

'Yes. She's good at what she does. I just wanted to know a bit more about her.'

He finally took his coat off and started looking at the papers on his desk. 'That's all I know, Eddie. As I said, it wasn't my decision.'

I left him and went into my own room. Both Boniface and Sarah were there. Boniface was talking to Sarah's expressionless face as she got on with typing a report.

'Burglaries,' he addressed her from the doorway. 'Curious. String of them. All in the Sixteenth Arrondissement. Rich pickings. Investigation's going nowhere, so Commissioner Dax has called me in.'

'You do know you're talking out loud,' I told him, sitting down at my desk. If you didn't stop Boniface in his tracks, he'd talk you into the desire for an early grave.

For the first time, it registered with me that he was holding a wooden crate full of files and junk. He sauntered into the room and put it down on the third desk.

'What are you doing?' I asked him.

He turned and beamed at me. 'I'm working in here now. With you. Spare desk.'

I pointed at the door. 'Out.'

'No can do, Eddie. Orders of the commissioner.'

As if to support his claim, Dax walked into the office and looked around.

'I see you're settling in, Boniface, good.'

'What's going on?' I asked.

'As I told you, Detective Boniface has been assigned the investigation into the burglaries in the Sixteenth, so he's going to need more space. And as this desk is going spare, I decided he could have it. You've had too long on your own in here.'

I made a show of looking at Sarah. 'Are you serious?'

Dax gave one of his shrugs that went from paunch to shoulders. 'You're the senior officer in this room, Eddie. Your responsibility.'

'Boniface is not my responsibility.'

'He is now.'

He left before I could say another word, and Boniface began to take papers and folders out of his crate and pile them on his desk. When he'd done, he was all but hidden behind four towering stacks. I watched him work. Engrossed in what he was doing, he lost all the cockiness and self-obsession he usually displayed and systematically went through the files, sorting them into new heaps, considering documents and photographs. Observing him, I had a brief moment of panic, knowing I was going to miss his skills in my attempt to free Firmin and Jacquot from Judge Rambert's clutches.

I caught Sarah looking at me studying Boniface.

'Everything OK?' I asked her.

She turned back to her work. 'All well, Inspector Giral.'

'Eddie,' I tried to correct her again.

35

Getting on for noon, I had a call from downstairs telling me I had a visitor. I went down to find Peter, the jazz-loving Wehrmacht officer I'd last seen at Otto Abetz's fraught soirée. He was in uniform and I beckoned him as far away from the door and desk as I could. Just as I couldn't let the Germans see me with Dominique, neither did I want too many cops – or French people in general – seeing me with German soldiers. It was yet another tightrope the Occupation had strung up.

'I have come to see if you would like to go for lunch,' he told me.

I was taken aback.

'It would be my treat,' he added.

That decided it. Hunger will go a long way towards overcoming principles.

'Just give me a moment.'

I left him in the entrance and went up to the third floor to get my coat. Sarah was putting the cover on the typewriter, ready to go for her lunch. I waited a few minutes for her to go downstairs and leave the building, so she wouldn't see me with Peter.

On the way, he and I spoke of jazz and of concerts we'd seen. I mentioned seeing Sidney Bechet and Dooley Wilson.

'Wilson is a wonderful drummer,' he said. 'I saw him play in London some years ago. But I've never seen Sidney Bechet. Or Josephine Baker.'

'That's unlikely now,' I told him, immediately feeling it was a cheap comment.

'Sadly, true.' He'd taken no offence at my words.

'Where do you have in mind for lunch?' I asked him.

We'd already crossed to the Left Bank and had passed two restaurants with a *Man Spricht Deutsch* sign in the window. I'd hoped to go into one of those. Restaurants were subject to strict restrictions – menus and prices had to be displayed and adhered to and you had to use your ration tickets to get a meal – but the ones where the waiters had learned to speak German tended to attract German officers. That meant they could ignore all the rules without the fear of being investigated by the police. Like most things, when you were outside it, it was an annoyance. When you were able to benefit from it, that was altogether different.

'Le Catalan,' he finally said as we entered the Rue des Grands-Augustins, in the Sixth. 'I thought you might appreciate some home cooking.'

'Hardly my home cooking. But that does sound good.'

He was right. It did sound good, as the food would be excellent and with little attention paid to the finer points of rationing, but I had to predict whether anyone there would know me. Being from the south of the country, I'd been to Le Catalan quite a lot since living in Paris – and once or twice since the Occupation had started – so I was worried I'd run into someone I knew. Like the waiters, for a start.

'Eddie,' one of them said the moment we walked in, a fisherman's son from Collioure. 'How are you today?'

A second one showed us to a table in the middle of the restaurant. I didn't know him so well and his expression was impassive as he took our coats, although I saw him hide a reaction to Peter's uniform. I decided not to order the soup just in case.

Peter and I spoke of jazz a little more, and it struck me once again how I would never have met such a kindred spirit had it not been for the war, yet it was the war that meant we couldn't or shouldn't be kindred spirits. The Occupation hadn't just brought us the pleasures of hunger and compromised principles, but the ambiguity of friendship – or simply coexistence – with people we were told were our enemy.

'Have you heard any news about Bonsergent?' he asked me after we'd given our orders. I recalled the conversation at the ambassador's dinner table about the Frenchman sentenced to death for jostling a German NCO.

'His lawyers have lodged an appeal, but we don't yet know the outcome. It's not looking good.'

'It's a bad thing.' He lowered his voice to almost a whisper. 'It reminds me of the Grynszpan affair, the young Jew who killed vom Rath here in Paris. The Nazis used that as a pretext for Kristallnacht. We have to hope this doesn't cause similar problems.'

Despite his candour, I still felt I had to watch my words. He was a Wehrmacht officer, after all. 'I don't think so. They're still trying to appease us. I think if they were going to use it as a reason for more widespread retribution, they'd have done it by now.'

'Reason? They don't need a reason, they need an excuse. You have to hope no one gives them one.'

He looked around guiltily, worried that a table of four German officers nearby might have caught his words. I glanced in the same direction and saw Johannes Thier, the naval officer I'd seen with Hochstetter, seated at another table in the corner of the room. I couldn't see his lunch partner as they were hidden behind a screen. Intrigued, I leaned out slightly, but I still couldn't make out who was sitting opposite him. Thier glanced sideways and caught me looking across. He seemed surprised but recovered quickly and raised his glass at me. I did likewise and turned my attention back to my conversation with Peter.

'The attitude of many of your soldiers here appears to have changed.' I kept my voice low as well and considered his words. 'A lot of Parisians used to describe them as "correct", but that's no longer always the case, and sentences like the one given to Bonsergent aren't helping. It's affecting our attitude towards you.'

'I said "excuse", Eddie. That may be what the Party wants.'

I looked at him thoughtfully. Privately, I welcomed the change in attitude from both sides. It might mean that more people would lose the apathy that had quickly set in after the Germans invaded the city and stand up to the Occupation. Whatever that involved. But it could also lead to the response from the Nazis that Peter feared. Another, more dangerous tightrope we were forced to walk.

Jacquot and Firmin were never far from my thoughts at the moment – curiously, I felt a responsibility for them, as I'd arrested them so often in their youth – and the sight of Thier reminded me of something he'd said. Summoning up the courage, I asked Peter.

'Does the name Otto mean anything to you?'

He considered for a moment. 'Ambassador Abetz obviously springs to mind. It's a common name. Do you have a surname?'

'No. Just the name Otto. I heard a Kriegsmarine officer mention it to Major Hochstetter.'

Peter looked serious. 'Major Hochstetter? Of the Abwehr?'

'That's the one.'

He paused and looked around. There was a nervousness to him. 'Then I think that might be your answer. Otto isn't a who, it's a what.'

I sat back, surprised. 'A what?'

He hushed me. 'I don't know much, but I think it concerns a buying agency. One run by the Abwehr.'

We were silent as the waiter brought our first course. My mind tumbled through the options as I watched steaming dishes of fish and vegetables being placed in front of me. My stomach ached with hunger.

A buying agency run by the Abwehr. The pain I felt in my stomach wasn't just from the lack of food. Of all the gangs and villains that had sprung up since war had been declared last year, the Occupier was turning out to be the biggest and most dangerous. If the sleazy businessmen who followed in the Wehrmacht's wake, out to make an easy Reichsmark, were the icing on the cake, the army of so-called buying offices set up by the various military and civil authorities to gobble up French goods at prices they set for themselves were the cherry on top. In that, they were at least as big a bunch of gangsters as the best that Paris had ever had to offer. With the difference that when they fleeced the people of the city, they had official backing and we couldn't touch them.

If there was any chance that Morvan was working with them, that made him a far scarier proposition. It occurred to me that it might also put Lafont back in the frame, as I knew he worked with a buying agency operated by the Abwehr. At least it probably meant that Adolf's ambassador to Paris wasn't involved. Every cloud.

'Have you been invited to this evening's celebration by Ambassador Abetz?' Peter asked, changing the subject when we were alone again. I had to gather my thoughts.

'No, I haven't.' I wondered if and when Hochstetter would be summoning me for that. 'At Maxim's again?'

'No, an altogether grander affair.'

'Grander than Maxim's?'

'At the embassy. By all accounts, there is no expense spared at these evenings.'

I put my fork down for a moment. The food on my plate

suddenly tasted of wormwood. Looking up, I spotted Thier leaving the restaurant. His guest was in front of him, already outside the door, and I still couldn't see who it was, or even if it was a man or a woman.

Peter pointed at my plate. 'Eat up, Eddie. Don't let it go to waste.'

36

Leaving the restaurant, we heard the shouting before we saw the crowd of young men gathered at a crossroads. They were bunched outside a shop, all looking in at it.

'Filthy Jew,' one of them called.

Peter and I turned to look at each other and quickened our pace.

'I'll deal with this,' I told him.

'No, I will help.'

As we approached, one of the young men bent down and began to try and prise a cobblestone loose. I reached him and tapped him on the shoulder to make him stand up.

'What do you want?' he asked. He had teeth like a weasel, hair like a badger and breath like a rat.

'For you to do something. I'm in just the mood.'

A couple of his friends gathered around me, but looked warily at Peter in his uniform.

'What's it to you?' one of them asked, although not as sure of himself as he would have been had I been alone.

I showed him my police ID. 'That's what it is to me.'

'We're just doing your job, *poulet*.'

'Not my job you're not. Move on.'

Behind him, I noticed the shop-owner looking at us fearfully. He was elderly, with a yarmulke over white hair and tired eyes.

'Are you going to try and make us?'

The young man and one of his cronies advanced towards me, so I slapped him across the side of the face. He instantly stopped in astonishment. A slap is a funny thing. When you punch a thug like this one, their immediate instinct is to punch back. A slap, though, especially across the ear, takes them by surprise. It stings like hell and it reminds them of teachers and parents. He just looked at me dumbfounded.

'Yes, I am,' I told him.

The second one turned to Peter and spoke in slow French so Peter would understand. 'I'd have thought you'd be all right with this.'

Peter's reply in decent French took him by surprise. 'Then you are wrong. Leave now or I will call the German authorities.'

The one trying to get at the cobblestone finally lifted it out and hurled it at the shop. The glass in the door shattered, the sound echoing in the narrow street and shocking us all motionless. His friends cheered. It seemed to embolden them. The stone-thrower and three others ran over to the elderly man and began to shove him. One of them punched him to the ground and stepped forward to kick him.

Pushing the two in front of me out of the way, I ran across the street and stood between the group of men and the shop-owner. Before I had a chance to reach for my gun, one of them lunged forward and gripped me in a bear hug. He was big, a head above me and a shoulder's-width wider, and my arms were pinned firmly to my sides. A second one punched me in the stomach. He made to hit me in the face, but I was able to lash out with my right foot and stamp on his knee. I heard something pop. He cried out in pain and the heavy crushed me tighter, the breath squeezed out of my chest.

I heard a shot fired, then a second. Behind the group crowding around me, I saw that Peter had pulled his Luger out and let off two warning shots into the air. He began to lower his gun to cover the gang, but one of the thugs near him managed to knock it out of his hand. A second one held him, while the first went scrabbling in the gutter for the firearm. I could feel my head begin to swim with the lack of oxygen going into my lungs.

Another shot was fired. In my haze, I looked over, expecting to see that they'd shot Peter. Instead, the one with the gun dropped it to the ground and put his hands up. A German soldier came into view and smashed his rifle butt into the young guy's face.

I felt the grip on me loosen, and I stamped on my captor's foot with my heel. He yelped and let go. I staggered forward to catch my breath. For the first time, I saw the German military lorry. So there was a point to them driving around the city all day.

A feldwebel with an old Prussian-style moustache and bullet head organised a dozen armed soldiers into rounding the thugs up. One of them prodded me with his rifle and began to herd me in with the gang.

'Not him,' I heard Peter say. 'He's a policeman. He's with me.'

I stood up fully, my breath back, and looked around me. The rabble had been corralled near the back of the lorry, some of the soldiers eyeing them up hungrily. I'd seen their sort before in the last war, eager for any excuse.

The feldwebel was standing by Peter. I pushed against the soldier who'd been shepherding me with his rifle and went to join them. Peter was replacing his Luger in its holster.

The feldwebel was smirking at him. 'I hope you had a nice lunch, Hauptmann. Good job a non-commissioned officer was here to save you.'

'For which I thank you, Feldwebel,' Peter replied, running his hand through his hair.

The NCO looked scornfully at the shop-owner. 'And all for a Jew.'

Peter waited until the man's gaze had turned back to him. 'Your name, please.'

'No need to thank me.'

'I'm not. I'm going to report you to your senior officer for insubordination and conduct unbecoming a German soldier.'

The feldwebel looked at him in disbelief. 'We just saved your arse.'

Peter gazed at him coldly. 'And in return, I might just save yours. By not recommending you be court-martialled. If you leave now.'

The two men stared at each other, the feldwebel obviously wrestling with an urge to go the whole hog with the insubordination and land a punch on Peter's nose. Instead, he turned and shouted a few terse orders at his men to put the thugs on the truck. Wordlessly they did so and retreated, with one last look of hatred at us both and another glance filled with venom at the shop-owner.

'They'll probably take that lot away and pat them on the back,' I commented, holding my ribs gingerly.

'Possibly. Though with any luck, they'll take out their anger at me on them.'

'You're a bad man, Peter.'

I slowly crossed to the shop-owner and asked if he was all right. He simply pointed at his window, where a red poster sat like an open sore. In October, the German military authorities had decreed that all businesses owned by Jews that gave onto the street had to be sold or signed over to a non-Jewish administrator by the twenty-sixth of December and a red poster put up to replace the yellow one that Jewish-owned businesses had been forced to display previously.

'This will never be all right,' the elderly man told me and turned to go inside.

37

'I've eaten far too much.'

The tightness in my ribs hadn't yet gone, making it difficult to digest my food. It was a strange problem to have. When you normally have little to eat, a meal that would have been normal only a year ago suddenly became a gluttonous feast that was hard for your body to cope with. At my desk in Thirty-Six, I felt uncomfortable in more ways than one.

Only those words weren't mine.

Sarah stood up and held her stomach.

'Far too much,' she repeated.

I stared at her, silhouetted against the weak sunlight through the window. 'Where did you go for lunch?'

She hesitated. I couldn't see her face. 'Over the river.'

'Everywhere's over the river from here.'

'The Left Bank. Excuse me.'

She hurried out of the room. In search of the bathroom, I imagined. Or away from my questions. I stared at the door through which she'd just left and recalled Judge Rambert knowing about her helping in Charonne and Bel Air.

'You're imagining things,' I said.

'Imagining what?' A voice came from behind a citadel of files on the desk opposite me. Boniface peered out.

'Talking to myself.'

He disappeared back behind his castle walls, but the voice continued. 'Another flat's been burgled.'

'Solve it soon and you can go back to the detectives' room.'

He reappeared, putting his coat on, ready to go out. 'Changed their MO slightly. They always carry out their burglaries during the day. That hasn't changed. And always when the concierge is out, if the building has one. That's a ditto too. But this time they've gone for a flat requisitioned by the Germans. Taken a whole load of stuff. Risky business. Or they didn't realise. Whatever the reason, they've upped the stakes.'

He left and I was suddenly alone in my room. It felt much too quiet, but it would have taken a team of Hochstetter's best interrogators with thumb screws and genital clamps working around the clock to get me to admit to that. Instead, I took it as my cue to go out too. There was a major in the Abwehr I had to see.

Unfortunately, Hochstetter wouldn't come out to play when I asked for him at the Lutetia. All around me Abwehr types milled and looked industrious in a military intelligence sort of a way.

'Inspector Giral,' I insisted. 'Major Hochstetter is the liaison with the criminal investigation department of the French police.'

'I know.' The young hauptmann behind the desk had the look of bored officialdom everywhere, which only goes to show that Adolf needn't have invaded as we'd already had plenty of those of our own.

'Then you'll also know that he always sees me.'

'And you will also know, Inspector Giral, that Major Hochstetter is a very busy man. He is not always available to receive French civilians.'

'I hope you have a lovely Christmas.'

I retreated from the grey-soaked desk in defeat. An officer emerged from the lift, carrying a heavy parcel. From the wrapping paper that the Germans had had printed especially, I could see it was a package of things he'd bought here and was sending home. I watched him hand it over to the hauptmann who'd dealt with me. To accommodate all the stuff their soldiers were buying on the cheap and sending back to Germany, the Occupiers had set up a designated postal service just for them. The parcel would be stamped and shipped in its special paper to ensure it wasn't held up at customs.

'That's what I call taking control,' I said under my breath. Special rules created to exploit the damage they were wreaking on the rest of us.

I considered taking the lift while the hauptmann was distracted, but he looked up and gave me a hard stare as I loitered near the sliding door. Two tall, blond officers with firm jaws and a tall, blonde secretary with a firm gaze beat me to it while I was waiting. I looked down at my oversized suit and worn hands and decided I probably would have been ethnically excluded from taking a ride with them anyway.

'Inspector Giral.' A voice from somewhere over my shoulder called my name.

I turned to scan the lobby to see who it was. The old bar looked increasingly like an officers' mess. Not that I knew what an officers' mess looked like. I ended the last war a sergeant and in a mess of my own.

It was Dietrich Falke, the trader I'd met at Ambassador Abetz's cosy little dinner on Friday night. He was seated alone at a low table with a huge glass of brandy in front of him. He stood up unsteadily and beckoned me over, his skeletal hand movements exaggerated. I had a feeling the brandy hadn't led a solitary existence.

'Inspector Giral, come and join me,' he invited.

I recalled the way he'd entered my thoughts the other night when I'd been looking through the files for the man I now knew to be Morvan, and I decided to take him up on his offer. Any opportunity to get some information out of one of the Occupiers was an opportunity never to be missed. I'd also seen the whisky bottles on the shelves behind the bar.

'Brandy?' he asked, clicking his fingers at a waiter.

'Whisky. Thank you.' Temptation is as temptation does.

'Well, what brings you to the Abwehr?' His words were said with the slow deliberation of someone trying not to sound drunk.

'I was hoping to see Major Hochstetter.'

He tapped the side of his nose. 'Ah, the good major. You and me both, Inspector.'

'You have business with him?'

We had to wait a moment while the waiter served me my whisky. Instinctively I went for the ration tickets in my wallet, but stopped myself in time. Not that there were ration tickets for whisky. Or indeed any whisky. Not for us. Well, not legally.

Falke had forgotten my question by the time the waiter had left us.

'You have business with Major Hochstetter?' I repeated.

He snorted and finished the first brandy. The waiter had brought him a second one to keep the first one company.

'Don't talk to me about business.'

'Not going well?'

I took a drink of my whisky and closed my eyes, letting the flavour wash through me.

'That looks like it hit the spot,' he said, clinking his new glass against mine. 'I'm glad to see you're a man of pleasure, Inspector.'

'Whisky is not easy to come by these days.' He nodded at that, but I was determined not to let him get sidetracked. 'Business not going well?'

He let out a low belch and leaned in towards me. 'It might be now.' Again the tap on the side of the nose. I had to resist an urge to swat it for him.

'So what would that be, Herr Falke?'

'You French. You don't know how to do business.'

'Is that right?'

He shook his head and almost spilled his brandy. 'Damn right. Greedy. That's what you are. And inefficient.'

'I'm most dreadfully sorry.'

'Don't be.'

He stared into space, his train of thought gone.

'Édouard, such an unexpected pleasure.'

I looked around to see that Hochstetter had arrived. He was taking off his army coat and folding his scarf meticulously. He really had been out, like the barking hauptmann had said. Thing being, I could have done with him waiting a few minutes longer while I tried to get something more out of Falke. Hochstetter and I both turned at the sound of the trader snoring in his armchair. So much for that.

'I think we shall leave your companion,' Hochstetter said.

We took the lift to his office and I sat down on the chair opposite his desk.

'Otto,' I said.

He sighed. 'I thought you would be back to insist on this. I have no idea to whom Korvettenkapitän Thier was referring.'

'Not a whom, a what.'

'Then you know more than I, Édouard.'

'I doubt that very much. I know that Otto is the buying agency run by the Abwehr. I just need to know who's in charge of it to help me with my investigation.'

'The murder of this black marketeer? As I said, I have no idea. It is not an area of the Abwehr's business that concerns me.'

'You must know who runs it.'

'Must I? I can assure you I do not.'

I tried changing tack. 'Judge Rambert. He was the other Frenchman at Ambassador Abetz's dinner last week.'

'What about him?'

'He wants to wrap up the Cartier murder investigation as quickly as possible so he can impress Abetz. And the German authorities in general. The problem is, he's arrested two men who I think are innocent.'

'In what way should that concern me?'

'He's a Vichy appointment. With German backing. I need you to use your influence to make him wait until we find who really is responsible for Cartier's murder.'

'How could I possibly do that? I presume his German backing, as you call it, is in fact Otto Abetz. If that is the case, my influence is not appreciably greater than yours. I'm afraid the matter of who your judge wants arrested for the murder is a French matter.'

'Except the judge is making it a German one.'

Hochstetter finally lit a cigarette. As I watched the match die in the ashtray, I knew it was his way of dismissing me.

'Either way, Édouard, I am afraid I am not in a position to be of assistance.'

'I'll remember that. Will I see you tonight at Abetz's dinner?' My invitation had arrived shortly after Peter had mentioned it.

'More than a dinner, I hear. But no, I'm afraid you won't be able to count on my presence there this evening.'

'You've decided not to go?'

'I have not been invited. It appears our ambassador no longer feels the need to curry favour with me.'

I put my coat on ready for the onslaught of cold outside.

'And that is always a mistake,' he added.

38

'Canapé?'

I looked at the tiny morsel of fish on a slice of bread that was far thicker than the ones in the posters telling us how to make our food go further and decided not to go with the biblical reference. Instead, I couldn't help working out how many ration tickets that alone would have cost. I also wondered why, with all the food our Occupiers had to play around with, they would serve up these stingy portions. No doubt more to follow, I imagined. Unless our host really did believe he was the second coming.

'No thanks,' I replied.

The French waiter moved on, his eyes gliding off me like his shoes on the floor. He at least still owned a pair of leather-soled footwear. As I watched the tray of food slip away with him, I knew I wouldn't be able to hold out much longer. Especially when meat that looked nothing like the label on my tin at home was carted out. In the meantime, my resolve was steely.

'Champagne? Whisky?'

I looked sternly at the waiter of temptation and picked up a glass of whisky. I'd do my penance tomorrow with my tin of indeterminate gristle.

The moment's tussle with temptation was just a brief respite from the conversation around me. I turned back to where some overstuffed Ober-something with a walrus moustache and more medals than we've had wars was holding court.

'Reprisals. The only language these people understand. I was in Poland and I know first-hand that it works. For every act of disobedience or insubordination by the French, we take twenty hostages. For every one of our soldiers killed, we take ten of those hostages and we execute them.'

I stared at him over my glass. It was my first whisky and I was being careful with my tongue. Miserably, more than a few heads around the officer were nodding along. One of them belonged to Judge Rambert.

'But it can't be indiscriminate,' the judge replied. 'The hostages must be targeted. The same social class and neighbourhood as the perpetrators.'

'Nonsense,' the officer replied, his bells and whistles jangling in irritation. 'The first twenty off the street, that will suffice.'

'Hardly diplomatic.' Rambert gestured at the people around us. 'Look at the number of French citizens in this room. These are the people we need to be winning over. We won't do that if you simply arrest all and sundry. You might be arresting the wrong sort.'

I was saved from myself by the arrival of our host. For some reason, he singled me out for special treatment.

'Inspector Giral,' Otto Abetz greeted me with the false warmth of the seasoned diplomat. 'So good to see members of the police accept the hand of friendship we have extended.'

'Isn't it just?'

I extended my own hand and took a second glass of whisky off a tray borne by the same expressionless waiter as before. He glanced at me for a moment, a brief flicker of odium crossing his face. You're accepting their silver too, I wanted to say to him.

Abetz spoke to the group I'd been lumbered with for the last endless ten minutes, specifically the Ober-thingy in his stuffed shirt.

'Did I not tell you that France was wonderful? This is the policeman I was telling you about. Only in this city could you find a police officer capable of quoting the country's great writers. And some not so great, of course, such as your beloved Paulhan, eh, Inspector?'

By the time I could be bothered to reply, Abetz had already seen someone far more interesting over my left shoulder and moved on. Most of the party went with him, dragged along by a desire to be part of his world. Complying with Judge Rambert's invitation to look around, I spotted all the French people in the room, all just as eager to be a part of the universe that Abetz and his like were offering. An observation struck me. None of the French in the room had the sallow skin and sunken eyes that everyone else I saw in my day-to-day had. Collaborating obviously worked wonders for the complexion.

As it was, I was stuck in a conversation I thought had ended before the German officer had started up with his execution-of-hostages small talk. The only two of us left were me and a French journalist with *Paris-Soir*, which had reappeared in the kiosks little more than a week after the Germans had entered the city. Like every other paper allowed to continue, it was entirely Berlin-on-Seine. He was young and earnest and wore his hair crinkled and oiled in this year's fashion.

'It is still a French newspaper,' he persisted in insisting to me, his voice slurred. I was going to have to catch up with my drinking if I wanted to keep up with Otto's other guests. Except I was realising it was better not to drink, but to listen instead. 'Produced by French people. Just like Paris, it is French through and through. France is still France and Paris is still Paris.'

'If you say so.'

'I do.' He did. 'Look at you. You're a policeman so you know I'm right. Paris is still policed by Frenchmen.'

'Look around you.' I nodded at the Germans in their uniforms and their French hangers-on lapping up every word, all framed by swastikas placed about the room. 'That's how you've just lost whatever argument you had and how you always will.'

He finally gave up and left in search of a kindred soul, so I found myself standing alone in the middle of the German embassy. More trays had appeared while I'd been caught up in my own conversations. None of the microscopic portions of earlier, but full-bodied platters of meat, fish and cheeses. Hochstetter had been right. It was even grander than Maxim's. I wished I'd kept my coat on with its big pockets. As it was, I was uncomfortable enough in my least disreputable suit and shoes, standing awkwardly isolated amid the Empire splendour of the embassy building. It was always the way of these things. Hours of feeling isolated punctuated by endless minutes of talking to someone who at best doesn't care and at worst patently dislikes you. And I was doing it in a ballroom stuffed with Nazis and with a self-styled French elite who thought the Nazis were a good thing.

'You look as out of place as I feel.'

I turned to see that it was Peter who had spoken to me. So there was one friendly face at least. Unfortunately, he didn't look out of place in his Wehrmacht uniform, although it was in so many ways at odds with the man I knew.

'So Major Hochstetter summoned you after all?' he continued.

I shook my head. 'I actually got an invitation from Abetz himself. The good major hasn't been invited.'

Peter was that bit too drunk to register what I was saying. He was also more verbose than usual. 'Lunch together was very pleasant, don't you think? Although the incident after less so.'

And that was the problem. That incident and everything that had led to and from it was represented by the uniform he was wearing. He leaned across and plucked a glass of champagne from a passing waiter.

'I feel most out of place,' he repeated, gesturing with his glass at our surroundings. He lowered his voice. That's when it's time to listen. 'Our good host has long wanted Jews and Jewish shops to be forcibly identified. You and I have seen where that leads. He also wanted to ban Jews from entering the Occupied Zone from the Unoccupied Zone as early as August, when we'd barely got here. So much for diplomacy.'

One of Peter's Wehrmacht colleagues called to him from another group and he made his apologies and went over to join them.

A wallflower again, I looked around. No matter how much you want to be alone at these things, it's impossible not to feel slightly foolish when you are. Standing equally alone, Martin Hochstetter was holding a glass of champagne and eyeing the room in disdain. The event evidently offended something in him, so I thought I'd add to it and joined him.

'I have nothing to say,' he told me without making eye contact.

'Few people do at these things. You should blend right in.'

He maintained an impassive glare in front of him before, surprisingly, breaking into a laugh. 'I see why my brother finds you entertaining.'

'We're here at your service. Apparently.'

He was prevented from replying by the arrival of Falke, who weaved up in conversation with a German officer even drunker than the trader was. 'I much prefer the Jardins des Champs-Élysées,' he was saying. 'They are so much more charming and less pretentious than Les Tuileries.'

'I have to agree with you,' his companion said. Falke clapped him on the back and sent him on his way so he could stop and talk to Martin. He hung his drink-free arm around the younger

Hochstetter's shoulder, who looked like he'd walked into a cobweb.

'Let me buy you a drink, Hauptsturmführer Hochstetter.'

'They are free.'

I really must learn to put that much ice in my words.

'Nevertheless, do me the honour of drinking with me anyway.' Falke glanced up at me and began to steer himself and Martin away. 'You are a hero of the Reich and I will not take no for an answer.'

'Catch you later, Dietrich baby,' I murmured after their departing backs. Since Peter's comment about Otto and the buying agency, I wanted a word with Falke to see if my half-formed suspicions about some involvement of his in the black-market trade and even Cartier's murder had any foundation.

'Inspector Giral.'

I turned to find Judge Rambert at my shoulder. He was drinking whisky. I pointed at it, ignoring my own glass in my hand.

'Isn't that against the law now? Are we going to see reprisals for such flagrant criminality?'

'Don't talk nonsense.' He wasn't as drunk as everyone else seemed to be getting, but he wasn't entirely sober either. 'There is a difference between a drink or two among friends and terrorism among the lower classes.'

'The Bouvier brothers. I want a word about them.'

He held his hand up. 'Monday, Inspector. In my chambers. This is neither the place nor the time.'

To stop any objection, he walked off quickly and began to talk in earnest to the officer who'd advocated reprisals earlier. I began to wonder when I could safely make my exit, but I was joined again by Falke and Martin, who'd evidently walked a circuit of the grand room. Both were much drunker than when they'd left me just a short while ago. Ideally, I wanted to separate the two so I could talk to Falke. Curiously, I seemed to be a respite for Martin from the trader's prattle. I saw him look once again at the opulence in the room and the people fawning over each other. The anger was bubbling barely beneath the surface.

'I've just been talking to that man over there,' I told him. 'He's French. Very much opposed to the indiscriminate taking of hostages.'

'That is no concern of his.'

'Actually, it is. He's a judge. Working closely with the German authorities and Ambassador Abetz. He doesn't seem at all happy with the idea of reprisals against certain groups.'

That much at least was true, I thought as I watched junior Hochstetter stumble across the room towards the group containing Judge Rambert, the German officer and the *Paris-Soir* journalist. Either way, it got him out of my hair so I could talk to Falke.

'Herr Doktor Falke,' I said, snatching another glass for him off a tray. This time, the waiter made eye contact with me and almost seemed to nod. 'How's business? You weren't happy with French businessmen the other day, I remember.'

Falke did that thing again with the side of his nose. Across the room, I saw Martin bowl up to Judge Rambert and start talking into his face. Falke tapped his glass against mine. I'd been nursing my whisky for so long, it had gone warm.

'It's all sorted now,' he told me, trying to focus his attention. 'I had a partner lined up. A French one. It could have been lucrative for us both, very lucrative, but he got greedy. Wanted more. Too many demands. "You're not in any position to make demands," I told him. So now I've got another one. Partner, that is.'

'Who's your new partner?'

Before he could reply, I registered a noise coming from the other side of the room. We both turned to see Martin prodding the judge on the shoulder. I could see the spittle as he spoke from where we were. It was going better than I'd intended.

I turned back to Falke. 'Who's your new partner?' I asked him again.

He laughed. 'Wouldn't you like to know?'

Martin had spun Rambert around, to the horror of the rest of the group. A silence spread out across the ballroom.

'What happened to your old partner?' I asked, my voice low.

I'd barely got the question out when I saw Martin punch the judge full in the stomach. Rambert collapsed, his face contorted in shock and pain.

'What happened to your old partner?' I said again.

Falke tore his gaze away from the spectacle and looked at me, his eyes blank with drink. He ran his finger across his throat and laughed, a coarse sound, and uttered one word.

'Gone.'

39

'This way.'

I followed the waiter along a corridor away from the ballroom. I figured that with Martin judging the judge, it was better for me to make my exit, but when I'd tried, the doors out had been blocked by half a dozen German soldiers. I'd turned back amid the hullabaloo to see the waiter who'd been serving whisky all evening beckon me over.

'Nicely done,' he said as we disappeared into the entrails of the building.

'Went better than I'd expected,' I had to admit.

'Anything to get one over on the Boches.' He looked up and down and motioned to me to follow him through a service door. 'This way.'

'What is it?'

'You'll see.'

Despite myself, I followed, intrigued. We followed a path through corridors and down stairs to what I guessed must be the rear of the building. On the way, we went through a kitchen busy with waiters and chefs stuffing what food they could scavenge into bags. I heard all accents in there: southern, Alsace, Breton, Auvergne, the melting pot I'd grown to love. The waiter picked up a couple of cloth bags, the sort you stored bread in. Emerging cautiously through another door, he led us across a small courtyard.

'Just had a delivery,' he told me cryptically. 'Help yourself. We all have.'

He handed me one of the bags and opened a wooden door to reveal the boiler room. The heat inside was sweltering. To one side was a pen containing a mound of coal. He motioned to the bag he'd given me.

'Just in. Go on.'

Without waiting for me, he filled the second bag for himself and hid it by the door. I hesitated a moment, the sight of the enclosed space in the dark and the heat and the smell of the coal dust almost too much for me. I nearly backed out, but recalled the cold at night and succumbed. As quickly as I could, I began filling my bag, wedging the door open to let some cool air in. The room glowed red and a light flashed somewhere nearby in the growing dark.

I wandered the streets away from the embassy with my bag of coal and wondered what I was going to do with it. I couldn't take it to Dominique's flat. I didn't think she'd take too kindly to stolen coal. Lost in my thoughts, I realised I was heading for the Fifth and my own apartment. I carried on. It felt good to be in familiar streets in the heart of night.

Curfew hadn't yet fallen, so I took a small detour through the Jardin du Luxembourg. It was as though I had the park and all the city to myself for a brief moment. I slowed my pace and breathed in the scent of the winter paths, enjoying the sensation of leafless trees vanishing into the dark sky. In the summer, I used to come here to sit in the shade of the horse chestnut trees and read. For a brief moment, I felt panic at the thought that they might never come into leaf again, not while the city was under Occupation.

It seemed like there were no longer the usual sounds of the park at any time these days – birds, traffic, children, lovers – but

I became aware of one noise cutting into my thoughts. The sound of a voice raised in anger. Following it to its source off the path among the trees, I found a uniformed cop berating a middle-aged couple. In their arms they each held a bunch of fallen branches that they'd gathered. As I approached, I made out the cop's words.

'Scavenging for firewood is a serious offence. The courts don't look kindly on it.' He was inspecting their papers and scowling at them.

'It's dead wood,' the woman argued. 'It's just lying here.'

'It's the law.'

'Well, it's a stupid law.'

I held my bread bag of coal behind my back and walked up to the tableau.

'What is it?' I asked the cop.

He was about to give me some lip, but recognised me in time. I have to admit, he wasn't an officer I knew by sight.

'These people were scavenging for firewood, Inspector.'

'Are you planning on charging them?'

'Yes.' He brandished their papers as though that were a reason for arresting them.

'Well, it is a serious offence, Officer. Well done.' I held out my hand and he gave me their identity documents. I took a quick look at them. 'OK, Officer, well, if you want to leave this with me, I'll take over. As you say, the courts take a dim view of this sort of thing.'

He looked uncertain, but followed my implicit order and left us.

'The law is an ass,' the woman told me.

I watched the cop disappear from view. 'I entirely agree.'

She looked shocked at my answer. I took one last look at their papers. They each bore a single word added to them in a bright red stamp – *Juive* in hers and *Juif* in his – and I handed them back. The way things were going, the courts would have taken an even dimmer view in their case.

'Then why are you upholding it?' The man finally spoke.

I felt the coal weigh heavily behind my back.

'I'm not. If I were you, I'd wait here until our young friend has gone and take your wood home.'

'Are you serious?' the woman asked.

'Yes, I am. And next time, be more careful.'

I went home for the second night in a row. My flat was cold, but I got a fire going with my coal purloined from Otto Abetz, which made the warmth slowly permeating my home all the sweeter. Unlike last night, my stomach was full and I had the taste of whisky in my mouth. I sat in my armchair and watched the fire in the grate begin to take hold, its heat embracing me like no blanket ever could.

Paulhan's book was on the table in front of me, but I left it there. Instead, I took out a business card from my wallet. It was the one Dietrich Falke had given to me the first time I'd met him, with the address on Avenue Foch. Another Occupier who didn't skimp when it came to luxury.

The thought of Otto and an Abwehr buying agency was uppermost in my mind. There were dozens at least of these agencies in the city that I knew of. All set up by German civil and military authorities, they bought up everything from French producers dirt cheap and sold them back in Germany for a vast profit. In some cases, they even sold them to themselves, for an even bigger profit. And then they sent the bill to the Vichy government to cover the cost they incurred in occupying us, so we ended up paying for it twice. Who said war wasn't profitable?

Oddly, Thier had immediately mentioned Otto when I'd asked Hochstetter a simple question about any new criminals in the city. Now, for the first time, I began to fear German involvement in the black market, Morvan's gang and Cartier's death. I recalled Falke's drunken comment at the embassy about his partner and saw again his hand pulled across his throat. I had nothing to tell me that Falke's old partner was Cartier, but I had to admit that it was a possibility. Which begged the question as to whether Morvan was the German's new partner.

And that brought another wolf back into the fold. Henri Lafont. A small-time crook who used his gang to act as muscle for the Abwehr's buying agency. Every now and then, the French producers didn't want to sell to the buying agencies, which was where he came in, forcing them to sell to the Germans at knockdown prices. I knew nothing about Morvan, but I knew that Lafont was more than capable of force-feeding Cartier his own butter. And while I didn't welcome the prospect of him resurfacing, he did at least provide a feasible alternative to the Bouvier brothers as suspect for Cartier's murder.

A chain forming in my mind slowly took on a possible shape. It went from Otto, a buying agency run by the Abwehr, possibly to Lafont, who acted as enforcer, to Falke, a German trader here to buy up French goods cheaply, to Morvan, the partner who had replaced Cartier.

And any one of them could be responsible for Cartier's murder.

Deuxième Plat

40

'What are you doing here? It's Saturday morning.'

Sarah didn't look up from her typewriter. 'I agreed to come in to make up for the work I missed on Tuesday.'

There wasn't much I could say to that. The temperature outside had plummeted almost as much as the chill in my office. Ice had formed inside the windows. I'd kept my coat on, but the cold still seeped through to my bones. It was nothing compared with the frozen wastes coming from Sarah.

'Eddie, could I have a word?'

I looked away to see a strangely welcome interruption. Boniface was standing in the doorway, the expression on his face not the usual mocking calm.

'What is it, Boniface? I'm busy.'

'There's something I think you should see.'

I studied his face. Normally I'd dismiss him out of hand, but I knew that when he lost the cockiness, he usually had something worth listening to.

'What's this about?'

He glanced at Sarah and back at me.

'Just something you need to see.'

Another cop drove us to the American Hospital in Neuilly.

'What's it about?' I asked Boniface, but he turned to me and signalled to me to keep quiet. That was a first.

We travelled in silence through the expensive suburbs in the west of the city, seeing more and more Germans as we drove through the streets of the Eighth and the Sixteenth. Unsurprisingly, most of their troops – and all of their officers, I imagined – were billeted in the more salubrious parts of town. The poorer parts and Communist strongholds of the north and east weren't so much to their liking, which made it odd that they should be using the girls' school on Cours de Vincennes as a barracks. They were most likely the regiments that had come too late to the party to nab the best beds.

The cop pulled in through the hospital gates and parked among the skeletal trees in the grounds. The last time I'd been here was a hot summer's day little over a week after the Germans had marched into Paris. It was also the last time I'd seen Jean-Luc, my son.

An American doctor met us inside and led us along a snowy-white corridor to a private room. Two cops out of uniform were on duty outside the door. I looked at Boniface in puzzlement. The doctor showed us into the room.

'Not too long,' he said in heavily accented French before closing the door behind us.

The figure in the bed was pale. One cheek was bruised and swollen, the right eye almost closed. I didn't recognise him until he opened his left eye and slowly focused on me.

'What's going on?' I asked Boniface.

'I saw the name,' he told me, 'and thought you should see it. He was brought in last night, but nothing's been registered yet with Thirty-Six. The two cops outside are friends of mine; they won't say anything out of turn.'

'What's the problem? Why was he brought here?'

Boniface led me to the window, as far away from the bed as possible.

'I arranged it. There's another guy in the room next door.

His injuries are much worse. We found them together in an apartment that had been burgled by this gang I've been after. They'd both taken a hell of a beating.'

I turned to look at the figure in the bed. His good eye was staring at me with a cold malevolence, but he hadn't yet said a word.

'What happened? They surprised the burglars?'

'Or the burglars surprised them.' Boniface lowered his voice a tone. 'We were tipped off by the concierge. Someone had heard noises during the day, so she went in, found what she did and called us.'

'What was it she found?'

'This one in the bed and the other guy on the floor next to it. They'd obviously been in bed together when the burglars broke in. It's a huge apartment and the bedroom is at the other end from the front door. If they were otherwise engaged, they wouldn't have heard anything.'

I couldn't help glancing at the patient again. 'I see why you brought him here.'

'As I said, I saw the name and thought I'd better tell you first.'

I approached the bed for the first time.

'How are you feeling?' I asked.

'How do you think I feel?' Martin Hochstetter replied.

'A visit on a Saturday, Édouard, I am honoured.'

Hochstetter stood up when I was shown into his office at the Lutetia and asked the leutnant for some coffee for us.

I sat down and wondered how I was going to tell him. At the American Hospital, Boniface had taken me in to see the other man who'd been attacked. Just as Boniface had said, he'd been beaten much more severely than Martin Hochstetter had. Still unconscious, he was in no state to be questioned, but we knew from his ID that he was French. Boniface had discovered that he worked in a bar near the Champs-Élysées.

'It's about Martin.'

Hochstetter waited until the leutnant had served the coffee and left before speaking. 'What about him?'

'He's in the American Hospital. I'm sorry, but he's been attacked.'

Hochstetter lit a cigarette, his actions slow and deliberate. There wasn't the slightest tremor in his fingers. He took a deep drag.

'Can you tell me the circumstances, please?'

I told him everything we knew about his brother's attack. Where he had been found and who he was with.

'And he is in the American Hospital, you say?' he asked me when I finished. 'May I see him? Discreetly?'

'I'll have one of our cars take you there.'

'And can you assure me that he will remain there? I fear far too many questions will be asked if he is transferred to a German military hospital.' He looked away and gazed out of the window. For the first time, he displayed some sign of emotion. 'It is bizarre how people can be convinced to support a system that is detrimental to their own lives, their own well-being. I love my brother, but I am unable to agree with him in so many aspects.' He looked at me warily, his voice barely audible. 'Not his sexuality, his political views. And it is precisely because of his political views that his sexuality places him at even greater risk.'

'It does seem odd that he would be such a believer in the Nazis.'

'It has sometimes caused me much consternation.' He looked like he was going to say more, but decided against it. Instead he shifted to the front foot. 'May I remind you that my brother is in a Paris hospital because of his sexuality? At the hands of Frenchmen, from what you tell me.'

'The other man was beaten more severely. We think the motive was more that he was a Frenchman fraternising with an occupying soldier rather than their sexuality.'

'And that justifies it?'

'Not in the slightest. But that isn't the problem at hand. The problem is that we have to keep this from the German authorities, for your brother's safety.'

Hochstetter stubbed out his cigarette heavily. He was so agitated, it had burned almost to his fingers.

'I apologise. I believe that in France you decriminalised two men loving each other a hundred and fifty years ago. In Germany, the Nazis recriminalised it and began to persecute those involved less than one twentieth of that ago.'

'I'll take you to see him.'

He came out from behind his desk. 'Thank you, Édouard, I am in your debt.'

I stood up and put my coat on, all the while looking at him.

'Yes. You are.'

41

The phone was ringing when I opened my front door. I'd left Dominique sleeping in Montmartre and taken myself home. I'd told her the previous night that I wanted to check on my flat, but the truth was I wanted a Sunday morning of books, not records.

I checked my watch. Eight o'clock. I knew I should have woken her, but I didn't want her to tempt me into staying. I'd left without shaving or washing. I shivered. The flat was freezing. The copy of Paulhan was sitting neatly on the low table in front of my chair, where I'd left it on Friday night. Even cold and tired, I knew to look after my books. It was people I wasn't so good at taking care of. I closed the door and stood in the hall, where the phone was shrilling insistently.

'Only got yourself to blame,' I said out loud. My voice rang lonely in the flat. I paused before picking up the phone. 'And now you're going to pay for it.'

I put the handpiece to my ear and braced myself for an argument with Dominique. I wondered where she'd be calling from at this time on a Sunday.

'Inspector Giral?' A male voice spoke. I recognised it as one of the sergeants from Thirty-Six. 'You're needed. The Rue de Buci market. There's a huge queue forming and it looks to be turning ugly.'

'Can't you send uniforms?'

'There are already a handful there, but we need someone senior.'

'Why not a senior uniform?'

'You're the nearest.'

'Nice to know I'm needed.'

I hung up and went to the bathroom to see if I'd do. I was unshaven and unwashed, but at least I was dressed. That's half the battle some mornings. I poured icy water from the tap over my face and neck and waited for the shock to hit me. It all but killed me, but at least it woke me up. No breakfast. I'd have to see what I could pick up at the market.

The brisk walk to warm myself up took less than ten minutes. The scant few Parisians who hadn't seen their cars requisitioned by the Germans were banned from driving them on a Sunday, so the roads were even more devoid of traffic and noise than usual. The Rue de Buci had become well known among Parisians as one of the few places where you had a chance of finding food to buy when everywhere else had failed. I turned the corner into the street and stopped in my tracks. Normally overrun with desperate shoppers from dawn to dusk, the pavements were teeming, a seething mass of hunger in ill-fitting overcoats. And of anger. Here of all places, the queues for food were a pot waiting to boil over. It looked like the waiting was about done.

Strung out along the road under crumbling buildings held up with huge wooden struts and decorated with fly-blown posters for shows and concerts advertising a Paris that now seemed long gone were hundreds of people, all jostling and vying for position. A swell of noise was steadily growing, a chorus of resentment.

'Two thousand,' a sergeant I recognised from Thirty-Six told me.

'How many?'

'You heard, Eddie. A good two thousand, easily. Queuing for three hundred pieces of rabbit.'

'And how many cops have you got?'

'About twenty.'

As we talked, I watched two of his men vainly trying to shepherd an offshoot queue into the back of the original one. I heard voices raised, but no one was pushing back at the two policemen. Yet.

The sergeant and I both heard a tidal wave of angry shouting coming from the front of the queue. Hurrying to see what was happening, we found five German soldiers, who had gone to the head of the line.

'Haven't they got enough food of their own?' the sergeant asked me in disbelief.

I went over to the soldiers and spoke to them in German. On hearing me, a few in the queue started muttering 'collaborator' and 'lapdog'.

'This is a queue for French people,' I told the soldiers.

'We have been allowed to come to the front,' one of them replied.

He pointed at a harassed-looking stallholder, who shrugged apologetically. I felt sorry for him; he'd been put in an impossible situation.

'Don't you have your own canteens you could go to?'

'They don't have rabbit.'

I could see from his attitude that the calm, unreasonable logic of his argument was more than enough justification for him and his friends. Behind them, three women began to raise their voices; the words they were using were ones I hoped the soldiers hadn't learned yet. The German I was talking to, a ruddy-faced feldwebel who looked every bit the country boy, turned to glare at the women. The expression on his face only served to rile more of the would-be rabbit-buyers around our little group. Another dozen voices began to be raised in anger.

One of the three original women suddenly pushed the arm

of another of the soldiers. My immediate image was of Jacques Bonsergent in his prison cell waiting to be executed for jostling a German soldier. I could feel a bead of sweat run icily down my spine. The police sergeant with me tried to calm the woman down.

'Please don't push them,' I told her and the others around her.

'Doing the Boches' work for them?' a voice said.

'I'm trying to protect you.'

A second woman prodded her finger into a soldier's chest, more forcefully than the first one. A couple more of the police sent to manage the situation gathered around us.

The feldwebel looked at me. 'Are you going to allow German soldiers to be harassed like this? What is your name?'

'If you would leave, that would greatly ease the situation.'

'We are not going to leave. I asked for your name.'

Behind him, his companions were beginning to get edgy. Each was armed, and I started to worry about what they might do if they felt any more threatened.

'Inspector Giral,' I told him.

'Collaborator scum,' one of the women muttered.

The feldwebel pointed at the pair who had touched the soldiers. 'I demand that you arrest these two women.'

I glanced at the sergeant by my side. He stared back at me blankly. The decision was mine to take, I realised. Initially I tried to resist. 'That may cause a greater disturbance.'

The feldwebel gave me a cold look. 'You are aware of the repercussions of assaulting a German soldier, I take it?'

'Only too aware.' I tried to keep the ice out of my own expression.

'Then you will arrest these women.'

The two of us looked intently at each other in an impossible stand-off. His eyes were blue and chillier than the morning, a farm boy given a gun and a uniform and determined to make the most of them both. I exhaled slowly, my breath misting between us.

'Arrest them,' I told the sergeant. 'But do it quietly.'

The sergeant and two of his men pulled the women out of the queue and quickly walked them away. I had to admit, he did it well, without too many of those further back realising what was happening.

'You can't do this,' one of the women protested.

'We're doing it to protect you,' I heard the sergeant counter. 'Don't make this any worse.'

The sight seemed to sober up those at the front in an instant. The noise subsided to a bitter murmur, and every face followed the women for a brief moment before turning down to stare at the pavement at their feet.

I turned to the feldwebel. 'I believe that will be enough.'

'Arrest that woman as well.' He pointed at a young African woman in the queue.

'She wasn't involved.'

'Arrest her.'

'She did nothing.'

'I have your name. Arrest her.'

Struggling with my own anger, I signalled to a couple of uniformed cops and gave the order. By now, no one was looking at us, and the poor woman was led away quietly. She glanced at me, her expression a mixture of fear and incomprehension. I watched her impassively before turning back to the feldwebel.

'That will be enough, I take it,' I told him.

42

'We'll try and get you out of here as soon as we can,' I promised.

The woman in the cell sneered at me. 'You should be ashamed. Doing the Boches' dirty work like that.'

I considered having one more go at explaining how I'd had her arrested to stop the situation at Rue de Buci from worsening, but I didn't have the heart. I knew deep down that we'd got lucky. Arresting the three women could have gone either way. It was just fortunate for them – and for me – that it went the right way.

Checking with the sergeant on duty that they'd get a meal, I knew there was nothing more I could do. I tried phoning the Palais de Justice to see if Judge Rambert was there, but he wasn't. Nothing would happen now until tomorrow morning.

In need of a wash, I went home to shave and shower. Part of me was tempted to spend the rest of Sunday reading, but I realised I wanted to see Dominique. It was time to go to Montmartre and face the music. Literally, as it turned out.

The jaunty voice of Charles Trenet singing 'Boum' was playing on Dominique's gramophone when she opened the door. It was far too cheerful. I was in a mind to turn around and go back home to Paulhan.

She leaned out and kissed me before opening the door wide to let me in.

'How are you, Eddie?' She closed the door and ushered me into the living room. A fire was burning in the grate and I felt a pang of shame. 'Everything all right with your flat?'

'I got a call when I was there, so I had to go into Thirty-Six.' I didn't mention the morning's escapades with hungry Germans and angry French. Best not to.

'I thought it had to be something like that. Well, never mind, you're here now. I'll get some lunch on. I don't know what, though.'

'Let's go out,' I said on impulse.

She looked surprised. 'Out? To a restaurant? Do you think that's a good idea?'

'Why not? There must be somewhere you know in Montmartre where it won't matter.'

She cocked her head and smiled. 'Why not?'

We locked up and she led me through streets I hadn't walked in years to a narrow alleyway near Place du Tertre. At a double door next to a high wall that didn't seem to have a building behind it, she pushed and took me into a tiny restaurant. The aroma of cooking was like before the Occupation. I paused a moment to take it in.

'How come you've never brought me here before?' I said.

'You've never asked.'

The owner, a woman our age with long grey hair and a smile that would open a block of ice, gave Dominique a hug and greeted me with the caution of someone meeting a best friend's new beau. She showed us to one of just half a dozen tables and told us what food she had to offer.

Since the Occupation, restaurants had been placed into one of five categories, ranging bizarrely from a D, which could only charge a maximum of eighteen francs, to an E, which was allowed to sting you for seventy-five. In reality, they all got away with what they could. This place was firmly in the D class, but none the worse for it, judging by the smells coming from the kitchen. The best bit about it was the lack of grey uniforms.

The menu the woman had recited had been the usual nowadays of a vegetable soup starter and egg or fish with vegetables or pasta. There was no butter allowed on the table by law, which was a relief as Dominique and I had had more arguments about my butter than Pétain and Laval going on a date with Adolf. I'd had moments when I'd been tempted to come clean about it, that I'd stolen it from a dead man's zinc bathtub, to see if that made it any more palatable to her. Today was also one of the meat-free days the government had imposed long before the Germans had shown up, so there was no meat on the menu either. I had a brief memory of the platters of food at Maxim's and lunch at Le Catalan with Peter, and felt even more guilt than I needed. I could tell her none of that.

We ordered and the food came. When the woman put the second course of fried eggs and vegetables down in front of us, she gave a little wink and Dominique smiled.

'What was that about?' I asked her.

'Check under your egg.'

Puzzled, I lifted the fried egg with my knife. It was nestling on a small beefsteak. I let the egg flip back guiltily in case anyone at another table saw. Dominique laughed.

'Everyone's got steak,' she said.

For the first time, I noticed that all the other diners were eating meat. She started to cut into her own steak. I couldn't yet bring myself to slice into mine, despite having forgone my unappetising tinned meat last night and breakfast this morning.

'And you complain about my butter,' I said.

'What?' Her mouth was full.

'You complain about my butter, and you're eating meat when it's illegal.'

She shrugged. 'They're just trying to help.'

'Help. And my butter isn't trying to help? Isn't all graft these days based on trying to help?'

'It's different.'

'It's hypocrisy.'

She put her knife and fork down. 'With all of them here in their grey uniforms eating the finest food that none of us can afford and you worry about a tiny piece of meat hidden under a fried egg? And what about all the French people, the rich and the right-wing, who suck up to them and take their food? What about them, Eddie? *That's* hypocrisy.'

I had nothing I could say to her.

She picked up her knife and fork again. 'Eat your food. Just this once, please. Without an argument.'

43

'It's Bonsergent,' Dax told me on Monday morning. 'His appeal's been turned down.'

I sat down heavily on the chair facing him.

'So what happens next?'

He stared at me, his silence horribly eloquent. I looked out of the window. The buildings across the river from us stood out sharply in the stark light of a biting-cold day. I tried to imagine Jacques Bonsergent in his cell in Cherche-Midi, and thought of Marie Ferran.

'I can't see the Germans allowing another appeal, can you?' Dax finally said, pulling me out of my grim thoughts.

'God only knows where this will lead.'

'Talking of which, we've just received this. Intercepted by us. You can be sure the Germans will have seen a copy by now.'

He picked up a flimsy pamphlet that was lying on his table and threw it in front of me. It was four pages of letter-size paper, the typeface rough and ready. Across the top in large handwritten letters was the single word *Résistance*. It claimed to be the official journal of the National Committee for Public Health and was dated the fifteenth of December.

Its first word was a repeat of *Résistance*, followed by a message saying that this was the cry of all of you who had not given in and who wanted to do your duty.

'Stirring stuff,' I said.

I looked up at Dax to see him looking at me intently. Neither of us really knew how to respond to the magazine in front of the other.

'We don't know who's doing it or where they're doing it from.'

'Do we want to?'

I instantly regretted letting the words slip out. Dax didn't react in any way.

'The Germans will, you can be sure of that. An informant found it in the Sorbonne. It had been circulating among the lecturers and students. It's the only one we've found so far, but you can be sure there are more. And not just in the Sorbonne, I'll wager.'

'Nice sense of humour,' I commented, looking at the last line on the second page. It was done in the form of a 'latest news' headline. I read it out to him. '"General de Gaulle and his collaborators have been stripped of their French nationality. Monsieur Laval has not yet been given German citizenship."'

He grunted and reached out a hand for me to give it back. Getting up, he unlocked the safe in the cupboard behind him and stowed it securely there.

'Don't want it falling into the wrong hands.'

I couldn't help thinking it already had.

Dax made to dismiss me, but I had a couple of things of my own I needed to tell him, starting with the near-riot at the Rue de Buci the previous day and the arrests we'd been forced to make.

'You had no choice,' he decided. 'Risky, though.'

'I'll see Judge Rambert this morning. Try and appeal to his better nature to get the three women released without charge.'

That won a snort from both of us. I also told him about Falke's drunken comment about his partners – new and old.

Dax hung his head. 'For Christ's sake, Eddie, can't you

investigate anything without seeing German involvement in it?
Why a German?'

'You'll have to take that up with Adolf. We're under German
occupation, so pretty much everything we do is tied up with
them.'

'You're right, though. It does put this Falke in the spotlight.'

'I want to have him followed. See where it might lead us. The
only problem being that Falke knows me, so I can't. Normally
I'd use Boniface for it, but he's busy on this other investigation.'

'Don't even think of using Sarah again.'

'Don't worry, I wouldn't.' Not while I had doubts about her,
anyway. 'So who *do* I use?'

He waved a hand at the room outside his door. 'There's a
whole team of detectives out there. Use them. That's their job.'

I glanced out of the window set into the top half of his door.
The only detectives I saw were Lafitte, who'd probably try and
shoot me if I were ever desperate enough to ask him to do anything, and Courtet, a spotty kid who'd failed to get into the
army and who thought the Popular Front was another name for
the Folies Bergère.

'Courtet? He couldn't find his own arse if he were sitting on
his hands.'

'Plenty of other cops, Eddie.'

I left Dax and went in search of an elusive tail. I wasn't spoilt
for choice. In the detectives' room, Lafitte was on the phone,
although he found the time to pause and sneer at me. Courtet
was reading a newspaper. The right way up this time. Two other
cops had come into the room. Tavernier, who'd worked himself
up to a casual disgruntlement with the Germans for messing up
his retirement, and Barthe, who used to keep a bottle of brandy
in his desk drawer but was now having to fire on air since Vichy
had banned pretty much the one pleasure he had. He at least

was politically sound and was not a bad cop when he was off the booze. I went over to him.

'Job for you,' I told him.

I explained who Falke was and what he looked like. Unfortunately, I had no pictures of him. Fortunately, he was distinctive with his skeletal look. It would have to do. I also had his address. I handed Barthe the business card.

'I want you to follow this guy. I want to know where he goes, who he sees. I want to know any business partners, any French people he meets, anything you can find.'

Barthe looked at the address on the card and tapped it against his forehead by way of a salute. I watched him put his coat on.

'And be discreet,' I told him.

Both Sarah and Boniface were in my office when I returned to it. I could sense a quiet tension in the room.

'Been asking Sarah about her husband again?' I asked Boniface. I could tell from the noises they both made that I was right. 'Well, don't.'

Secretly I welcomed Boniface being an arse. It diverted Sarah's scorn away from me. The phone on his desk rang, a merciful release for us all. Sarah typed in silence as Boniface spoke and I began to get my coat to go out and plead with Judge Rambert. Boniface hung up and peered out from behind his battlements.

'That was the American Hospital,' he said. 'We can go and question—'

'OK,' I interrupted him. I glanced at Sarah and he cottoned on.

'I'll meet you at the front door,' he told me, reaching for his own coat. 'I'll get a car.'

Sarah stared in silence at the typewriter, tapping away at some detective's words. She didn't look up in acknowledgement when I left to join Boniface.

44

'Not sure you can trust Sarah?'

I considered Boniface's question before answering. Despite my belief that she'd be a good cop if only the powers-that-be would allow it, there was something I couldn't put my finger on. A nagging doubt at the back of my mind about her.

'No, I think we can trust her,' I said, crossing my fingers. 'It's just that I don't want too many people knowing about Martin Hochstetter.'

Boniface headed west away from Thirty-Six, crossing the Pont Neuf over the Seine to the Right Bank. He waited patiently while a German staff car motored past, its driver riding rough-shod over the 40 kph speed limit the Occupiers themselves had set.

'Does Dax know?'

'No, I haven't told him yet.'

He took his eyes off the wheel for a moment to glance at me. 'Is that wise?'

'Probably not.'

'I want to know where her husband is. And what he's doing.'

I was surprised at the turn of the conversation back to Sarah.

'Is that because you don't trust her, or because you're thinking with your dick as usual?'

He laughed. 'Bit of both, perhaps. Don't say you're not tempted, Eddie.'

'I'm really not.' I paused to stare out of the window. Paris was grey and gloomy, with the heart skewered out of it. It could not have felt less like Christmas if Pontius Pilate had come down and stabbed Père Noël to death with a model of the Eiffel Tower. 'I don't know anything about her home life, but I think you should leave it to her to tell us when she wants to. And you can take that as an order.'

He met that with silence. I reckoned he would pay as much attention to it as I would. I knew I had questions about Sarah that I wanted answers to, but for very different reasons from the ones Boniface harboured in his trousers.

'This Martin Hochstetter,' he said after he'd been silent for a blessed while. 'Don't forget there's also a Frenchman lying in a hospital bed, and in a much worse way. We should be finding out who did this to them for his sake, if not for the German's.'

'What do you want to do?'

'I think we should ruffle a few feathers.'

There were times when Boniface shocked me with how similar to me he was in some ways. Part of me wanted to shake a branch or two, but I hadn't yet come up with a valid reason why that should be at all a good idea.

'What good would that do? I thought you said it was the burglars who attacked them. It's not like we don't have clear suspects or think the Nazis had any involvement. From what you've told me, they were simply in the wrong place at the wrong time. If that's the case, we'd just be putting the French guy in danger of arrest by the Germans for no reason. Not to mention the trouble Martin Hochstetter would be in.'

'Are you worried about the trouble he might get into?'

'Not really. But it gives me leverage with his brother. And believe me, I need it.'

*

A German staff car was parked under the twisted winter trees in the car park at the American Hospital when we turned in through the gates.

Boniface and I looked at each other in concern, the implications obvious.

We both checked the vehicle after we'd parked and were on our way inside the building. There was no driver inside or gefreiter among the trees having a crafty cigarette.

'How would they have found out?' Boniface demanded.

Neither of us could help hurrying along the corridor to Martin Hochstetter's room. A doctor I didn't recognise walked past us in the other direction, but otherwise it was deserted, the doors leading off it all closed, the hospital hushed.

I reached the room before Boniface did and pushed open the door. There were three men in the room, who all turned in unison, startled by my intrusion. I stopped dead. Boniface barged into the back of me.

'Édouard, you look perturbed.'

Boniface nudged me gently forward and closed the door behind him. I stood and looked at the tableau before us. Hochstetter, as calm and collected as ever, was seated on a high-backed chair by the bed. His brother was sitting up facing him, much of the bruising on his face having gone down considerably. He'd even had a sort of a smile on his face when we'd walked in. The third figure, standing by the window, was the doctor who'd met us the day before. He was the only one to look at all concerned.

'Detective Boniface,' he said, hurrying forward to greet us. 'I'm glad you got my message.'

Hochstetter began speaking to the doctor in English, but then looked at me and switched to French.

'Would you be so kind as to leave us while the inspector questions my brother, Doctor?'

Showing some relief, the doctor recovered his professional

mien. 'Please don't tax the patient, gentlemen, he is still some way from being fully recovered.' He nodded at the room in general and left.

'What are you doing here?' I asked Hochstetter.

'Visiting my brother. Surely you can have no objection to that.'

'We'd like to ask Martin some questions,' Boniface said. 'Would you mind waiting outside?'

For a brief moment, I almost loved him.

Hochstetter looked at him in surprise, and then at me. 'They breed you hardy in the Paris police, I see. I think I will stay here.'

'No, I would prefer to speak to them alone.' Martin spoke for the first time. His voice was stronger than I thought it would be, but it lacked the arrogance I remembered from the last time I met him. It was the first time I'd heard him speak French, and it was even better than his brother's.

'You are certain of this?' Hochstetter asked him in German. He glanced at me, aware that I could understand him. 'Very well, I will leave you to it. I shall be outside.'

Once he'd left the room, Boniface took his place on the chair by the bed. I stood by the door. Boniface started by asking Martin how he was.

'As well as can be expected. I would prefer to be treated by a German doctor, but this will have to suffice.'

I almost felt like giving him up there and then to the care of the Nazis, but Boniface managed to stay cool.

'Can you remember the men who attacked you?' he asked.

Martin put more scorn into his laugh than most of us could manage in an insult. 'Do you think if I recognised them I would still be here? They would be strung up with piano wire by now.'

'Nice.' That was me, I couldn't help myself. Boniface shot me a look to silence me. That was twice now.

'Did you see your attackers? Can you remember what they looked like?'

'I didn't see them. They were wearing scarves over their faces, and caps.'

'Can you remember anything they said?'

'They called my friend a collaborator.'

Boniface glanced at me, our supposition about the motive for the viciousness of the attack on the Frenchman seemingly confirmed. He chose his next words carefully.

'How did you meet your friend?'

Martin looked at me, then back at Boniface, apparently weighing up the lesser of two evils. Some of his self-assuredness was gone. 'I would prefer to address my answers to you alone.'

Boniface glanced at me and shrugged.

'I'll wait outside,' I told him.

I found Hochstetter in the trees near his car, smoking a cigarette. On the ground at his feet were two fresh dog-ends. He was nothing like as calm as he wanted to appear. His fingers shook very slightly.

'You drove here alone, I take it?' I asked him.

'I am not foolish. What is my brother saying?'

'He didn't want me in the room either.'

He nodded and drew deeply on his cigarette. Its companions on the ground wouldn't have long to wait for company. 'I suppose it's understandable. If you mix with others who denigrate your way of being, you begin to believe them. Despite his bravado, he is my younger brother. I know him. He's afraid.'

'Of what the SS would do if they found out?'

'Of that. And of my feelings for him as a brother. He needn't worry on the second count. On the first, he is right to be very afraid. Is your Boniface a good detective? Can he be trusted?'

I thought of how much Boniface drove me up the wall and how fervently I wished he'd be sent to another station. 'He's a very good detective. And he's probably one of the cops I trust the most these days.'

'I am glad to hear it.'

'Although that might not always be such a comfort. He's keen to pursue the investigation more vigorously, to find the perpetrators.'

'You know I wish to avoid that.'

'I do, and I'm doing my utmost to deter him, but a good cop is a good cop.'

'I trust I can count on you, Édouard.'

He finished his cigarette and immediately reached inside his coat for his silver cigarette case and box of matches. I stood back while he went through his lighting-up ceremony, sucking keenly on the new cigarette and flicking the spent match away from him, watching its smoke-trail spiral to the ground.

'I wish for this affair to be kept quiet,' he insisted. 'You would do well to remember that.'

I waited until he'd removed the cigarette from his lips and held it by his side before moving back towards him. It was the closest I'd ever stood to him and I could see he was taken aback.

'And there are all sorts of things I wish for, Major. I want Marie Ferran released from Cherche-Midi prison and I want some information about Otto and its possible involvement in the black market and Cartier's murder. If you want my cooperation in ensuring your brother's safety, perhaps *you* would do well to remember that.'

45

In the car back to Thirty-Six, Boniface filled me in on how his questioning had gone. Martin Hochstetter had told him that he'd seen two attackers, but he couldn't swear that there weren't any more. He'd sometimes borrowed the apartment for the night. The Germans had requisitioned it shortly after they'd entered the city, but it wasn't used permanently, just by visiting officers and officials. Boniface was certain the burglars couldn't have known that and possibly thought they were burgling an empty flat.

I asked about the Frenchman.

'He worked in a bar that Martin Hochstetter visited after a dinner with the German ambassador at Maxim's. They'd seen each other a few more times since then.'

I told him to drop me off by the Palais de Justice before returning the car to Thirty-Six. Judge Rambert made me wait half an hour before seeing me. No one left his chambers while I was waiting, so he'd evidently wanted to put me in my place. That was never going to work.

'How's the gut, Judge? Quite some thump, wasn't it? Must have been something you said.'

He looked at me sternly and bade me sit down. He poured himself a glass of whisky and took a sip of it, savouring the afterburn. None for me, evidently. I nodded at his drink.

'Illegal act, Judge. I could arrest you.'

He laughed, a cold sound like a distant shell firing. 'That simply doesn't apply to certain of us.'

'I'm here about the incident at the Rue de Buci. I was the officer who made the arrests of the three women.'

He stared at me, forcing me to continue talking. It was a tactic I used every day, which annoyed me all the more.

'I made the arrests to prevent greater damage being done. I'm sure you'll appreciate how much we need to avoid confrontation in light of the Jacques Bonsergent matter.'

'I am aware. Unfortunately, these people have brought it on themselves with their petulance. They made the Germans act robustly.'

'See what you've made us do, in other words. An interesting angle for a judge to take.'

'Do you have anything further to offer on the matter, Inspector Giral?'

'Just that there's no need to make an example of these women.'

'I gather one of the suspects is African. Which further strengthens my resolve that hostages should be of the same class and background as the perpetrators, wouldn't you say? A deterrent to others.'

I stopped myself from speaking while I let my anger calm. For one moment, I wondered if he somehow knew about Dominique.

'Any action against these three women would serve nothing.'

The judge took his time over another sip of his whisky. I could smell the aroma from the other side of the desk.

'I disagree with you, Inspector Giral. Unfortunately for me, the Germans would agree with you. They have urged me to allow all charges to be dropped.'

He paused, making me wait. I held my tongue.

'Given their magnanimity,' he continued, 'I have decided to

accede to their wishes. The three women will be released from custody this morning and no further action will be taken. I'm sure you will agree with me that we should thank the Germans for their show of goodwill.'

I hid a sigh of relief. 'I can never express how grateful I am.'

He nodded at that and gestured to the door, indicating that my audience was over. I stood up and made to leave.

'Actually,' he added, 'I thought you were here regarding the Bouvier brothers, since you've been very insistent on arguing their innocence. Sentence was passed earlier today. They are to be guillotined on Saturday morning.'

46

Judge Rambert had refused to talk any more on the matter, and had called a court official to have me escorted from the building.

I'd gone straight from the Palais de Justice to Thirty-Six, but there were no cars available, so I'd hurried home to fetch my own car. At Fresnes prison, I decided to talk to Firmin rather than Jacquot. He was the one who seemed to have a better grasp of what was happening and what the brothers had been doing the night Cartier was murdered.

'You have to remember something,' I told him. 'They've passed the death sentence on you and Jacquot. They will execute you on Saturday if I can't find who killed Cartier.'

'I don't know of anyone, Eddie, I swear.'

He was shocked at the news but not the wreck I would have imagined. He was tougher than I'd thought.

'What about this Morvan?'

'I don't know. We only met him that night, he was offering us work. I don't know how to get hold of him.'

'And the name Falke doesn't mean anything to you?'

He shook his head. 'You've got to help us, Eddie.' Sitting upright in his chair, he seemed strangely calm. I hoped he really did appreciate what he and Jacquot were facing.

'I promise you, Firmin, I will.'

At Thirty-Six, Dax was just as horrified as I was at the death sentence passed on the brothers. The judge had left us just five days in which to save Firmin and Jacquot from the guillotine.

'I know justice is a moveable feast now we're under Nazi rule,' he said, 'but I really didn't expect such a summary decision.'

'I suppose we'd better get used to it. More so now with Judge Rambert in town.'

I dropped into my office to find my phone ringing.

'*Message for you, Inspector Giral,*' the sergeant from the entrance to Thirty-Six told me. Politically cast in Lafitte's mould, he was a humourless desk bully from the northern suburbs of the city.

'I haven't got time for this now.'

'*Major Hochstetter of the Abwehr. Popular with the Germans, aren't you?*'

'Direct line to Adolf. I'll put in a word if you want.'

I hung up and rang the Lutetia. I was put through to the man himself.

'*Édouard, would you mind coming to Abwehr headquarters, please, and retrieving your officer?*'

'My officer?'

'*You might need to bring a car. He is rather drunk.*'

I put the phone down and sighed. Hochstetter had been next on my list to visit, but not like this.

'He's in the bar,' Hochstetter told me when I showed up at the Lutetia.

He'd been waiting for me in the foyer. His attitude was different from usual. Normally this would have gone one of two ways. Either mocking sarcasm or cold and coruscating anger. In their place was a slightly absent sense of anxiety. It was no doubt the result of his brother's woes. In anyone other than Hochstetter, I would have mistaken it for a mild outbreak of humanity.

He led me to a table, where Barthe was sitting slumped in an armchair. Fast asleep next to him was Falke. A pair of well-used brandy glasses stood on the table in front of them.

'They appear to have been getting on like a house on fire,' Hochstetter told me.

'May I ask what happened?'

'From what I have been able to ascertain, Herr Falke here noticed your officer following him, no doubt on your orders, so he invited him in for a drink. It seems your policeman was unable to resist.'

I looked at Barthe and could have kicked him senseless if he weren't already there. Instead I kicked him awake. He focused first on me and then on Falke in the chair next to his. Even in his stupor, he had the grace to close his eyes in shame.

'My car's outside,' I told him. 'Go and wait for me there.'

Hochstetter indicated that I should follow him to his office. I watched Barthe stumble across the lobby and then followed the major up the stairs.

'If you will excuse me for a moment, Édouard,' he said, briefly leaving me alone while he spoke to the junior officer in the ante-room.

I took the opportunity to steal a couple of sheets of headed paper from his desk and fold them carefully before putting them in my jacket pocket. I had a feeling I might want to put them to use before very much longer.

Hochstetter returned to the room. 'I gather the incident at Rue de Buci has been resolved to everyone's satisfaction.'

His chosen subject surprised me. 'Have I got you to thank for that?'

'I am afraid not. It is the work of Ambassador Abetz. I imagine you should expect to be forced into giving him something in return.'

'Just out of curiosity, why aren't these women being tried? The same leniency wasn't shown to Jacques Bonsergent.'

'Precisely because of that, I should hazard a guess. We have our example in Bonsergent, we do not need to make another example of these three unfortunate women. For the time being at least. And that is not my thinking, I would add. But I will say this, the next step in a similar incident would most certainly be greater reprisals. You and I do not want that, but there are many others who do.'

'How can there not be other incidents? You've forced us into this. Would you be so calm about any reprisals that Martin might face from the SS?'

Hochstetter lit up his first cigarette of our meeting and let the match die in an overflowing ashtray.

'A rather cheap way of reminding me of the dilemma I face. I do, in fact, have something for you. The affair with the young woman at Cherche-Midi. I have spoken to the Gestapo about the matter.'

'Will she be released?'

'That is all I can tell you. You know that with the Gestapo, there is little more I can do but make requests.'

'Thank you.'

I went on to tell him about the Bouvier brothers and the sentence that had just been passed on them, but he held his hands up.

'I have no influence over this Judge Rambert, and even less over Herr Doktor Abetz. You know that. I am afraid that this is one matter in which I can have no say.'

'In that case, I want to question Dietrich Falke. I think he knows something about the murder for which the Bouviers have been sentenced.'

'I am unable to help with that either. I know you find yourself in an ascendant position in our working relationship, Édouard, but there are some things I simply am unable to do for you.'

I studied him. His expression was impassive.

'I'm in a similar situation. I'm trying to deter Detective Boniface from investigating Martin's attack too closely, but there's also a limit to how much I can influence that.'

He looked at me through his cigarette smoke. 'The winds of war blow first one way then the other. They will blow the same for you, Édouard. This circumstance will not last. It will come back to haunt you.'

I watched the tendrils of smoke twist in the no-man's-land between us. 'In the last war, the gas would turn with the wind. You attacked and gained ground when the wind was in your favour.'

'Only to lose it again when the wind changed.'

'But the air smelled so fresh for that brief moment. You weren't in the last war, you don't know how that feels. Or how important it is.'

He sighed. 'I may be able to offer one more concession to you. I am unable to arrange an interview with Herr Falke, but I can tell you about Otto.' He paused a moment. 'Hermann Brandl. If you are looking for Otto, then look for Hermann Brandl.'

'An Abwehr officer?'

He nodded once. 'That is all I can give you. What you do with that knowledge is up to you. As you know, I have little enthusiasm for some of the activities of officers like Brandl.'

'Thank you,' I finally said. 'That is helpful.'

I stood up to go. For the first time, I chose when to leave. He stayed seated and lit another cigarette, his hand trembling.

47

'I'm sorry, Eddie.'

Barthe had been asleep in the passenger seat of my car outside the Lutetia when I'd returned from talking to Hochstetter, so I'd woken him gently. Now he was rubbing his head and wincing from where I'd woken him gently.

'You screwed up, Barthe.'

'I haven't had brandy in months, Eddie. You know what that's like.'

I pulled out onto the deserted Boulevard Raspail, which should have been humming with cars and buses but had become a ghostly field grey since the Germans had come to town. I almost felt sorry for him. I'd sold my soul for a whisky or two lately, I thought. But I hadn't got clocked by a suspect for murder, so I reached across and slapped him across the back of the head again.

'That's an end to it,' I said as he rubbed away the smarting in silence. 'No one at Thirty-Six will get to know of it.'

'Not Dax?'

'Especially Dax.' I drove slowly back towards the Île de la Cité. 'Did you at least find anything out from Falke?'

Barthe paused and looked disconsolately at a German staff car lording the middle of the road. 'Not so much from talking to him. He mentioned a new partner and seemed pretty cheery about that. That's why he bought me a drink.'

'A drink? How come you let him see you?'

'On the steps outside the Lutetia. He suddenly turned around and came back out as I was going in. He thought he'd dropped his wallet, but he hadn't. Only he recognised me. I'd been asking about him at the Avenue Foch address on his business card just as he'd decided to show up there.'

I winced. That was bad luck, I had to admit. 'What was the set-up at the address? Has he got anyone else working with him?'

'It's not his business, just a poste restante office. He had some documents that he seemed to be dropping off. Everyone who uses the place has a locker as well as a mail service.'

'Did he go anywhere else apart from the Lutetia?'

Out of the corner of my eye, I saw Barthe nodding. 'He dropped by his flat, on Avenue d'Eylau. Then he went to Place de la Concorde. The Hôtel de la Marine.'

'The Hôtel de la Marine?' I waited at a junction, even though no other car was in sight, and took a deep breath. 'You know who's there, don't you?'

The French Admiralty, that was who was there. Only they weren't there now. Another navy had taken over the building for their own headquarters.

'The Kriegsmarine,' Barthe confirmed.

I saw again Korvettenkapitän Johannes Thier, Hochstetter's Hamburger buddy, at Le Catalan with an unknown guest. Thier, who seemed to be spending a lot of his time lately at the Lutetia visiting his childhood friend.

'So is Falke trying to trade with the Kriegsmarine as well as the Abwehr?' I asked.

'He'd be raking it in if he does.'

'Such a dreadful man,' Thier said as he led me up a flight of stairs to his office.

'Did the Kriegsmarine get to Paris before the Abwehr did?'

He looked surprised by my question. 'I really don't know.'

Don't get me wrong, the Hotel Lutetia is about as sumptuous as they come, but by the time I'd climbed my first wrought-iron and tile staircase and been led along a gilded hallway to an office with a ceiling so high the Eiffel Tower would scarcely have scraped the bottom of the glass chandelier, I'd come to decide that Hochstetter's lot had really missed a trick.

I'd dropped Barthe off at Thirty-Six and driven to the Hôtel de la Marine. Before entering the building on Place de la Concorde, I'd stood a minute or two in front of it and marvelled at the sight. As long as you could blot out the huge swastikas and the layers of grime blemishing the ornate eighteenth-century façade, even in the cold of a grey winter's day and with a weak sun behind it casting it in shadow it was a stunning building. It had been inspired by the Louvre and even been so bold as to improve on it with the addition of a loggia running along its entire front. I counted twelve huge Corinthian columns lining the external gallery.

And it had a twin. The Hotel Crillon, sandwiched on the Place de la Concorde between the Jardin des Tuileries to my right and the Jardins des Champs-Élysées to my left. That had been requisitioned by the German High Command.

'You don't believe in slumming it, do you?' I'd muttered as I walked up to the gate. The guards on duty had inspected my police ID and eventually allowed me in.

Up on the first floor, Thier showed me into his office and closed the door behind him. He rang a bell and asked an orderly for a pot of coffee. It was a leap of faith every time you entered one of their buildings to talk to one of their officials, but at least you got a good cup of coffee out of it. There were days when that was the best you could hope for.

'How can I help you, Inspector Giral?' he asked. He had the

same urbanity as Hochstetter and more than a smidgin of the unsettling authority his Abwehr friend had. I wondered if it was a Hamburg thing.

'Dietrich Falke. I was interested in your dealings with him.'

'May I ask why?'

'I'm investigating the murder of a Frenchman, a black marketeer.'

He looked shocked. 'And you think Herr Falke could be responsible?'

'No, not at all,' I lied. 'But he might be working with people who I do suspect may be responsible, so I'd simply like to know what dealings you've had with him. To build up a picture of his business.'

'Well, I hadn't met him until that evening at Maxim's with Ambassador Abetz, and I spoke very little to him that night. He was on the opposite side of the table from me. Next to you, I believe.'

'You haven't had lunch with him?'

'Lunch? Good Lord, no.'

'May I ask who you were with at Le Catalan on Friday?'

He smiled slightly as the orderly poured the coffee and left.

'You may, but I am not disposed to tell you.' Like Hochstetter, he had the polite manner with the underlying cold entitlement. 'I am afraid it is not germane to your line of questioning.'

'Has Falke been here to see you?'

He paused a moment to sip his coffee. 'Yes, I'm afraid to say he has.'

'May I ask what for?'

'You may indeed. The awful man was labouring under the misapprehension that the Kriegsmarine would want to avail itself of his services. He came here offering to sell us goods he'd be buying from French producers and manufacturers.'

'And you weren't interested?'

'We sent him packing. I know we say "to the victor the spoils", but I don't see that we should be pandering to the greed of men such as Dietrich Falke. We are perfectly able to work with the French on more equal terms without having to resort to consorting with the worst sort of profiteer.'

'I would like to question him. Would you be in a position to allow that?'

He shook his head. 'As I say, I have no dealings with the man, so it is not something I would be able to arrange. You would have to take the matter up with the German High Command. Or with Major Hochstetter. Surely all requests like this go through him.'

I took a sip of my own coffee. It was real, as I knew it would be. Studying Thier over my cup, I wondered if he was.

48

I had one more job to do before dropping my car off near my flat and catching the Metro to Montmartre and Dominique.

Bouchard, the pathologist, was listening to some bunch of people warbling on his gramophone player in the Institut Médico-Légal, in the Twelfth, on the banks of the Seine, a short way upstream from Thirty-Six.

'Do you reckon this is why they invented opera?' I asked him. 'To show there's still something worse than cutting up dead bodies in a building that looked like it was meant to be a prison for the terminally morose?'

He looked at me over the top of his semi-lunettes. 'You, Eddie, are a philistine.'

'Just the one question for you, Doc. Joseph Cartier, the black marketeer with a taste for Breton butter. What was his time of death?'

'Hold this.' He handed me the scalpel he was using and went to a cabinet near a desk, lit gloomily by an old lamp. Taking out a file, he read from it, while I stood over a corpse with all sorts of bits where they shouldn't be. He sometimes did this to me when I'd annoyed him. 'I've told you this before, but he died sometime between six p.m. and midnight on December the twelfth.'

He returned everything to its place and came back to reclaim his scalpel. I backed away. 'Thanks, Doc, just wanted to be sure.'

'What's it about?'

'The new judge, Rambert, wants the Bouvier brothers to meet the guillotine for Cartier's murder. I don't think they did it.'

'I've heard about that. Bit of a bastard by all accounts, this new judge.'

'Good to get a medical opinion.'

Leaving him, I used up some more of my precious petrol to drive to Thirty-Six to check for messages or in case there was any news about the brothers. On the way, I looked at the fuel gauge and seriously considered weeping.

'Inspector Giral.' The bullish sergeant who'd told me about Hochstetter's call earlier in the day was still on duty. He called me over. 'The Gestapo were here for you.'

'And I missed them. Pity. What did they want?'

'They brought a prisoner. A girl. Said she was your responsibility.'

I jolted like I'd been shocked.

'What's her name?'

He searched for it in a ledger, seeming to take an age. 'Marie Ferran.'

The sergeant showed me into an interrogation room. A young woman looked up when I walked in. Her expression was an appalling mix of fear and resignation.

'Marie Ferran?' I asked her. I needn't have. She was the spit of her brother, Pierre, although all the worse for a month and a half of Cherche-Midi and the tender care of the Gestapo.

Her hair was unwashed and her face grimy. She sat in the chair and shivered. All she was wearing was a thin blouse and skirt, no doubt the ones she'd been wearing since her arrest, judging by the dirt ingrained in them.

I turned to the sergeant. 'Didn't it occur to you to get her a blanket? And something hot to eat? Get something now.'

He left and I spoke to Marie. 'My name's Inspector Giral, but everyone calls me Eddie. The Gestapo brought you here?'

She stared at me. There was no emotion on her face. I looked around at the grim walls of the room. This wasn't the place to talk to a frightened kid.

The sergeant came in with a blanket and I watched him wrap it gently around her shoulders. His movements surprised me with their tenderness. He nodded at me and I thanked him.

'Don't worry about the food,' I told him. 'I'll take her home.'

I got her to stand up after a minute or two and she limped away from the table. It was only then that I saw she wasn't wearing any shoes. Her feet were black, with raw sores on the heels and toes. She caught me staring at them.

'The Gestapo took my shoes away.'

Outside, I managed to get her into my car, and drove in silence to Bel Air.

'You live above the shop, don't you?'

I had to turn to face her to see her nod. The comment about her shoes was the only words she'd spoken all the time I'd been with her.

The Ferran electrician's workshop was closed and no one was answering the bell for the apartment above.

'Do you have a key?'

I didn't for one minute think she would, and she shook her head to confirm that. Not just her shoes; the Nazis had taken everything she'd gone into prison with but the clothes she was wearing.

'Is there a neighbour you can go to?'

She shook her head again. I couldn't expect her to think straight. From next door, I heard the sound of a lock turning and I saw Ulysse shutting up his bar for the night, the lights down low. He saw Marie and ran towards her. He hugged her tightly and she finally began to lose some of her fear.

'Where's my father?' she asked him.

'Out working. He and Pierre have been out all day. I think he said it was in a factory somewhere, but I don't know where.'

'Can we come in?' I asked him.

'Of course.'

He led us into his café and locked the door behind us.

'The coffee machine is still warm,' he told Marie, his smile warm but worried. 'Fancy a cup? And I've got some bread and cheese and ham. Bugger rationing.'

She smiled for the first time, a tentative childlike softening of the anxiety etched into her face.

'And a brandy,' I added.

'Three brandies coming up.'

He led us to a table away from the window and got on with preparing supper. I asked if I could have some too. It had only just occurred to me that I hadn't eaten since breakfast.

'My pleasure, Eddie. We look after our own around here.'

The first coffee and the first sip of brandy warmed us both and she began to appear more comfortable. I think Ulysse's ease with me allowed her to believe I wasn't a cop out to cause her harm. I had no doubt she'd seen enough of those over the last five or six weeks. I caught her studying me closely, her look oddly inquisitive.

In between making the first and second coffees, Ulysse disappeared and came back with a bowl of hot water and a flannel and some bandages. He bathed her feet, tending the sores, and put a pair of slippers of his own on them.

'Bit big for you, but they'll do,' he told her. 'They'll keep you warm at least.'

He brought the food over and a second glass of brandy. I don't know about Marie, but I was certainly welcoming the warming food and drink.

'You can talk to Eddie,' he told her. 'He's one of us. He was kept in a German prison for nearly two years.'

He left us to talk, and Marie took another sip of brandy and a mouthful of food. Ulysse had even found a couple of eggs for her.

'You were in a German prison,' she eventually said. It was more a statement than a question.

I nodded at the photographs of Ulysse in the trenches. 'Last war. I was captured at Verdun.'

'Horrible?'

'Not good. Maybe not as bad as what you've seen.'

She picked at the fried eggs on her plate.

'They pretended to execute us,' she told me. I tried to hide my shock. 'They told us we'd been sentenced to death and they lined us up against a wall inside the prison. They even put blindfolds on us and gave the order to fire. And then nothing. Just rifles clicking.'

I tried to imagine what that must have felt like. I'd suffered at the hands of prison guards during war, but I hadn't experienced that.

'They did it three times,' she went on. 'And each time I thought it was real.' She looked up at me, her expression intense and wild. 'I hate the Boches. I want every last one of them dead. To suffer the way they made us suffer.'

Her look and her words shocked me. Not because of what they said, but because I saw myself in them. I'd come back from a war and a prison camp with the same hatred, and it had almost killed me. It had certainly marked my life and my place as a father and a husband. And as a person. I had to choose my words carefully and I knew I could never say the right ones.

'Please don't let it take you over,' I said. It sounded vague and meaningless, but I had no other way of saying it.

'I won't go to prison again. I would sooner die. And I would make sure I took as many of the Nazis with me as I could.'

'The only person you take when you think like that is yourself. Believe me, I know.'

She shook her head and stabbed her fork into the last piece of egg. She wasn't in any place to listen. I knew what that felt like, too.

'I didn't know you knew Ulysse,' she said. 'From the last war?'

Her words struck me as odd. 'I'm investigating a murder.'

She looked up. 'Whose?'

'Joseph Cartier.'

'Someone finally killed him, did they? Good. He had it coming. He's as bad as the Boches. Why are you taking the trouble to investigate his death? There are better things you could be doing.'

'A murder's a murder. They all have to be investigated.'

'All of them? Really? Even a piece of shit like Cartier, who took advantage of everyone in the neighbourhood? We're poor here, no one has much money. The Boches have made that worse. They've created an even greater inequality between them and us. Between the haves and the have-nots. And they've created an inequality between proper French people and scum like Cartier, black marketeers who are just making that inequality worse for their own profit. All the rich in their homes in the Sixteenth cosying up to the Nazis and exploiting their fellow French.'

'You're a Communist? Like your father?'

'I'm a Communist, but not like my father. He talks, like all the older ones. All the old-style Soviet supporters who believed the Nazis when they said they'd be all right because of the fake pact between Hitler and Stalin. So what did they do? They showed themselves. They came out of hiding, and they got arrested for their troubles. By your police. Working for the Boches. We don't do any of that. We act.'

'And end up in Cherche-Midi.'

I knew the moment I said it that I sounded like every other

257

person who didn't understand me when I came back from the last war, shell-shocked and angry.

We were disturbed by a banging on the glass door. I turned to see Yves and Pierre Ferran struggling to get in.

'Wait a minute,' Ulysse shouted, hurrying to unlock it.

Marie turned to face me, again with the strangely probing look. 'I know who you are.'

Ulysse opened up, and father and son rushed in and held tightly onto Marie, who finally broke down and began to cry.

Set apart from the three of them, Ulysse and I looked at each other and gave a half-smile and a shrug. It was time for me to go.

But Marie's last words to me lurked quietly in my head.

49

I found the first poster when I went out in the morning to get a hot cup of bad coffee from Louis in the Bon Asile, the grimy café in a narrow lane behind Thirty-Six where all the detectives went. Louis no longer had any of the good stuff left and obviously couldn't get any from whichever black marketeer he dealt with. I was tempted to tell him to try whoever it was in Charonne that was selling to Claude at Les Quatre Chats.

My worries about coffee evaporated the moment I left the café and saw the first poster and a small crowd gathering around it. I edged myself into a position where I could read it and my heart sank, the coffee sitting heavily in my stomach.

Small and barely noticeable, it was dated the previous day and printed in German on the left and French on the right. It said: *Engineer Jacques Bonsergent of Paris was condemned to death by a German military court for an act of violence against a member of the German army. He was shot this morning.*

Looking at the other people reading it, I could tell that none of them had known about the case, as it had been kept out of the news. No one spoke. We all just looked at each other in silence, acknowledging the change we were witnessing. Two men wearing hats took them off and bowed their heads.

Next to it on the Morris column was one of the fly-blown and tattered hearts-and-minds posters that the Germans had put up across the city near the start of the Occupation, exhorting Parisians to trust the German soldiers and playing on the idea that we had somehow been abandoned by our own politicians and leaders. I noticed that someone had scrawled a cross of Lorraine on what was left of it. It was the symbol of de Gaulle and his form of resistance against the Germans. There were none of those to be seen in Communist Bel Air, I mused.

'Everything all right?' the same sergeant as last night asked me when I went back to Thirty-Six.

'Everything all right.'

It felt like a truce had broken out between us.

With no news about the brothers, I stole a lift to Bel Air from a couple of other cops rather than go through all the rigmarole of requesting and waiting for a pool car. They weren't going that way, but then they weren't inspectors either.

'Thanks, boys,' I told them when they dropped me off at the top of the steps leading to Rue de la Voûte. 'I can walk from here.' I was winning my own hearts and minds and being just as successful.

On the corner of Cours de Vincennes, I saw a Bonsergent poster that had already been vandalised and partly torn down. I was hoping that Marie Ferran wouldn't be tempted into doing her own version of that after her experience of the Gestapo in Cherche-Midi. I tried her family apartment first, but there was no reply, so I went next door to find Ulysse.

'Haven't seen her this morning,' he told me when I asked. 'I take it you've heard the news? Did you know about it?'

I had to be wary in my reply. 'I knew about the case and his appeal, but we've been excluded from the whole thing. I learned about it this morning from the poster just like everyone else.'

'It's a bad business.'

'Do you know where I might find her?'

He thought for a moment. 'Before she was taken by the Nazis, she was helping out at the school on Cours de Vincennes, but they've broken up now, so I don't suppose that helps.'

'I don't suppose it does.'

I didn't, but it was the only place I could think of to try. Oddly, the school doors were open, even though classes had finished for Christmas. I found Isabelle Collet blowing on her hands to keep them warm.

'Heating turned off for the holidays,' she explained. 'Not that there was much of it before then.'

Tiny threads of ice inside the windows bore out her words. She and a few other people were sorting tins and packets of food into tidy piles, itemising every piece they had.

'What's going on?' I asked.

She looked at the activity around her and suggested we went outside. 'It's warmer out there than it is in here.'

To get out of a cold wind blowing, we went to the side of the building facing the annexe that the Germans had turned into barracks for their soldiers.

'What was all that with the food?' I insisted.

She glanced back at the building over her shoulder. 'Food for the ones who really need it. Donated by people with whatever they had to spare.'

'Spare? How come anyone's got any spare food?'

'This is a poor neighbourhood, Inspector. We know how to save. And we know how to look after each other.'

I couldn't help feeling impressed. On the day the Germans had entered Paris, Prefect of Police Langeron had ordered former civil defence staff to open up any locked shops, requisition all the food they found and take it to local *mairies* to be sold at affordable prices. With the coming of the black market and everyone out to make a quick franc, that spirit had evaporated pretty much instantaneously, so it was a surprise to see it thriving in one part of town at least.

As we spoke, a lorry pulled up outside the barracks, followed by a second, then a third. A dozen or so soldiers came out of the building and opened the tailgates and began ferrying the trucks' contents inside. We watched them carry boxes of food, butchered chickens, hams of pork and trays filled with fish protected with ice. From the back of one of the lorries, four soldiers manhandled a giant Christmas tree out onto the pavement and carried it in. Another truck drove up and more soldiers came out to offload its contents. They gently lowered dozens of wooden crates to the ground. Even from where we stood, we could hear the boxes tinkling when they were moved.

'Wine,' I couldn't help commenting.

'And the rest. For their Christmas. It's going to be very different from ours, don't you think?'

Isabelle pointed to an alleyway between the two parts of the building used as barracks. I could see movement on the ground, but it was a moment before I realised it was rats. Dozens of them, fighting over bins and piles of rubbish.

'We can at least boast the biggest rats in the city. No one else has rats because no one else has the wasted food that the Germans do. You look all over Paris. The only place you'll see rats is around anywhere the Germans are quartered. The rest of us are too poor even for vermin to care about.'

50

I found Marie Ferran at home when I tried knocking again after leaving the school. She made me wait in the street while she came downstairs. She was still wearing the slippers that Ulysse had given her when she'd come out of Cherche-Midi.

'You can buy me a coffee in Ulysse's bar,' she said. 'You can afford it with the money the Germans pay you.'

'They don't pay me anything. I'm employed by the city.'

'Keep thinking that, why don't you?'

We took a seat at a table and I ordered coffee for us both. This time we didn't get a brandy. I didn't need to hear her words to appreciate her underlying anger. She stirred her coffee like she was brewing a poisonous potion for me to drink. Her breath came in sharp, loud sighs.

'What do you want?' she asked me.

'You said you knew who I was. What did you mean by that?'

'Just that you're a cop.' She looked at me challengingly. 'Why are you here?'

'Checking up. Seeing how you are.' That earned me a snort. 'OK, I'm here to make sure you don't do anything stupid.'

'Because of the Boches murdering an innocent man while the police stood by and did nothing? The only stupid thing to do in this case is nothing.'

'No, Marie. That is the one stupid thing we should be doing.'

'Spoken like a good little collaborator.'

I tried not to let my own anger show, but I couldn't help fighting back. 'Collaborator? Which one of us two has been shot at by the Germans? Lived in a trench among the piss and shit and blood of other young men too scared to know how to deal with it? Spent the best part of two years in one of their prisons, thinking every day they were going to kill me? Not two months. Two years.' I stopped, my anger wound down with my outburst. 'I'm sorry.'

She was impassive with the coldness of stored rage. 'So, aren't you ashamed now of what you've become? One of their lapdogs. At their beck and call.'

I had to avoid losing my temper again; that simply stoked her own.

'Look at Jacques Bonsergent,' I tried to reason with her. 'He was probably innocent, but they responded with this degree of severity. Why? To show us what they will and won't tolerate.'

'And we're supposed to accept it? They execute a Frenchman for not kneeling down in front of them and doing as he's told, and you think we should just go along with it?'

'No, I don't think we should go along with it. But if we respond to this the wrong way, they will take more French people as hostages and they will kill them.'

'Then we respond more. And we kill another ten Germans.'

'And they kill another five hundred French people in retaliation. Fifty of ours dead for every one of theirs. What in the name of anything you hold sacred does that achieve?'

She slammed the side of her right hand into the palm of her left one. 'Direct action. That is the only way we will ever rid ourselves of the Nazis.'

'Yes, I agree.' Instinctively I'd lowered my voice. Despite the anger rising from each of us, we'd both kept our voices down. 'But we choose when. Save up your anger. Wait and strike when the moment is right.'

She looked surprised. I'd surprised myself. I'd never openly expressed anything like that before, not even to myself.

'And when will the moment be right? How many more Jacques Bonsergents will there have to be before the moment is right?'

'And how many more will there be if we simply kill Germans tit for tat? There is a German. A man called Dietrich Falke. Another parasite I suspect of murder, but I'm being stopped from questioning him. If I take the law into my own hands, the Germans will retaliate, so my job is to bring him to justice. Legally. Random killings are worthless, both because they're exactly that – random – and because they just lead to greater reprisals. That's a war we stand to lose. We have to use our heads.'

'I am. It's just that my head thinks differently from yours.'

I sat back, spent, and rubbed my eyes.

'Well, at least that's one thing you've got to be grateful for.'

The scorn open on her face, she stood up and left. In the doorway, she paused and turned back to me for a brief moment, her expression thoughtful.

'It's not really you that I know. It's Jean-Luc.'

51

'New rule for us to uphold, Eddie,' Dax told me in his office.

I'd tried to catch up with Marie Ferran after her comment in the doorway, but she'd been too quick. She'd got through the door to their apartment and bolted it behind her. The shop was shut, probably out of respect for Jacques Bonsergent, so I couldn't get hold of Yves or Pierre either. I knew I had to give up for the time being, but I wanted to know how she knew Jean-Luc.

'After what happened at the Rue de Buci market, the powers-that-be have realised that every queue's a political demonstration waiting to happen,' Dax continued. 'So now they want us to regulate queues by making shoppers collect a ticket and come back at an appointed time.'

Even half listening, I could see the obvious flaw. 'But they still have to queue to collect a ticket? Hard to see how that one's not going to work.'

'Less of the sarcasm, Eddie.'

'You know I'm right.'

'That's what's so annoying.'

I shook my head. I was sure the world over there were decisions taken by people who didn't actually do the job, but it just seemed like we had more than our fair share of it. And for once, I couldn't even blame the Occupier.

'What do you know about Sarah?' I asked. 'Was she put here by Judge Rambert?'

Momentarily taken aback by my shift, Dax laughed. 'Hardly. I had a good chat with her last week and she seems all right. Everyone's wary about talking politics these days, but it didn't strike me as though she'd be playing on the judge's team.'

'When was this?'

'Friday. We went for lunch. At one of the places that serves Germans, so no rationing. She seems pretty capable. I think she'll fit in.'

The day clicked. 'Friday? She was with you?'

'Yes, why?'

'Nothing.'

I left him and went to my own office deep in thought. So Sarah's fullness was thanks to Dax taking her to one of the restaurants that paid little heed to the niceties of permits and food tickets. The doubt that had been forming in my mind that she had been Thier's lunch partner was unfounded. And Dax didn't see her as Judge Rambert's plant, either. I watched her typing up a document from one of the other cops. I couldn't help feeling a sense of relief, but there was still something about her I wasn't quite sure of. Even so, I felt slightly happier about the job I had for her. Taking out the headed paper I'd stolen from Hochstetter's desk and a handwritten scrap of paper I'd sweated over in the early hours this morning while Dominique was asleep, I stood in front of her desk.

'Can you do me a favour?' I asked her.

She looked up. Her expression was neutral. 'What is it, Inspector Giral?'

'Eddie. Can you type this up on this paper for me? It's in German.'

She looked at the two items and back at me. 'You don't want me to ask why, do you?'

'No. Can you do it as soon as possible?'

She was saved from answering by Boniface coming into the room.

'Martin Hochstetter has been discharged from hospital,' he blurted out.

Glancing at Sarah, I pulled Boniface over to the other side of the room to talk.

'Is he still here in Paris?'

'As far as I know.'

Personally, I could have wished the younger Hochstetter as far away from Paris as possible, but the longer he was here, the greater the leverage I had over his brother, which was no bad thing.

'Are you going to question him again?'

He shook his head. 'I can't. The Germans won't let me near him now. He's telling them he was attacked in the street at night.'

'Christ's sake. Let's only hope we don't get another Bonsergent. And for even less cause.'

Rambert had a visitor when I went calling. Sitting in a second armchair facing the window, drinking from fine bone china, Otto Abetz was sharing the time of day with the judge.

'Well, this is all very nice,' I said after I was shown in.

'It was, Inspector Giral,' Rambert said. 'What can I do for you?'

'The Bouvier brothers. I'd like a stay of execution for a week while my investigation continues.'

He looked scornfully at me. '*My* investigation, I think you'll find. I am the instructing judge in this case. The sentence stands.'

'One week. I want to verify the involvement of other suspects in Cartier's murder.'

He waved me away with his left hand and took a sip from

the cup in his right. 'The case is closed, Inspector, the verdict handed down. Please do not trouble me again.'

I turned to Abetz. 'Is this the winning-over of the French people you had in mind, Herr Doktor Abetz?'

The ambassador finally acknowledged me. 'It is precisely what I had in mind. This will win the hearts and minds of the French people that we need in the Reich. The rest can simply fall by the wayside.'

'If you'd really like to know, Inspector,' Rambert added, 'Ambassador Abetz and I are here to discuss the use of targeted reprisals. Actions such as these against specific groups are precisely what we believe to be for the good of France.'

'Whose France?'

'Exactly,' Rambert said. 'These petty criminals are vermin. And, like vermin, they need to be taken off the streets and exterminated.'

The one image that came to my mind was that of the rats scavenging outside the German barracks in Isabelle Collet's school. I knew I had nothing more to gain from this meeting, so I turned away from them.

'I would say it's the rats that are attracted to the Occupier that are the real vermin we need to be expunging.'

52

'I have a meeting with Hermann Brandl,' I told the young woman on duty at the reception desk in the Lutetia. I was relieved it wasn't the Rottweiler of the last few days.

I'd picked up the fake letter from Sarah on my way from the Palais de Justice. The woman was examining it now, her nose twitching as she read it.

'It's a letter of introduction,' I explained to her. 'From Major Hochstetter of the Abwehr to Hermann Brandl, recommending that he receive me.'

She looked up at me and back down at the headed paper I'd whipped from Hochstetter. The scrawled signature at the bottom was copied from one of the missives he occasionally sent me. It would by no means have passed muster if compared with an original, but I was keeping my fingers crossed it would get me to the lift and Brandl's office. I just had to hope that Hochstetter didn't decide to waltz up at that precise moment.

She snapped the letter shut and directed me to where I could find Brandl. I hesitated at first, unsure I'd got away with it.

I found my way to an office on the third floor, well away from Hochstetter's, which was welcome news. Getting past dear old Hermann proved to be a lot less fraught. He simply glanced at the note and invited me to take a seat. I felt offended on Hochstetter's behalf.

'I'm looking to speak to Henri Lafont,' I told him.

'And why would that interest me?'

'I know he works with you, but that's not what concerns me. It's simply a case of elimination. I need to know where he was on the twelfth of December to corroborate a witness statement.'

I hadn't been convinced I'd get this far, so I was making it up as I went along. I'd decided on the spur of the moment to start with Lafont while I worked out how to move on to Morvan and Falke.

'Where did you learn that he worked with me?'

I leaned forward and gave my best smile. It wasn't a weapon I wheeled out often. I also brandished the fake note. 'It's all right. I work very closely with Major Hochstetter of the Abwehr. He trusts me.'

'He might, but I don't know you from Adam. Why should I trust you?'

'I'm not asking you to compromise any operation. I simply want to know where I can find Lafont so I can ascertain his whereabouts on the twelfth of December.'

He sat back. 'In that case, you do not need to question him. I know where he was on the twelfth of December. He was in Algiers.'

'He was where?'

'In Algiers. Indeed, he still is in Algiers.'

'What's he doing there?'

'That is no concern of yours. But I can assure you, he was not in Paris, or even in France, on the twelfth of December. I know, as I am the one who posted him there.'

It was my turn to sit back, only a lot less relaxed than my dance partner. In a single move, Brandl had snatched away my hottest long shot at finding an escape for the Bouvier boys. If Lafont wasn't even in the country, then he couldn't have killed Cartier.

'What is this in relation to?' Brandl asked. 'Perhaps I can shed some light on it.'

I had to tread more carefully. I now suspected Abwehr involvement in the new operation in Charonne, but I couldn't just come straight out and ask about Morvan or Falke, my real reason for being there. This was even more circumspect than dealing with Hochstetter.

'We're investigating a murder, and a new black-market operation in the Charonne district of the city.'

He looked slightly surprised. 'Ah, the Charonne.'

'There's a Frenchman I wish to question about the murder.'

'That would be Morvan.'

His directness took me by surprise. 'Would you be willing for me to interview him?'

'I am afraid you have the wrong end of the stick. This Morvan is not someone I work with.'

'He's not part of any Abwehr operation?' I baulked at saying the name 'Otto'.

It was his turn for the smile and the forward lean. 'I know of this black-market operation and of how troublesome it is proving to be. To my own interests, you understand.'

'If it's troublesome, why don't you shut it down?'

'That is much more complicated than you think. In my position, I am unable to take certain actions. Official actions, at least, that would put an end to this operation. However, the French police would be in a position to do something about it.'

'Not if we don't know how to find where they're operating from.'

He smiled again. 'That is where I can help you. This is the Abwehr. I know exactly the whereabouts of the warehouse in the Charonne where these criminals are based.'

He wrote an address on a piece of paper and handed it to me.

'And now so do you, Inspector Giral.'

*

In the lobby on the way out, I ran into Hochstetter. Not my one, though, but the younger version. He was as dismissive of me as he always was.

'I have nothing to say to you,' he told me, which was odd, as I hadn't indicated I wanted him to. That changed.

'But I have something to say to you. Drop any hint that you were attacked by French people.' I gestured at the uniforms in front of us, at the Nazi insignia staining everything it touched red and black. 'You stand to lose too much.'

'You are threatening me? You really think anyone in Germany will believe a French policeman?' He got more venom into the word 'French' than a rattled snake.

'No, but there will be people who doubt, and it will sow the seed.'

'I also see why my brother despises you French.'

'If it were up to us French, you wouldn't have anything to worry about. It's the Nazis, who you support, who are your only threat.'

53

I re-emerged into the cold from the Buzenval station in Charonne and took up a position on the opposite side of the street. The entrance to the Metro was on the corner underneath the fine Art Deco Palais Avron cinema, but that wasn't what I was looking at.

All through the journey from the Lutetia to Charonne, I'd had the feeling of being followed. The sporadic clacking of a pair of armistice shoes somewhere behind me that stopped whenever I did to look around. I waited, but no one who struck me as suspicious appeared.

Seeing nothing, I burrowed into the heart of Rue de Buzenval. The address on the piece of paper that Hermann Brandl had given me was on Rue des Vignoles, between Rue de Buzenval and Rue Planchat. I pondered the names as I hurried, in an attempt to ignore the sweat cooling on my back. Buzenval was yet another battle between us and the Germans – or Prussians back then – and Planchat was a priest shot during the Commune uprising. Not prescient, persistent. Nothing ever changes.

At one point, I stopped suddenly, convinced yet again that I could hear armistice shoes behind me, but there were a few other pedestrians, so it could have been anyone.

Turning into Rue des Vignoles, I found the street I wanted halfway between Buzenval and Planchat – Impasse Bergame

– wondering what it was with black marketeers and dead-end alleys. There was a message there if any of us had the time. The number I had was a single-storey block in a row of uneven buildings, like headstones in a disused graveyard. Ancient metal doors shrieked open onto a dingy hallway with a wooden door on the opposite side. The new kids in town hadn't yet learned the need for the heavy-duty locks that old man Cartier had used. It took me a good quarter of an hour, but I managed to pick the lock and get in, pulling the second door to behind me. Some light came in through a window on the wall farthest from where I stood, but my eyes couldn't adjust to the dark. I found a light switch and flicked it.

The light cast by two rows of overhead lamps was feeble, but it was enough to make me let out a low whistle. They might not have had the locks and bolts that Cartier had had, but these guys had three times the room, and each shelf was packed to over-flowing. In awe, I moved along rows of tinned food, clothes and shoes. They had butter and cheese and hams; bacon, potatoes and wine. They even had real coffee. I had no doubt it would be the stuff I'd enjoyed at Les Quatre Chats a week ago. As criminals went, they were evidently a cut above the standard. I wondered if that was evidence of a link with Falke. It suddenly occurred to me that I hadn't asked Brandl about Falke's involvement with the Abwehr. He'd distracted me by giving me the address to this place before I'd had a chance.

It was a sound that had become familiar to me over the last hour or so that pulled me out of my longing. A harsh clacking of wood on concrete. Armistice shoes. And they were inside the building.

Pulling my gun out of its holster, I hurried deeper into the room. I was too far from the switch and it was too late anyway to turn the lights out, but I found a door that opened into a tiny cupboard. Normally, I imagined, it would have held cleaning things, but it was stacked floor to ceiling either side with crates of tins. Stencilled on all the boxes on one side was one word: *Sardines*. I managed not to laugh. Steeling myself, I took a deep breath and edged my way into the narrow gap between the two sides and pulled the door to, keeping my gun hand towards the opening. Through the crack, I got a glimpse of the warehouse but not the entrance, so I couldn't see who it was who'd come in. Or how many.

The sound of the shoes grew louder. I had no idea if their wearer was trying to muffle the noise, as that would have been impossible with wooden soles on this floor. The clacking stopped and I waited. When I heard nothing more, I edged out to try and see, my gun hand pressed up almost to my nose because of the confined space.

A face appeared right in front of me and I almost pulled the trigger in shock.

'What the hell are you doing here?'

54

She'd taken her armistice shoes off to kill the noise they were making. The new shoes she'd bought because the Gestapo had taken her old ones away from her when she'd been held in Cherche-Midi.

'What are you doing here, Marie?'

'I've been following you.'

I took in a deep breath so I could squeeze out from between the wooden crates. My right hand with the gun in it was the only part of me outside the door frame.

'Give me a hand out of here.'

She looked at me for the briefest of moments and then slammed the door into my wrist and tore the gun out of my hand, before opening the door again. I yelled in pain. She backed away, holding my gun on me, as I slowly eased myself out of the cupboard.

'Don't be stupid, Marie.' I held my left hand out. 'Give it back to me.'

She backed away even further and shook her head. I tucked my right hand under my left armpit to soothe the smarting.

'I wanted to see who you were with,' she told me. 'Which of the Boches you were working for.'

'It's my job. I don't work for them.'

'Their murder of Jacques Bonsergent. It's an end. The French people who fell for the myth of the courteous blond warrior come to save us have now seen them for what they are. And it's up to us to act. Now.'

'Not like this, Marie. We talked about it. This will never work.'

'Jean-Luc was right about you.'

That hurt more than the door on my hand. 'What do you know about Jean-Luc? How do you know him?'

'We were at school together. In Ménilmontant, before we moved to live above the shop.'

'When did you last see him?'

'In June, when he was trying to join de Gaulle. We argued about it. He always was too timid when it came to his beliefs.'

'In June?'

'But I've heard from him since.'

I was too stunned to answer at first, and by the time I'd pulled myself together, we were both startled by the sound of gunfire from the alleyway outside. Marie wavered for a moment, but then moved away from the door, to the window on the far wall.

'Give me my gun,' I told her. 'Quickly.'

She shook her head and edged further towards the window. Hearing more gunshots, I ran to the door and looked out to see what was happening. The street door was half open and a man was standing just inside. He fired a single shot out into the *impasse* and ducked back in. In the brief moment of light from the open door, I saw who it was.

'Why are you here?' I called.

Boniface turned and saw me, a look of surprise on his face.

'We'll work that out later. Where's your gun? I've only got one round left.'

Cursing, I went back into the warehouse to see the far window open and Marie gone. My gun was nowhere in sight. I ran back out to where Boniface was peering out of the door. A shot zinged against the stone of the outside wall and he ducked back in. Whoever was out there obviously didn't know how low he was on bullets or they'd have rushed the building.

'Where's your gun?' he asked me.

'Long story.'

He looked at me in disbelief. I peered into the alley and took in the view. It wasn't good. Another shot rang out sharply, a counterpoint to the background throbbing of a Renault Novaquatre blocking the mouth of the narrow lane. Both front doors were open, shielding men with guns. A third man was sheltering in a doorway, a pistol pointed at us. I didn't recognise him, but the man behind the passenger door popped up for a brief moment.

'Morvan,' I gasped.

'I thought it was. Just as you described him.'

We looked at each other. We both knew it was time to sound the retreat. Stepping back inside, we pushed the door shut behind us. There was nothing to wedge it in place, so it would only hold them for a few seconds. As we went through the second door, I heard the outer metal doors being pushed open.

Inside the room, we cast about for a weapon, but short of opening a crate or two and throwing tins of sardines and bottles of wine at them, there was nothing we could use.

'The window,' I called to Boniface in a loud whisper.

Unknown to him, he followed Marie's route out of the warehouse. The wooden frame was very flimsy. These new gangsters had all the backing but not a lot of the nous. The door opposite opened as he was climbing out into the courtyard behind the building. I looked back to see the man from the doorway come in. He pointed the gun and told me to stay still. Deciding to risk it, I dived head-first through the open window and landed on the cobbles outside in a forward roll. A gunshot sounded and a bullet zinged out of the window and into the brick of the wall opposite.

'This way,' Boniface called.

There was a tiny lane between two buildings on the other side. We ran into it before the racketeers got to the window to fire a second time. Our escape took us into a parallel *impasse*, this one too narrow for a car, so we made for Rue des Vignoles, only to see the Renault reverse out of the Impasse de Bergame and into the main road, pointing in our direction.

We ducked back into the alley and in through a door that was opening. An elderly lady was coming out as we ran in, narrowly bowling her over. Her flat door was open into a little kitchen, and we raced through that and into a courtyard beyond. From behind, I heard one of the pursuers still on foot shouting a question at the woman.

The courtyard led to a third dead-end alley, this time with a slender service lane that took us out onto Rue Planchat. We could run more easily here, but it also meant the car chasing us could follow us down the street. One of those moments of idiotic thoughts overtook me, and I reflected on the Novaquatre. It was good and modern, and powerful enough, but it wasn't the Traction Avant that the really well-heeled criminal about town favoured. So not doing that well, I thought.

I saw it behind us turning into Rue Planchat as we came to a junction, so we ducked right and headed for the Metro station on Boulevard de Charonne. We slowed down slightly as we crossed the main road, grateful once again for the lack of vehicles, and could see the entrance to the station just a hundred metres ahead. Which was when a Traction Avant slewed across the road in front of the Metro and growled to a stop. In the front seat, next to a driver I recognised as the one who'd been firing at us from the doorway, Morvan was scanning the street.

'Not doing so badly then,' I commented.

'What?' Boniface asked.

I looked back to see the Novaquatre turning at the junction.

I also saw another sight.

'This way,' I called.

Sitting astride their *vélo-taxi* for a quick rest by the side of the street were the pair who'd given me a lift the previous week. The one with the cigarette cupped in his hand recognised me. I pushed Boniface into the back of the sedan chair and jumped in.

'Stop smoking,' I shouted at the first one, 'and head for Quai des Orfèvres.'

'What?'

I looked to either side of me. Neither of the cars following us was in a position to cross to where we were. Yet.

'Just move. And take the narrowest streets Paris has to offer.'

55

The two men driving the *vélo-taxi* were slowing down, their breathing ragged. They'd taken us down the smallest streets to be found, slotted in front of what buses there were and crossed junctions that weren't built to be crossed, but the two cars were constantly snapping at our heels. As hard as they tried, the riders could never put enough of a distance between us and our pursuers before having to re-emerge onto a wider road, the route they were taking telegraphing to the drivers in pursuit where we'd come out again.

In one of the brief moments when neither car was in sight, we came to a Metro entrance. I shouted to the two young men to stop for a second and told Boniface to get out. We'd disappear into the station and get a train to Quai des Orfèvres. But by the time Boniface had got out, the Traction Avant had already come into sight to our right. Despite the lack of traffic, it had stopped at the traffic lights, Morvan no doubt unwilling to attract too much attention. The lights changed and it moved towards us. It was too late for me to get out and not be seen escaping into the Metro.

I watched Boniface vanish into the entrance and shouted at the two men to keep going. Rolling their eyes and gasping, they saw the Citroën bearing down on us and started to pedal. The first turn to the right was another narrow road, so they took it and turned left almost immediately. We were outside a cinema.

'Stop,' I called to them.

I jumped out and ran inside, turning to see my two knights quickly start up again and duck down a side street to their right. I hoped they'd get away. The black marketeers were too interested in catching up with me to worry about them, I figured.

I showed my ID to the woman in the ticket booth and went into the auditorium. Behind me, I thought I caught a glimpse of the street door opening, but I didn't stop to look.

Inside the darkened room, the newsreels were showing. Goering was looking at a piece of art and hitching his trousers up. A chorus of coughs and sneezes started up, their volume low. Behind me, the two doors either side of the central seats opened. Pétain looked severely at the camera and at some PoW wives working in a factory. It was the only look he had these days. The sound of persistent colds from the cinema seats slowly rose in crescendo. I hadn't taken a seat and I passed a nervous-looking usherette in the aisle. Finally, the man himself appeared, Adolf doing his party trick of standing up in the back of a slowly moving car, and the auditorium gave up any pretence of decorum and broke into jeers and catcalls.

The lights went up and caught me in their spotlight. Behind me in the same aisle as me was Morvan. His hand was in his pocket but I knew it was holding his gun. Across from us in the other aisle was the Traction Avant driver. His hand was also in his pocket. I looked up and down my aisle, searching for a way out.

Sitting in a group next to where I was standing were three young men, still laughing at the images on the screen. The manager hurried down the aisle and tried to get past me to the stage. I stopped him and showed him my ID. He looked panicked.

'Do you want me to close this cinema down?' I asked him.

He gulped and shook his head.

I tapped the nearest of the young men on the shoulder. 'You're under arrest,' I told him. 'You and your friends.'

They stood up and protested. I heard muttered oaths directed at me from other seats in the cinema.

'Filthy collaborator,' one voice said louder than the rest.

I glanced at Morvan. He looked at me hard and then at his colleague in the other aisle, but didn't move.

I spoke to the manager. 'Go and ring Quai des Orfèvres and tell them to send a paddy wagon. I'm taking these three in. And consider yourself lucky I don't report you to the German authorities.'

That earned me a low-level hum of jeers from the auditorium to rival Adolf's.

The three young men began to look scared and stood closer together.

I stared again at Morvan. Holding my gaze for a moment, he turned to the driver and nodded, and began to retreat from the stand-off. I watched them leave by their own separate doors.

The manager looked at me.

'Well, what are you waiting for?' I asked him. 'Do as I said.'

56

'OK, you can stop here.'

The driver turned to me in astonishment. 'What for?'

'To let them out.'

Sandwiched between the driver and another uniformed cop on the long bench seat in the front of the paddy wagon, I watched them exchange incredulous glances with each other from either side of me.

Without another word, they got out on their respective sides of the cabin. I followed the passenger out and scanned the road to the front and back of the van. We were in what passed these days for a busy street next to a Metro station. I saw cyclists and pedestrians, one bus in the distance, the odd car or two – many of them requisitioned by the Germans and carrying new licence plates – and the burgeoning breed of *vélo-taxis* and cars with gas tanks perched precariously on the roof or in the rumble seat.

What I didn't see were any Traction Avants or Renault Novaquatres. I thought of Morvan and the cars he appeared to have. To be able to own one of those, licensed and running on the road, would almost certainly have required the collusion of the German authorities. Falke's partnership or business relationship with the robbing hood and his merry men would explain that, as well as his relationship with the authorities. Military was my guess, with the Abwehr as front-runner, although given

Hermann Brandl's eagerness to shop the operation in Charonne, that was in some doubt. Unless our Hermann had a rival within the Abwehr, working with Falke, who he was trying to sabotage.

'Open up, then,' I told the passenger when we got to the back of the paddy wagon.

He looked as puzzled as the three young men when the doors opened. It wasn't a bright day, but they emerged blinking from the dark of the van's interior, reluctant to climb down at first when they saw they were in the middle of a street. The driver barked at them to get out, and they hurriedly jumped down onto the road and gathered next to the pavement.

'No need to shout,' I told him.

He gave me as filthy a look as he dared.

'Where are you taking us?' one of the men asked.

'You're free to go. No charges. Clear off.'

They looked at each other uncertainly, no doubt convinced it was a trap, until the one who'd spoken nodded at his friends and started to walk away. The other two followed, back in the direction of the neighbourhood where I'd pretended to arrest them.

'Now if you wouldn't mind,' I told the driver, 'I could do with a lift home.'

They dropped me off and vanished down Rue de la Harpe. It wasn't a wide street and the driver had to negotiate it carefully. By my reckoning, I hadn't made a couple of new friends today.

Inside my flat, I removed the loose tile from above the wash-stand in my bathroom and took out two guns I kept there. One was a Manufrance, a tiny little pop-gun I'd stopped keeping in my car at the same time I'd stopped being able to keep petrol in my car. Rejecting that one, I took out a heavy old Luger and felt its weight in my hand. I'd taken it from a German officer in the last war when he'd tried to kill me with it. Luckily for me, it had jammed. Sadly it hadn't gone quite so well for the

German officer, which was why I came to be the one to have it twenty-five years later. I checked the magazine and put the gun in my shoulder holster, grabbing a box of bullets for good measure just in case. I recalled Ulysse having one like it on the shelf behind the counter in his café. We all collected souvenirs.

Boniface was at his desk in my office by the time I got to Thirty-Six.

'You've just answered my question,' I told him.

'What was that?'

'Whether you got back here in one piece.'

'What happened to you? I heard something about a cinema. And why didn't you have your gun?'

I noticed Sarah sit up at his question.

'You heard right about the cinema. My gun? I'd just been to see Otto Abetz, the German ambassador, and I wasn't allowed to take my gun with me, so I left it here.'

Both he and Sarah seemed to be expecting me to retrieve my pistol from my desk, so we waited in a mutual stand-off. The Luger weighed heavily in my shoulder holster. It was the wrong fit and I was worried it would fall out.

'What were you doing at the warehouse?' I asked Boniface. 'You're off the Cartier case.'

He shook his head. 'A fence in Charonne was selling goods from one of the burglaries in the Sixteenth – well, the Eighth this time – and something he said led me to the warehouse. There's talk of a new Breton gang in Paris. I'm thinking they might be the ones behind the burglaries.'

'They've moved from Brittany to Paris? Now? That hardly makes them the brightest shells on the beach. But if it is a Breton gang, we have to assume that Morvan is at the head of it.'

'Do you think the same gang could be behind the burglaries and the black-market takeover?'

I paused to consider. 'A lot to take on. They may just be

fencing the goods from the burglaries. That could tie in with the black-market operation, but I don't know that they'd actually be doing the burglaries themselves.'

While we were talking, Sarah covered her typewriter and left for the evening.

'Happy Christmas,' she said to both of us.

Her words gave me a jolt. I'd forgotten it was Christmas Eve. For the last fifteen years, I'd barely been aware of the holiday, often choosing to work instead. But this year, I had Dominique and I'd given no thought to what Christmas Eve and Christmas Day might be like. The first time I might have made something of this time of year and we had Occupiers, rationing and an execution, and little spirit to celebrate anything with the nothing we now had.

And I knew that before I'd be going back to Montmartre, I'd have to have a word with Dax about organising a raid. On Christmas Eve. For Christmas Day.

'You are going to be a popular boy,' Dax told me.

After that particular job, I left Thirty-Six and tried to feel even vaguely like it was Christmas. Breathing in the night air, feeling its cold anaesthetise my head, I felt nothing. I had a gun to find, questions to ask Marie about my son, and a station full of cops whose Christmas I'd just ruined.

'Merry fucking Christmas,' I muttered, surprising the only other pedestrian on the Quai des Orfèvres, a muffled man who hurried away from me.

I took the Metro to Bel Air to look for Marie, my gun and some answers. Getting on the train, I saw Sarah sitting in the carriage next to mine. She hadn't seen me. I found myself staring at her. There was still something about her I couldn't fathom.

She got off the train after two stops. On impulse, I followed her.

The streets on the Right Bank were busier than they had been around Thirty-Six, and it wasn't difficult to track her unnoticed in the dark. She came to a café and went in. I waited outside and spotted her moving through the dim light behind the plate-glass window.

She found the table she was looking for and I watched her sit down opposite another woman. They greeted each other like old friends. I stared at them through the Christmas Eve night.

The woman laughing and chatting with Sarah was wearing the grey uniform of a clerk in the Wehrmacht.

57

'Out,' Yves Ferran told me.

'Where out?'

I'd been hunting for Marie for an hour. Dominique would be wondering where I was. I knew I'd have to give up soon, but I was desperate to retrieve my gun and to find out what she knew about Jean-Luc.

'Just out. It's Christmas Eve.'

'You think I don't know that?'

'If you see her, let her know I want a word,' I'd told Ulysse earlier when I'd tried there for the second time. It was the message I'd been leaving everywhere I could.

He'd made a half-hearted attempt at putting up some sort of jollity for Christmas, but it was flat. I'd seen other shops and homes with decorations, but it felt like all we were doing was painting the walls of our prison.

'I imagine she knows,' Ulysse had told me, his voice colder than his celebration. My days of free and illegal brandy the police mustn't get to hear of were well and truly gone.

'Were you the one who got her out of Cherche-Midi, or was I?' I asked him as I left. It was cheap, I know, but I was fed up with the attitude that all us cops were skipping through the daisies with the Nazis.

I stood outside the café on Cours de Vincennes by the barracks in the school building and pulled my coat tighter around me. The cold had set in. There were just a few people on the street, and the few there were had congregated around one of the posters announcing Jacques Bonsergent's execution.

I went to take a look. The Germans had added a second poster to go with the first one. It threatened anyone caught vandalising or tearing down the first poster with being condemned to death. The notion of winning hearts and minds was an even more distant dream than my glass of brandy from Ulysse.

'That should help,' I couldn't help murmuring.

Someone next to me heard me and sidled away.

'Another cop,' someone nearby whispered.

'Collaborator,' a second voice said, the hate dripping from the word.

Another cop. Standing in front of the poster, guarding it against vandalism, was a uniformed policeman I recognised looking very uncomfortable. He caught my eye and I could see the relief in his expression. Mine was probably the only halfway friendly face he'd seen since he'd been standing there. Yet again, the Occupiers had exacted their justice and then pushed us to the front to face the baying mob. Although in this case it was more of a sullenly hostile mob.

'You were the one who arrested those women at the market,' a woman shouted at me. She turned around to include the rest of the crowd in her accusation. 'At the Rue de Buci. I was there, I saw him.'

'Boche-lover,' a man snarled. He and two others took a step closer to me and the other cop.

From the back, a stone was lobbed lazily through the air at us. It missed, but a small cheer went up.

'*Poulets*,' another voice called. 'You're no better than the Boches.'

A second stone flew at us. Harder this time. The young cop

behind me had to dodge to avoid it. I took a step back and stood next to him. The crowd followed, taking two steps forward towards us. Out of the corner of my eye, I saw the other cop undo the flap on the holster at his belt. I closed my eyes for a second. If I brought out the Luger, a German pistol, who knew what the mob might do. I stared at them glowering at me in nascent rage and considered whether I was going to have to draw my gun.

Underneath the murmur of abuse, a sound other than that of intensifying anger grew in the night air. As it became apparent what it was, everyone clustered around the poster slowly unclenched and began to look at each other in astonishment. The sound of scornful voices stopped, to be slowly overwhelmed by something altogether more harmonious yet incongruous. We all glanced around, trying to find the source, until all eyes alighted on the same place. It was coming from the school. Not the main building, but the annexe where the German soldiers were billeted.

Through the darkness, we heard the sound of singing.

'They're singing carols,' a voice said in surprise.

From the doorway of the barracks, 'Stille Nacht, Heilige Nacht' gently built in crescendo, the tune filling the night.

I took my hand off the Luger in its ill-fitting shoulder holster.

Alone among the crowd listening in silence, I turned back to look at the poster. All I could do was stare at it in horror and sadness and wonder how we were ever to reconcile this beautiful and innocent sound with such a horrendous act of violence and hate as the execution of a young man for jostling a soldier. And what it had done to the rest of us trying to get by together in the city.

58

'What are you complaining about? Christmas Day's come early.'

'Five o'clock early.'

I was in the back of a cop car on the way to Impasse de Bergame. A couple of trucks and three more cars filled with cops bristling with guns and antipathy towards me straggled in a line behind us as we turned into Rue des Vignoles. The streets were blackened and everything was shut up against the dark and the cold. The cop I was talking to was a sergeant in the front passenger seat who looked like he'd been around almost since the last time the Germans came calling and he still harboured the grudge. Only now it was me providing safe haven for his ill humour.

'Think of Boniface,' the young detective next to me told him. 'He's got two families he's missing.'

The other three occupants of the car laughed, even Courtet once he got it. Boniface was a legend at Thirty-Six for having a wife and a mistress and children with both of them.

'Well, that's two families whose Christmas we're improving then,' I commented.

No one laughed. No one was of a mind to laugh at anything I'd had to say since gathering them all the previous evening to tell them about this morning's dawn raid. I'd tried to press-gang as many single guys as I could because it was Christmas, but

I was happy to make an exception in Boniface's case. Call me old-fashioned, but two families was one too many. Or in my case, two too many.

The only person less impressed with my news of the raid had been Dominique.

'I'll be back before you know it,' I'd told her.

'And if you're not, Eddie Giral, *you'll* know it.'

The first three cars entered the alleyway; the fourth stayed at the entrance, blocking it off. The trucks pulled up on Rue des Vignoles, waiting to be filled with all the goodies from the black marketeer's store. Minus whatever we could lift for ourselves. I'd promised Dominique I'd bring back a tin of sardines, which went some way towards mollifying her. Apparently, stealing from a black marketeer was the right thing to do. I wished I'd known that with the butter.

There was no delicate lock-picking this time, just a couple of the biggest bruisers putting their shoulders into it and acres of splintered wood on the concrete floor, even though they could just as easily have turned the handle. They stepped back and let me in first. I brushed past them and found the light switch and turned it on. The cops in the small hallway crowded in behind me, pushing me through the door.

'Joyeux crapping Noël,' the sergeant muttered.

The warehouse was emptier than my stock of goodwill.

Every single shelf had been cleared, with not a tin or empty box to show that anything had ever been there. I hurried to the cupboard where Marie had slammed the door on my hand and yanked it open. It was empty. This was going to be a seriously sardine-free Christmas chez Dominique.

'They've emptied the place,' I said, simply voicing a thought out loud to vent my frustration.

'You don't fucking say,' the sergeant replied.

In the next breath, he ordered the cops to leave the building.

'Or have you got any other ideas, Inspector?' he asked me.

I looked away in despair at the empty room and turned back to him. 'Send them home.'

I stayed. Not just because I didn't want to share a car with three cops who felt I'd ruined their Christmas, but because I had a gun to find. I tried calling at the Ferran family residence, but there was no reply. Either they were out or they weren't answering at this time of day on Christmas morning. I went for a walk in the cold for an hour, hoping that dawn would finally show, and tried again, but there was still no reply.

The sun was only just beginning to rise as I descended into the mouth of the Metro to face the ride to Montmartre and a Dominique without the sardines she'd been promised.

59

Some people are never angry in the way you expect them to be. And that's as ambiguous a statement as any.

'Don't worry about the sardines, Eddie.' Dominique greeted me with a hug and a kiss. 'I wasn't really expecting any. Anyway, we've got food.'

'We have?'

'We'll be fine.'

'I'm sorry I had to go out. If it's any consolation, half the Paris police force hate me more than you do right now.'

'I don't hate you.'

And that was about as good as it got. Dominique played the Sidney Bechet song again on the gramophone. I'd learned by now that the woman singing 'That's What Love Did To Me' was Lena Horne. She had a great voice, but it still wasn't my type of song. I wanted to read. I was finding this palaver of being with someone all day difficult.

'Can we turn the music off?' I asked her.

'What's wrong with it?'

'There's nothing wrong with it. I'd just like a break from it. I can't think with music playing all the time.'

She got up and turned the music off before sitting back down heavily on the armchair opposite me.

'All right, Eddie, what do you want to think about?'

'I don't want to think about anything, Dominique, I'd just like a bit of quiet for a while.'

I have no idea how it happened and at what stages it got progressively worse, but the conversation was one of those that steadily takes you down a path into a labyrinth that is only ever going to hold the Minotaur of your choice at the end of it. Mine was a question asked by Dominique when the acidity eating away at us had reached its boiling point.

'Does Sylvie know about Jean-Luc? About him being missing?'

'I don't know. Why are you concerned?'

'She has a right to know. Is she in Paris?'

I shook my head. 'She left before the Germans came.'

'Well, do you know if she came back?'

'I haven't got a clue.'

'And you haven't bothered to find out? To tell her about her own son?'

'Why are you worrying about my ex-wife? You don't know her, you've never met her.'

'She's Jean-Luc's mother, Eddie. She has a right to know.'

'So you keep saying.'

'Is that enough thinking for you now? Are you glad you made me turn my music off?'

I got up and went to fetch my coat. 'I'll go out. You can play all the music you want.'

I took the Metro to the Fifth. There was just me and some lonely guy riding the rails rather than face home. I didn't go to my flat, but to the Jardin du Luxembourg. I didn't go there to read but to walk. The bitter cold and emptiness of the park served my mood. The wind sent ripples across the water of the pond and I sat for over an hour watching the shapes shift and echo back and forth across the surface. I tried to find a pattern in them, but every time I thought I made one out, something happened to change it and send the various pools and waves skittering off in a false direction.

It became too cold to sit and I wanted to immerse myself in my streets. Leaving by a gate on the east side, some distance from my flat on Rue de la Harpe, I started to wend my way north towards home. I was in no hurry. The day was cold but crisp. I saw no more uniforms – ours or theirs – and I felt a longing to take my time, to stay.

Sylvie had criticised me for moving to the Fifth after I'd left her and Jean-Luc, saying it wasn't the right part of town for a cop, but it was the first Paris I'd known. It was the site of the hospital where I'd been sent from the front line in 1915 to recover from shell shock. The hospital where I'd met Sylvie. The one place I'd felt anything approaching safe when I'd decided to immerse myself in my own downward spiral of danger. Cocaine, me and the jazz clubs and Corsican gangs of Montmartre in the 1920s hadn't been a good mix. Part of me wondered if that was the reason for the slight unease I felt in Montmartre now, with Dominique; a reminder of that past.

I knew I wouldn't give up my flat, and I wondered if I'd be back soon, at least when spring came, if not sooner. In my heart, I knew I wouldn't be doing this if it weren't for the cold and the lack of coal. I imagined Dominique felt the same. Part of me hoped she did.

'Or you just don't know what it is you want,' I caught myself saying out loud.

My walk took me past the Sorbonne. On the corner of the square in front of the old university building and Boulevard Saint-Michel, the Café d'Harcourt stood dark and empty. There'd been a fight between students from the university and German soldiers on Armistice Day. Not so much a protest as a bar brawl. In response, the German authorities had closed down the café, along with all the other cafés in the area. The others had since reopened, but the Café d'Harcourt was completely shut up as I passed.

The moment stopped me in my tracks. I asked myself what it was about the Bonsergent case that should make it any different. German soldiers had actually been hurt in the incident in the café, rather than just one NCO being jostled – and not even by Bonsergent by all accounts, yet they'd singled him out for execution. He was an example. The initial charm and courtesy shown by the occupying soldiers in the early days had gone, and the Nazis were showing their teeth. They were in charge and they were going to bloody well make sure that we – and Vichy – knew it.

The moment gone, I went home and built a fire in the grate. As the room warmed, I looked at my bookshelves, but there was nothing I felt able to read. I still had the tin of unidentified meat I'd bought the last time I'd sought refuge from sound in my flat. I doubted I'd trouble the tin-opener this evening.

Sound came. A knock at the door. I sighed, knowing we had to talk.

I opened it expecting to find Dominique on the landing.

Only it wasn't her.

60

'I'm afraid I don't have any coffee. Not real coffee, anyway.'

Nonplussed, I hesitated at the door before standing aside to let my visitor in.

'That is of no matter. I bring a gift of my own.' Hochstetter went into my living room and held up a bottle of whisky. 'Perhaps you have glasses.'

I fetched two tumblers from the kitchen and went back to find him still on his feet, looking at my bookshelves. It was Christmas Day and he was in uniform. I wondered if he owned real clothes.

'This is a pleasure,' I told him, pouring us a glass each of his whisky.

'Is it?' He sat down – my good chair – and looked around. 'This is all rather bijou, as I think you would call it.'

I also took in a glance at my small flat. 'This is all rather normal, as we actually call it. Have you got nowhere else to go on Christmas Day?'

In reply, he held up his glass of whisky, before toasting it with mine. 'It is a goodwill call, Édouard. I hope you can take it as that.'

I felt oddly guilty. 'Thank you for getting Marie Ferran released.'

He nodded without saying a word. The thought suddenly struck me that Hochstetter – and possibly other German soldiers – were sad and lonely exiles in their conquered land. He was as much an outsider in Paris as I was, as much a prisoner as we were. And now, for once, he needed my understanding rather than vice versa. The guilt evaporated.

'I still want to question Dietrich Falke,' I added. 'You managed to get Marie Ferran released by the Gestapo. Wouldn't this be a less complicated matter?'

'Marie Ferran is a French citizen, a student. She had been held long enough considering the nature of her crime. Her release was not as complicated as you might think. Herr Falke, on the other hand, has the protection of the German authorities. As such, they would need compelling evidence of a crime to allow you to question him.'

'Will you at least try?'

He nodded again. His hand as he held the glass trembled almost imperceptibly. 'I heard about your incident with a Jewish shop in the Sixth.'

'How did you know about that?'

He smiled for the first time, a rueful half-smile. 'I am an officer in the Abwehr. Similarly, I am aware that you now know that this Morvan you are so keen to apprehend has nothing to do with the Abwehr. And that your Henri Lafont has a watertight alibi for the murder of Cartier. You met Hermann Brandl. Rather cunningly, I might add.'

'I'd still like to know Falke's relationship with the Abwehr.'

He very nearly allowed himself a smirk. 'Haven't you worked it out yet? Falke does not work with the Abwehr. He merely comes to the Lutetia to drink as he likes the bar there. Almost as much as he likes to drink, as your own officer will testify. The good Herr Doktor Falke works with the Kriegsmarine. He supplies them with goods in the way Henri Lafont previously did with the Abwehr. They are odious characters for us to be consorting with, but they are the reality now, unfortunately.'

'Why are you telling me this?'

'Don't be disingenuous. I have told you this because it is no skin off my nose for you to know – quite the opposite, in fact. It might stop you from pestering me with your nonsensical demands on my time and energies.'

We both took a sip of the whisky. I tried in vain to hide how good it tasted.

'Just some thugs,' I said, returning to his original comment. 'The incident with the Jewish shop.'

'I gather a Wehrmacht officer helped you defuse the situation. As I have said to you on previous occasions, you would do well to wish for my continued presence here. And that of the Abwehr and the Wehrmacht. Were Herr Doktor Abetz to have his way, the running of the city would be in the hands of staunch Party members. You would do well to continue to work with me against that possibility.'

'Is that why you're here?'

'As we are discussing dangerous bedfellows given the times we are living in, I would strongly recommend that you be very wary of getting into bed with Herr Doktor Abetz.'

'Better being screwed by the devil I know?'

'Crude, but accurate.' He reached out for the bottle and topped up our glasses. 'I am sure I am not giving anything away to you by now when I say that our institutions are riven with inter-departmental rivalries. Not to mention deep personal rivalries. Between Party and non-Party members of the Wehrmacht, as you saw Abetz trying to capitalise on at dinner, and between the Wehrmacht and Abwehr and the other branches of the military and civil organisations. You may be tempted by the bounties that someone like Abetz might appear to be offering you, but they are bounties that will come at a price and that will not last.'

'Divide and rule? I'm afraid we in France have more than enough experience of our own there.'

'That is as may be, Édouard, but I would strongly urge you to maintain your distance from Ambassador Abetz and his coterie. Theirs is a power struggle that will profit you in no way.'

I gazed at him frankly. 'I will do what I need to do to see justice done.'

He looked sad suddenly. 'I feel we have found a modus vivendi that is mutually beneficial. It would be a pity for either of us to take advantage of the current or any other dilemma that would alter that.'

I studied the rich gold of the whisky and the tears it left as it ran down the inside of the glass. I don't know how far I'd go in saying it was mutually beneficial, not normally, but his words struck me that just as I was forced to work with him, in his way he was forced to work with me. Our need for support was, if not mutually beneficial, then at least mutual.

'How is Martin?' I asked, in a move that was intended for my benefit. 'I understand he's been discharged from hospital.'

'My brother is all right, thank you, Édouard.'

'I understand he's claiming that he was attacked in the street. You do realise that that could lead to another situation like this one with Jacques Bonsergent?'

'I am all too aware of that. I am doing my utmost to ensure that he does not allow the matter to escalate. At the moment, he is saying that he cannot be certain his attackers were French, which is as good as we can hope for.'

'My hope is that you both remember what is at stake here.'

My words hung in the air between us, until we were both startled by the sound of a key in the lock. Fighting down panic, I turned to see Dominique walk into the room. She stopped, a look of shock on her face when she saw the colour of the uniform sitting next to me. I got up quickly and spoke first.

'Madame Mendy, I do apologise. I've got your money here.'

I brushed past her to fetch my jacket, hanging on the hook

in the hall, and took out my wallet. Both Hochstetter and Dominique remained silent.

'I'm sorry, I haven't introduced you. This is Major Hochstetter, of the Abwehr, and this is Madame Mendy, my cleaner.' I turned to Dominique, hoping her anger wouldn't rise. 'I'm so sorry, Madame Mendy, I forgot to leave the money last time you were here. I apologise for you having to come out on Christmas Day to collect it.'

I took five francs out of my wallet and handed them over to Dominique. She took them, her face impassive, and folded them into her coat pocket.

'Thank you, Inspector Giral. I hope you enjoy your Christmas.'

I saw her out, trying to make eye contact when we were out of Hochstetter's vision, but she wouldn't look at me. Watching her disappear down the stairs without a backward glance, I wanted to whisper something at her, but I didn't dare.

I returned to the living room, expecting Hochstetter to have seen through my charade. He regarded me wryly from my arm-chair, before looking around the room and speaking.

'You have a cleaner?'

As a last resort, I used my key.

I'd tried knocking on the door, but there was no reply, so I unlocked it and let myself in.

'Dominique,' I called.

For once, her flat was silent. It was an experience that was as unfamiliar as it was unsettling. I made a quick tour of the rooms, but they were empty. On the table in the hall I found the five francs I'd given her and swore. She'd obviously been home since I'd pretended to Hochstetter that she was my cleaner, and gone back out again. I tried knocking on the Goldsteins' door. Mr Goldstein answered nervously but said that he hadn't seen Dominique. Behind him, I glimpsed his wife with a tray bearing just two cups, so I presumed he was telling the truth when he said she wasn't with them.

Giving up, I took the Metro again. Not back home, but to Bel Air, where I banged on another door like a lovelorn boy. Only this time it was a gun I was searching for. There was no reply at the Ferrans'. Next door, Ulysse's café was shut up. I didn't know his address to ask him about Marie. I doubted he'd help if I did know where to find him.

Walking back up through the narrow steps to the Cours de Vincennes, I saw the same young cop on duty in front of the Bonsergent poster. He had a lonelier job than I did.

'Much trouble?' I asked him.

'Not now.' He looked cold and miserable. He gestured at the ground around him. 'No one comes near now, not with me here. This is what people did in the night.'

At the foot of the column holding the two posters, the original and the subsequent threat, was a bank of flowers, some real, many made of paper. There were tricolores and rosettes and messages of love and anger. I went to stand next to him.

'You go home,' I told him. 'I'll stay here until your relief comes.'

61

The morning after Christmas brought news of three deaths –
one that had happened and two that were going to.

'Jean Fabre is dead,' Boniface told me in Dax's office.

'Who?'

I was distracted. I'd spent the night in my own flat but couldn't
decide on what book I wanted to read, so I'd sat and stared
instead at the shadows and flames of the ill-gotten fire burning
in the grate. I'd woken shivering at four in the morning, the fire
burned out, and couldn't get back to sleep. In the morning, as
I had no gramophone, I listened to the radio for the first time
in over a week. When the Germans had first arrived, *Radio-
Paris* had played music and tried to make us believe that life was
going on as normal, but as winter approached, they'd dropped
the façade and become more political, tending not surprisingly
towards the Nazi. They'd even told us we'd forgotten how to
smile and were taking advantage of the magnanimity of the
victor. I switched off almost immediately, preferring the heavy
sound of silence. I was missing Dominique's endless music, but
at least I'd had the bottle of whisky that Hochstetter had left to
sing me a soulful tune.

'Jean Fabre,' Boniface repeated. 'The Frenchman who was
attacked with Martin Hochstetter. So now it's a murder investigation.'

'Can you run it alongside the investigation into the burglaries?' Dax asked him.

'Yes. We have to assume the burglars are the ones who beat the two men, so it's the same case.'

'All right by me,' I commented, racing in my head through the implications for my own investigation.

'Eddie and I were discussing the possibility of some new Breton gang being behind both the burglaries and the black-market operation in Charonne,' Boniface added.

'Maybe not the burglaries themselves, but fencing the stolen goods,' I corrected him.

Dax looked at me. 'Is this the Breton gang you want for the Cartier murder? Do you think the Bouvier brothers are involved?'

'I think the Bretons, specifically Morvan, are definitely in the frame for the black-market set-up, and for Cartier's murder, but I can't see the brothers being part of that. They're too lowlife to be working with Morvan.'

'What about the brothers for the burglaries?' Boniface asked.

'Can't be them. They were in prison when at least one of the burglaries was committed. The one where Fabre was killed.'

'Could still be them working with the Bretons,' Dax commented. 'Either way, the murder of Fabre is your priority, Boniface, with the burglaries alongside that. Eddie, you're still to focus on the Cartier murder and the black-market operation.'

'Suits me,' I said.

Boniface spoke to Dax. 'I want to interview Martin Hochstetter again.'

Dax sighed. 'Not a German, Boniface. And SS.'

'What on earth for?' I asked Boniface. 'You've already questioned him.'

'Because it's a murder inquiry.'

'He's unlikely to have any more information just because the other guy died.'

CHRIS LLOYD

'I've got to agree with Eddie,' Dax said. 'I don't see what new information you'll get from him. It's going to be more trouble than it's worth.'

You can say that again, I thought. The last thing I wanted was Boniface's heavy boots trampling over the delicate situation with Martin Hochstetter and ruining the leverage I had over his brother.

Boniface was angry, the first time I'd seen it. 'It's a murder. We would always go back to interview a key witness.'

'That was before the Germans came to town,' I reminded him. 'Those rules are long gone, especially where they're concerned.'

We both looked at Dax, waiting for his judgement. I still had my coat on and was actually getting uncomfortably hot. He'd had a small stove put in his room and had even managed to get a coal ration from somewhere, but I couldn't remove my coat as the Luger was the wrong shape for my holster. It had a longer barrel and a thinner butt than my service pistol and moved about in there. I didn't dare let it attract Dax's attention and have him asking where my proper gun was.

Dax looked thoughtfully at Boniface. 'Leave it for a day or two. We'll reconsider then if you're not getting anywhere with it.'

Boniface looked annoyed as we left Dax's office. I did my best to hide the relief I felt. I couldn't have Boniface rocking my sleigh while I had the upper hand with Hochstetter.

'You know it makes sense to interview Martin Hochstetter,' he told me. 'You would.'

'You heard Dax. Give it a day or two.'

'This is my case, Eddie. The first I've led. I don't want you fucking it up for me.'

We were at the threshold to my office and I grabbed hold of his arm. 'Careful how you speak to me, Detective.'

In the office, Boniface put his coat on, ready to go out. For once, he wasn't talking.

'You don't need to go through interviewing Martin Hoch-stetter again,' I told him. 'And believe me, if you try, it will only bring you headaches from his brother and from the Nazis.'

'When did that ever stop you, Eddie?'

62

Sarah left the room when I had my visitor.

He sat in the chair opposite my desk with his grey uniform and silver cigarette case and looked incongruous. Behind him, Boniface's desk was empty too, the door to my office shut. He looked at me quizzically; his expression had little of his usual ridiculing sense of power, but it had regained a lot of the underlying confidence that had been missing yesterday.

I'd summoned Hochstetter to my office, just like he'd sent a brace of soldiers for me so many times. I'd called him at the Lutetia, but I hadn't sent a car for him. The Abwehr could pay for its own fuel.

He sighed and lit a cigarette, looking around for an ashtray for the spent match. He picked one up off Boniface's desk and put it down in front of him on mine.

'What is it you wish to see me about, Édouard?'

'I wanted to help, Major. To keep you up to date with the investigation into the attack on your brother.'

'I thought all that had been settled.'

'I'm afraid that Jean Fabre, the man in bed with your brother at the time of the assault, has died.'

He winced, hiding it behind eyes half closed by tobacco smoke. 'I fail to see how I might help with that.'

'I'm not working on the investigation, Major, which is

unfortunate for you and your brother as it means I'm unable to determine which way it goes. I know that my colleagues here want to question Martin again, and Commissioner Dax is keen to request that of the German High Command. I imagine it's in your interest for me to prevent that as far as I can.'

'You are being vulgar, Édouard. What is it you want?'

I'm also lying through my teeth, I thought, but you're not to know that.

'Korvettenkapitän Thier. You know him well, don't you?'

'Since our school days.'

'So you'd have some influence with him. You told me that Dietrich Falke works with the Kriegsmarine. I think it's possible that Thier might be able to shed some light on Falke's activities. Can you use your relationship to sound him out? Find out what you can about his knowledge of Falke's involvement in the black market. And Cartier's murder.'

'Abuse a friendship, in other words?'

'To continue to make sure that we're both protected. This information will help to ensure that the wrong knowledge doesn't fall into the wrong hands.'

'My brother, you mean.'

'I didn't say that.'

Hochstetter took a final drag on his cigarette and stubbed it out, his eyes locked on mine at all times. He made to light another, but thought better of it, slowly replacing it in the silver case and returning that to his jacket pocket. He paused, his gaze unsettling.

'You see, Édouard, I know your secret.'

He looked at me, inviting me to break cover. He'd evidently seen through my charade with Dominique.

'We all have secrets,' I told him.

'That is quite true. I don't doubt you have more than the one I now know.'

'As do you. Your divorce, for instance.'

'That is hardly a secret. It is simply that you have only recently become aware of it.'

He changed his mind and took his cigarette case out again. The wait while he went through his lighting-up ceremony was interminable. I sat back, digging my nails into my palms to remain calm. This was the power of Hochstetter.

'I'm sure you have other secrets waiting to be discovered, Major.'

He pulled on the tobacco and squinted at me through the smoke. 'You have a son, Édouard. His name is Jean-Luc and you have been estranged from him for most of his life.'

I kept cool and held his gaze. Not Dominique. Worse. 'That's no secret. You simply could have asked. As you say, we're estranged. I haven't seen him since he was a child.'

'We both know that is not true. He came to see you shortly after we liberated Paris.'

'Liberated?'

'From yourselves.' He slowly inhaled, making me wait. The urge to slap the cigarette out of his mouth was almost unbearable. 'You helped him escape the city. When he was a deserter. On the run from both his own army and the German army.'

I slowly exhaled, relaxing the grip of my fists, and looked out of the window. It was a dark day, the roads quiet, the trees skeletal.

'I know Martin's secret,' I reminded him.

'Indeed you do.' He calmly stood up and put his army coat on. 'But one day, Martin will no longer be in Paris and I will still know you have a son. How do you think that might work out, Édouard?'

63

Dax had another piece of information for me the moment Hochstetter left my office.

'The Bouvier brothers. Their execution has been set for seven o'clock on Saturday morning.'

I looked at him. His face registered the same disbelief I felt.

'I'll go and see Judge Rambert.'

He shook his head. 'Don't waste your time. He's never going to listen to you. You go and try and find this Morvan. I'll pay the judge a visit.'

On the way to Fresnes, I stopped at a telegram office. The Occupiers had finally allowed us to send telegrams from the Occupied Zone to the Unoccupied Zone. Post between the two zones had been one of the first things the Germans had banned, but they'd reinstated it of sorts in September. At the time, I'd sent my parents a ninety-centime official card, which was all we were allowed, a standard form with words to cross out that allowed you to say very little. Just that you were healthy or ill, wounded or dead. It didn't go far in bringing us any closer to-gether. I'd had one back in reply, basically telling me they were still alive. This month, though, the Germans had allowed us to send telegrams, so I sent a carefully worded one simply asking how Jean-Luc was. I'd wait to see if they got it and if they'd reply. I gave Thirty-Six as the return address.

At the prison, I had to compose myself. My mind was still

reeling from Hochstetter's revelation, but I knew I had to focus on the brothers and finding out who really did kill Cartier. The one problem was that I couldn't see Firmin, so I had to make do with Jacquot.

'Firmin's got it wrong,' he insisted. 'We were arrested in the Eighth.'

'No you weren't, Jacquot. I've seen the charge sheet from your local nick. Forget it. This Morvan, the Breton I saw you with, you must have some way of getting hold of him.'

Impatiently I watched him rack his brains. 'I don't know, Eddie. He just came and offered us a job. Then you came along. He said he'd see us in Les Quatre Chats.'

'And the name Falke really doesn't ring a bell? You've got to help me, Jacquot. Where were you the night Cartier was killed?'

'I told you, the Eighth. In the local nick. We were drinking.'

'For Christ's sake, Jacquot, no you weren't. And that's why you're here now. You were caught outside after curfew by the Germans last Tuesday and taken to your local nick. I want to know about the night of Cartier's murder.'

He looked thoughtful. 'I told you. The Eighth.'

'You know you're for the blade on Saturday morning, Jacquot. Tell me where you were, and don't say the Eighth again or I'll throttle you before you get anywhere near the guillotine.'

'We were in the Eighth. It was our local nick last week.'

I held my head in my hands. 'What do you mean, your local nick last week?'

'That's why we're here now.' His expression was bright, eager to please. 'But we were in the Eighth when Cartier got killed.'

I looked at him sharply. 'Are you saying you've been arrested twice?'

'Yeah. Once last week; we were drinking in Les Quatre Chats and then down by the river and lost track of time, so the Boches took us in.'

'I don't care. When was the other time? The night of Cartier's murder?'

He looked like he was counting the days. 'Yes, I think so. That was in the Eighth. We were arrested by the *poulets* that time. Bastards.'

'So you were in a cell all night?'

'Yes.'

'The night Cartier was murdered? Thursday the twelfth of December?'

He smiled. 'No, the night before. It was the Wednesday night we were arrested in the Eighth.'

I closed my eyes and cursed. He'd found and lost an alibi for them both in the swish of a blade.

'Oh Jacquot.'

My next call was as hopeless as my last.

From across the road in a back street by the Gare d'Austerlitz, I watched someone who wasn't doing his job properly. If he had been, I wouldn't have been watching him. Crossing the road, I grabbed him by the scruff of his neck and shouted, 'Boches.'

His two friends running the find-the-lady scam quickly picked up their cards and money from an upturned wooden box and legged it, leaving behind half a dozen gulls looking wistfully at their losses.

'Morning, Pepe,' I told my new companion.

'Nothing to do with me, Eddie. I'm as offended by con artists as you are.'

He even managed a harrumph. He surreptitiously straightened the cloth cap that was pulled low over one eye – his gang code – and shrugged further into a stolen coat that had been made for someone ten meals bigger.

'Don't care. What do you know of this Breton gang and its

leader, guy called Morvan? And let's take the honest-Eddie-I-don't-know-anything bit as read, shall we?'

He looked around to make sure none of his scam pals was listening. 'Just that they're new in from Bretonia.'

'It's called Brittany.'

'That's the place. What I heard is that they decided there were rich pickings here with the black market and came for a piece of it.'

'They into anything else, Pepe? Burglaries? Fencing?'

'Not that I've heard. They're setting up big in a small way, if you know what I mean. Good stuff in just one part of the city.'

'With a view to expanding, I imagine. How about a German called Falke? Know him? Tall, thin as a miser's dog. Looking to work with some of our local philanthropists.'

He shrugged.

'Know anything about these burglaries in the Sixteenth?' I asked him.

'Nothing. I haven't heard any of the usual lot bragging about them.'

'Could it be the Bretons?'

Again the shrug that made him vanish inside his oversized coat.

'You hear anything, you let me know,' I told him.

He wiped his nose copiously on his purloined sleeve and nodded. 'You have my word, Eddie.'

'Good enough for me.'

The evening was already drawing in by the time I got to Charonne, and I had one more hopeless call to make.

The city smelled different. There was no petrol or diesel clogging up the light night mist, but that also meant no life on the streets. No scent of perfume on diners passing by, no strong aroma of food coming from homes or restaurants, no smell of coal burning in grates as everyone eked out what little they had. A necrosis of everything that made Paris what it once was, even in the poorest parts of town.

I stopped short of Les Quatre Chats before going in and took one last look around me. One of the first things that always struck me in certain parts of the city was the lack of Germans. My job took me from one end of Paris to another. In all sorts of ways. From the Sixteenth and affluence in the west to Charonne and gaunt people barely scraping a living in the east. From fine houses and apartments coveted and commandeered by the Occupiers to dirty streets and crumbling blocks that held no interest for them. The Germans rarely set foot in what they probably saw as the more dangerous working-class – and Communist – suburbs of the north and east of the city unless they had the misfortune to be billeted there. Instead, they quite wisely chose to stay in the smarter, arguably less tense areas. The girls' school on Cours de Vincennes where some of the German troops were garrisoned was so far south of this street that I imagined the soldiers would rarely venture out into the local neighbourhood. It was easy at times almost to forget they were here.

But then I pushed open the door into a grim café to try and find out what I could about a German trader who'd come here with the sole intention of fleecing the city and a gangster willing to get into bed with the Nazis to skim off whatever was left, and find out which one of them had killed yet another leech before two innocent dupes were executed for a crime I knew they didn't commit.

'Good evening, Inspector Giral,' Claude announced in a loud voice before the door had closed behind me.

The place hushed in an instant.

'And a good evening to you all,' I told the room, taking advantage of Claude's getting everyone's attention. So much discomfort in such a concentrated space was almost as much of an aphrodisiac as whisky. 'Don't mind me, I've seen who I want to see.'

I walked along the line of wine-drinkers at the bar. Just four of them this early in the evening, two separate and two together. One of the two men who were sitting together, hard-faced with pockmarked skin and nicotine fingers, rang a bell. Stopping next to them, I asked if I could see their papers. They showed them to me. Sure enough, the one I recognised was a name I'd nicked in the distant past for thieving, François Janvier. Back in the day, he'd run in a gang with the Bouvier brothers.

'Working for Morvan?' I asked him.

'I went straight years ago.'

'So you've got a job then?'

He shook his head. 'Renault. Laid off because of the Boches.'

'How are you earning a living?'

I sensed rather than heard a noise from the end of the bar nearest the door. I looked up in time to see the farthest of the four drinkers disappear and hotfoot it across the road.

'Shit,' I cursed.

I shoved Janvier's papers back at him and ran out after the man. Looking left and then right, I saw him at the wheel of a car, quickly accelerating away from Les Quatre Chats. It was the Renault Novaquatre that had chased me and Boniface on Christmas Eve.

'Shit,' I repeated.

64

I was drinking whisky alone in Thirty-Six. It was Dax's whisky. It was Dax's room. That was the sort of day it had been.

'Whisky's illegal,' a voice said from the darkened doorway, making me jump. It was Sarah.

'What are you doing still here?' I asked her. 'I thought everyone had left.'

'Catching up on the typing.' She nodded at the whisky again. 'It's illegal.'

'A present from Hochstetter. That makes it legal somehow. Anyway, it's Dax's. If anyone's breaking the law, he is. Can't tempt you to one?'

She shook her head. 'I'll be off then. Goodnight, Inspector Giral.'

'Eddie.'

I watched her leave. The same impulse that had made me follow her on the train two days earlier made me drink up the whisky and turn the lights off in Dax's room. Somehow, Hochstetter knew I had a son. I wanted to know how, and I still had my doubts about Sarah.

This time, I followed her to Montmartre, but not to the same flat she'd taken me to, to show me the guinea pigs kept in a bathtub. I still hadn't worked out why Cartier had had them. It was the least of my concerns.

Instead, she went into an old building on Rue Germain-Pilon, at the Pigalle end of the mountain. It looked like one of the businesses that had been abandoned when two thirds of the city had fled before the Germans got here, only these people hadn't returned. I stood across the narrow street and pondered whether to follow her inside. There was nowhere outside to hide if she were to come back out.

The sounds of a clarinet and a piano wafted my way from a club a few doors further down. Glancing along the street, I recognised the *Paris-Soir* journalist I'd spoken to at the German embassy. He was sharing a bottle of champagne with a group of French yaw-yaws, high-society creatures who would always rise to the surface. Among them, a woman with the hair and teeth of a dressage horse clung to the arm of this season's matching accessory – an SS officer. They disappeared inside the club, evidently slumming it for the night as close to Pigalle as their faux boldness would allow.

Making up my mind, I crossed the narrow street and pushed through the door I'd seen Sarah go into. She was standing inside, her arms folded, leaning up against an interior door jamb.

'Come to see how the other half lives, Inspector Giral?'

Before I could answer, she turned and vanished into the room beyond the door. I followed and found myself in a large room the size of a warehouse. All around, women were sitting talking. Looking more closely, I saw that some were helping others fill in forms or write letters. More were sorting through old clothes on racks, some bringing, some taking. In one corner, a pen had been set up with children inside, under a dozen watchful eyes.

'Their mothers are working,' Sarah explained. 'They'll pick them up on their way home.'

'Who are they?'

'Prisoners' wives, mainly.'

I looked at her and she nodded.

'My husband's a prisoner of war. In Germany.'

I turned back to see a pile of tins of food on a table. 'Black market?'

'Some is. Most of it's grey market. Stuff people make at home to sell to friends.' She pointed to the far corner, where the woman she'd taken me to meet the other day was handing out parcels wrapped in brown paper. 'Guinea pig meat. Hardly the black market you're talking of.'

'The source of all our woes, according to the radio this morning.'

She laughed bitterly. 'The result. It's not the black market causing shortages, it's the Occupation.'

'And our marvellous government in Vichy.'

'I've got to agree with you there, Inspector Giral. But they've got to blame the black market so we don't realise it's their own incompetence in distributing what little food there is fairly.'

'Dangerous talk, Sarah. Sounds almost like Communism. And it's Eddie.'

'I'm no Communist. But do you know how much German soldiers get paid for being here? Fifty Reichsmarks spending money. At twenty francs to the Reichsmark, that's a thousand francs. Do you know what the Vichy government pays the wife of a PoW with one kid? Less than thirty francs.'

'How do you know all this?'

'With all due respect, Inspector Giral, how do you not know all this?'

We were interrupted by a hubbub of hushing running across the room. At the far side, I was surprised to see the pianist who'd played at Pilou's bar last week, when Dominique had refused to sing. He took his place at an old piano perpendicular to the far wall. When I couldn't stop myself from gasping was when Dominique appeared and stood by him. He played the opening bars of 'Un Jeune Homme Chantait' and the room fell completely silent in anticipation.

'They perform for free,' Sarah explained to me in a whisper.

Dominique's voice when it came was like molten gold poured from a silver chalice, her tone conquering the cold and hunger we all felt, her harmony vanquishing the Occupation and its world in an instant. I had to look down at the floor and breathe in slowly.

'Don't worry,' Sarah whispered to me again. 'I know.'

'What are you doing here, Eddie?'

'You sang beautifully, Dominique.'

I'd caught up with her outside after she'd finished her song. She said goodbye to the pianist and was about to set off up the hill to her flat. My words stopped her.

'You were inside? You heard me?'

'It's great that you're singing.'

'I don't want to sing, Eddie, not if I can't sing for a living any more. I just do this to help. It's what people do. We work together in what way we can and look after each other. It's the only way we're going to survive this. You should try it sometime.'

'I'm sorry about yesterday.'

She snapped at me. 'A cleaner?'

'What would you have me do?' I could feel my own irritation rising. 'That was Hochstetter, the German I'm forced to work with that I've told you about. You want me to tell him we're breaking who knows how many of their laws? That we're to-gether? You want me to put you in that sort of danger?'

'You had a Nazi in your home?'

'And how am I supposed to stop him from coming in if he wants to? Anyway, I'm not convinced he's a Nazi.'

That seemed to annoy her more than anything else. 'He's one of them. An Occupier. And you allowed him in your house and you turned me away.'

I threw my hands up in exasperation. 'Fine, Dominique. Let's just go to the Abwehr now, shall we? Tell him we're an item. Ask for you to be arrested while we're at it. Talking of which, does Sarah know about us?'

'Yes, she does.'

That stopped us both in our tracks.

'Come to my flat, Dominique. Let me cook for you. I've got a tin of something in my kitchen that might not kill us.'

Despite herself, she laughed. She caught her breath. 'All right, but not tonight. Tomorrow. I want to be on my own tonight.'

We didn't embrace or kiss as we parted. We never could. I watched her walk away from me and I turned to catch the Metro home. After so many nights needing my own quiet, I was surprised at the thought that Dominique evidently needed the same.

'Maybe she's not too sure either,' I said out loud.

In the Metro home, I considered the fact that Sarah knew about me and Dominique and how no one else seemed to. Not Judge Rambert, not Hochstetter, not Otto Abetz. They would have used that knowledge had they known it. Which had to mean that Sarah had kept it to herself.

I climbed the stairs to my flat and hunted for my key. A figure was sitting on the steps up to the next floor, outside my door. I slowed to a halt when it slowly stood up.

'Hello, Édouard.'

It was a voice I hadn't heard in fifteen years.

65

She hadn't changed in all that time. Older, like me, but still the same light-haired and gentle beauty I'd fallen in love with when I was a broken, vulnerable young man in the last war. She'd been equally vulnerable, a nurse having to cope with young men like me, shell-shocked and in pain, and I'd only made her more vulnerable. The realisation of that was what had made me leave her and Jean-Luc. The realisation that no matter how much I tried, I'd make their lives as sad and unstable as my own was at that time.

'Where's our son?' Sylvie asked me.

After I'd found her waiting for me on the landing, I'd hurried her into my flat and made us both some coffee while I gathered my thoughts.

'He escaped. He left Paris.'

'I know that. He telephoned me to say he was in the Unoccupied Zone.'

She brushed her hair off her forehead in a gesture I'd known and loved and never stopped loving. I had to look away, pretending to concentrate on stirring my coffee.

'Where in the Unoccupied Zone?'

'He wouldn't say.'

'How was he able to telephone you?'

She looked irritated. 'At a hotel we used to go to in the school holidays. In Collioure, near your parents in Perpignan. He knew when he joined the army that he could always get messages to me there if I wasn't in Paris. But that doesn't matter. He said he was going to try and cross the Pyrenees and get to Lisbon.'

'He was on his way to London. He wanted to join the Free French. I tried to put him off, but I couldn't stop him.'

'Did you even try, Édouard?'

She, Hochstetter and my parents were the only people who called me by my full name.

'Of course I did.'

I had to think. Did I really? I thought at the time that the safest bet for him would be to get out of Paris, so that's what I'd done, I'd helped him escape the city. Beyond that, perhaps I hadn't given enough thought to what crossing the Unoccupied Zone, the Pyrenees and Spain to Lisbon would entail. And after that, to London and the Free French and becoming a soldier again.

'He would have been safer in Paris,' she hissed, echoing my own doubts. The anger in her voice was barely contained. 'At least I would have been here. To look after him.'

'He might have been arrested. Sent to a prison camp. I couldn't risk that happening.'

She sighed, calming momentarily. 'Your parents are hoping he'll turn up in Perpignan.'

'You're still in touch with them, aren't you?' I recalled something Jean-Luc had said in the summer about spending the holidays with them. As I saw less of my parents, Sylvie and Jean-Luc appeared to have seen more of them.

'Not for my benefit. They wanted to see Jean-Luc growing up. They know he's on the run and are hoping he'll know he'll be safe with them.'

'He could cross the Pyrenees from there.' I knew the moment I said it that it was the wrong thing.

'And go and fight? And get killed?' The anger was back in her voice. 'He should stay there with them until this is all over.'

'And when will that be, Sylvie?'

'This can't last for ever. What are you doing to find him, to get him back?'

I looked at her helplessly. 'What can I do? I got a message to him last month and he was safe. That's all I know.'

'That's all you know.' She mimicked my voice. There was a bitterness underlying it that shocked me. 'He can thank God I'm here, Édouard. I've only just got back from the south.'

'Only just got back? How? The Germans only gave you until the end of September to return.'

She looked slyly at me. 'It's not just you who can get things done. I paid someone to smuggle me back across the demarcation line.'

I looked aghast. 'Do you know how dangerous that is? What if they'd caught you?'

'They didn't catch me.'

'But why didn't you stay? If my parents are hoping Jean-Luc will go to Perpignan, wouldn't it have been better for you to stay there and wait for him?'

She shook her head vigorously. 'And who would be here in Paris looking after our son's interests? You wouldn't have been. So I've come back. And I've been to see the French authorities and the German authorities to find out what I can do.'

'You've done what?'

'One of us has to do something. I've asked the Germans to be lenient with him if they find him. He's only a boy. I've said his father's a policeman, not that that's ever been any help to him.'

I hung my head a moment. 'Oh Sylvie, that's not how this works.'

'What are you going to do, Édouard?'

'No, Sylvie, what have *you* done?'

I recalled my meeting with Hochstetter that morning. Now I knew how he'd found out I had a son. Whoever Sylvie had seen had made sure that word had got back to him. And now he had a hold over me that would never break.

Unless something happened to Jean-Luc.

66

I had a request waiting for me at Thirty-Six the next morning. It was from Firmin, in Fresnes prison, saying he needed to speak to me without delay.

Nice to see you getting some sense of urgency, I thought.

I'd planned on going to the police station in the Eighth to check up on Jacquot's story. Not that it gave the brothers an alibi. It was for the Thursday night that they needed one. I was planning on making the trip out to Fresnes after that, but given Firmin's message, I swapped them around.

'Jacquot was right,' Firmin told me in the prison interview room an hour later. 'It was the commissariat in the Eighth when we were arrested two weeks ago. Our local nick was last week.'

I sighed heavily. 'It's no good, though. The dates are still wrong. You were arrested in the Eighth on the Wednesday night.'

He hung his head. 'I'm still confused. Jacquot's always doing this.'

I leaned across the table and held his face up so I could look him in the eyes. 'Firmin, we need an alibi for the Thursday night. That's when Cartier was killed. The Wednesday night's no good. Is there really no one who saw you on the Thursday? No one who can say you were nowhere near Cartier's warehouse.'

'It's no good, Eddie. We've got no one.'

'Where were you? If you tell me that, I might find someone who can vouch you were there.'

He shook his head. 'It's no good, I told you. We were still in the nick on the Thursday night.'

It took a moment for his words to register. 'What do you mean, you were still in the nick?'

He looked at me forlornly. 'We've got no one we know to give us an alibi. We were still in the nick, so none of our friends saw us.'

I calmed him down with my hands. 'Wait a minute, Firmin. What are you saying? Which night were you in a police cell? Wednesday or Thursday?'

'Both. They were going to release us on the Thursday morning, but Jacquot called the cop releasing us a bastard. So they kept us in a second night.'

I could happily have taken a swing at him. 'Let me get this straight. You were arrested on Wednesday the eleventh and kept in the cell in the Eighth until when?'

He did the sum on his fingers. 'Friday morning. We were starving, so we went to a café just down the road from the nick for some breakfast. They had bread, it was really good. And the coffee wasn't bad.'

'I don't care what you had for breakfast.' I was shaking with frustration. They'd never been the brightest stars in the night sky, but this was dim even by their standards. 'And then what did you do?'

'Then we got the Metro to Bel Air and started trying to nick people's butter. We were worried Cartier was going to be mad at us.' He brightened up. 'You know we were there. We tried robbing you.'

The police station in the Eighth was a much grander affair than most arrondissement cop shops. An imposing mansion on Rue du Faubourg Saint-Honoré, it obviously catered for a better class of delinquent than we did at Thirty-Six.

With the exception of the Bouvier brothers.

'Here they are,' a sergeant told me. He was looking through a register he'd taken from a cupboard behind his desk.

I tried to take a peek at the entry he was squinting at. 'So what happened?'

'Arrested on Wednesday the eleventh of December at ten p.m. Drunk and causing a disturbance.'

He put the register down and called a colleague over.

'I remember them,' the newcomer, a lugubrious Parisian with a waxed moustache, said. 'Mouthy little runts, especially the younger one.'

'That the one that called you a bastard?' the sergeant asked him.

'And worse. We put them both back in the cells for another night.'

'When were they released?' I asked.

The sergeant checked the register again. 'Friday the thirteenth. Six o'clock in the morning, after curfew ended.'

I took the ledger from him and looked at the entries for the brothers. It was all there. I held onto the book. 'I'm going to need this. I'll get it back to you later.'

Before they could object, I hurried out of the station and looked for a café nearby. I struck lucky in the second one I tried. I started describing the brothers to the owner, a bluff Basque with a hare-like head and long teeth, only for him to finish my description with words of his own.

'Scruffy little bastards with bad breath and no table manners. I remember them. Tried to use fake ration tickets.'

'What day was it? I need you to be precise.'

'The Friday,' he said without hesitation. 'My wife was check-ing the till when they came in and she only does that on Friday mornings. They in trouble?'

'You could say that.' I pointed at a notebook he had behind the counter. 'I need you to write a witness statement saying what you just told me. And one from your wife, if you can.'

Armed with all the bits of paper, I began the walk to where I'd parked the pool car. On the way, I passed a young woman of roughly the same age as Marie Ferran walking the other way. As she tightened her scarf, I spied a cross of Lorraine on a chain around her neck. She saw me notice it and quickly covered it up.

'Not a Communist part of town, then,' I said quietly to myself.

'This proves the brothers couldn't have killed Cartier,' I told Dax.

I'd laid all the documents out on his desk in front of him and explained what I'd learned. I'd also added Bouchard's pathology report giving the time of death.

'They couldn't have been at Cartier's warehouse at the time Bouchard said he was killed,' I added. 'This is a rock-solid alibi.'

'Not even Judge Rambert could ignore this sort of evidence,' Dax agreed.

'Let me take it to him.'

'Not a chance. He'd still find fault if it's you presenting this. Leave it with me.'

I shook my head. 'I'm coming with you.'

'No you're not, Eddie. We can't risk the judge refusing to accept the evidence because you and he don't see eye to eye. I'm going.'

Circumstances agreed with him.

'Major Hochstetter,' Sarah said when I went to retrieve some more documents from my office to take to the Palais de Justice.

'What about him?'

'He rang a short while ago. He asked if you'd go and see him. He said he had some information for you.'

I stared intently at her, weighing up the documents in my

hand. Anything Hochstetter had for me had to be about my son. I nodded and took the documents to Dax. He was just sending Courtet out to build a sandcastle or something.

'I'll join you when Hochstetter's finished with me,' I told him.

He hefted the pile of papers and looked sharply at me. 'No you won't. Stay away, Eddie.'

67

'You said you had some information for me,' I reminded Hochstetter.

He looked momentarily surprised. 'I did? Oh, no, I said I had something for you.'

The Lutetia had had its usual frown for me from the slanted eyebrows of its upper balconies when I'd got there, which was good as it had irritated me, replacing the usual trepidation I felt when crossing Hochstetter's threshold. In his room, he'd taken an age to order us both a coffee. Under other circumstances, I would have welcomed it. Not today.

'What is it?'

'I failed to give you your Christmas present.'

I simply stared at him. 'My Christmas present?'

Before coming to join me on another sofa, he picked up a book from his desk and placed it on the low table in front of me.

'For you.'

Warily I looked at it. I recognised it. A cheery working-class family beamed at me from the front cover, their smiles painted on, as that was the only way any poor families would be smiling these days. Behind them, a factory belched out smoke and production, evidently not one of the many that had had to close down since the Occupiers had come to grace us with their presence.

I picked it up and turned it over, looking at him in surprise. I had to stop myself from shaking with anger and frustration. On the back cover was a peasant family, also smiling. So too was Hochstetter, a faintly unnerving grimace that was at odds with the menacing smirk of the Hochstetter that I knew.

Turning it back, I read the title. *Agenda de la France Nouvelle.*

'It's an appointment diary,' he explained. 'For 1941.'

'I know it is. Why?'

It was another form of Vichy propaganda. I flicked through it. It was filled with illustrations and articles justifying Pétain's actions and attacking the Freemasons, and supposedly helpful advice on coping with food and energy shortages. I had to stop myself from hurling it out of the window. They were so venal they'd even try to turn the hardships we were all facing into some sort of positive, a new way forward of challenge and opportunity. One illustration in particular showed a gust of wind of a new France blowing away the symbols of the Third Republic, such as Marianne and the Chamber of Deputies, and what they called the elites of the old regime who had supposedly landed us in this mess.

'An offering. To formalise our working relationship in the coming year. Appointments and friendly phone calls in place of summonses and demands.'

'I don't know what to say,' I told him.

'Thank you, perhaps.'

He sat back and lit a cigarette. We both watched the match burn itself out in an ashtray on the table. He'd failed to snuff the flame with his usual shake.

'Well, this is all very nice,' I finally said, getting up, 'but I really must be going.'

He banged his forehead. 'But of course, I do have some information for you. It concerns Jean-Luc, your son.'

I sat down again. 'What about my son?'

He took a pull on his cigarette, drawing out my agony. 'It appears that he is in custody. German custody.'

I felt my skin go cold. 'Where is he?'

'He was detained at the beginning of November. He is currently being held at Gestapo headquarters in Bordeaux, awaiting shipment to a prison camp in Germany. Providing he is lucky, of course.'

'I want to see him.'

'I'm afraid that will not be possible.'

'I demand to see him.' My voice was low. 'Don't forget I know Martin's secret.'

'Ah, another piece of information that I have for you. You see, Martin has returned to Berlin. He decided to go back to duty early, which I think was best for us all. With the possible exception of you, Édouard.'

'His being back in Berlin doesn't alter the fact that I know his secret and how the Nazis would view it.'

'No, it doesn't. But it does alter how much use that information is to you. As you say, he's back in Berlin, where you have no jurisdiction or influence. Which is rather like your situation at the moment in Paris, don't you think? You may briefly have held some measure of power while Martin was here, simply because of your position as a police officer, but that has now gone. You have no evidence, no suspects, just hearsay. Your only witness is dead and you have a victim who is no longer here to defend your absurd accusations.'

'I can give away my secret here. It will get back to Berlin.'

'And who precisely do you think will believe you? A damaged French police detective who ran out on his family, is largely ostracised by his colleagues and helped a deserter escape the law. You may make accusations, but who do you think in the Wehrmacht, the SS or the Party will believe you over me and my brother? And what effect do you think such an accusation will have on your career?' He sucked deeply on his cigarette. 'And, indeed, on your safety?'

'I want to see my son.' My fists were clenched in my lap.

'That's as may be, but as I said, it is impossible.'

'I will use what I know about Martin so I can see my son, and to hell with the consequences.'

'Strong words. But picture this if you will. Another German soldier, this time an officer in the SS, is cruelly attacked by Frenchmen, and the Paris police are dragging their heels in apprehending the guilty party. We have all seen what can happen in such matters. Your poor Bonsergent is a case in point.'

'You can't be serious. That would be one provocation too many right now.'

'Would you be willing to risk it? I would strongly suggest you resist the temptation to use my brother in your games. Now, if you don't mind, I have to prepare myself for Herr Doktor Abetz's reception this evening. Have you been invited?'

'No, I haven't.'

'Oh my, how quickly fortune and favour can change.' He gestured at the book on the table. 'Don't forget your Christmas present.'

68

Sylvie was waiting for me inside the entrance when I got back to Thirty-Six. My heart sank.

'Come upstairs,' I told her. I wanted to see if Dax had returned from the Palais de Justice.

She shook her head. 'I don't want to stay in here.'

Instead, we crossed the road and stood by the wall overlooking the Seine. She had a coat on but I shivered, despite the weather not being as brutally cold as it had been until now. The mercury felt even more all over the place these days than I was.

'Where's our son?'

I closed my eyes and sighed. 'He's in prison.'

'He's what?' Her voice was a screech imbued with panic and pain. 'Where? Here?'

'Bordeaux. The Germans have him. They're sending him to a camp in Germany.' I kept from her that it was the Gestapo that was holding him.

She slapped me across the face. She slapped me a second time and I took it.

'What are you going to do about it, Édouard? You can't do nothing like you always did.'

'I am doing something, Sylvie, believe me.'

She dried her eyes from the tears that had started to fall. 'You will do. Or I'll tell the Germans your secret.'

'What secret?'

'Dominique.' She paused to let her words sink in. 'Don't think I don't know. I'm sure they won't be happy about one of their policemen living with an African woman.'

I rubbed my eyes, suddenly tired. 'Please, Sylvie. You're better than that.'

She slapped me again. On the arm this time. 'Don't tell me what I am. I know what I am. I'm a mother who brought her son up on her own, and you're the father who's never lifted a finger to do anything when he needed you. I'll do what it takes to get Jean-Luc back.'

'Telling them about Dominique won't help that, Sylvie. Really it won't.'

She turned and began to walk away. 'We'll see, Édouard.'

Shaking my head, I glanced up to see Sarah at the window, looking down at me. A couple more cops were at the windows of the adjacent detectives' room. Lafitte's cold face stared at me before turning away.

'What was all that about?' Sarah asked me when I got back upstairs.

We were alone in my office and I was controlling my anger. Lafitte had been on the phone in the detectives' room, so I hadn't been able to take it out on him. Boniface came in and took his coat off the hook before I could answer her.

'Another burglary,' he told me. 'Over Christmas, most likely, but they've only just found it this morning.'

'Do you really think I have the time for this?'

'You're the inspector. I thought you should know.'

'Yes, well, don't.'

He went out without a word.

'My ex-wife,' I finally told Sarah. 'I have a son and I've heard that he's in a Gestapo prison in Bordeaux. They're sending him to a camp in Germany.'

Every time I spoke the words out loud, they sounded worse than the last time. She got up from behind her desk and stood in front of mine as I took my coat off. I pulled out the Luger before it fell out and placed it on my desk while I hung the coat up.

'Will they let you see him? Or talk to him?'

I shook my head. 'Hochstetter told me. He's using it as leverage over me.'

'Is there nothing you can do?'

'There was. But that's changed. Now he's the one with the hold over me.'

'Forgotten something,' Boniface said, bustling back into the room.

Sarah quickly dropped the files she was holding onto my desk, covering the Luger up. I watched as Boniface found what he was looking for and hurried back out again. Sarah removed the files and I placed the pistol in my drawer.

I nodded a thank-you at her.

69

'What's happening?' I asked.

Dax was sitting on a hard wooden chair in the corridor outside Judge Rambert's chambers.

'Still waiting. He's got someone in there with him.'

'Not a chance.'

'Don't do anything stupid, Eddie.'

I turned at the judge's door to look back at Dax and shoved it open. Rambert did indeed have a guest.

'Herr Doktor Abetz,' I greeted him.

'The policeman.'

'You have a nerve, Inspector Giral,' Rambert objected.

Dax had followed me into the room. He put his hand on my arm to keep me quiet. 'We have evidence regarding the Bouvier brothers,' he said. 'It throws substantial new light on the case and proves without any doubt that they are innocent of the murder of Joseph Cartier.'

Rambert turned to Abetz. 'I'm most sorry, Otto. You have met Inspector Giral. This is his superior officer, Commissioner Dax.'

Abetz bowed to Dax. 'A pleasure to meet a senior French police officer. We have been expecting you.'

'You have?' I asked.

Rambert ignored me and shook his head at Dax. 'This is not normal procedure, Commissioner. The verdict stands.'

I made to answer, but Dax kicked me lightly on the ankle. He set out the documents we'd put together in front not only of the judge, but also of Abetz. 'This evidence is incontrovertible.'

'It is not evidence,' Rambert said. 'If you wish to submit new evidence, it will have to wait until Monday.'

'You know full well that that will be too late,' Dax said. 'The Bouvier brothers are scheduled to be executed tomorrow.'

I saw Abetz looking at the police ledger.

'You may leave, or I will call an officer to have you removed,' Rambert told Dax. 'Understand that I will not be browbeaten like this.'

Abetz picked up the two statements by the owners of the café where the brothers had had breakfast.

'Herr Doktor Abetz,' I said. I sensed Dax groan next to me. 'You spoke eloquently at your dinner of winning the French over. This is a chance to do that. Show that German justice is more flexible than French justice.'

He looked at me thoughtfully, but spoke to Rambert. 'I think the Parisian people have seen enough executions for the present, don't you think? I believe it would be in our interest to accede to their wishes and accept this new evidence.'

'But Otto,' Rambert argued, 'this is hardly correct procedure. The verdict must stand.'

'I don't think you quite understand,' Abetz told him, his voice calm. 'I believe it would be in our interests – mine and yours – to show mercy.'

'It's too late. The execution is scheduled for tomorrow morning.'

Abetz dropped the police station register heavily on the table.

'It is not too late, Judge Rambert, wouldn't you agree?'

'We owe you, Eddie.'

'Just try and stay out of trouble, boys.'

Dax and I had waited with the judge until he'd signed the order to release the brothers, which he'd done while Abetz was still there. The ink hadn't yet dried when Dax and I left for Fresnes, but by the time the prison authorities had gone through all their rigmarole to unlock two cell doors, it felt like the paper it was on had turned to parchment.

It was just an hour and a half before curfew when I dropped Firmin and Jacquot off at their mother's flat. Jacquot stopped and turned at the door to look at me. His eyes were clear.

'Seriously, Eddie. We owe you.'

I went home, tired out after a long day. I still had some of the whisky Hochstetter had left waiting for me. What I didn't need was Sylvie waiting for me on my landing.

'I'm tired,' I told her. 'Can't this wait?'

'Don't worry, Édouard, I won't come in. The Gare de Lyon tomorrow morning. Eight o'clock.'

'What about it?'

'You'll be there. I've arranged for someone to get us both across the demarcation line. You're finally going to do something about finding our son.'

'Are you mad? I can't do that. I'm a police officer.'

'You'll have to do it. Or I'll make good on my promise to tell the Germans about you and Dominique.'

She began to go downstairs.

'Be reasonable, Sylvie.'

She didn't even turn to face me. 'No, Édouard. You be at the Gare de Lyon tomorrow morning.'

I'd barely gone inside and got a fire going when she knocked on the door again. I jerked it open.

'What do you want now?'

'Well, I thought I was coming for supper.'

I winced. It was Dominique standing on the landing.

'You've forgotten, haven't you? You said you'd cook me a meal.'

'It's been a tough day.'

I stood aside to let her in. Even though I'd forgotten my promise, I'd never felt such relief at seeing someone as I did at that moment. She stopped a few paces before reaching me. Neither of us reached out to touch the other.

'If you won't come to see me, Eddie, then I thought I'd have to come and see you.'

'I'm glad you did.'

She looked at the fire burning in the grate. 'I thought we were going to pool our coal rations.'

I couldn't help glancing at the flames while I thought of my reply. 'I stole it.'

She looked disappointed. 'Why, Eddie?'

'From the Germans. I took it from the German embassy.'

She laughed, a generous peal that filled my little room. 'In that case, I suppose I can't argue. Were you stealing for me as well, or just yourself?'

'Would that make a difference?' I was genuinely puzzled.

'It might.' She took a paper parcel out of her bag and opened it. There were four rashers of bacon wrapped up inside. 'A peace offering. I thought we could eat it together.'

'Where did you get them?'

She took them into the kitchen and called to me. 'A neighbour. They've just been to see family in the country and brought them back.'

'Generous of them.'

She re-entered the room. 'Oh, I had to pay for them.'

I stared at her. 'On the black market?'

'No, I told you. A neighbour.'

'Did you have to give them a ration ticket for it?'

'Of course not, Eddie. What's the problem?'

'You criticise me for taking a gift from a black marketeer, but not for stealing from one. You criticise me for buying on the black market. You applaud me for stealing from the Germans. And here you are, buying from the black market yourself. Make your mind up, Dominique.'

'This isn't black market, Eddie. It's just some people who went to the country and came back with some food to sell.'

'That's the black market.'

She ran her hands through her hair. 'No, it's not. What's got into you? The black market is gangs and corruption. This is just harmless. People helping their neighbours out. The grey market.'

'You bought food from someone who sold it to you without declaring it. You didn't go to a proper shop to buy it, you didn't give them a ration ticket. That's just as much the black market as people like Joseph Cartier and every other thug who exploits our hardships.'

She paused for a moment, the silence hanging between us. 'So what do you want me to do with it? Throw it away? Will that help anyone?'

I looked at her, angry with myself for getting us to this point. I longed for her to stay and talk to me like I'd never longed for anything in my life.

But I remembered Sylvie and her threat to tell the German authorities about us. And about what that might do to us both. Especially to Dominique. I took a deep breath.

'You should probably go home, Dominique.'

70

I stared at myself in the mirror the next morning. My flat had grown cold, the embers of last night's fire having died in the grate. I was wearing my coat to shave and looking hard at my reflection.

This was a mistake.

After drying my face, I checked my watch. I had over an hour before I had to meet Sylvie at the Gare de Lyon. She'd arranged for the person who'd smuggled her across the demarcation line to return to Paris and take us both across the boundary going the other way. Into the Unoccupied Zone and from there to Bordeaux and, she hoped, to Jean-Luc.

I shook my head and dressed slowly.

It was a mistake, but I had no choice. I had no idea whether Sylvie really would make good her threat to tell the Germans about Dominique, but she was desperate. I knew the bad decisions people took when they were in that position, and I owed it to Dominique to protect her from harm. Reluctantly, I also had to admit that I needed to do something to find Jean-Luc, no matter how ill-fated.

Taking one last look around, I locked my door and began the descent.

'It's happening,' Monsieur Henri told me on the stairs. 'Thirty thousand Gaullists. They're massing outside the city. They're already attacking the Boches.' He closed his door.

'Is that right?' I murmured, carrying on downstairs.

He opened his door again and peered out. 'I'd stay in if I were you,' he added, quickly slamming it again behind him.

'I wish I could.'

I went by Thirty-Six with the idea of checking up on things. It was Saturday, so Sarah wouldn't be there and I doubted that Boniface would either. I couldn't shake the feeling out of my head that it would be the last time I saw the place. I took a deep breath before going in. Crossing the demarcation line in the hope that the Germans would release Jean-Luc was a fool's errand at best.

'Eddie.' The sergeant in the entrance hall called me over. 'I've been trying to ring you at home. You've got a visitor.' He nodded to the benches behind me.

I hoped for a moment that it was Sylvie, saying she'd decided against going through with her plan, but I turned to see someone else. He got up and hurried towards me.

'It's Marie,' Pierre Ferran told me. 'She's got a gun.'

I know.

'Where is she?'

'That's the problem. She wasn't in her room this morning. We all had a drink last night at Ulysse's. She's only a kid and she's not used to drinking much, but you know Ulysse with his brandy.'

'I used to. So what happened?'

'She was saying she was going to kill a German soldier. We all thought it was just the drink talking, but when we went to bed, she showed me the gun.'

'Where's the gun now? Did you take it?'

He shook his head. 'She locked herself in her room with it, and by the time I'd fetched my father and we got in, she'd climbed out of the window and gone. She's been out all night. She's always done that.'

'Where's your father now?'

'He went looking for her.'

'How does he know where to find her?'

'She said last night that she knew where she was going to kill a Boche.'

'Where?'

'In the Jardins des Champs-Élysées.'

I stared at him for a moment. Behind him a couple of cops were heading for the rear of the building and the courtyard where the pool cars were kept.

Glancing at my watch, I saw I had less than an hour before I had to get on a train with Sylvie to try and secure my son's release. I looked back to see the worry evident on Pierre's face.

'Go home,' I told him. 'Wait for news there.'

'Don't tell my father I asked for your help. He doesn't want us to have dealings with a cop who works with the Boches.'

I stopped and looked back at him. It was pointless arguing, so I simply shook my head at him. 'Just go home.'

'Find her,' he begged me. 'She's not the same since she was arrested.'

I ignored him and spoke quickly to the sergeant on duty. 'Get as many cars and cops as you can to the Jardins des Champs-Élysées. We're looking for Marie Ferran. She's armed and wanting to kill a German.'

'Good,' the sergeant muttered under his breath.

Another argument not worth having, I thought, even if I'd wanted to. Instead, I ran out into the courtyard and caught up with the two cops just as they were pulling out in their car. I flagged them down and got in the back.

'Jardins des Champs-Élysées,' I told them.

'We've got an arrest in Vaugirard to make.'

'Good for you. And you've got the Jardins des Champs-Élysées to go to on the way.'

'It isn't on the way,' the driver argued.

'It is now. Drive.'

I stuck to the edge of the path, following the line of wintry bushes forming the border between the pathways through the gardens and the broad swathes of grass under the branches and leaves. During the summer, the trees would have provided shade and respite from the heat – and cover for Marie – but in the winter, they writhed in the bitter wind snaking through their boughs and roots. They gave no shelter. My breath misted in front of me like an elusive fog.

The two cops had dropped me on the corner of Avenue Gabriel and Place de la Concorde and left me to venture in on my own. I figured that Marie would know to steer clear of most of the areas in the gardens. Some parts were just too near the main avenues running through them and she'd be caught before she could do anything. The south-western end was the site of the Grand Palais, which the Germans had turned into a giant military lorry park. That meant there were always German soldiers there for her to find, but she would have been too smart to give that a go – there were too many of them coming and going and working on the lorries.

Which meant there was only one part of the gardens that would serve her purpose – the narrow strip between Place de la Concorde and the Élysée Palace, empty since the Germans had arrived with their guns under their arms and our government had left with its tail between its legs. There were large areas of trees set back from the paths to escape into, buildings in which to take cover, and it was closest to the Metro station that would have brought her here – and would take her away again after her job was done. More importantly, it was also where she'd be most likely to find a German soldier walking alone, seeking solace from his daily exile in a land he'd helped make hostile.

It would be where I would choose to come to kill one of the Occupiers.

In the cold morning air, there were just one or two people about. I heard French voices and stepped back to see who they were. Two young women with prams, preferring to brave the chill of the outdoors over the cold of their homes. They talked of their PoW wives' allowance and rising costs and how much they hated Laval. Oddly, their comments reminded me of the joke in the *Résistance* pamphlet about Laval not yet getting his German citizenship.

I watched them pass me until my sight was distracted by a blur of grey in the distance. A uniform. It was impossible to tell at this distance if it was army or navy, but it was a soldier alone. He was by the Diane Fountain, exposed on the open path. I looked around, but no other cops had arrived yet. No sirens of cars on their way.

Scanning to right and left of the path, I followed him, my pace brisk to catch him up and put myself between him and Marie. Wherever she was. I passed the Ambassadors Theatre to my right and heard a sound. A clack-clacking on the gravel, the noise muffled by the cold.

Almost directly alongside me, Marie slowly emerged from the side of the theatre. She was heading for the statue. She hadn't seen me. She was holding something in her hand, down by her side. It had to be my gun. I looked ahead to see that the German, an officer I now saw, had stopped for a brief moment to look up at Diane before moving on, in the direction of the Élysée Palace.

Marie walked slowly at first, then stopped and pointed. Almost straight away, she lowered the gun and walked forward again. She'd seen the distance was too far. I didn't dare call out as that would alert the German, so I broke into a trot, keeping as quiet as possible.

She quickened her own pace and was now within a scant ten metres of the soldier. In the felted cold air, he hadn't heard her footsteps, or had thought nothing of them.

She stopped again and raised her arm. I was running now, reaching to put myself in her line of sight without having to call her name and endanger all three of us. I was just too far away and almost stumbled in my haste to get to her in time.

I watched as she waited, her hand shaking. She finally saw me as I came towards her from her left, from the other side of the fountain. The soldier was moving further away and still she hadn't shot. I stopped, out of breath, and looked directly at her. The German was behind me. For her to take aim, she would have to step to one side or shoot me.

I held my hand out for the gun and took a step towards her. I could see she was crying, tears running down cheeks that looked as delicate as a child's. I took another step, but was jolted by someone barging into me, knocking me off my feet.

Getting to my knees, I could see that Marie had a clear shot on the officer. I tried to stand up to get to her, but a hand pushed me back down. I looked up to see Yves Ferran silhouetted against the sky.

'You can't let her do this,' I told him, keeping my voice low.

Expecting the report of a gunshot, I looked to where Marie was, just as her father did the same. While he was distracted, I pushed him away and got to my feet, ready to run back into her firing line, but he grabbed hold of me again, pulling me back.

Together we looked at Marie. Glancing over my shoulder, I saw that the German had vanished from view. Breathing a sigh of relief, I turned back to see Marie flee the gardens, the gun still in her hand. I began to give chase, but Yves tripped me, sending me crashing to the ground.

'You'll get your daughter killed,' I shouted at him, any concern about keeping quiet gone.

'Collaborator scum,' he hissed at me. 'You'd save a Boche?'

'No, I'd save your daughter. Maybe you should be doing the same.'

I tried to get up, but he kneeled on me, pinning me to the ground. From where I lay, I saw Marie disappear behind the theatre and escape through the trees as the first police sirens rang out in the misty air.

71

I was nursing a graze on my knee, but I was more worried about my trousers. A hole had opened in the leg where I'd fallen, and I sat down and poked my finger through, wincing when it touched the tender skin. I had one more pair of trousers and no real idea how easy it would be to find new ones. I sighed an angry sigh. The new world of rationing and shortages was so twisted that I worried more about clothes than about Marie still being at large with my service pistol, the ache in my knee and having to let Yves Ferran go. I'd had no choice.

'Arrest me,' he'd invited as the first cops had broken through the trees. 'I'll tell them how come my eighteen-year-old daughter got hold of a gun.'

'Tell her to come and see me. Or I can't protect her from the Germans.'

He'd spat on the ground before walking away. 'Collaborator.'

A man about my age with thick glasses and a toothbrush moustache that had gone out of fashion for most people as quickly as Adolf's lot had invaded France studied me from the seat opposite me. I was on the Metro, which was the real reason I was fretting about my trousers more than I was about real problems.

I checked my watch for the dozenth time. I'd let the other cops return to Thirty-Six without taking up the lift they'd offered.

I'd said I'd make my own way back. Instead, I'd waited until the last one had gone from sight and then taken the Metro from the Tuileries for the Gare de Lyon. A straight line, thankfully, but taking an age. My watch told me I'd be cutting it fine to meet Sylvie and make the train, the first part of the illegal trek across the demarcation line. There are few things more unnerving than rushing to do something you don't want to do.

I ran up the steps and into the railway station, hunting for the platform I needed. The air was thick with steam and coal. Nice to know someone had some, not that the trains had much. The soot clung to my throat and the inside of my nose, making me want to retch. Quieter than it would have been just a few months ago, the Gare de Lyon was still bustling with noise and with people in my way as I tried to get past them. I squeezed past a couple looking around nervously and wondered if they were embarking on their own illicit journey.

Turning my head in one direction and another as I ran, I suddenly felt myself collide with the back of someone. I bounced back, but they fell heavily to the ground. Instinctively I leaned forward to help them to their feet. When I saw the uniform, I recoiled and he got up under his own steam.

Dusting himself down, he was joined by two more German soldiers, a feldwebel and a stabsgefreiter, a lance corporal. From the buttons and squeaks, the man I'd run into was evidently an officer. They were patrolling the station with at least a dozen more soldiers, who quickly gathered around their officer and NCOs.

'I apologise,' I said to him. 'I wasn't looking where I was going.'

Inside, I was raging with myself. With the memory of Bonsergent in my mind and the fact that I was racing to start a clandestine act, the last thing I needed was to knock a German officer to the ground.

We were next to a queue for tickets, so there was a ready-made crowd of French onlookers. I sensed the unease in their hubbub.

'I am an officer of the German Reich,' he said to me slowly. He had the blond hair of Adolf's wet dreams and the fanatic's eyes of my dry nightmares.

'I apologise,' I repeated. 'I was running for a train.'

Behind him, I'd finally found my platform. The train was releasing steam, ready to pull out of the station. I watched it in dismay. It was too far to make out faces, but there were a few heads stuck out of windows looking back at the platform.

The feldwebel, a bullet-headed thug who'd evidently found his calling and his ideal playmate in the officer, poked me in the shoulder.

'I don't think an apology will suffice,' the officer said.

The noise from the crowd of onlookers began to rise. 'Filthy Boches,' one voice muttered, loud enough to be heard. The officer nodded to his men to start searching for the person who'd said it. A young Frenchman pushed back at one of the soldiers, and three of them pulled him out of the crowd.

'There's no need for this,' I told the officer. I showed him my ID. 'I'm a police officer.'

'Then you should be upholding the law, not breaking it.'

'It was an accident. I have apologised.'

The noise of anger rose. Out of the corner of my eye I saw the Frenchman throw a punch. Luckily it didn't land. A second soldier lashed out at another man in the queue, and someone spat on the ground at his feet.

'Please,' I said to the crowd. 'Don't provoke them.'

'Collaborator,' someone shouted at me.

The feldwebel went over to the first Frenchman and slapped him across the face, standing back to taunt the young man into retaliating. Quickly I stepped forward and put myself between the two of them. The officer wandered over and studied me.

'So you wish for there to be no problem. Perhaps you might have thought of that before assaulting a German officer.'

'I didn't assault you, I ran into you by accident.'

He smirked. 'We have seen all too many of these "accidents" where someone walks into us or closes a door in our faces.'

'That isn't the case here.'

'Are you just going to let them do this?' the young Frenchman said to me. He was stabbing his finger over my shoulder at the feldwebel.

'Calm down,' I told him.

I heard a rifle being cocked. Some of the soldiers had raised their weapons and were pointing them at the crowd of onlookers. No one was giving way, but there was an edge of fear among the French.

'Please stay calm,' I told them.

Behind me, I felt the young man being dragged away. I heard a slap as one of the soldiers hit him. The crowd bristled, the tension running through it like an electric volt.

The feldwebel and the officer were up close to me now, both of them staring me directly in the face. I could feel the heat of their breath against the cold of the station.

'So what are we going to do, police officer?' the feldwebel asked me.

I heard the undertone of French rage begin to bubble over. 'Do what you want with me, but leave these people alone. It's nothing to do with them.'

The officer seemed to accept that, and I saw him smile slyly at the feldwebel. 'I suggest you do as our policeman says,' he told him.

Without warning, the feldwebel headbutted me in the face. He mistimed it, so it didn't connect with my nose, but it hurt my cheek like hell. I did nothing, and he punched me in the stomach. Doubling over, I caught my breath and stood up straight again. He hit me a third time, an open slap across the face, a humiliation.

'See what your French police are worth,' the officer said to the crowd.

In reply, they were silent.

The feldwebel hit me again, a full-bodied punch this time. I kept my feet and looked at him. He was enjoying his time in Paris. Glancing to his officer for approval, he dished out one more punch, to the side of the head, and I staggered, losing my footing, and fell. The crowd gasped. Stemming the blood from my lip from the previous punch, I got up and faced him.

The officer looked at the crowd and then back at me. 'Let this be a lesson. The German Reich will not tolerate this behaviour.'

He ordered his men to withdraw and nodded to the feldwebel, who hit me one more time, knocking me to the ground again. They walked away to averted gazes from the French onlookers. I got to my knees. My trousers had taken even more of a beating than I had, with another hole in the other knee.

I saw people turn away, unsettled by the whole incident. A man came out of the queue and put his hand out to me. I thought he was going to help me up, but he pushed me down again and looked at me in disdain.

'Coward,' he said.

I climbed back up to my knees to see the train pulling out of the station.

Dessert

72

'Do you know him?' Bouchard asked me. He set down his pathologist's bag of tricks on the cold, hard ground.

'I do indeed.'

The body was lying face-up under the trees in the Jardins des Champs-Élysées. He'd been found early on Sunday morning by a baker crossing the gardens on his way to work, just a bare half an hour after curfew had lifted at five thirty and the Metro started running. Fortunately, I'd been at home, so I was there to answer the telephone call from Thirty-Six telling me what had happened. It was another reason why living at Dominique's flat wasn't such a good idea. At least that's what I told myself.

Rushing out, I'd forgotten my scarf, which was now a mercy. The temperature had risen sharply. Bouchard had been caught out by the sudden change in weather and was sweating in a heavy old coat and whatever delights lay underneath.

'Nice bruises, by the way, Eddie. What happened this time?'

'There were these two dozen German soldiers and a runaway train.'

'I don't want to know. Who is he, then? Any danger you might let me in on it?'

'It's not so much who that's a problem, but what.'

He looked at me quizzically. 'All right, it's far too early to be putting up with cryptic comments. Who or what is he?'

I looked down at the man. He really was cadaverous now. In death and swaddled in an expensive overcoat, Dietrich Falke looked like his face had finally come to rest and he no longer had to keep up the tired, hangdog look he'd worn the few times I'd seen him in life.

'He, I'm afraid, is German,' I told Bouchard.

'Oh fuck.'

Curses always sounded so much more enjoyable when they came out of Bouchard's bygone-academia mouth in his educated accent, but I had to agree with him.

'Isn't it just? His name's Dietrich Falke. He euphemistically called himself a trader.'

'How do you know him?'

'I've been trying to get permission to question him in relation to the murder of Joseph Cartier, the black marketeer in Bel Air.'

'I remember. Liked his butter neat.'

'That's the one. I suspected our Dietrich here was trying to take over Cartier's business, along with some charmer of our own.'

'For all the good it did him.'

We both stared at Falke for a moment and at the neat bullet hole in the middle of his forehead. I didn't imagine the hole we'd find in the back of his head when we turned him over was going to be quite so neat. Only we didn't get the chance. From behind, the sound of boots on the compact earth and shouts and the jangling of metal made us both turn around at the same time.

'Ooh, look, more Germans,' I said.

'Do you think they've come to help?'

Heading a group of soldiers, some of them with rifles slung over their shoulders, was Korvettenkapitän Thier. He had a stern expression on his bow, like a ship cutting through waves of shipwrecked sailors. They were heading straight for us. Smaller groups to right and left of them were busy ordering other French cops back from the scene.

'I could hazard a guess.'

'Inspector Giral,' Thier announced when he reached us. 'This is a German investigation. You and your men will withdraw from the area.'

'We will? This is a crime on French soil. The Paris police will be responsible for investigating it. The French Institut Médico-Légal will examine the body.'

He smiled coldly. It was another thing I reckoned they'd all learned in pre-war Hamburg. He was almost as good at it as Hochstetter.

'I really don't think you understand. This is a crime that involves a German citizen, as I know you are aware. That means that the German authorities will be responsible for any investigation into the circumstances.'

'I'm not sure that was in the armistice, Korvettenkapitän.'

'It does not have to be. It is in my power to take over this investigation. And this corpse.' He pointed at Falke in case we weren't sure which corpse he was talking about. He turned and issued an order to a junior officer behind him to organise the removal of the body.

'I trust you will respect the principles of forensic science?' Bouchard asked him. It was a great moment even if Thier didn't think so.

'I can assure you we will apply the same principles as recognised by your institute, Herr Doktor.' Even in his superciliousness, Thier couldn't help being impressed by Bouchard's innate authority.

His men began to remove the body and scan the ground for any evidence. One of them found the shell, where it had rolled under a bush. Inwardly I cursed the fact that one of our cops hadn't found it before the Germans had got here. I held my dismay in check as I watched them wrap it in a handkerchief and place it in a leather bag carried by a gefreiter. If there was one item I hadn't wanted the Germans to find, it was the bullet casing.

Because if my suspicions were correct, there was every likelihood that it had come from my gun.

73

I tried to follow Thier into the Kriegsmarine building, just a short walk across Place de la Concorde from where Falke had been found, but the guards at the door turned me away. The body had been taken away in a military ambulance, in the opposite direction to the navy building. I had no idea where they would take it for examination.

All I had was to sit tight and see what they turned up. That didn't bode well. I wondered for a moment if they even would investigate. Part of me hoped they wouldn't, as that way they wouldn't worry about the bullet casing that they'd found at the scene. As far as I could see, we were damned if they did and damned if they didn't. If they chose not to investigate, they could just as easily decide it was a random attack by a French person and take the retaliatory measures they wanted to. If they did investigate, and if my suspicion that Marie had gone through with her wish to kill a German was correct, it was more than possible that the bullet was from my service pistol. It would be a short distance from there to wanting to check the shell against my gun, especially with Thier in charge. That is, if they could find it. I couldn't. But that wouldn't help me either, as they'd assume I'd got rid of it precisely to avoid it being examined. And if they did find Marie and my gun and it matched the bullet, what would I do? Take the blame, the way Jacques Bonsergent had? Or point the finger at the real killer.

Either way, it would still lead to retaliation. How many had Martin Hochstetter talked of in Poland? Forty or fifty local people shot for every soldier killed. We'd already had a glimpse with Bonsergent how much the Occupation had hardened and changed and how far the Occupier was willing to go.

There was only one thing for it. Matters had taken a turn for the worse with Hochstetter, but right now he was the only game in town if I wanted any chance of influencing Thier's investigation.

I was surprised to find Thier with Hochstetter when I got to the Lutetia. The pair of them were chatting like the old friends they were and drinking coffee. There was no offer of a hot drink for me today.

'You could just as easily have stayed in Hamburg to do that,' I told them. In for a centime. 'It would have saved us all a lot of bother.'

'You have heard Édouard's attempts at humour, I take it?' Hochstetter asked Thier.

'Not yet.'

His reply appeared to please them both, and they laughed, the malicious and conspiratorial sound of the officers'-mess bully. In an instant, Hochstetter stopped and looked at me, the change in his demeanour shocking, his expression as cold as I'd ever seen it.

'Do not suppose for one minute, Édouard, that I am amused. What have you come to request of me today?'

I looked at Thier uncertainly before replying. 'Dietrich Falke. I gather by now you'll know of his murder. I'm requesting that his death be investigated by the French police.'

'Denied. Your next request?'

Unnerved by his abrupt answer, I had to think on my feet.

'In that case, I want to be kept informed of the progress of the German investigation.'

'Denied.' Hochstetter turned to look at his companion. 'Should Korvettenkapitän Thier so wish, you will be apprised of the results once it has been concluded.'

'Unless we require you to assist us in apprehending the individual suspected,' Thier added.

All this while, I was standing like a raw private facing a reprimand from his senior officers. I looked around for a seat. They'd taken up all the space on the two sofas, and short of dragging one of the heavy upright chairs across the carpet, I was stuck where I was. Taking another look at the two grey judges in front of me, I decided what the hell and made them wait as I pulled a chair to the other side of the low table from them and sat down. I looked from one to the other.

'Do you have an individual you suspect?' I asked Thier.

It was Hochstetter who took up the reins in their double act. There'd be a job for them both at the Folies Bergère if the soldiering didn't work out. 'Yes, Édouard, there is a suspect. Are you aware of a Hauptmann Schlegel?'

Luckily, I think my look of surprise hid my relief. 'A German suspect?'

But Hochstetter held his hand up. 'No. Not a German suspect. Hauptmann Schlegel was walking in the very same Jardins des Champs-Élysées yesterday morning when he became aware of an incident.'

My heart sank. With it, my expression, evidently.

'You would do well to look disappointed,' Hochstetter carried on. 'What Hauptmann Schlegel witnessed appeared to be an unsuccessful attempt on his life. He described a young Frenchwoman, and two Frenchmen tussling with each other. One of the men he described fits your description.'

'If he saw something, why didn't he take any action? This sounds very circumstantial.'

'He didn't take any action,' Thier joined in, 'because of the delicate situation with the French public at present. He very intelligently didn't want to aggravate that situation any further. So he left the gardens and reported the incident to his senior officer. Who reported it to me once he learned of the murder this morning.'

'Hauptmann Schlegel was unable to furnish us with an adequate description of the young woman,' Hochstetter added, 'but I think we all know who she was. Are you prepared to deny it?'

'Of course I am.'

He made me sit through one of his interminable cigarette rituals and leaned forward. 'I'm not convinced you are aware of the trouble you might be in.'

I thought of the bullet casing that one of Thier's men had picked up and thought I was only too aware of how deep my woes could possibly go. It was the one question I didn't dare ask – any news on the type of gun used.

'And of the trouble you have caused me,' Hochstetter carried on. 'I assisted you in getting this Marie Ferran released from the Gestapo. You gave me your assurances that she would not be a threat to German lives. And now that we know she made an attempt to kill one of our soldiers yesterday, we can only assume that she is responsible for the murder of Falke.'

'You have no evidence of that.'

'Yet,' Thier replied. 'But when we find that she is behind it, the full force of German justice will come down on her.'

'And we've all seen how that works.'

'Maybe you need to see it again.'

'Not only that, Édouard,' Hochstetter said, 'but you may be regarded as having colluded in Falke's murder, as you were the one who so vigorously sought her release. Had she not been released, Falke would be alive today.'

Hochstetter was nearer than he knew to the truth. I had colluded. I had my share of the blame, because I'd been the one who'd told Marie about Falke, in an unguarded moment on Christmas Eve. I was the one who had led her to him.

It was my turn to lean forward, showing a confidence I most certainly didn't feel. 'That is not necessarily the case. I've been trying to question Falke in relation to the murder of a French black marketeer. You have both denied me access to him. And he is now dead. I suspect the gang he was working with is responsible not only for Cartier's death but for Falke's too. I don't believe that Marie Ferran is responsible for this.'

I sat back and took a deep breath. Even I almost believed my own words – I had genuine suspicions where Morvan and his gang were concerned – but deep down I had to agree with the two men in front of me. When it came to Falke's death, Marie held all the numbers to be the winning lottery ticket. With a single shell from my gun rattling around inside the tombola drum.

Unless I could find someone else to pin it on before Thier could pin it on her. And me.

Thier looked at Hochstetter and sighed. 'This is all very well, but I have work to do.' He looked back at me. 'And an investigation to hand over to the Gestapo.'

Getting up, he took his leave of Hochstetter and nodded at me.

Hochstetter waited for him to go before shaking his head at me. 'Oh, Édouard, you really do have to hope the Gestapo never learn that the young woman responsible is the same woman that they released at my request and your urging.'

'We stand and fall together.'

'I'm afraid not. You will be the one to fall.'

He looked at me expectantly, but I had one last subject I had to bring up.

'My son. I know my ex-wife has been asking your authorities for leniency for him. I can only ask you the same, just as I've shown understanding in the matter with Martin.'

'You regard your behaviour as showing understanding?'

'I put my own officer off investigating too closely, including the death of the Frenchman attacked with your brother. I ensured Martin's apartment wasn't searched as thoroughly as we would normally have done.'

'It wasn't his apartment. He was staying here with me at the Lutetia.'

'I also made sure he was kept away from a German military hospital.'

'I will take that into consideration.'

'I want permission to see my son.'

He looked coolly at me. 'Denied.'

74

'They will come for Marie and they will come for her through you.'

'With your help?' Yves Ferran sneered.

'I'm the one trying to put them off.' I couldn't hide the exasperation from my voice.

Father and brother had been ferrying boxes from their van to the shop when I'd showed up, straight from the Lutetia. Yves had slammed the van door angrily when he'd seen me.

'You need to tell Marie to come and see me,' I insisted. 'I'm her only chance.'

He folded his arms, a muscle twitching in his right forearm. 'We look after our own here.'

'You're not going to be able to look after Marie with the Kriegsmarine and the Gestapo coming after her, believe me. And trust me, you need to stay somewhere else for now at least. Until I can find a solution.'

'Trust you? A collaborator?'

'I'm not a collaborator. I'm a cop. Would you rather the Germans were doing my job?'

For some reason, that last remark seemed to get in under his defences. He almost saw sense.

'We're staying put. In case Marie needs us.'

I did say almost.

'You call me if she comes home.'

*

The kitchen smelled stale, the living room musty. It was evident that Sylvie had only recently returned to Paris.

Evident, too, that she wasn't here now.

This was the second time in as many days that I'd been in the home I once shared with Sylvie and Jean-Luc. I'd come here last night, after missing the train at Gare de Lyon. It would have been pointless me catching the next one hours later, as Sylvie hadn't told me where we were going or who we were meeting. So I'd got into our old flat late last night to see if she'd returned. She hadn't.

I wandered the once-familiar rooms and felt nothing. I'd been here just once before since leaving fifteen years ago. That was in June this year, when I was looking for my son when the Germans first came to Paris and he hadn't found Sylvie there. Just me with bitter memories and the need to flee.

Leaving a note on the kitchen table for her to ring me when she got back, I took one last look at the gloomy hallway and closed the door behind me. I had no idea if she'd crossed the demarcation line or turned back when I failed to make the train, or if she'd been caught. Another waiting game. Outside, all I could do was stand and breathe in the air and consider my next move.

Only someone else considered it for me.

I didn't notice the Traction Avant until it pulled up alongside me and the snake-hipped man I'd first seen at Les Quatre Chats got out. A second man followed him, the thickset heavy with the wayward nose who'd been with him on that magical night.

'Get in the car,' snake hips told me.

His accent was so enchanting and Breton, I could only do as he asked. He also had a gun pointing at my belly, which carried a bewitchment of its own. I climbed into the back seat and sat next to a man.

'I've been looking for you,' I told him.

'You've found me.'

For the first time, I noticed his Breton accent. I also noticed the scent of Gomina Argentine. I couldn't help it. The strong, over-sweet aroma filled the back of the car, making my eyes water.

'Would you mind if I opened a window?'

'So why have you been looking for me?' Morvan asked me.

'Oh, you know, death of one black marketeer, new black-market operation opening up, death of a German trader in a public garden. The usual. You're very hard to find, by the way.'

'Not really. I'm here now.'

'And the Bouvier brothers were no help. I thought that since they probably worked for you, they'd lead me to your door, but they didn't.'

He laughed and pointed at the pair in the front of the car. 'Those two work for me. You really think Jacquot and Firmin work for me?'

He laughed again, his two companions joining in. I stayed out of it; I figured it was a private party. They were driving me down Rue des Pyrénées, the road where I used to live, in the direction of Cours de Vincennes. There was a long way to go yet. Rue des Pyrénées was a very long road, stretching from Belleville, through my old part of Ménilmontant, all the way down to Charonne.

'So where are we going?' I asked when we'd crossed into the frontier land of Père-Lachaise, separating the two ends of the road, and were still going.

'You'll see.'

The thickset one drove off Rue des Pyrénées into the warren of streets in Charonne. He pulled up outside an old warehouse, a factory that had closed down by the look of it. We weren't that far from the one they'd had to abandon on Impasse de Bergame.

'Good going, by the way,' I told Morvan. 'Clearing out your old place so quickly.'

'Yeah, well, we've got you to thank for that, haven't we?'

They led me into the building, through a better class of door this time, and into a giant room, laid floor to ceiling with shelves creaking under the weight of paradise. I couldn't help looking up and down the rows in wonder.

'I'll take one of everything,' I told them.

'This way.'

The other two stayed where they were, and Morvan led me to a wooden door halfway down the space on the left. Knocking once, he opened it and went in.

Two men were sitting in the room, one behind a scuffed desk, the other in a baggy armchair.

'One cop to see you, boss,' Morvan announced.

I looked from one to the other of the room's occupants.

'Well, this is a surprise.'

75

'We want to take you on a sightseeing tour, Eddie.'

'That's OK, boys, I've seen all I want to see.'

I was still staring in wonder. Jacquot was sitting behind the desk, Firmin was in the armchair. I saw now why Morvan had laughed when I'd thought the brothers worked for him. He worked for them.

'The perils of underestimating people,' Jacquot told me, apparently reading my thoughts.

'Shouldn't you be the other way around?' I mimed the action of swapping their respective positions over.

'I'll say it again, Eddie. The perils of underestimating people. You of all people should understand that.'

'Rude.'

Jacquot got up abruptly, followed by his older brother. 'Come on then, off we go.'

I followed with a meekness born of stupefaction. Jacquot still looked like the same undernourished punk he always had, with wonky and missing teeth, unkempt hair and the dress sense of a stoat, but he had an authority over Firmin and the three Bretons that was simply at odds with his aspect.

They led me back out of the door to the Traction Avant. A fourth man had joined the others in the outer room. I recognised him as the one who'd given me the slip at Les Quatre Chats.

Morvan and the heavy Breton sat in the front, Jacquot, Firmin and I bunched up on the back seat. They started off and I sat back for the ride.

'I noticed you've got German plates on the car,' I said. 'I was wondering how come you were allowed to drive on a Sunday.'

'We've got Morvan's charm to thank for that,' Jacquot replied to me across his brother. 'Worked wonders on the Boches.'

'Did it now?'

'You wondering why I wanted to see you, Eddie?' he continued.

'I'm wondering quite a lot of things, to be honest.'

He laughed. 'The thing is, we haven't yet thanked you properly for getting us off the murder charge. That judge really had it in for us.'

'Glad to help. I think.'

It was Firmin's turn to laugh. 'Came a bit close, that did.'

'I was wondering if you spoke.'

'You were the only one who ever looked out for us, Eddie.' Jacquot took up the reins again. 'Our mother never did. We appreciate that.'

'Nice. You're not telling me you planned it all, I hope.'

'Course not. We never thought we'd be arrested for Cartier's murder. It was all true, by the way. We really did find him like that. But it was our chance. Cartier was a nobody. He really did pay us to steal back his butter. Can you believe that? That's no way to run a business. His death was no loss.'

'Not to you two, anyway.'

'Very true.'

'But we decided to use it in our favour. While our Breton friends were setting things up, you couldn't associate us with the deal if we were in prison.'

'You needn't have worried. I would never have you thought you capable.'

'Underestimating people again, Eddie.' Jacquot laughed. 'Mind you, it did come close. You know, the guillotine. Never thought that would happen. But we knew you'd come up with the goods.'

'Once we gave you the right information.' Firmin joined in the laughter.

'Also,' I added, smarting at how I'd been played, 'it diverted our attention away from the burglaries.'

Both brothers looked surprised. I nodded pointedly at Morvan, who'd turned to look at us as we spoke.

'I haven't got a clue what you're talking about,' Morvan said.

We were crossing the city, into the Sixteenth. The driver turned us into Avenue Foch and down to the end, where he pulled up between the tree-lined central garden and a gateway into an open courtyard. A table had been set up inside, manned by two German soldiers, while others roamed around the space between the buildings. Half-hearted queues of civilians formed, carrying crates and sacks of all sorts of goods, from clothes to tools, leather to stationery. In front and behind us on the avenue, trucks were pulled up, stacked high with machinery and heavy items.

'Know what this is, Eddie?' Jacquot asked me. 'It's one of their *bureaux d'achats*, a buying agency, where the Germans buy every item you can imagine from these poor fools.'

'Why are you showing me?'

'Because this is where the money is. The black market's all very well. We can make a good living out of it. But if you want the real money, this is the place to be. Work with the Germans to buy up goods from French producers. The mark-up is amazing.'

'I ask again. Why are you showing me?'

Firmin told the driver to move on before answering me.

'Because this is the reason we would never have killed Falke. We've nearly been under the blade for Cartier's death, so we don't fancy any more of the same for Falke's murder. Especially when we didn't do him either. He was the golden goose. Our only way to get into all this. With him dead, we're back to square one. On the outside, looking in.'

'You were trying to edge Falke out,' I told him, nodding at Morvan. 'That's why you had your man here go and see Thier from the Kriegsmarine. You were after cutting out the middle-man.'

Jacquot smiled. 'Ah, you and me, Eddie. We're smarter than we look. You're right. But Thier wasn't buying it. He refused to work directly with us. He's too stuck-up for the likes of us. Not that that stops him from skimming off part of the profits for himself.'

'I thought as much.'

'The operation back there was your friends at the Abwehr. Thier claims to be buying for the Kriegsmarine, but they're buying things the navy couldn't possibly need. It's a racket and Thier is up to his neck in it. And he's the one who makes the rules. So you see, we still needed Falke. There's no way we would have killed him.'

'Why do you want me to know this?'

'To keep you off our backs. The more you know, the more you're involved. Now that you've seen our operation, we own you even more. That'll come in useful to us. We've got a business to run and we don't want you going around accusing us of murders we didn't commit.'

'An illegal business, Jacquot, don't forget that. I could just nick you for that.'

I glanced out of the window. We'd crossed the river and were heading for the Fifth. I wondered where they were taking me next.

'Yes, you could, couldn't you?' He turned to his brother. 'Had we thought of that, Firmin?'

Firmin took a small piece of card out of his coat pocket and handed it to Jacquot. 'Yes, we had.' He turned to me and smiled.

Puzzled, I looked at what Jacquot was holding. It was a photograph. I closed my eyes.

'So you recognise it, then?'

He held it up. It was a souvenir of the night I'd been shown to the area in the courtyard at the German embassy where they kept the coal. In it, I could clearly be seen holding a bag and placing pieces of coal inside. Jacquot turned it so he could see and played at humming and hawing at it. I recalled a flash in the darkness at the time.

'A cop stealing coal. Not good. And it's the Germans' coal too. I imagine your friend in the Abwehr would have something to say about that.'

Taking one last look, he carefully placed it inside his coat pocket. The car pulled up at the end of my street, and Jacquot opened the door to let me out.

'I think I preferred you when you were thick,' I told him.

76

On Monday morning, Dax's office was filled with grey.

Thier was there, along with Hochstetter and a third man, a bull-headed senior officer with more braid than hair and a hard career soldier's body running to fat. Hochstetter announced him as General Niederberger, from the German High Command, a bigwig without the wig but with a malign presence that seeped into every corner of Dax's little office. They'd called me in to make the place even cosier.

Niederberger sat in one of Dax's chairs in front of his desk. Dax sat in his own chair. The three of us remaining stood. It was Niederberger who was doing most of the talking. He gestured over his shoulder without looking at Hochstetter and Thier. He was giving us an ultimatum.

'I have bowed to the judgement of my fellow officers here.' Hochstetter exchanged a glance with me, but Thier stared at the back of the general's head the whole time. 'I would like you to know that for me, I would be taking action immediately. The death of a German citizen on French soil is a very serious crime. My response would be swift and decisive, but Major Hochstetter and Korvettenkapitän Thier have managed to convince me otherwise. Marie Ferran.'

'We don't yet know that Marie Ferran was responsible for Falke's death,' I said.

Dax looked at me, imploring me to keep quiet, and Hochstetter and Thier remained stony-faced. Niederberger didn't appear to have noticed my words. I think he was the sort of person who simply didn't notice my sort of person. He carried on looking at Dax and talking as though I hadn't interrupted, like an army truck running over a mouse.

'Unless Marie Ferran is handed over to the German authorities, we will arrest thirty citizens from the Bel Air district as hostages. We will not search for her or take any hostages for forty-eight hours to give the French police time to find her first and surrender her to us, but after that, my men have orders to act. They will round up thirty hostages and hold them for a further twenty-four hours. If Marie Ferran is not surrendered to us in that time, we will execute the hostages.'

'Do you know what you're saying?' I asked. 'This will tip local people over the edge.'

Niederberger's voice remained the same monotone as he stared at Dax. He hadn't once looked at me. 'If you are unable to control your inferiors, Commissioner, I will have him removed. We will then arrest another thirty hostages every twenty-four hours after that and execute them after twelve hours. Their fate now lies in your hands.'

As abrupt as his message, he stood up and crossed the room to leave. Dax gasped like a landed fish. I was standing by the door and I instinctively moved aside, such was the malevolence in the general's movements. Looking uncertainly at each other, Hochstetter and Thier put their caps on and followed him.

I caught up with Hochstetter by the door to the stairs. Niederberger and Thier were already descending them.

'You can't allow this to happen,' I told him.

'I have no choice.' He looked at the general's retreating figure, with Thier in his wake, and gave the slightest of shakes of his head. 'I have done what I can. The solution now is yours to find.'

*

'How are we going to do this, Eddie?' Dax asked me in his room.

He took the bottle of whisky out of his drawer and looked surprised at the level. He brandished the bottle to ask if I wanted one. I shook my head. It was early even by Dax's standards.

'Differently. We have to put everyone into finding Marie Ferran. Detectives, uniforms, everyone we've got. Target Bel Air and Charonne and find her.'

'We can't hand her over to the Germans.'

'And we can't not.' He looked surprised. 'Don't worry, I've got no intention of letting the Gestapo have her. We just need to find her before they do.'

'Do you believe she killed Falke?'

'I think there's a strong possibility,' I had to admit.

His face fell. 'Then how do we find a way out of this that doesn't involve giving her to the Germans?'

'We find someone they'll be just as happy with.'

Dax and I called all the cops we could lay our hands on – plain-clothes and uniformed – and brought them into the detectives' room. They were sitting on the desks and standing in the aisles. I explained the situation. Who Marie Ferran and Dietrich Falke were and the ultimatum given to us by the Germans that morning. A hum of anger went around the room at that last bit.

'So we're dividing you up into teams. Half of you will take Bel Air, the other half Charonne. You need to find her. And do not tell anyone you speak to about the German ultimatum. That will do nothing but terrify the local people. If I find that anyone has breathed a word of this threat outside this room, I will come for you like Dantès after Danglars.'

They began to disperse, unsure at my last comment if I'd

actually threatened them or not, and began checking with a couple of sergeants which team they were with.

'One more thing,' I told them. 'She's armed and she's scared.'

'How did she get hold of a gun?' someone asked.

'That doesn't matter. All you need to know is that she's got one.'

I watched them disperse before returning to my office. Boniface was at his desk.

'Not out searching for Marie Ferran?' I asked him.

'Another burglary. I've got my own case to worry about.'

I was prevented from replying by a uniformed cop coming in. He was a holding a piece of paper.

'Telegram for you, Inspector Giral.'

I took it from him and read it. It was from my parents, in reply to the one I'd sent them on Thursday. All it said was: *Weather in Pyrenees. Fine.*

I let my hand holding it fall to the desk and stared out of the window. The message I got from their words and their strange punctuation was that Jean-Luc was in the Pyrenees and he was safe. I read it again and wondered how they'd know that and if it was true. Which begged the question as to whether Hochstetter was lying, and why. Unfortunately, I felt I had to believe Hochstetter.

In frustration, I got up and burned the piece of paper in the heater in the detectives' room before going downstairs. All the way down the three flights, the doubts filled my head. And the hope, which was worse.

77

I stood outside and watched the various cars filled with cops leaving Thirty-Six to look for Marie Ferran, and had to stifle a yawn.

After my grand tour of Paris with the Bouvier brothers, I'd been up most of the night reading Paulhan. The bits where he spoke of language as an aid or as an obstacle to expression. I'd worked out that I could hunt for Marie with all the other cops, or I could find another way of solving the problem. Of solving various problems. When clarification becomes obfuscation. Or so I was hoping.

'I am as uncomfortable with this situation as you are. And as Major Hochstetter is. I think hostages and reprisals serve no purpose other than to turn the French against us.'

'I also think Marie Ferran is innocent,' I told Thier in reply.

He drank some coffee and sat back at his desk in the Hôtel de la Marine. I finished mine to wake myself up and hoped for a second cup. Since the start of the Occupation and rationing, and the incompetence of our government and the work of the black marketeers, so much of what had happened had ended up creating whole new currencies by which we lived. In my case, coffee was stronger than any Reichsmark they could ever have tempted me with.

Thier nodded. 'I would like to know more about this Marie Ferran and your reasons for not suspecting her.'

'She's a kid. With a lot of bravado and a lot of anger. She was held by the Gestapo for nearly two months after the Armistice Day events. They staged a mock execution.'

Thier had the grace to look shocked. 'They really are a law unto themselves. Excuse my words at Abwehr headquarters yesterday. I would prefer not to have to pass this investigation on to the Gestapo. It would get a result, of that I have no doubt, but maybe not the correct one.'

'I don't think she'd be capable of killing Falke. I saw her at this incident with Hauptmann Schlegel. She had opportunities to pull the trigger but didn't.'

'Easy to say, not so easy to do,' Thier agreed.

Secretly, I didn't. I couldn't put my hand on my heart and say that Marie had had a clear shot at any time. And even if she had wavered, that didn't mean she wouldn't have pulled the trigger at her second attempt. With Falke. I was walking a thin line.

'We don't have to be in this situation,' I told him. 'Of reprisals.'

'Meaning?'

'In my investigation into the murder of Joseph Cartier, a French black marketeer, a number of people have come to my attention. They're people that you know. One of them is called Morvan, a Breton. And two associates of his, brothers.'

He exhaled heavily. 'I know these people.'

I looked around to buy some time to think of how I was to continue. Through the window, which gave onto Rue Royale, I could see the entrance to Maxim's, where I'd had supper at the German embassy's expense a lifetime ago. And where I'd first met Falke and Thier. For the first time, I noticed a rug on the floor and an ornate mirror on the wall opposite the window. They were both antiques, but new in this room since last time. I knew the Occupiers earned more money from our government and reparations and the fee they charged us for occupying us than they could ever spend, but I was surprised to see so many new purchases. Hochstetter's office had remained untouched in the six months I'd been going there.

'The brothers have an alibi for the murder of Cartier, but Morvan doesn't. The three of them are involved in a business where they've taken over Cartier's black-market operation. I know that they were also working with Dietrich Falke to get into the buying agency business. With the Kriegsmarine.'

He looked sharply at me but didn't deny anything. 'What has this got to do with Falke and Marie Ferran?'

'I think Morvan has killed at least once, possibly on the orders of the Bouvier brothers, to remove the previous black-market operation so that they could take it over. I know that Falke was an associate of theirs, and I suspect they are more ambitious than he suspected.'

'But why would they kill him?'

'Because Falke was a middleman, taking a substantial part of their profits that my suspects wanted for themselves. For which they'd have to trade directly with Falke's clients.'

Thier looked thoughtfully at me for a moment. 'As you have no doubt learned, I have had dealings with these people. I refused their advances. They were far too much of a liability for such a delicate matter. And now it appears I have lost the trader I was dealing with thanks to them.'

'I know you refused. The problem is that these are not the sort of men to take no for an answer.'

'Their ambition?'

'And greed. Enough to want more of the profits that Falke was going to be taking from them.'

'And enough to kill him if he stood in their way?'

'Cartier was killed so they could take over his business. I don't think Falke's death would have caused them any heartache.'

He glanced out of the window. In profile, his brow was creased. He turned to face me. 'Do you believe this to be true?'

'I believe it could be. And I believe it could offer us all a solution to circumstances that could present far greater problems.'

He nodded.

When clarification becomes obfuscation.

78

'Is Sarah there?'

'Why do you want her?'

'Just put her on.'

'She's gone to lunch.'

I was in a café on Rond-Point de Longchamp that had a big friendly painted sign on the window advertising that they had a telephone. Which I was using now to become frustrated with Boniface.

'Any news on Marie Ferran?'

'Not that I've heard.' Then silence for once.

'I need an address, Boniface. It's on a piece of paper on my desk.'

He muttered something in complaint. I heard him put the phone down and rustle about a bit before picking it up again. He sounded angry. *'This is my case, Eddie, not yours.'*

'What on earth are you on about?'

'You know perfectly well. This address on Avenue d'Eylau. That's where Martin Hochstetter was attacked.'

I was stunned silent for a moment. 'What? It's also where Dietrich Falke was staying in Paris. Why didn't you tell me about Hochstetter?'

'The German authorities just said it had been requisitioned. They didn't tell me who was living there. How did you find out?'

'Long story.'

I hung up. I'd recalled Barthe mentioning Falke's address and I'd come here straight after seeing Thier. I had to hope that Thier would go along with my plan, but in the meantime, I wanted to follow up Falke just in case that offered another solution.

Leaving the café, I walked down Avenue d'Eylau in search of the apartment block. The Eiffel Tower stood proud at the end, a view many Parisians would have given their eye teeth for. Obtusely, the fact that Falke – and for some reason Martin Hochstetter – had been staying on this street appealed to me, as it commemorated one of Napoleon's victories over the Russian Empire, backed by the Prussians. I wondered how long it would be before Adolf wanted the name changed.

Finding the number I wanted, I thought for the thousandth time how the Germans really didn't wish any hardships on themselves while they stayed in Paris. The hallway was bigger than my whole apartment, only with none of the damp patches.

I showed my ID to an elderly lady who wore an ancient feather boa and carpet slippers and introduced herself as Madame Renée, the concierge. I asked to be shown up to Falke's flat.

'What a to-do that was,' she told me as we made our slow way up two flights of stairs.

'Wasn't it just?'

She searched through a giant ring of keys and opened up.

'I haven't cleaned. I'm not sure the Boches would allow me to and I haven't heard from that nice Detective Boniface about whether I should.'

'Not a problem, Madame Renée.'

'I'll leave you to it then,' she said, starting the laborious return journey downstairs.

Inside, I closed the door and got a sense of the geography of the flat. It was huge, the rug in the hallway worth a year's salary for me, the floor polished and buffed over decades to a mirror shine. Boniface had told me at the time of the attack on Martin Hochstetter that the owners were Jewish but had fled the city before the Germans arrived. Theirs was one of so many flats that the Occupiers had taken for their own.

I had no real idea what I was looking for. I was just surprised that Martin Hochstetter should have been using an apartment allocated to Dietrich Falke for his non-Nazi-permitted *liaison dangereuse*. A small suspicion began to form in the back of my mind.

Madame Renée had warned me that the bedroom where the attack had taken place hadn't been cleaned, but it was still a surprise to see the extent of how much it had been left alone. The sheets were strewn on the floor, a bedside lamp on its side, the bulb broken. A patch of dried blood marked where Jean Fabre had been beaten. I knew we hadn't searched the flat as thoroughly as we normally would – partly my doing – but it appeared that the Germans had done nothing to reclaim the place since Falke's death either. I was sure they soon would, so this would possibly be my one chance to find anything that had so far gone unseen.

I opened a few drawers, but they were all empty. It evidently wasn't the room that Falke had used for himself. The wardrobe was bare and an ottoman at the foot of the bed bore nothing more than a pile of old sheets and blankets. I looked around at the ornately carved ceiling adornments and the Zuber wallpaper that cost more than my flat, but I couldn't see anything that shouted out to me. Except for the wealth shown in the decorations, more than I'd see in a lifetime of scraping criminals off the street.

Falke's bedroom was obviously the one next to this one. The same expensive and tasteful decor, but lived in by someone who wouldn't know his Watteau from his Fragonard. The bedside drawer contained a bottle of pills and a pornographic magazine. A row of suits and shirts hung in a wardrobe, with a small three-drawer mahogany cabinet at the bottom of it filled with underwear.

Inside the wardrobe, on the left-hand side, was a taller cabinet for trousers that had a lock. Looking at it more closely, I saw that it had been forced, the wood splintered around the metal. I pulled it open and looked inside. A tape recorder stood on the floor; the metal spindles where the tapes should go were empty. The suspicion that had been forming began to take shape.

Finding the cable that emanated from the back of the tape recorder, I followed it from the wardrobe, along the wall where it had been clumsily tacked, and into the first bedroom. I ripped at the wire so that it came away from the wall, and the wave led me to the head of the bed and disappeared underneath. Getting down on my hands and knees, I looked under the bed and pulled at the cable. Attached to the end was a microphone. I sat back on my haunches and inspected it.

'Dietrich, you seedy little bastard,' I said out loud.

I returned to his bedroom, but there were no tapes hidden anywhere. I tried the living room and the kitchen, emptying the drawers and cupboards, figuring that the Germans or whoever came to clean up wouldn't know it had happened after the attack.

I didn't find a tape, but I did find one thing, mixed in with the cutlery in a drawer. A key. I recalled Barthe's comment about everyone using the poste restante office having a locker.

Dusting myself off and taking one last look, I closed the door and went downstairs. The suspicion was firmly in place now. Falke had lent his apartment to Martin Hochstetter for his tryst with Jean Fabre, but had then recorded him. It was no great leap to picture him blackmailing Martin, especially with what was at stake for him as a member of the SS. I had the sudden image of Falke insisting on talking to Martin at the event at the embassy, walking off with him, his arm planted firmly around his shoulder.

'Now all you need is proof,' I told myself.

Madame Renée had a pot of coffee on in her little kitchen. I could smell that it was *café national*. I shuddered.

'Would you like a cup, Inspector Giral? I don't get to talk to many people. Not really.'

'I'd love one, thank you.' I sat down at her table while she poured me a drink before sitting down herself. 'Aren't you having one, Madame Renée?'

She slapped her forehead and got up again. 'Honestly, mind like a sieve.' She poured herself a cup and sat down again.

'Not to worry. So when did you last see Herr Falke?'

She cocked her head to one side, searching through her memory. 'That would be Saturday evening. He was just going out. Awful gentleman.'

Saturday. The night he was murdered. 'Was he with anyone? Did you see anyone follow him when he left?'

'No. He was on his own. The other man was here on his own too.'

'What other man?'

'The German. The one who was attacked. He was just leaving on Sunday morning when I was opening up.'

'Sunday?' When Martin Hochstetter had supposedly left Paris two days earlier. I leaned forward. 'Don't you mean Saturday?'

'I think so. What day is it today? It's Saturday today, isn't it?'

My heart sank. 'Today's Monday.'

She looked doubtful. 'I thought it was Saturday. Never mind. A mess, isn't it?'

'What is?' I was struggling to keep up.

'The apartment. Such a pity.'

'I'm sure you'll be allowed to set it right very soon.'

'I hope so. Your Detective Boniface did at least say I could have the lock repaired.'

'The lock?'

'Yes. Didn't he tell you? A hole clean through the middle of it.'

If she'd punched me in the jaw, I couldn't have been more shocked.

'A hole? Was there any broken glass on the landing?'

'No. No broken glass that I can remember. How's your coffee?'

'It's lovely, thank you.' I couldn't help feeling disappointed. 'Was the light bulb broken, perhaps?'

'Clean through the middle, like I said. No, it wasn't broken. Although the funniest thing. Someone had taken the bulb out of its socket and left it lying on the floor up there. Don't even ask me why. It was the middle of the day when they broke in. So I put it back in before your police got here. So they could see what they were doing.'

79

'I just need to check Herr Doktor Falke's locker,' I told the young German woman with a severe bun and sharp cheeks who was eyeing me warily.

'I cannot allow you in.' She spoke in a voice as unforgiving as her hairstyle. 'And it is my lunchtime, so I am closing.'

Falke's poste restante office was just a quarter of an hour's walk from his apartment, a third of the way down Avenue Foch. It was on the opposite side of the road and a good few blocks from the Sicherheitsdienst, the Nazi intelligence service, which was a relief. It was always a good idea to put as much concrete between you and the SD as you could.

As the woman turned me away, a Wehrmacht officer who could only be described as dashing showed up and went inside. Five minutes later, he re-emerged with the woman. She wore a glow to match his dash.

I waited for them to disappear from sight and went back inside the building. The door to the office was no black-market stronghold and I got past it in less than five minutes.

The reception room was tiny: a desk and chair, an array of pigeonholes behind them for post and a trio of tall metal filing cabinets that looked like they'd seen action at the Meuse on the way here. A window on the left-hand wall cast a meagre light that would depress a mole. Next to a blotter on the desk, a tiny wooden Christmas tree had flopped over to one side. I had to resist the urge to put it up straight.

Two doors gave off the room. I tried the one to the right, which led into a large office with a desk, some shelves and a window that overlooked a garden at the rear of the building. It looked like the room a boss would sit in.

Trying the door straight ahead, to the left of the desk and filing cabinets, I struck gold. Or some sort of metal at least. This was the business end of the operation, with two rows of lockers, a table that I supposed clients could use to count whatever it was they put in the lockers, and a couple of chairs. A window matching the one in the anteroom was set into the wall on the left.

I found the locker I wanted from the number stamped into the key and tried it. It opened without a squeak. I leaned my forehead against the cold metal and breathed out. I hadn't realised I'd been holding my breath.

Inside, I found half a dozen folders stacked untidily at the bottom, resting on something bulky. Lifting the folders, I found a large envelope left underneath them as though to hide it. Pulling it out, I knew straight away from the feel what its contents were. I shook out a tape and held it for a few moments, looking at it as though it could give its secrets away like that.

The phone in the anteroom rang out shrilly and I nearly jumped out of my skin. Absurdly, I imagined the woman suddenly rushing in through the door to answer it. It rang for what seemed an age before the caller gave up. The silence left in its wake was almost more disturbing.

When the echo had died down in my ears, I turned back to the tape, replacing it in the envelope and putting it in my coat pocket. Checking through the folders, I saw that most of their contents were copies of letters between Falke and his office in Germany, but halfway down the pile, I found another, smaller envelope. I took out the letter that was inside and scanned the first couple of lines of text, expecting to find more commercial correspondence, but my head suddenly felt light at what I was reading.

Printed on both sides of a flimsy piece of paper was a record of events left by Falke, from his first meeting with Martin Hochstetter to his last. There was a second piece of paper, a carbon copy of an original. I read it and put both documents back in the envelope. Looking at the address written on the front, I saw that it was in the same handwriting as the notes inside. I guessed that Falke had addressed the envelope to himself at this office as insurance. He'd received it in time to store it in his locker.

'For all the good it did you.'

I replaced all the other items in the locker and locked it again. I put the second envelope inside my coat with the one containing the tape, and took one last look around the room before turning the light off and closing the door. As I was crossing the reception room, I heard voices outside and a bunch of keys jangling. There was an urgency to the sound that matched my own. I quickly ran to turn the light out before retracing my steps into the room where the lockers were just as I heard the key going into the landing door lock. I was closing the door gently as the office door opened.

Listening out, I heard voices and laughter and the unmistakable sound of kissing that was as energetic as it was wet. After that, silence. I tiptoed to the window and looked out onto the street. It would have been climbable had it not been so public. And had the bars on the window not been quite so sturdy. Walking silently back to the door, I heard another door open, the one into the main office, I assumed. The sounds the couple were making were taking on a different insistency.

Opening the door a crack, I looked through. All I saw was

that the door into the office was open and the light on. Stepping out and pulling the locker room door shut behind me, I took one last look around the anteroom to make sure I hadn't left anything and crossed to the outer door. Glancing to my left, I saw that the couple were enjoying a Beer Hall Putsch of their own on the boss's desk, so I quickly opened the door and clicked it shut behind me as silently as possible. Although I imagined that not even a marching band playing outside the window would break their magic spell right now.

I walked down the stairs smiling to myself.

Before leaving, I'd put her little Christmas tree upright. It seemed only fitting.

80

It was a tough call which piece of pornography Falke would have found more delectable, the magazine in his bedside table or the recording he'd made in the bedroom next to his, no doubt when he was out. The magazine had involved lots of women, sometimes alone, sometimes with other women. The tape recording was of one man with another. I recognised one voice as Martin Hochstetter's; the other had to be Jean Fabre. Not that there was a great deal of talking. I wound the tape back to the start of its original spool and took it off the tape recorder.

Mayer, the sergeant in the evidence room, had found me a machine to play the tape on. He was one of the few cops not out looking for Marie Ferran, but I always wished the elegant, fine-featured man from Alsace worked with us upstairs in the detectives' room. He had a keener intellect and sharper insight than the vast majority of the detectives who graced the office heater, but he was stuck down here in the bowels of the building.

'Any help?' he asked me when I returned the tape recorder to him.

'I hope so.'

I climbed back up the three flights to find Sarah in my office but Boniface mercifully absent. I held out the two pieces of paper from the smaller envelope.

'Could you get these photographed, please, Sarah? It's urgent. Give me the originals and keep the copies in this room.'

I watched her go and pondered my latest dilemma.

Although I still feared that it was Marie who'd killed Falke, plucking up the courage to pull the trigger on him after Saturday's dress rehearsal, I now also had another very credible possibility. Only it wasn't the easy one I would have liked. I now had a clear suspicion that Martin Hochstetter had killed Falke. The tape recorder, the scene at Ambassador Abetz's celebration, the possibility that Falke had been blackmailing Martin.

But that was all it was. A suspicion.

There was also the unreliable word of Madame Renée that she'd seen Martin at Falke's flat on what may have been Sunday morning against Hochstetter's claim that his brother had left Paris on Friday. Martin had the motive and the means, but by all accounts he didn't have the opportunity.

I tried to imagine taking it to the German authorities without cast-iron evidence. Without any evidence. And even if I did have proof, I really couldn't see them accepting one of their own – an officer at that – being responsible for Falke's murder. Even if they believed me, they'd make sure it was hushed up, with Marie as the scapegoat.

And then there was Hochstetter.

Martin being guilty of Falke's murder would exonerate Marie, but if I were to accuse his brother officially, Hochstetter would double his efforts to cover it up. It would quite simply be opening the floodgates of reprisals for Marie and the people of Bel Air.

And then he'd come for me. With a vengeance. And, more importantly, for Jean-Luc. My son, who as far as I could tell, was in a German prison at the mercy of whatever wrath I inspired in Hochstetter.

I was damned if I did and damned if I didn't. Only it would also be Marie Ferran or thirty of her neighbours who were damned if I didn't.

81

'We need more time.'

I was in the lion's cage, only the lion was the one holding the whip and the chair.

Hochstetter studied me. It was time for another of his cigarette epics. He chose his moments. Aeons shifted and he answered. A simple shake of the head.

'Can you ask Niederberger to give us another forty-eight hours?' I was hoping for twenty-four.

'I am afraid that will not be possible, Édouard. Korvetten-kapitän Thier and I have already staked our reputations to assist you in your cause. There really is no more we can do.'

'New information has come to light,' I said warily. This was where the lion got hold of the revolver as well if I wasn't careful.

'What new information?'

'The criminal gang that has been working with the Kriegs-marine. There's credible proof of their involvement in not only the murder of Dietrich Falke, but that of Joseph Cartier as well.'

Which was true as far as it went, but not really the whole story. Or even that true.

'May I see this information?'

'I've passed it on to Korvettenkapitän Thier. He's dealing with the matter.'

Hochstetter took one of those drags on his cigarette that seemed to turn his cheeks hollow. 'I know.'

'Have there been any reports of arrests of French people crossing the demarcation line?'

'Why? Do you suspect Marie Ferran of having attempted to cross the line?'

'Yes,' I lied. I pictured Sylvie being caught trying to cross the border. I needed to know. 'Sometime on Saturday or possibly Sunday morning.'

'I will check.' He called up someone on the intercom and asked them to look into it.

'How is your brother?' I asked.

'He is well, thank you. But please do not think this is an opportunity for you to take advantage of that affair. I am afraid that for you that ship has sailed.'

'Is he back in Berlin?'

'Indeed he is.'

'When did he return?'

Hochstetter cocked his head to one side and studied me. I thought for a moment that I'd shot my bolt, that he'd clam up. But he gave the appearance of having decided my question was not a trick one.

'On Saturday morning.'

'You said he left on Friday.'

'I am aware of that. I told you that simply to prevent you from causing a nuisance before he had time to leave.'

I kept my frustration in check. Saturday morning still gave Martin an alibi for Falke's murder.

'I'm asking you again about my son. May I see him?'

He sighed. 'I understand your concerns. And in this matter of Marie Ferran, I am equally dissatisfied with the idea of reprisals, but regarding your son, I am afraid it is really not in my gift. It is a matter between the Gestapo in Bordeaux and the military district that will be the site of the camp to which he is sent. I have no involvement or influence even if I wanted to.'

A knock on the door preceded the arrival of the person at the other end of Hochstetter's intercom. He handed the major a piece of paper and a file. Hochstetter thanked him and waved him away. I waited an age while he read the note.

'It would appear that Marie Ferran did not attempt to cross the demarcation line. There are no reports of arrests at the times you said.'

'Or just that she wasn't caught.'

My words hid my relief that Sylvie either hadn't crossed into the Unoccupied Zone or had crossed into it safely.

He tapped the folder. 'The post-mortem report on Herr Doktor Falke.' He opened it, studying a document inside without letting me see it. I had a greater urge to grab it than I'd ever had to fling his cigarette out of the window.

'What is it?' I asked him, masking the impatience I felt.

He read out some of the contents, the usual pathologist detail, before coming to one point that shocked me. 'It seems that Herr Doktor Falke was killed with a single bullet fired from a Luger.'

'A German weapon.'

'Plenty of French people with Lugers,' he commented, without breaking his stride.

He carried on reciting from the report, but I wasn't listening.

If Falke was shot with a Luger, then it wasn't my gun that had killed him. And if it wasn't my gun, there was every possibility it wasn't Marie. I looked at Hochstetter as he came to the end of the report and exhaled slowly.

The problem was, I was still unable to tell him any of that so they'd call the dogs off Marie. He could never learn that she'd stolen my gun and that I'd suspected her of using it to kill a German and tried to cover it up.

I had one last question to ask before leaving. But it wasn't for Hochstetter.

At the front desk of the Lutetia, I put my hand in my inside pocket as though I was reaching for something. The hauptmann wasn't on duty this morning. His place had been taken by a young woman. Another severe bun, this time with a uniform and a smile that was discordant with everything else about her and her setting.

'I have a document for Martin Hochstetter,' I told her.

'I am so sorry, but Hauptsturmführer Hochstetter has left. He was only here on leave for the Christmas period.'

'Oh, that's so disappointing. I must have just missed him. Do you know when he left?'

She checked a ledger that was on the desk. 'Saturday.'

'Saturday?'

I couldn't help feeling dashed. My poor old Madame Renée with her feather boa and faded slippers had been wrong. I turned away.

'Oh no, wait a minute,' the woman suddenly said. She was looking at another part of the ledger. 'Hauptsturmführer Hochstetter was supposed to leave on Saturday, but he was able to find a Luftwaffe transport flight instead of the train. He left on Sunday.'

I stared at her, trying to see the ledger from which she was reading.

'Sunday? You're certain of that?'

'Yes.' She smiled, which was almost better than the news she'd given me. 'Sunday morning.'

I thanked her and left, emerging onto the cold of Boulevard Raspail, outside the Lutetia, deep in thought. I looked back to where I thought Hochstetter's office window must be and took a deep breath.

A diesel engine juddered to a halt alongside me. I glanced at it.

German staff cars, like dilemmas, were coming thick and fast.

'A word, Inspector Giral.'

Thier sat in the back of the car, a gefreiter at the wheel and a feldwebel holding the rear door open for me.

'Thirty-Six, Quai des Orfèvres,' I told the feldwebel and climbed in. 'Not the scenic route.'

He didn't react. He had a face that wouldn't register an emotion if Adolf and Heinrich were to dance a cancan past him in tassels and top hat.

'Do not confuse me with Major Hochstetter,' Thier told me.

'That's not as easy as you think.'

Thier nodded at the feldwebel, who tapped the gefreiter on the arm, telling him to drive on. We drove across the river, where Thier told the gefreiter to pull over to one side of the Place de la Concorde. He ordered the two men in the front to get out. I watched them stand on the pavement some distance from the car, stamping their feet to keep warm. There were no other people on the darkened street, no cars jostling for space, just one bus rumbling by.

'A sad sight,' he suddenly said.

'There's a simple solution.'

'There's never a simple solution. Have you found Marie Ferran?'

'Not yet.'

He paused while a three-wheeled contraption with a gas cylinder strapped to the back thundered by, another of the new inventions made necessary by rationing and shortages.

'I have arranged a meeting with the Bouvier brothers and their associates for tomorrow evening.' He nodded at the Hôtel de la Marine opposite. 'In my office. At seven p.m. This means we should be able to come up with the solution we discussed and prevent reprisals against innocent civilians.'

'I want reassurances they'll be treated as prisoners.'

'You have my word. They will go into the German system and be treated fairly.'

'Will they be charged with Falke's murder?'

'No, as that would mean the death sentence.' He turned to face me. 'In both our interests, we will find a more suitable perpetrator of this crime. One who compromises neither of us.'

'Who?'

'Falke himself.'

He indicated that I should get out. I watched the two Germans get back in and make the short journey to the Hôtel de la Marine.

There was just one thing that puzzled me.

Why I could smell Gomina Argentine in Thier's car.

82

'I've found Marie Ferran.'

It wasn't the message that shocked me, it was the source.

The next morning, Dax had forced me to direct operations from Thirty-Six while all the other cops were out looking for Marie again. Even though I had to hope that Thier would be as good as his word, we still had to find her before the ultimatum ran out, just in case. Dax had even drafted Sarah into searching. She was the one on the phone to me now.

'Where are you?'

'I'm at a café on Rue de Vignoles, in Charonne. I tried to think of one place she wouldn't think anyone would look for her. The warehouse you raided, the one the new gang had taken over and abandoned. She's there.'

'We looked there.'

'That's where she is.'

'Wait for me. Don't go in, but keep an eye on the building.'

I drove as far above the Germans' speed limit as I dared to the Right Bank and across a Place de la Bastille so quiet it still unnerved me, through streets to the dead-end lane where Boniface and I had been chased by the Bretons. Sarah was waiting outside the café.

'Stay here,' I told her. 'She knows me.'

Inside the building on Impasse de Bergame, I trod carefully

and opened the door as silently as I could. The lock wasn't repaired from where we'd broken it during the raid, but I noticed some string hanging down from the interior handle. It looked like someone was using it to fasten the door when they were inside. The light was on, so if it was Marie and she was in, she'd failed to hook it up.

Edging forward, I froze when I heard a noise. Wood on concrete. Armistice shoes. The sound was coming from behind a bank of empty shelves to my left, separated from me by a dividing wall. A chair scraped and it sounded like someone had sat down. Moving slowly around it, I came upon a figure sitting at a table before I'd realised what was happening.

She looked up at me.

'Hello, Marie,' I greeted her.

'Jean-Luc said he wanted to kill a German,' Marie told me. 'But you stopped him.'

I was sitting at the table opposite her. She had a piece of stale baguette she was trying to eat with a glass of water.

'Let me buy you breakfast.'

She looked thoughtful for a moment but shook her head. 'You won't stop me.'

'Did you kill the German in the gardens?'

'What do you think?'

I tried to hide my exasperation. 'I don't know what to think, Marie. That's why I'm trying to help you.'

'By handing me in to the Germans?'

'I'm not going to hand you in. I'm here to protect you. But you're only going to be safe with me. The Germans are going to come looking for you, and I won't be able to do anything if they find you before I can get you somewhere safe.'

'And what's this somewhere safe? A prison cell?'

I had to be honest. 'Yes, but with us in the police station. And the Germans won't know about it. But I need to know if you killed Falke or not.'

'So what if I did?'

'That's no answer, Marie. I need to know. But I'm going to try and make the Germans think you didn't do it.'

She chewed a piece of bread and looked puzzled. 'Why?'

'I told you. It's the only way I can see that will keep you safe. And everyone you love.'

'Everyone I love?'

She pulled out a photograph and turned it on the table to face me. I immediately felt my throat constrict. It was a photo of her and Jean-Luc, laughing at the camera. I picked it up. It was a Jean-Luc I'd missed.

'How old were you?' I asked her.

'Sixteen.'

He looked like Charles, my older brother. The same thoughtful look, the eyes that were sad even when they were laughing. My brother Charles who had died in the last war when he was little older than Jean-Luc now. I had to put it back on the table face-down.

'He's safe, you know,' she said.

'How do you know?'

She took a form postcard from her pocket and showed it to me. It was dated the beginning of December, after Hochstetter claimed Jean-Luc had been arrested. Unfortunately, that didn't have to mean anything. The post was notoriously slow. The card just had the standard lines that the sender crossed out as appropriate. One in particular jumped out at me.

'This doesn't tell you anything. Anyone could have sent it.' My hand trembling slightly, I pointed at the line that had drawn my attention. 'It says he's a prisoner.'

It was her turn to point at it. 'He's added an exclamation mark.'

'That doesn't mean anything.'

She shook her head sadly. 'It was a private joke between us. He used to send me a note when he was going to bunk off school to see me. It always said he was a prisoner, with an exclamation mark. It means he's free.'

I took it from her and studied it. The exclamation mark seemed both bigger and to diminish, almost disappear.

'Are you sure about this?'

'Completely.'

I set my hands down on the table to stop them from shaking and gave the card back to her. 'Then you have to stay safe for him.'

She put the card and the picture back in her pocket. 'How do I do that?'

'Give me my gun.'

'So now we get to the reason why you're here.' She laughed, an oddly joyous sound.

I held my hand out on the table. 'Hand it over, Marie, please.'

She nodded and reached into her lap. I hadn't seen it resting there. But instead of handing the gun over to me, she held it to her own head.

'I will die rather than go to prison. I don't care if it's the Gestapo or your nice safe cell, but I won't go to prison again.'

She stood up and pushed her chair back.

'If you kill a German, Marie, they will kill thirty of your neighbours.'

'All the more reason to kill myself.'

'Don't do anything stupid.'

She took the gun from her head for a brief second to look at it. 'Don't worry. If I'm going to kill a Nazi, I'll do it in a Nazi way.' She gestured at the cupboard where she'd trapped me the last time. 'In there.'

I looked at the narrow closet and quailed. 'I can't.'

She cocked the gun and pressed it harder against her temple. 'All right, all right.'

I backed into the cupboard and she closed the door. I was immediately engulfed in a darkness blacker than a night terror. I heard the key turn in the lock. It clattered on the floor when she threw it away.

'Marie, don't be stupid. Let me out.'

I heard nothing for a few moments, and my breath began to come in short gasps. After a while, I heard her shoes clacking on the floor. I banged the door as hard as I could, but it barely seemed to make any noise.

'Open the door, Marie.'

The longer I could hear her, the longer it was before the fear would completely set in. In the dark, I heard her scrabbling around outside, and then there was silence. I banged again, but I knew she'd gone.

Memories of rats and water came back to me. Dust and darkness. Rocks and earth closing in. It was a memory, but not of the trenches.

I heard more scraping. I almost called out, but didn't in case it wasn't Marie returning. Someone else was moving about in the warehouse, their steps sounding like they were trying to make as little noise as possible. I listened intently at the door. There was no sound of wood on concrete, just of metal rasping on the floor. The new footsteps were louder now. They approached the door.

The key in the lock made me recoil, injecting a strange blend of fear and relief into my veins. The door opened tentatively, and light from the bulbs and the window seeped in. I could see out and it felt sweeter than the moment in the last war when you got back to your trench and sat in the mud with your head in your hands and your rifle between your knees. Until you counted the dead.

The door opened wider. I saw the shock on Sarah's face.
'What happened?'

I gestured at my surroundings with my eyes. 'This did. Help me out.'

83

'What was the problem with the cupboard?'

For the fourth time I picked my gun up off the table where I'd been sitting with Marie. The moment Sarah had released me from the cupboard, I'd seen it lying there.

'Did you get this from Marie?' I'd asked her.

'It was there when I came in. Marie had gone.'

I'd looked at the window she'd used the last time to escape and knew she'd been swallowed up in the lanes and alleys of Charonne. It was now Sarah and me who were sitting at the table, in my case calming my nerves. I glanced back at the open door of the cupboard.

'I was a prisoner in the last war.' I heard her give a sharp intake of breath. 'Most of the time I was bored, some of the time I was afraid. But then the Germans put me to work in a coal mine. Ten hours a day, crouching, digging coal for their war effort. I never got used to it.'

'I'm sorry. How long did they hold you?'

'Two years, nearly. I was taken prisoner at Verdun and released after the Armistice. Then our army wouldn't demob me for another year. It still felt like a prison.'

'How long did it take to get back to normal after you came home?'

'I'll let you know.'

'So you understand what my husband's going through.'

'I've got some idea.' I looked again at my gun. It was fully loaded, not one bullet missing. 'Why?'

'You should probably put it in your holster before you lose it again.'

I swapped the Luger for my service pistol and put the Luger in my coat pocket. When it was done, I looked at her.

'I saw you with a German woman in uniform.'

'Following me again?'

'I like to know who I'm working with.'

She took a deep breath. 'The hotel next to where I live has been requisitioned by the Germans. They've billeted all the grey mice there.'

Grey mice. The nickname that Parisians had quickly given to female clerks in the German army because of their grey uniform.

'I've got to know some of them.' She looked at me frankly. 'I've made it my business to get to know some of them. Most of them are young women away from home for the first time. They're lonely and no one in the city apart from their own soldiers wants to know them.'

'So you talk to them?'

'So I talk to them. Some of them are like me, married to men who've gone away to war and are fighting somewhere. Or in a PoW camp, in my case. They need to see a friendly face and I give them that. I meet them in a café next door to their hotel. I don't go anywhere else with them. I don't want to be seen.'

'So why is it your business to get to know them?'

'Because who knows when what they tell me might come in useful. They all work in the various military organisations. They learn things that the officers and men discuss without worrying about them overhearing. And they tell me because I ask them and I show an interest in them.'

'There has to be more of a reason than that.'

'Isn't that reason enough? The only way we're going to get our country back – and our husbands – is with knowledge. And the use of that knowledge.'

'When the time is right.' My reply hung in the air. 'The Gaullist argument.'

'I'm no Gaullist. Or Communist.'

'So what are you?'

'Nothing. I'm just doing what I can, whatever that means.'

'We all are. And none of us knows what it means. Not yet. Not really.'

She studied me for a moment. 'We should never underestimate what we can be capable of. What any of us can be capable of. In a situation as extreme as this.'

'I don't.'

'Are you sure of that?'

I stood up. Her question smarted. 'I'd better go and look for Marie's family. See if she's turned up there.'

Sarah remained sitting. 'I'll stay here a while. See if she comes back.'

I nodded. 'Good idea. See you later, Sarah.'

'See you later, Eddie.'

I turned and left.

'Eddie,' I said quietly to myself before realising.

'Anything?'

'Nothing.'

The uniformed sergeant I asked looked exhausted, but at least he'd worked up a sweat despite the cold. He'd been searching for Marie Ferran for nearly two days in Bel Air.

'Keep looking,' I told him. 'She's nearby.'

I didn't tell him she'd got away again, or that she was no longer armed. No one needed to know that.

'One thing, Eddie. The people we're talking to think we're

after Marie Ferran to punish her. They don't realise we're trying to save her, so they're obstructive. If we could only say what was going on, they might be more helpful.'

'I agree with you, but we can't. If we tell them thirty of their neighbours are likely to be executed, we'll just panic them. What the Germans did to Bonsergent will be a carol concert compared with what they'd do if people here started rioting.'

Another cop joined us, one of the young detectives who'd been called up during the fighting as a reservist and then de-mobilised without seeing action. He was one of those I'd asked to find Pierre Ferran and try to reason with him.

'Pierre Ferran,' he told me now. 'He's in a café on Rue de la Voûte. He said he's willing to talk to you.'

Following the detective's instructions, I found Pierre in Ulysse's café. He was sitting alone at a table in the window. He looked as miserable and worried as I felt.

'I'm waiting here in case she comes in,' he told me when I sat down next to him. 'My father and all our neighbours are looking out for her.'

'Have you seen her today?'

He shook his head and looked at me mournfully. 'What's going on? Why are the cops suddenly so keen on finding her?'

I understood the sergeant's words of a few moments ago. It would be so tempting to tell Pierre, to make him see the urgency of the situation. Instead, I just gave him words. 'She's a young kid. She's not safe and she's got a gun. We just need to get to her before the Germans do.'

That bit at least was true.

'My father doesn't want me talking to you. He says you're only after Marie so you can turn her over to the Germans.'

I hung my head and silently cursed Yves. 'I'm the only chance you've got of making sure Marie comes out of this alive. Your father's going to get her killed, Pierre. And others.'

84

'The Bouvier brothers. I want to question them.'

I looked dumbfounded at Boniface behind his piles of folders. 'You want to what?'

'You heard, Eddie. I want to question the Bouvier brothers. They were in the Eighth when they were arrested. That puts them in the frame for the burglaries.'

I looked at him then surreptitiously at my watch. I had just a few minutes before I had to go out on my own job while Thier met the brothers at the Kriegsmarine.

'Are you mad? They were in prison for most of them.'

'Only the recent ones. You said yourself they're working with this Breton gang. I can get to them through the Bouviers.'

'Boniface, I don't want you messing things up talking to the Bouvier brothers.'

'That's not your decision to make. This is my case and I choose who I want to question for it.'

I nearly punched the desk in frustration. 'No, I've got them in my own frame for something else.'

They also had me in a frame, one of me stealing coal from the German embassy. And any minute now, the Kriegsmarine was going to be helping set them up for their involvement in screwing up Thier's business with Falke. Coincidentally getting them off my back if I played my part right.

Boniface leered at me across the room. 'Found your gun yet?'

I paused to calm myself before replying. 'All right, Boniface, truce. Henri Lafont's the one you need to go after. That's the word I'm getting. You need to talk to Hochstetter about him. I'm sure he'd be happy to help.'

I left. My service pistol stayed firmly hidden in its holster.

'It's cold, Eddie.'

'Quit your moaning. You'll be back in the warm soon enough.'

I was standing on the street corner facing the warehouse where Morvan had taken me on Sunday for my audience with Jacquot and Firmin. I still found it hard to believe that the two punks I'd known since they were in stolen short trousers had grown up to become highly immoral villains. I almost felt a touch of pride.

'Bloody freezing.'

Next to me, Isaac l'Aveugle, Isaac the Blind, started stamping his feet to stave off the winter, making a hell of a racket.

'Will you stop doing that? You know we're not supposed to be here.'

With the face of an angel, the beard of an elf and the soul of a magpie, Isaac was the best safe-cracker I'd ever arrested, but he was as cantankerous as they came. He'd gained his nickname after a shell had exploded near him during the Boxer Rebellion in China, blinding him.

'It's New Year's Eve. I should be home in the bosom of my family.'

'Don't give me that. You know you miss this.'

I looked at my watch, trying to catch the light from a chink in a curtain. Thier's meeting with the Bouviers and the Bretons should be just starting. I nudged Isaac on the arm.

'Let's go.'

I guided him across the cobblestones of the courtyard towards the main door into the warehouse. I could have unlocked it myself, but Isaac would have it open and the coffee on by the time I'd decided which pick to use.

Inside, we crept past shelves piled high with tins and boxes to the room that the brothers used as their office. None of the gang members was there, so Thier was keeping that part of the bargain at least.

'In the corner,' I told Isaac.

'That means fuck-all to me.'

I steered him to a free-standing safe set against the wall in the left-hand corner behind Jacquot's chair. I'd spotted it when I'd been there on Sunday.

'Do your stuff,' I told him.

I knew better than to leave him to it while I went to nick some of the food from the warehouse. The dishonest bugger would have taken whatever he could from the safe before I'd got a look-in.

'There you go, Eddie. We're in.'

Reaching inside, I found piles of cash, which I left, apart from a stack I handed over to Isaac for his time. On a small half-shelf on one side, I found what I was looking for. The photo of me stealing coal. I rummaged around for any other copies, and found the negative lying underneath.

'Jackpot,' I muttered.

'Anything else, Eddie?'

'I'll grab us a bag each, Isaac. There are tins of food aplenty in the room outside. Fancy some coffee and sardines?'

'Ugh, sardines. Haven't they got any pâté?'

'You do know there's a war on?'

I took Isaac back to his home, a dingy flat in the Marais where he lived with his daughter, and drove back to Charonne. I had no idea what I expected to find, but I wanted to make sure everything had gone smoothly. The first thing I saw was that the outer door was open. I knew for certain that I'd closed it behind us when we left.

Checking up and down the *impasse*, I pulled my gun out and went in. From the brothers' office, a dim light shone through a gap in the door, but I didn't need to push it open to know what I'd find. The smell of cordite hung heavy in the cold air.

I holstered my gun and cursed. Jacquot was in his chair, Firmin on the floor in front of the desk. Both had a single bullet wound to the head. I looked more closely. Thier had staged it to look like Jacquot had shot Firmin, then himself. I recalled his words about making it appear that Falke had killed himself.

'Problem solved,' a voice said from behind me.

I turned to see Thier standing behind me. He was alone, but I had no doubt there'd be a German or two not far away.

'This isn't what we agreed.'

'No, but you have to admit it works. Both our headaches have gone away in one fell swoop. I have a new partner, who is far less problematic than these two chancers.'

'Morvan?'

'Morvan.'

'Your mystery lunch partner at Le Catalan. The one you were dealing with all along behind the Bouviers' backs.'

He gave a grudging nod. 'And you are rid of whatever it is the brothers had on you.'

'You sent me off after Otto to distract me from your own operation.'

'We all protect our interests.'

'And Marie Ferran?'

'As we agreed.'

In reply, I pointed to the two dead bodies.

'You have my word,' Thier said.

85

At home, I made up a fire and took out the last of the whisky that Hochstetter had left me. I'd wanted to share it with Dominique, but I never knew how she'd react to it. And now Dominique wasn't here and I wasn't in Montmartre. Staring at the flames starting to take shape, I took a sip and closed my eyes. It was good. Only it didn't taste good.

If I closed my eyes, I saw Jacquot in his chair and Firmin lying on the floor in front of the desk. And I saw Thier's calm logic appraising the sight. I opened them again and stared instead at the flames steadily licking the blackened sides of the grate, their heat reaching my legs.

What had I honestly thought would happen? That Thier would arrest the brothers on some vague lesser charge and send them to Germany, where they'd receive a gentlemanly trial and a fur-lined prison cell? The moment I threw in my lot with the Kriegsmarine, I signed Jacquot and Firmin's death sentence. I either hadn't seen it or hadn't wanted to see it. That guilt washed over me.

But so did another emotion. Relief. Their death served me. It had saved me. I'd sold Jacquot and Firmin down the river for the good of others. For Marie Ferran and Martin Hochstetter. For Thier and Hochstetter. For Morvan and the Bretons. But most of all, for me. Jacquot's photo of me at the coal face had been a wasted venture, just like his black-market ambitions. I'd sacrificed them all on the altar of my own safety. I'd used Thier and his own ambition to get the Bouvier brothers off my back. They hadn't killed Cartier or Falke, I knew that, but if anyone had to be the lamb to the slaughter, it was them and the hold they'd tried to get over me.

I took a drink. It tasted no better.

I had suspicions but few certainties. I think I knew who had killed Falke. From the tape and the two documents that he had left, I knew that he was blackmailing Martin, so I suspected Martin of killing him and then returning to Berlin. The uncertainty there was how I was going to use that to my advantage with his brother. Another uncertainty was how many others Falke had been blackmailing, and how many other potential suspects lay unknown to me. Or if I was wrong and it wasn't Martin at all – Falke had simply been another victim of Thier's greed and machination. As had I, the thought crossed my mind.

Joseph Cartier. I didn't yet know who his killer was. Oddly, I believed Jacquot and Firmin, which meant that Cartier's killer was still a mystery. Falke? With Thier? Morvan with either? Morvan was, perhaps, the obvious one as he was the beneficiary, but now there was a new uncertainty as I'd seen the extent of what Thier was willing to do for his own ambition.

And behind it all was my other motivation, the one altruistic reason for me doing what I'd done – to ensure that Marie Ferran went free and no hostages were executed. I had to believe that that made it worth it.

That deserved a drink of Hochstetter's whisky. It still tasted bitter.

The fire glowed brightly now and warmed my face. It was almost painful. Almost as much as another New Year's Eve on my own in my armchair and no sound of another person's voice. Or music.

'Happy New Year,' I said, my voice echoing unhappily in my little flat.

86

The new year awoke to a heavy fall of snow on the ground. I trudged ankle-deep through a good fifteen centimetres of it from home across the Pont Saint-Michel to Thirty-Six. On an empty Île de la Cité, my footsteps crunched loudly under a white sky. It was the only noise in the muffled air. I'd forgotten to remove the Luger from my coat the night before, and it weighed heavily in my pocket.

I stood for a full quarter of an hour by the heater in the detectives' room, getting any part of me warm that I could and scowling at anyone who came near. I spied Lafitte staring at me, the scorn in his eyes as dark and empty as the sky outside the windows. Opposite him, Courtet was on the phone, oblivious to the world. Lafitte picked up the phone next to him and a connection was made in my memory.

Waiting for him to speak to the person on the other end, I strode over and took the receiver from him.

'Judge Rambert?' I said into the mouthpiece.

Only it was a woman's voice on the other end. Lafitte snatched it back from me. 'My wife.'

Shocked, I looked up to see Courtet whispering into his phone, looking like he wanted to hang up. Lunging across, I grabbed the receiver and listened. It was Rambert's voice I heard.

'Detective Courtet can't come to the phone right now,' I told him. 'He's about to face some summary justice of his own.'

I hung up and Courtet blanched. I was about to open my mouth, but he was saved by Dax, a temporary reprieve, who called him into his office.

I returned to the heater to wait, as lonely in my anger as I had been before. The one person who dared to join me was Sarah. Her comment about underestimating people weighed heavy. The one person I'd overestimated throughout the investigation had been Morvan, his presence blinding me to other, more real threats, like the Bouvier brothers. And even then, I'd ended up underestimating him, when he'd connived with Thier under everyone's nose. I stared moodily at the stove. Sarah's presence next to me at the heater was a sharp reminder of all that.

'I went out with one of my grey mice on Sunday night,' she said, her voice low so no waggling ears could pick up her words. 'Her name's Karin and she works in the High Command. She lost her husband in Poland and she's no fan of the Nazis.'

'Why are you telling me this?' I couldn't help a note of impatience creeping into my question.

'Just hear me out. She's lonely here and needs someone to talk to, so I took her for a drink and got her to open up a bit. She has access to PoW records.'

'Is this because of your husband?'

She shook her head. 'Your son. I asked her if she could arrange for you to visit him in prison.'

I stiffened, nervous at what she might say. 'And can she?'

'That's the point, she can't.'

I hung my head. The let-down felt unbelievably cruel.

'You don't understand,' Sarah continued. 'I had dinner with her last night. She's been looking through all the PoW records, including the ones held by the Gestapo in Bordeaux, and there's no record of your son.'

'What does that mean?'

'It means he's not a prisoner. Your Major Hochstetter is lying.'

'Is there any chance she might be wrong?'

'She double-checked. And all the records she has are up to date. You know what they're like – everything in its place. The fact is, your son hasn't been captured or imprisoned.'

I stared into the flames in the heater, the emotions of the last few minutes impossible to bear.

'Hochstetter lying?' I thought of his assertion that his brother had left Paris on the Saturday. 'Who would have thought it?'

'It means he doesn't have this hold over you.'

'Only if I can prove he's lying.'

'Call his bluff.'

She handed me the papers I'd given her to have photographed.

'Why are you doing all this?' I asked her. 'You sure you're not Resistance?'

'Hardly.'

Before going, she looked at the untidy handwritten scrawl in German on the first sheet of paper and laughed. 'What do they say? Has Laval's German citizenship come through?'

Deep in thought, I watched her leave the warmth of the heater for the office we shared.

'Which is exactly the line from the *Résistance* pamphlet,' I said to myself.

Dax called me into his room. I was still warming the backs of my legs and absorbing Sarah's words. He closed the door behind me. Courtet was nowhere to be seen, but Dax had other things on his mind.

'German bigwigs on the way,' he told me.

'What do they want?'

We only had to wait another ten minutes to find out. The same trio of aces as Monday came in. Hochstetter, Thier and

Niederberger. The first two looked like New Year's Eve had worked its magic on them. Niederberger was as fresh as a nettle.

'We have a declaration,' Niederberger announced. 'In light of new information that has come to light with regard to the death of German citizen Herr Doktor Dietrich Falke, French citizen Marie Ferran is no longer suspected of his murder. The order placed on her head and the ultimatum delivered here on Monday is rescinded.'

He stood up, a bare thirty seconds after sitting down, and began to leave the room. Despite the hangover snarling in his head, Hochstetter spoke up before he could go.

'I would like to commend Inspector Édouard Giral for his actions in assisting the German authorities. We have ascertained that Herr Doktor Falke's death was due to suicide.' He stared pointedly at me. 'A more thorough search of the area uncovered the weapon.'

'I'm sure it did.'

He nodded at me. Niederberger grunted. Not once had he looked at me. So Falke was a suicide and the Bouvier brothers no longer existed – in any sense. Carrying their hangovers with them, Hochstetter and Thier slowly followed the general out of Dax's office.

Boniface joined us in Dax's office. If I'd expected any plaudits from Dax for averting reprisals in Bel Air, there were none coming.

'You know Lafont is not behind the burglaries,' Boniface told me. 'Stop wasting my investigation. I want the brothers for this.'

I sighed and looked at him. I'd expected a mouthful of Dax's whisky at least. 'You're right. It's probably the Bouviers. I suggest you go after them, although they might have gone to ground.'

He snorted, but it was Dax who spoke.

'I need to see your service pistol, Eddie.'

I hesitated a moment and looked at them both before pulling it out. 'You mean this one?'

I could sense the disappointment Boniface felt.

'Out, both of you,' Dax told us.

'Classy,' I muttered to Boniface as we left.

87

Yves and Pierre Ferran were ferrying tools to their van outside their shop.

'Working today?' I asked them.

'Just sorting,' Pierre told me. He was replacing fuse wire in a box in the back of the van and replenishing ceramic casings. 'Only chance we get.'

Yves was struggling with a large crate with rope handles at either end. Inside, I could see some tool or other. He grunted, either at me or the weight of what he was carrying.

'I'm just here to tell you that Marie isn't under suspicion any more. The Germans have decided Falke's death was suicide, so she's completely in the clear.'

Yves put down his load and jumped out of the back of the van. He stood in front of me, eyeing me up and down, before going back inside for more equipment.

'Excuse him,' Pierre said. 'He finds it hard to back down. Especially where Marie is concerned.'

I watched him for a moment, counting lengths of electrical wire and ticking them off against a list.

'I still need to see Marie.'

Yves came back out of the shop at that moment. 'Why? Want to arrest her for being a Frenchwoman?'

'A Frenchwoman you're going to get killed one day.'

I turned away and left them to their work. I was angry with everyone.

Which is always a good mood to be in to go and see Hochstetter. And he was in pain from his hangover, which would be a bonus.

'Another coffee,' he ordered a young gefreiter who'd drawn the short straw that morning. 'And do not spill it this time. And bring one for Inspector Giral.'

I sat down and studied him. 'You've already cheered me up.'

'I am delighted to hear that, Édouard. What can I do for you? I imagined we had said all we had to say. The affair with this Ferran girl has been cleared up.'

'Not entirely.'

'What is it you want? I am not in the mood for your meanderings this morning.'

'In that case, I'll get to the point. We both suspect that Martin killed Falke.'

Hochstetter held his hand up for me to be silent when the nervous gefreiter brought the coffee in.

'You have no knowledge of what I might suspect.'

'I admit I diverted attention from Marie Ferran to help her cause,' I continued regardless, 'but I also diverted it from Martin to help yours.'

'Why would you help mine?'

'As you said, we've found a modus vivendi that is mutually beneficial. I aim to keep it that way. You suspected Martin was guilty of killing Falke because Falke was blackmailing him. You lied about when he returned to Berlin.'

'Martin protested his innocence regarding Falke's death,' he said.

'But you don't believe him.'

He sighed heavily and took a drink. 'It doesn't matter what I believe. He is my brother and I will do what I need to do to protect him. Besides which, he had already left Paris when Falke was killed.'

'We both know that's not true. I've no doubt you insisted on his returning to Berlin before it came to light, only he didn't. He waited until Sunday morning to take a Luftwaffe flight. Which means he had the opportunity as well as the motivation.'

He lit a cigarette, taking his time to gather himself. The fight had gone out of him. 'He's young. The SS leads these young men to believe they are invincible when they are not. It was my duty to protect him. Just as yours is to protect your son.'

'Who is not in a Gestapo prison.'

He was evidently not in the mood to argue today. 'Maybe so. But I still know you have a son who is on the run from the authorities. There is nothing to stop me from doubling our efforts to find him.'

'Except I know about your brother killing Falke.'

'Without evidence, you really do not have much.'

'That's quite true. Only I do.'

I took out the photograph of the two pages that Falke had left in his locker and showed them to Hochstetter. The first detailed Falke's blackmail of Martin Hochstetter. The second was a carbon copy of a note he had sent to Martin, arranging to meet on the Saturday night for Martin to make a payment. The meeting place was the Jardins des Champs-Élysées.

Hochstetter read them and handed them back to me.

'I imagine you have copies,' he said. 'Only they prove nothing. Just that Falke was blackmailing my brother. Not that Martin killed him.'

I brandished the papers before putting them back in my pocket.

'There's also a tape recording of your brother with Jean Fabre that Falke was using to blackmail him. You know I have a son, but you also know that I have these documents. Are you prepared to risk it?'

'Evidently not. Perhaps you should leave now.'

I got up to go. 'So we're quits.'

He waited until I was at the door before replying. 'Until I find another secret of yours, Édouard.'

'Or until I find another of yours.'

88

I sensed a figure fall into step with me as I crossed the lobby on my way out of the Lutetia. My mood wasn't the brightest, so even though it was Abwehr headquarters, I was preparing myself for a frank exchange of views. Idly I hefted the Luger in my coat pocket before letting it go. The temptation was too great.

'Happy New Year, Eddie,' a voice over my shoulder said. 'Always on duty, eh? Even today, on New Year's Day?'

I stopped and turned to see Peter smiling at me. His cheery voice instantly disarmed me. I wanted to dislike him for his uniform and his country and his leaders and for his being in Paris, but I couldn't.

'Aren't you?'

'Yes, I suppose I am. Errands. First here with the Abwehr, and now I have to go to the High Command.'

I realised I didn't actually know what Peter did in the Wehrmacht. That had never seemed important.

'Errands,' I repeated. 'You and me both.'

'Then we'll do them together. I thought I'd make the most of the opportunity and walk there. It's not so terribly far.'

I thought for a moment. I had no real desire to return to Thirty-Six just yet, and I was tired of hunting for Marie Ferran and of conversations strewn with mines. 'Why not?'

On the way, we talked of jazz and books. I tried again to find a reason to dislike him, but he loved Sidney Bechet and Georges Duhamel, whose work had been banned by the Nazis, and again I couldn't.

It was gone three o'clock and the streets were deserted. After the success of the Armistice Day demonstrations the previous month, Gaullists in London had broadcast a message on the BBC calling on everyone to stay indoors on New Year's Day between three and four in the afternoon. Looking around me, I'd say it was a success. We passed a table manned by German soldiers offering free potatoes in an attempt by the authorities to entice people out of doors to break the protest, but they were having no joy. Silently, I applauded.

Crossing the Seine over the Pont Royal, we walked through the Jardin des Tuileries to get to Place de la Concorde and the German High Command.

'I much prefer the Jardins des Champs-Élysées to Les Tuileries,' Peter said. 'They are so much less regimented.'

The deep snow underfoot made walking difficult, the rhythmic crunching hiding all other sounds in the gardens. Snow lay in drifts under bushes and at the foot of statues on their plinths. The bare trees seemed to reach for an unyielding sky that mirrored the bleak whiteness of the ground.

Peter suddenly stopped and snapped his fingers, the sound like a gunshot in the cold air.

'That African singer we heard when I first met you,' he said. 'Dominique something. I loved her.'

I stopped and faced him. 'So do I.'

'I haven't seen her since. Do you know if she still performs?'

I didn't reply, just a small shrug.

Something over his left shoulder had distracted me.

It was a person, bundled up against the cold, walking towards us, labouring as their feet sank into the snow with every slow step. They came nearer, drawn towards us. I moved out from behind Peter to get a better view. He turned with me, a puzzled look on his face.

It was Marie Ferran.

She raised her right hand and I heard the crack of a gun. Smoke plumed from the barrel of the weapon she was holding. The shot was aimed at Peter but went wide. She was too far away still and moving.

'No, Marie,' I shouted.

She fired again. She was getting closer, the shot less wild. I heard it thud into a tree behind us.

Next to me, Peter unfastened his holster and began to draw his gun. I looked at him in panic.

'No, don't,' I told him.

'She is firing at us, Eddie.'

Marie fired a third shot. Instinctively, both Peter and I ducked. With every shot, she was drawing nearer to where we were standing, her aim getting more accurate.

I took my own gun out and fired it into the air. She didn't flinch or falter.

'Please stop, Marie,' I called again.

From our right, I heard the sound of crunching and turned to see two German soldiers who'd been at one of the potato stands pushing urgently forward through the snow. They stopped to unsling their rifles.

'Stop, Marie,' I tried one more time.

Peter took aim.

'Please don't shoot, Peter,' I begged him. 'Put your gun down, Marie,' I yelled. I could hear the desperation in my own voice.

In my mind, I saw the 'prisoner' line on Jean-Luc's postcard. The exclamation mark that was a private joke between him and the young woman with the gun. She was someone who had loved and been loved by my son, and now we stood and faced each other across a cold waste of snow.

She shouted something back that I couldn't hear. She shouted again.

'I won't be taken prisoner. I will take a Boche with me and die.'

She took one more shot. I fired a second bullet into the air, but it had as little effect as the first one.

Next to me, Peter was slowly sighting down the barrel of his gun. He was expressionless, a soldier defending his position.

Marie came ever nearer, appearing to quicken over a stretch where the wind had thinned out the snow on the ground. She shouted her cry of not being taken prisoner again, a chant to drive herself on. Her hand was shaking, but she was close enough now to hit Peter.

I could see her eyes. No longer filled with the laughter she'd shared with my son, but angry and determined. I tried to plead with her with my own eyes. She was my only connection with Jean-Luc, possibly my only way of finding him. I needed her to put her gun down.

She took aim.

I had an instant's thought of Jacques Bonsergent and of Niederberger calmly talking of reprisals. Thirty innocent deaths or more. In exchange for one.

And I lowered my gun and forced myself to aim it at Marie as she fired one last time.

As if in echo, four shots replied simultaneously, and she fell to the ground. She was motionless.

Next to me, Peter kept his gun trained on her as I lowered mine to my side. Glancing over to the right, I saw the two soldiers each load another bullet into the breech and slowly edge forward, their rifles trained on her.

Exhaling slowly, I walked over to where she lay.

The white snow was corrupted red as blood seeped into the ground from a single wound to her head.

It was another execution, another firing squad. There, one soldier at random is given a dud bullet. They don't know who, but it means that each one in the squad can believe their bullet didn't kill the victim.

Marie had just the one wound.

In our firing squad, one of us could never know if it was our bullet that killed her.

I kneeled by her before the others could reach her and touched her forehead.

'I'm sorry, Marie.'

I looked at the gun in her hand and hung my head.

Before Peter could join me, I removed it and exchanged it for the one in my coat pocket.

Café et Cognac

89

I stood outside Ulysse's café, looking in.

Snow still lay on the ground five days after Marie's death, and I stamped my feet to stave off the cold. Light shone from the inside of the café with a warmth that belied the occasion. I hadn't gone to Marie's funeral. I knew I wouldn't have been welcome. I wasn't going to be any more welcome at the wake, but there were things I had to do.

In the glow of the lights, I could see that the whole community was crammed in there. Yves and Pierre Ferran and Ulysse, of course, but Isabelle Collet from the girls' school, the man from the bicycle shop, the elderly women I'd spoken to, the people from the local businesses and the families whose doors I'd knocked on. They were all inside, drinking Ulysse's wine and eating his ham and cheese.

Shaking myself out of those thoughts, I went to the rear of the Ferrans' van. It was parked outside their shop, not in front of the café. I tried the handle at the rear, but it wouldn't give, so I picked up a rock from the ground and broke open the lock.

Inside, the item I was looking for was lying in plain view. I lifted the lid off the crate with rope handles that I'd seen Yves carrying on the day of Marie's death and peered inside. A huge metal cylinder with air vents and an electrical cable coming out of it.

'What the hell are you doing?'

I turned to see Yves standing at the back of the van, his face red with grief and anger. Pierre stood next to him. His eyes were raw, but there was another concern underlying his expression.

I looked back at the tool in its crate.

'I've never seen one of these before. What is it?'

'Get out,' Yves shouted at me.

'Although I think I know what it is.'

'It's a drill,' Pierre explained. 'For our work.'

'A portable one? I didn't know they existed. I've only ever heard of the big industrial ones.'

'They're new,' Pierre said, turning to his father. He seemed to need to talk. 'We only got it just before the war.'

I delved into the crate, following the lead to its end, and found a screw plug attached to it. I held it up to show them.

'That would go nicely in a light socket, wouldn't it?'

'What do you want?' Yves asked. 'Have you got no respect? I've just buried my daughter.'

I stood up inside the van and looked out at them. 'You have my deepest sympathies. I wish it could have ended differently.'

He grunted, too angry and grief-stricken for more words.

'Just leave, please,' Pierre said.

'You know I can't. Just as you know what this is about.' I nodded at the drill in its crate. 'I saw this the other day but didn't know at the time what it meant. Now I do. This is what you used to break into Joseph Cartier's warehouse and steal all his goods. You plugged it into the light on the ceiling and drilled through the lock. You and Ulysse and all the good citizens of Bel Air in there right now. That's why the light bulb was broken. You'd taken it out and left it on the floor, but in the rush, it got stamped on and scattered.'

'He was robbing us blind,' Yves said. 'He deserved what he got.'

'That's how come the new gang weren't selling here in Bel Air, only in Charonne. You'd divvied up all of Cartier's stuff between you. That's where all the food for the community in the girls' school came from. So what happened? And it's pointless lying at this stage.'

'We broke in,' Pierre said. 'All of us, like you said. We found out where he was keeping the stuff and we decided to take it for ourselves.'

'Only Cartier came back and caught you at it,' I guessed.

'We didn't mean to kill him,' Pierre went on. 'It just happened. People lost their tempers with him after everything he'd put us through and we just started hitting him.'

'The butter was a nice touch,' I told them. 'And the guinea pigs.'

Yves spat on the ground. 'One of the locals who'd had to breed them because they couldn't afford to pay the evil bastard left them for him. It's what he deserved.'

'So what are you going to do about it?' Pierre finally asked.

I sighed and jumped out of the van.

'What can I do? Arrest a whole community? See you all tried and executed? I have to ask myself what good that would do, and I really can't think of one positive thing that would come of it.'

'You're letting us go?'

I looked at them both, weighing up all the thoughts that had been in my head ever since Marie had died in the gardens.

'The problem is, you're not the only family in mourning, are you? Jean Fabre's family are also grieving over their lost son. Because you're also the ones behind this spate of burglaries of wealthy flats in the Sixteenth.'

The look they exchanged with each other confirmed I was right, even though I'd known it. Ever since I'd worked out the meaning of the tool I'd seen Yves carrying and the light bulb on the landing.

'You haven't just taken part in the murder of Cartier,' I told them. 'Or stolen from homes that their owners were forced to abandon or that were requisitioned by the Germans. You beat Jean Fabre to death and you attacked a German soldier. An SS officer and a member of the Nazi Party.'

'Collaborator scum,' Yves said.

Pierre looked worried at my mention of who exactly Martin Hochstetter was. 'What are you going to do?'

'What can I do? You'll be executed for Fabre's death. Frankly, I can live with that. But your attack on a German officer is another matter entirely. It won't just be you two who suffer, but who knows how many innocent French people taken by the Nazis as reprisals and shot like Jacques Bonsergent. I can't let that happen.'

'So you're not turning us in?'

I glanced away momentarily to quell my anger. 'No, I'm not turning you in. I can't.'

Father and son looked at each other. Incredulity gave way to relief before an undertone of triumph seeped into their expressions. I had to turn away. I walked instead towards the café.

'Where are you going?' Yves asked after me.

'One more thing to do,' I called back over my shoulder.

'You're not going in there.'

'And you're not stopping me.'

I stepped inside. The hush was instant. I nodded at the people assembled in the room and walked over to the counter. Ulysse was standing on the other side, his arms folded. The volume in the room slowly rose again. I heard the door open and close behind me, no doubt Yves and Pierre following me in.

'You've got a nerve,' Ulysse told me.

Reaching into my coat pocket, I pulled out a Luger and placed it on the bar. He hurriedly unfolded his arms and scooped it up. I glanced at the empty place on the shelf where it was normally kept.

'When did you realise Marie had taken your gun?' I asked him. 'Before or after she killed Falke?'

My mind went back to the vision of her lying on the ground and the Luger in her hand. The same sort of gun that had been used to kill Falke. I remembered her words. A Nazi way to kill a Nazi. A German gun, not a French one. Again I had a suspicion, but not a certainty. Although Ulysse's reaction made me believe that Martin Hochstetter had been right to protest his innocence.

I'd removed Ulysse's gun from Marie's hand and replaced it with the one in my pocket. Another Luger, but one that wouldn't match the weapon possibly used to kill Falke. Insurance for the day Thier or Hochstetter might decide that Falke hadn't committed suicide.

Shamefacedly, Ulysse replaced the gun on his shelf and turned to look at me, the defiance gone. No one in the room had heard our conversation.

'What are you going to do?' he asked in a low voice.

'Nothing. We all killed Marie one way or another.'

He nodded and reached under the counter. Pulling out the bottle of brandy, he poured a glass and placed it in front of me. I looked at it and back at him.

'No thank you.'

I turned away from him and walked out of the café into the snow and the cold, leaving the lights and noise behind me.

I went in search of the Metro. I had one last dilemma to face.

With Sylvie gone from Paris, and with it her threat to report Dominique to the Germans, I could go to Montmartre and hear music and drink whisky with Dominique.

Or I could go home.

Author's Note

Although *Banquet of Beggars* is a work of fiction, a number of the stories in the book were inspired by real events and real people. When you write historical fiction set in a relatively recent period, one of the decisions you have to take is whether or not to include real people in your books. In the case of Occupied Paris, it would evidently be impossible not to include references at least to the senior Nazi officials whose decisions and roles affected the lives of everyone, but there are times when the demands of the story I'm trying to tell call for these and other figures to become characters in the book. I've tried as impartially as possible to ensure that, even though the stories, scenes and dialogue that include these people are fictitious, the traits that I ascribe to them are as accurate as possible, based on descriptions of them by others who knew them, and that they were actually in Paris at the time the story is set.

The story of Jacques Bonsergent is true, and I wanted to commemorate him and keep his memory alive, but out of respect, I only make reference to him in the book rather than have him appear as a character. As told in *Banquet of Beggars*, he was involved in a minor incident with some German soldiers on an evening out with friends. This occurred shortly after the demonstrations of 11th November 1940, Armistice Day, when the Occupiers had been shaken by the strength of feeling against the Occupation. While walking home, one of Jacques Bonsergent's friends accidentally jostled some German soldiers. This led to an argument, in which one of the Frenchmen is said to have raised his fist to one of the soldiers. By all accounts, Jacques Bonsergent was very much a spectator in a particularly trivial incident rather than being actively involved, but he was the one arrested and tried. At his trial, a German military tribunal, he bravely refused to name his companions and took responsibility for what had happened. In an appallingly fast process, he was handed down a death sentence, his subsequent appeal was turned down, and he was executed by firing squad on 23rd December, the first civilian to be executed in Paris under the Occupation. He was twenty-eight years old. It would appear that the Occupiers wanted to make an example, and chose this incident, despite the occurrence of other more serious ones, such as the brawl at the Café d'Harcourt that Eddie reflects on in the book. A square and a Metro station are named after Jacques Bonsergent in the Tenth Arrondissement, close to where he lived at the time.

A character taken from real life that I have used in the book is Otto Abetz, the German ambassador to Paris under the Occupation. A self-professed Francophile married to a Frenchwoman, he worked hard at winning over the French elite through favours and lavish receptions at the top Parisian restaurants, the German Embassy and his residence in Chantilly, and through his use of the French media. A die-hard Nazi party member and protégé of Joachim von Ribbentrop, the Nazi Foreign Minister, Abetz set out to undermine Wehrmacht military authority in Paris from day one and feather his own political and personal nest. Regarded as a charming, urbane man, he was also said by both his supporters and detractors to have had a vicious temper that could turn at the drop of a hat.

Rationing in France during the Occupation is seen as the

most stringent of the systems put in place anywhere in Europe. By Christmas 1940, most people were restricted to 1,200 calories a day. Evidently, the black market flourished during this time, from the neighbour trying to make a bit of extra money – often referred to as the grey market – to highly organised criminal gangs, which I've tried to reflect in this story. All of this was hugely exacerbated by the role played by the Occupier. A huge amount of everything that was produced in France was being sent to Germany at a vast profit, leading, among other things, to even more desperate shortages in France. One of the most blatant examples of the exploitation of the French economy by the Nazis were the bureaux d'achats, central buying offices set up as a racket by various branches of the German civil and military authorities. At one point, there were some two hundred of these agencies operating in Paris. As part of the armistice agreement forced on the French in June 1940, the French had to pay the costs accrued by the Nazis in occupying France. Using these reparations paid by the Vichy government, the buying agencies bought up French goods cheaply and sold them on to the German military in France or to businesses in Germany at vastly inflated prices. Many of these goods were sold at rock-bottom prices to the agencies by French producers under coercion, mostly enforced by French criminal gangs, who gladly got into bed with the Nazis. Very often, the Vichy government was then charged a second time when the German authorities presented it with the bills for all the goods they'd bought from the buying agencies. While Parisians struggled to put food on their table, the people in charge of the buying agencies and their accomplices were raking in the money.

One of the most uncomfortable aspects of writing about this period is having to reflect some of the ideas and attitudes that were in evidence at this time. One such scene was when Lafitte shows Eddie the *Au Pilori* newspaper, which actually did run a competition asking its readers what should be done with the Jews in France. As appalling and shocking as they are, the replies shown in this story were actually published, although there is some debate as to how many of them were genuine readers' replies and how many were fake replies made up by the paper's editorial team.

Other real events were the ceremony to bring Napoleon II's ashes from Vienna to the Pantheon in Paris. This was a gesture that Hitler thought would please the French, but that left the vast majority of Parisians entirely indifferent. Eddie's comment about wanting coal instead of ashes was a saying that was making the rounds at this time.

The incident at the Rue de Buci was based on a real event, in which a handful of German soldiers went to the head of a queue of around two thousand French people hoping to buy one of three hundred pieces of rabbit. Fortunately, unrest that could have ended in a riot and tragedy was averted, but it was a sign of the growing tensions. The arrests that Eddie found himself forced to make were invented for this story.

Equally true were Eddie's comments at the Abetz dinner about the causes of the deaths of German soldiers in the early days of the Occupation, and the desire by some factions among the military and civil authorities to use them as an excuse for reprisals. The proposals mentioned in the book about possible reprisals and their nature are based on reports of recommendations made by senior officials at the time.

Finally, the Germans did indeed set up street stalls offering free potatoes on New Year's day to try and prevent Parisians from observing the protest of staying indoors between three and four p.m. On the whole, they proved not to be a temptation to the vast majority of people, although the Occupiers argued that the bitter cold contributed to that.

Acknowledgements

This is that bit of the book where I get to thank everyone for all their help and support, and it's always an impossible task to do justice to how much I owe so many amazing people and how grateful I am for it all. But, here goes …

First of all, the readers. A huge thank-you to all the fabulous readers who have taken Eddie to their hearts and for buying or borrowing this book – I very much hope you've enjoyed it. A special thank-you as well for all the lovely emails and messages you send me, for coming to see me at book events and festivals and for all the support you show me in recommending and reviewing my books. It really means a lot.

The same holds true for all the great bloggers, who very often don't get the credit they deserve, but who do an immeasurable amount of good work in promoting books and authors. I've been lucky enough recently to meet some bloggers in real life who I've known for years only on social media, which has been a tremendous pleasure, and to keep up contact with some who have already become friends – a big shout-out here to Simon Dalton, Jill Doyle, Gordon McGhie and Noel Powell.

Crime and historical fiction writers are as friendly and supportive a group of people as you're ever likely to meet. I'd like to thank my lovely Crime Cymru for all the friendships I've made and all the wonderful writers I've met through the Crime

Writers' Association and the Historical Writers' Association. As a member of the group behind Wales' first international crime fiction festival – Gwyl Crime Cymru Festival – I've also come to appreciate the enormous amount of work and thought that goes into organising a festival. A big thank-you to all the festival organisers who have invited me to appear at their events and to all the writers, readers, bloggers and booksellers I've met there.

Booksellers and librarians are a writer's lifeblood. The support they provide is enormous, and I'd like to thank all the wonderful bookshops and libraries for all your tireless work in putting my books in readers' hands and in organising events and signings. I appreciate how much extra work that involves. I'd like to say a special thank-you to my local bookseller – Griffin Books – and to Mel and her amazing team for all their support and for hosting my book launches. An equally special thank-you to all the Waterstones in Wales for choosing *The Unwanted Dead* as Welsh Book of the Month and for always showing me such warmth and professionalism. A big shout-out here to Steve and his team in Swansea, Chloe and her team in Aberystwyth, Sol and his team in Abergavenny, Beth and everyone in Carmarthen, Tom, Megan and everyone in Cardiff, Dee and everyone in Newport, Stacey and all the Llandudno team, and all the team in Wrexham. Thank you too to Kerry, Rhodri and everyone at my local library and to the Bridgend libraries for all your support for me and Welsh crime writers in general.

A big thank-you to my German, Spanish, Dutch and US publishers, who are an absolute joy to work with and for believing in Eddie. My German editor Thomas Wörtche and translator Stefan Lux and everyone at Suhrkamp. My Spanish editor Claudia Casanova, Ana Pareja, Fernando Alvarez and translator Iris Mogollón and all the team at Principal de los Libros. Jill Luites, Hajnalka Bata, Marc van Biezen and translator Tasio Ferrand at my Dutch publisher Meulenhoff Boekerij. My US publisher Claiborne Hancock, Jessica Case, Nicole Maher and everyone at Pegasus.

This one's for the dream team. I am unbelievably lucky to work with the nicest and best people in publishing. The most heartfelt of thank-yous to everyone at my lovely UK publisher Orion. To the most gifted and brilliant (and patient) editors – Emad Akhtar, Celia Killen and Sarah O'Hara, who make writing and, more importantly, rewriting a pleasure. To the wonderful Becca Bryant and everyone in the PR team, and to the equally wonderful Lucy Cameron and everyone in the marketing team – I am forever grateful for your amazing energy and talent. And to everyone in the Credits section of this book, who work so hard and so brilliantly. Thank you for everything you do.

If anyone ever asks the secret to getting published, I will always bore them rigid with stories of how brilliant my agent Ella Kahn is and how she doesn't just make the difference, she is the difference. The most profound thank-you to you, Ella.

And finally, my wife Liz, who fills my world. Thank you as always for your love and support, your insight and wisdom, and your belief in me. And for knowing where the wine is kept. Thank you with everything I have.

Credits

Chris Lloyd and Orion Fiction would like to thank everyone at Orion who worked on the publication of *Banquet of Beggars*.

Editorial
Emad Akhtar
Sarah O'Hara
Millie Prestidge

Copy-editor
Jane Selley

Proofreader
Simon Fox

Audio
Paul Stark
Louise Richardson
Georgina Cutler

Contracts
Dan Herron
Ellie Bowker
Oliver Chacón

Design
Nick Shah
Nick May
Joanna Ridley
Helen Ewing

Editorial Management
Jane Hughes
Charlie Panayiotou
Tamara Morriss

Inventory
Jo Jacobs
Dan Stevens

Marketing
Lucy Cameron

Operations
Sharon Willis

Finance
Nick Gibson
Jasdip Nandra
Elizabeth Beaumont
Ibukun Ademefun
Afeera Ahmed
Sue Baker
Tom Costello

Production
Ruth Sharvell
Fiona McIntosh

Publicity
Sian Baldwin
Ellen Turner

Sales
Catherine Worsley
Victoria Laws
Esther Waters
Frances Doyle
Ben Goddard
Jack Hallam
Anna Egelstaff
Inês Figueira

Barbara Ronan
Andrew Hally
Dominic Smith
Deborah Deyong
Lauren Buck
Maggy Park
Linda McGregor
Sinead White
Jemimah James
Rachael Jones
Jack Dennison
Nigel Andrews
Ian Williamson
Julia Benson
Declan Kyle
Robert Mackenzie
Megan Smith
Charlotte Clay
Rebecca Cobbold

Rights
Tara Hiatt
Ben Fowler
Alice Cottrell
Marie Henckel